A War of Wyverns

Books by S. F. Williamson

A LANGUAGE OF DRAGONS
A WAR OF WYVERNS

A War of Wyverns

S. F. WILLIAMSON

First published in the United Kingdom by Harper Fire,
an imprint of HarperCollins *Children's Books*, in 2026
HarperCollins *Children's Books* is a division of HarperCollins*Publishers* Ltd
1 London Bridge Street
London SE1 9GF

www.harpercollins.co.uk

HarperCollins*Publishers*
Macken House, 39/40 Mayor Street Upper
Dublin 1, D01 C9W8, Ireland

1

Text copyright © S. F. Williamson 2026
Cover illustrations copyright © Ivan Belikov 2026
Cover design copyright © HarperCollins*Publishers* Ltd 2026
All rights reserved

HB ISBN 978–0–00–865231–9
WTS HB ISBN 978-0-00-880771-9
EXPORT HB ISBN 978-0-00-880314-8
TPB ISBN 978–0–00–865232–6
PB ISBN 978–0–00–865236–4

S. F. Williamson asserts the moral right to be identified as the author of the work.

A CIP catalogue record for this title is available from the British Library.

Typeset in point size10/leading 15 by Berlington LT Std
Printed and bound in the UK using 100% renewable electricity at CPI Group (UK) Ltd

Conditions of Sale
This book is sold subject to the condition that it shall not, by way of trade or otherwise, be lent, re-sold, hired out or otherwise circulated without the publisher's prior consent in any form, binding or cover other than that in which it is published and without a similar condition including this condition being imposed on the subsequent purchaser. No part of this publication may be reproduced, stored in a retrieval system or transmitted in any form or by any means, electronic, mechanical, photocopying, recording or otherwise, without the prior permission of HarperCollins*Publishers* Ltd.

Without limiting the exclusive rights of any author, contributor or the publisher of this publication, any unauthorised use of this publication to train generative artificial intelligence (AI) technologies is expressly prohibited. HarperCollins also exercise their rights under Article 4(3) of the Digital Single Market Directive 2019/790 and expressly reserve this publication from the text and data mining exception.

This book contains FSC™ certified paper and other controlled
sources to ensure responsible forest management.

For more information visit: www.harpercollins.co.uk/green

For my siblings.
I would burn the world for you.

One

THE SKY IS DARK AND FULL OF DRAGONS.

I hurry through the streets of London, my umbrella tilted at an angle not to shield my face from the rain but to hide it. There are almost as many Guardians of Peace on the ground as there are Bulgarian Bolgoriths in the sky. A small mound of rubble blocks my path, left over from one of last week's attacks. It could have been caused by rebel bombs *or* by the army of Queen Ignacia, Britannia's dragon queen. Both groups are locked in their own individual battles with the Prime Minister. But judging by a stone pillar knocked clean off its base by what could only be the swipe of a tail, I'd guess the latter.

As I reach the Tube station, the first rays of sunlight stretch up over the grey buildings, bringing the capital's night curfew to an end.

Rebellion happens in the shadows, after all.

I climb on to the Underground train, my fake class pass hanging around my neck.

> **Penelope Hollingsworth**
> **Age 17**
> **First Class**

I sit opposite an elderly man in a singed coat. He peers at me from beneath bright posters plastered above the carriage seats. Two women in military dress link arms in front of two buildings – I recognise the white stone of 10 Downing Street and the red brick of the Academy for Draconic Linguistics. They are encircled by a string of words in a looping, feminine font.

Wyvernmire and Hollingsworth United In The Fight Against Rebels

I bury my face in yesterday's copy of the *Pimlico Bulletin* – a non-partisan newspaper – and am met with another slogan.

'The Truth for Every Class,' I mutter under my breath as I scan the headlines.

PM Allies Britannia to Bulgarians

Where is Queen Ignacia? Possible Sightings on Page 3

Western Drake Gutted on Kent Farm: Human Remains Retrieved From Its Second Stomach

I open to the first page and see a black-and-white photo of a familiar manor house.

BLETCHLEY PARK: A NATION'S SECRET?

A lump rises in my throat as I toss the paper to the ground. Memories surge: a gunshot, blood beneath my fingernails, a face crowned with dead leaves. My hand reaches for the wooden swallow around my neck. If Atlas were here now, he'd mock the Prime Minister for thinking she can manipulate Europe's fiercest dragons to extend her empire. For thinking that Britannia would bow to dragons who had massacred their own human population. If Atlas were here, he'd be slipping into the public houses and coming out with new recruits to the rebel cause, using nothing but his courage and his crooked smile. But he's not here.

Because he's dead.

All I can do now is continue what he started at Bletchley Park and help win the war for the Human-Dragon Coalition. Only a skilled linguist can obtain the secret weapon the rebels need.

And if languages can honour Atlas's memory, then I'll learn a hundred tongues and more.

The sun has risen as I reach Claridge House, the home of Rita Hollingsworth. She lives in Mayfair, only a few streets away from the Academy for Draconic Linguistics, which she founded at the age of thirty-five. I insert my key in the lock of the servants' door. A thick, spiked tail trails down the wall above me. It belongs to Clementius, the Western Drake on the roof, one of the few British dragons who hasn't fled the encroaching Bulgarian presence in London and who is secretly Hollingsworth's rebel guard.

I head straight for the stairs, counting the yellow diamonds on the patterned carpet as I climb several floors. Hollingsworth insists I travel between my home and hers before the morning rush hour. If anyone were to recognise me, my cover as her visiting niece could be blown. The walls feature portraits of her extended family – pretty cousins and ancient uncles stare out into the quiet house. I hear a scullery maid lighting the fires and a creak from the top floor. I imagine the Chancellor of the Academy for Draconic Linguistics rising from bed, her hair still in rollers.

The image is so ridiculous it makes me snort with laughter.

I open and close the office door softly. The room is vast, with high windows that overlook the street below. A large desk stands beneath a painting of a pair of Sand Dragons basking on a beach, the pearly moonlight captured in delicate brushstrokes. Beside it is an ornate mirror and for a moment I stare at my reflection. My thick hair is cut so short that it only just grazes my collarbone and dark shadows lurk beneath my eyes, making my skin even paler than usual. I tread across the maroon rugs towards the door in the corner, past the desk littered with empty cigarette boxes and books about Bulgarian dragons, one opened to an index page with the words *blood, blue diamond, Bolgorith*. Something catches my eye. A sketch in black pen, half-hidden beneath the Remington typewriter.

It's me.

And beneath it, a title.

Vivien Featherswallow, Draconic Translator

My fingers linger over the paper, but I don't touch it, my mind not quite believing it's real. The depiction is different to the government's Wanted posters of me, the ones Hollingsworth has collected and burned every day before they can be seen. My face is prettier, my eyes large and doe-like, whereas the Wanted posters depict me with a long, lank braid and a frown. Neither sketch is quite right, each telling a story that is not quite true.

'For the Coalition newspapers,' says a voice.

I spin around. Hollingsworth is standing in the doorway, wearing a blue silk dress and a belt embroidered with silver dragons. She looks me up and down like she has done every morning for the last three months, taking in my man's mackintosh and donated leather brogues, as if she expected me to arrive with a limb missing or my hair aflame. My decision to find my own accommodation rather than live here with her is not one Hollingsworth understands.

'Morning,' I say, my face growing hot as I realise she probably thinks I was snooping around her desk. 'I'm supposed to be undercover. What do you want rebel newspapers printing a sketch of me for?'

She gives me a thin-lipped smile. 'A rebellion must have a face, must it not? People need to know they're in good hands.'

I raise my eyebrows in surprise. Me, the face of the rebellion? Has Hollingsworth forgotten that a mere few months ago, I was trying to translate a secret, ultrasonic dragon language called the Koinamens to win the war for Prime Minister Wyvernmire?

'We won't publish it until you're safely out of London,' she says, her voice as deep as treacle.

Safely out of London.

Does that mean she finally thinks I'm ready?

I stare at the words beneath the sketch again and let out a small sigh. Draconic Translator. The title is one I've waited for my entire life. It's oddly satisfying to see who I am printed in black and white, to be given a distinct definition of myself, a neat box to fit in amid the chaos my life has become.

The door in the corner leads to my own workspace, an office within Hollingsworth's that used to be a cupboard. I set my satchel down on my small, pokey desk. The four walls that box me in like a dracovol in a cage are plastered with research papers – maps of various islands, handwritten pronunciation guides and lists of dietary habits. And tacked on top of them is a rudimentary drawing that Hollingsworth sketched in front of me. Three Bulgarian Bolgoriths, two black and one red.

General Goranov and his siblings.

Britannia has been in a three-way civil war between the human government, the rebels and Queen Ignacia since last year. And now that the Prime Minister has allied with the Bulgarian Bolgoriths – betraying her promise of peace to Queen Ignacia – barely a day goes by without a rebel attack on London.

I know a Bolgorith, but she was born in Britannia. Chumana, the pink dragon who set fire to 10 Downing Street before following me to Bletchley Park.

'If we eliminate Goranov and his siblings,' Hollingsworth told me a few weeks ago, 'the Bulgarian presence in Britannia will crumble.'

The servants and Hollingsworth's secretary think I'm here after having jumped at the chance to spend the war working for Britannia's beloved Chancellor instead of sewing shirts for the soldiers like other First Class girls. And it's not exactly a lie. I *am* working for Hollingsworth. But my true reason for being here, my mission, isn't to help Britannia fight the rebels. It's to help the rebels fight Prime Minister Wyvernmire and her army of Bolgoriths.

It's to learn the language of the Hebridean Wyverns.

I've met wyverns before, thanks to my parents' work in dragon anthropology. But the Hebridean species is different. They're small, two-legged dragons with a cultural heritage that rivals that of any human community. They can supposedly be found on the Isle of Canna in Scotland, although they haven't been sighted in years. It's my job to learn everything about them, from their traditions to their tongue, so that when the rebels find them – and Hollingsworth seems adamant that they will – then I will somehow be able to communicate with them.

And convince them to help the rebels win the war.

Of course, the minor detail of *how* these wyverns can make the Human-Dragon Coalition the victor in a three-way civil war has not yet been disclosed to me.

I sit down as London's traffic screeches outside and reach for a scrap of paper on my desk. It's a note from Hyacinth, Hollingsworth's secretary and another debutante working for the war effort to escape the dutiful drudgery of First Class girlhood.

> Dearest Pen,
> Party? Tuesday at 8 o'clock, 36 Churton Street in Pimlico.
> Pretty please.
> H

She's invited me several times already, ignoring my protests ('It's after curfew') and my excuses ('I can't leave my roommate, she gets lonely'). Her insistence is mildly annoying and the invitation goes against every rule in the how-to-be-an-undercover-rebel book, but part of me is glad that Hyacinth wants me around. She's been a good friend to me these past three months.

Of course I can't attend the party. What if somebody recognises me?

The journal of Patrick Clawtail, Oxford Fellow of Celtic Languages and dragon enthusiast, lies open on the desk where I left it yesterday. Hollingsworth gave it to me when I started working for her, right after Marquis landed our plane on Eigg. I only spent a few days on the island that houses the Coalition Headquarters before Hollingsworth sent for me.

Leaving my cousin and my sister, Ursa, behind was almost as hard as losing Atlas.

The journal details Clawtail's interactions with the Hebridean Wyverns over the course of four years, ending abruptly in June 1866 when he was executed by the government for 'inciting unrest between humans and dragons'.

It's made of black leather and written in faded ink. Random clippings – a feather, a tuft of fur and a leaf that is still green but has long since lost any odour – are dispersed between daily entries, descriptions of the island and recordings of the Hebridean Wyverns' complex language, which Clawtail named Cànan-Channaigh – Scottish Gaelic for 'language of Canna'. He coined an English word for their language, too: *Cannair.*

I have managed to grasp its basic grammatical rules, but Clawtail fills several pages with his attempts to convey the meaning of many complicated words, so many that I lose myself in them. It seems he eventually gave up on the task.

The later pages of the journal are entirely dedicated to the wyverns' culture and customs, with not a single reference to language.

It doesn't give me much to work with.

Clawtail and his family were supposedly the last people to lay eyes on the wyverns before they retreated further inland when the government came for the Clawtails and while his journal begins with enthusiasm at being able to study the wyverns' tongue, it ends with a hurried, unfinished entry.

A voice behind me says, 'Tensions between humans and dragons in Britannia were on the verge of explosion when that was written.'

Hollingsworth has appeared silently in the doorway, her eyes on the journal.

'Clawtail had a history of campaigning for the recognition of Celtic languages such as Scots, Scottish Gaelic and Norn, and he began doing the same for dragon tongues,' she continues. 'He sent his written recordings of Cannair to several universities by dracovol, thinking the wyvern protection would keep him and his family safe, but the government decided that his highlighting of individual heritages was intended to create division and therefore a threat to British unity. They executed him for treason on Canna just as the corrupt Peace Agreement was signed.'

I nod, trying to ignore the creeping feeling of annoyance. She's already told me all this. Clawtail was the first person ever to study dragon tongues. He was an anomaly.

'You, with your uncanny ability to learn languages at an impressive speed, can learn Cannair. That's why you are the face of the rebellion, Vivien. Because you will be the one to go to the wyverns and request an alliance. They are our only hope of winning this war.'

You've already told me that, too, I glower silently. *And yet here I am, still in London, still ignorant as to why these wyverns are so important.*

I cannot send you to the wyverns until the wyverns have been found, Hollingsworth tells me every time I ask why I can't go to Canna *now*.

I can't wait to be there, to rally the wyverns to the cause and to see Wyvernmire's face as the rebels bring her and her Bulgarian Bolgoriths down. She's the reason for the suffering of the Third Class, for the segregation of humans and dragons, for this war that has already killed hundreds.

She's the reason Atlas is dead.

Hollingsworth hands me a sheet of paper.

It's my latest translation for the Academy – I do a few each day just in case a wartime inspector ever asks to see Penelope Hollingsworth's work. It's a statement in Drageoir sent over from France, condemning Wyvernmire's alliance with the Bulgarian dragons. Hollingsworth has taken a red pen to it, scratching out and underlining words.

'What's wrong with it?' I say.

'Your translation is too literal, Vivien.' She pats her silver, corkscrew coils. 'You can hardly expect it to be approved.'

'Too literal?' I stare at her corrections.

The Dragons of the French Third Republic are ~~incensed~~ disappointed by the British alliance with the ~~immoral~~ controversial dragons of Bulgaria.

'But . . . you've changed the meaning,' I say. 'You've mistranslated the statement.'

'I have interpreted it differently to you, which is a translator's right.'

I scan her face for a trace of humour, any indication that she might be testing me.

'It's a translator's *duty* to translate in context, to give the words the meaning intended by the source language, or at least get as close to it as we can,' I tell her. 'The Academy is obligated to translate and publish any communications that come in from foreign dragons.'

'You forget the Academy is currently being run by Wyvernmire's government,' Hollingsworth says sharply. 'Her definition of duty is not the same as yours.'

I throw the paper down. 'So you're going to let this pass?'

'If I want to maintain my persona, I must,' Hollingsworth replies.

She walks back to her desk and sits down, her eyes lingering on the sketch of me. 'Language is a weapon, Vivien. Wyvernmire is using it and you will too, soon. In fact, it may be the last weapon the rebels have.'

'When are you going to send me to Canna?' I ask. 'I've learned the wyvern tongue as best I can. Have the rebels found them yet?'

Hollingsworth takes a sip of her tea and grimaces.

'Cold,' she mutters.

She rifles through a stack of papers, ignoring my question. I feel my neck flush with anger. Has she forgotten what she told me when she brought me here? *Your linguistic capabilities are the best chance the Coalition has.*

I turn back to the journal. My years of studying, my languages, my translations have all been building up to this. To making contact with the Hebridean Wyverns and saving Britannia. Atlas believed that my languages are a way I'm called to love and Dad once told me that they would save me.

So what is Hollingsworth waiting for?

She expects me to work for the Coalition yet treats me like a child.

My eyes fall on Hyacinth's note and I wonder if my black skirt and jumper would pass as party clothes.

If it's a rebel Hollingsworth wants, a rebel she shall get.

Two

ONE OF THE PERKS OF BEING Penelope Hollingsworth is that I can commandeer any of the Chancellor's cars, which are driven by her most loyal Guardians. They have no idea the woman they serve is secretly the leader of the Human-Dragon Coalition. At nightfall I say goodbye to Dr Hollingsworth, but she barely looks up from her desk as she mutters to herself from inside a cloud of cigarette smoke. The Guardian in the driving seat of the motorcar gives me a nod and a smile when I slide on to the back seat, the leather cold against my legs.

'Out to dine, Miss Hollingsworth?' he says as the engine roars to life.

'Yes,' I reply. 'Churton Street please, Johnstone.'

My heart flutters in my chest, but Johnstone doesn't flinch at the fact that I'm out after curfew.

Clearly, the latest restrictions don't apply to the First Class.

Hyacinth's friend George lives in the top half of Pimlico – First Class and bordered by Belgravia and Westminster –

while I live in the bottom half, closest to the Thames. The car drives through the streets of London, past Hyde Park where Guardians and dragons are lifting some sort of statue from a lorry in the dusk. I peer out of the window as an Irish Basilisk hoists the gleaming white stone on to his back and wonder if he's working *with* the Guardians or *for* them. The difference is crucial when you're a dragon. We pass by countless Underground stations and I think about how I could easily step on to a train and ride it all the way to Highfall Prison, where my parents and uncle are still being held. But Hollingsworth has made me promise not to. She says the only thing keeping my parents alive is Wyvernmire's hope that I'll go looking for them.

The Prime Minister's lies about me have spread among her Guardians and politicians, and the general public might soon start believing them, too. That the Human-Dragon Coalition is working with a young translator who is against Britannia and against peace, a translator who will use her Draconic tongues to help the dragons take over.

Thanks to Wyvernmire, *I* am London's most wanted rebel.

I slip a small, square photograph out of my pocket. Ursa's round, rosy face, framed by blonde pigtails, stares back at me. A gift from Dr Hollingsworth, stolen from the government's files on my family. I've already kissed the glossiness of the paper away.

We come to a stop outside a house flanked by stone pillars. I spot Hyacinth and her brother, Edward, outside. I know Edward well enough now, although he was suspicious of me when Hy told him I was Dr Hollingsworth's niece. I don't think he entirely believes it, but if that's the case, then surely seeing me arrive in a Guardian car will convince him of my lie. And lie I must, even though it bothers me to deceive them both. If anyone were to find out that the Chancellor's assistant was a rebel, the scandal would be huge and Hollingsworth's true identity as the leader of the Coalition would be uncovered.

'Thank you, Johnstone,' I say. 'No need to wait.'

'Pen?' Hyacinth sings. 'Oh my goodness, you came!'

I force a smile and stop myself from pulling awkwardly at my skirt. It's plain next to the pink satin dress Hyacinth is wearing.

'Evening, Penelope,' Edward says uncomfortably.

He's wearing a gold watch and a pinstriped suit in an unflattering shade of yellow. His hair is the same pale blond as his sister's and his eyes are too wide apart. A single paintbrush pokes out of his breast pocket.

'He fancies himself a starving artist,' Hyacinth joked to me a few days ago. 'That's why he dresses like the Third Class.'

I didn't bother telling her that the Third Class don't wear suits. I've snuck out to meet with Hyacinth before, but she doesn't know I've been doing the same with her brother. She doesn't know I've been meeting him after dark.

'No roommate?' she asks casually.

I hesitate. 'No. She's not really the party type.'

We ring the doorbell and a maid answers. There's barely time to stuff our class passes into the pockets of our coats before they're taken away.

'Ready to meet some friends, Penelope?' Hyacinth says. She taps my nose with her perfectly manicured finger.

'You are going to be *quite* popular.'

The maid leads us through a quiet hallway lit with old gas lamps. A grandfather clock stands tall and imposing on the panelled wall and the maid pushes open the door beside it. Music erupts into the hallway as Hyacinth takes me by the hand and leads me inside. Heads turn to look at us through clouds of cigarette smoke and modernity contrasts with the hallway we just came from: a chandelier gives out pretty, electric light and several girls are sprawled across the green velvet sofas, all bare arms and long legs.

'Hyacinth, darling!' one of them screeches.

Two young men, playing cards with roll-ups smoking in their mouths, look up at the sound of Hyacinth's name. Before I know it she's kissing the girls and they are kissing me, pressing their sticky lips to my cheek and asking my name, their skin carrying the warm scent of champagne and expensive perfume. I'd never spent much time with the First Class before I met Dr Hollingsworth and Hyacinth – unless sharing a dorm with Serena at Bletchley counts – but now I find myself surrounded by them. I catch Edward's gaze and he rolls his eyes. His sister evidently insisted on *his* presence tonight, too.

'Penelope is a colleague of mine,' Hyacinth says.

'Oh, another secretary,' one of the girls giggles.

'Niece to the Chancellor of the Academy for Draconic Linguistics, actually,' Hyacinth replies, her seductive gaze suddenly cold.

The girl sinks back down into her seat and I offer her an apologetic smile. Hyacinth, I know, only has a job because she wants one. As a First Class heiress to her father's successful printing business, her future is that of the wife to an equally wealthy First Class man. But for now, at least, she seems to like pretending otherwise.

A boy with tousled hair strides towards us and Hyacinth allows him to kiss her cheek, too. I feel myself blush – I had no idea so much physical contact was normal among the First Class. The boy offers me his hand and I shake it.

'George Beecham,' he says with a warm smile.

'Penelope Hollingsworth,' I say, my mouth dry.

What if he's seen the Wanted posters of me?

'I hope you don't mind me coming along with Hyacinth,' I add quickly.

He gives me a bemused look. 'Not at all.'

Other boys abandon their drinks and games to greet us, all dressed smartly with slicked back hair and accents that are surely the product of a lifetime of elocution lessons. They're handsome, all of them, but not in the same way Atlas was. Not one of them even comes close. Hyacinth lets out a small sigh and suddenly a dozen cigarette cases are conjured from pockets and offered to her. She takes her time, lingering over each, and then chooses one from a brown case with a silver clasp. Its owner smiles smugly and I raise an eyebrow.

'You're scandalous,' I whisper in Hyacinth's ear.

She grins. George puts a glass of champagne in my hand and I nod in awkward thanks. Can he tell I'm not one of them? What sort of small talk do the First Class make?

'Are you at university?' I ask him.

Of course he is. All First Class men study something while

waiting to take over their fathers' estates.

'I'm reading Law,' he says wryly. 'And you?'

One of the girls shrieks with laughter, spilling half of her champagne on to the arm of the boy pulling her down on to the sofa.

Think before you speak, Viv.

'I assist the Chancellor with the writing of the Babel Decree articles,' I say.

It's not true, but it sounds impressive. And here in this big house with all these First Class people, I suddenly feel the need to impress. That's how it's always been, hasn't it? Impress your parents or be punished. Impress your teachers or be demoted.

George lets out a low whistle. 'Hy says you're Hollingsworth's niece?'

I nod.

'Where are you from?'

'Oxford,' I reply, another lie slipping from my mouth.

He nods thoughtfully. 'Can I ask you something?'

I swallow.

'If your aunt is the Chancellor of the Academy for Draconic Linguistics, which exists for the learning and preservation of dragon tongues, then why is she writing the Babel Decree at all?'

I blink, then scan his face for a hint of emotion that might tell me where his First Class loyalties lie. He gives me a gentle smile.

'I don't mean anything by it. It's just that she founded the Academy to facilitate human relations with dragons. So why would she ban us from speaking their tongues, when it's the very thing she has devoted her life to?'

'*She* hasn't banned them,' I say before I can stop myself. 'The *Prime Minister* has. My aunt—'

Be careful.

'My aunt is simply following instructions.'

'Of course,' George says good-naturedly. 'Makes you wonder what Wyvernmire is thinking.'

I feel myself warm to him. I take a sip of champagne and the bubbles pop in my mouth.

'Ever met her?' he asks. 'The PM, I mean.'

I take another sip. 'A few times. She doesn't understand the importance of dragon tongues. She doesn't even speak any.'

George's eyes light up. 'Do you?'

'A few,' I say with a shrug.

He grins. 'So you really *are* Hollingsworth's niece.'

The champagne has created a pleasant glow that suffuses my whole body and I suddenly feel braver, more convincing. I'm an undercover rebel having a conversation at a First Class party and nobody has looked at me twice. Except George. I glance up at him through my eyelashes.

'Of course I am,' I say sweetly. 'Do you speak any languages?'

'Some French. My favourite word is *dépaysement*.'

'What does it mean?' Hyacinth asks, appearing at my shoulder.

'To be disoriented, in a homesick sort of way,' I reply. 'But it's more intense than that. I can't think of an English word that quite captures it. Translated literally, it means *out of country*.'

'Like alienated, or adrift?' Hyacinth says.

'Almost,' I reply eagerly. 'But not quite.'

'The word's untranslatable, then?'

I shake my head. 'Nothing's untranslatable. Just let me think . . .'

'It doesn't matter,' says the boy providing Hyacinth's cigarettes. I think his name is Stephen. 'Not in light of the new Babel Decree article.'

What is he talking about?

'It's going to be announced in the morning. My brother's a Guardian, he told me all about it,' Stephen says. 'Making Slavidraneishá Britannia's national dragon tongue? The language of the Bulgarian dragons? What's the PM playing at? English and Wyrmerian are the languages of the Empire, not some Slavic babble.'

I freeze.

Slavidraneishá is the new national dragon tongue? That can't be true. I would know, Hollingsworth would have told me.

George lays a hand on my arm. 'Are you all right? You've gone rather pale.'

I nod hurriedly.

'This is news to you, too?' he asks gently.

'No,' I almost snap. I meet his gaze and force a smile. 'But the rest of you aren't supposed to know.' I nod towards Stephen. 'If his brother knows what's going on in the Chancellor's office, then what's to say the rebels don't?'

'That's what comes from having a woman Prime Minister, I suppose,' Stephen drawls.

I open my mouth, then close it again as Hyacinth slaps his arm. He grins and plants a kiss on her cheek before she can stop him.

George tops up my glass. 'Stephen here thinks Wyvernmire should be impeached. Thinks she's unfit to rule, that her Bulgarian alliance and Babel Decree are proof of it.'

'The majority of the First Class support the Babel Decree,' I say.

Don't they?

Stephen gives me an icy glare. 'We're not *all* dragon haters.'

'Of course not,' I say quickly. 'But the First Class are the ones who put Wyvernmire in power in the first place. They are –' I pause and correct myself – '*we* are the reason Britannia is now ruled by language restrictions, even though its linguistic diversity is centuries old.'

'My father says we're all collaborators now,' Stephen replies.

'Nonsense,' says George. 'The Prime Minister is in control of the Bulgarians, not the other way round.'

I swallow my champagne. This conversation is getting dangerous and the drink has gone to my head. It has me dancing along the knife-edge of the truth. It has me wanting to tell that idiot Stephen exactly who I am.

'Have you ever met a Bulgarian dragon?' I ask George. 'I mean up close, in the flesh?'

He smirks. 'Yes, actually. My father deals with them every day.'

'Ever spoken to one?'

'Yes.'

I hold his gaze as he fills my glass again. 'Flown with one?'

George's eyes soften and I know I've got him.

'Of course not.' He grins. 'Are you about to tell me *you* have?'

'No,' I lie.

'I've heard Wyvernmire has!' says a girl.

George shakes his head. 'Of all the dragons, the Bulgarian Bolgoriths would be the last to allow a human to ride them. And Wyvernmire doesn't need to. She has them to guard her, to keep her safe somewhere in the city while she devises the battle plans that will take the rebels down.'

'Not for long,' Stephen interjects.

I sense everyone in the room turn to him, see the pleasure of the attention flood his face.

'What do you mean?' Edward says coldly.

'General Goranov will want her out of the way, won't he? So that the Bolgoriths can take over the capital.'

George scoffs loudly. 'Goranov takes his orders from Wyvernmire, you skrit. He might be in charge in Bulgaria, but in Britannia the humans rule. The PM is merely using the Bulgarians to her advantage. The alliance is a carefully calculated one, and once—'

'But that's where you're wrong, Beecham,' Stephen says. 'Wyvernmire isn't Goranov's Prime Minister, she's his puppet.' He sneers. 'How else do you think he convinced her to make him Dragon Chief of State?'

Dragon Chief of State.

'They're erecting a statue of him in Hyde Park.'

'Pen, are you all right?'

I stare at the bubbles in my glass, my vision swimming. Wyvernmire has created a title – a sovereign position – for General Goranov? Why would she give a Bulgarian dragon control over how the country is run? I feel myself sway.

'Is she going to faint?' someone whispers.

Do the rebels know? Does *Hollingsworth* know?

'Oh, give her some space for goodness' sake!'

Hyacinth's breath is sweet on my face. 'Darling, are you all right?' Her cheeks are flushed with heat or alcohol and her hair is curling at her ear.

She has no idea what this means.

'I'll take her outside for some air,' George says.

But Hyacinth is shaking her head. 'No,' she says firmly. 'Edward will.'

Edward appears in front of me and holds out his arm. I take it and let him lead me out into the hallway. As the door closes behind us and the maid hands me my coat, someone turns up the music. Outside, streetlights have been extinguished for the post-curfew blackout, to make it harder for the rebels to attack. My head spins with the fresh air. Edward lights a cigarette.

'Want one?'

'Yes,' I mumble.

Edward hands me a cigarette and offers me a light. I place it between my lips the way I've seen Hollingsworth do, then inhale. The end of the cigarette glows orange and my lungs fill with smoke. I panic, choking and gasping for breath.

'Pen, shut up,' Edward hisses, glancing at the sky.

I muffle another cough with my sleeve, eyes streaming.

'That's disgusting,' I croak.

He plucks the cigarette from my hand and puts it in his mouth so that he's smoking two.

I wipe my eyes. '*You're* disgusting.'

'Thanks.'

I lean back against one of the pillars and close my eyes.

'Your aunt didn't tell you, then?'

My eyes snap open. 'Do you think she knows?'

Edward stares up into the dark clouds and shrugs, the two cigarettes still smoking between his lips. 'She and Wyvernmire are supposed to be as thick as thieves. It would surprise me if she didn't know the Prime Minister has instated a Bulgarian dragon as Dragon Chief of State – whatever that's supposed to mean.'

You don't know how wrong you are, I want to say.

He looks at me. 'I thought you were about to teach Stephen a lesson back there.'

I roll my eyes. 'He's an ignorant skrit.' I pause. 'Do you have the . . . ?'

Edward pats his pocket with a nod, then pulls out a bundle of pamphlets and gives them to me. They're printed in black ink on creamy paper, unfolding in my hands like a book. Edward and I discovered we had the same disdain for the Babel Decree during a heated debate about dragon family dialects a couple of months ago, but neither of us dared declare it outright until the truth became blatantly obvious.

In Defence of Wyrmerian, the cover of the pamphlet reads.

This is how I rebel. I write the pamphlets defending the importance of the banned dragon tongues, and Edward uses his father's printing press to produce them. So far we've also done Harpentesa, Drageoir and Drogarti – Britannia's most common Indian dragon tongue – and the Guardians are no closer to figuring out who is responsible for the illegal publications that appear every fortnight.

Here Wyvernmire is banning languages left, right and centre, unaware that they are the very thing her most wanted rebel is using to undo her hard work. This deliciously ironic fact helps me get out of bed in the morning.

If Hollingsworth knew I was risking discovery in this way, she might think twice about making me the face of the rebellion.

'And are you going to tell me how you'll be distributing these ones?' Edward says.

'No.' I slip the pamphlets into the waistband of my skirt and close my coat. 'Will you let Hyacinth know I had to leave early?'

'You've had a bit of a shock. Perhaps it's best I walk you.'

'I'll be fine. Thanks, Ed.'

I hurry back across Pimlico, keeping to the shadows to avoid any Guardians enforcing curfew. Across the street is a Third Class quarter. It's littered with signs protesting the Babel Decree, covering the exteriors of the houses in such quantities that the Guardians can't keep on top of taking them down. A few months ago this would have surprised me, as the Third Class have never been permitted to study languages at university level. But now the idea that these people would be uninterested in linguistics or the right to free speech is ludicrous. Second languages, dialects, slang . . . they come naturally to those who inhabit the poorest corners of society, where people take care of each other, where community is made by talking and cultural melting pots give birth to new words in the wink of an eye. The Third Class – discarded by the Empire because they are not educated, wealthy or white – are linguists in their own right.

I turn to walk along the River Thames as a boat horn blares. I look up, just in time to see a huge figure on the path ahead. It's a Bulgarian dragon, head bent down to talk to the pair of Guardians standing in its shadow. I feel a swoop of dread. I slip into the obscurity of the nearby trees and walk as quietly as I can, studying the dragon in the moonlight. It's slightly bigger than Chumana, probably male, and a silver crown sits atop its head, peaking down into a triangular shape between its eyes. I'm only half-surprised that the Bulgarian dragons agree to wear such an evident marker of their alliance with Wyvernmire. Their magpie tendencies towards wealth and decoration have clearly won over their disdain for humans.

'You dare abandon your post?' the dragon snarls at the Guardians. 'Only Bolgoriths patrol the streets between here and the South Bank. You should not be here.'

I stop, surprised at his tone. These are Wyvernmire's Guardians of Peace.

'We have orders to search this part of Pimlico for rebels,' one of the Guardians says. 'A dragon cannot fit inside the houses.'

There's a whoosh like a breeze and flames lick in a straight line along the waterfront, engulfing the Guardian in a blazing cloud of orange. He doesn't even have time to scream before he's dead. I drop to the ground, trying to hold in my gasp. I feel my muscles tense with terror – I want to run but I don't dare. The other Guardian stares at the Bolgorith for a second, then turns and flees. A low growl emanates from the dragon's chest as he turns to stare across the Thames. He walks past me, his long, spiked tail dragging up dust, and I catch the acidic scent of burning meat. I don't move, my knees damp from the grass, as I wait for my heartbeat to slow. Then I get shakily to my feet and run the rest of the way, trying not to think of who might be watching me from the sky. Are the Bolgoriths above Wyvernmire's own army now that Goranov is Dragon Chief of State?

Sweet Street is empty, but I still wince as I push open the heavy iron door to the sugar house, its screeching even louder in the silence. I climb up the metal staircases of one of London's oldest factories and into a huge derelict space. Then I fumble in the dark for a match and light the lantern I keep hanging on a broken nail in the wall. An orange glow fills the dark, illuminating splintered floorboards and beams that cross each other above me. The smell of smoke and sugar syrup and something else mingle in the air and I'm suddenly aware of the champagne swishing in my stomach. I hear a crunching sound.

'I'm home,' I call out, shrugging off my coat.

The floor shakes and dust falls from the rafters as a huge shape emerges from behind a rusting, ten-foot sugar tank.

My roommate.

Chumana.

IN DEFENCE OF WYRMERIAN

It befalls to us now to approach the unlikeliest of vernaculars, one it never occurred to us to defend due to its status as Britannia's national dragon tongue and its assured place as the Draconic twin to the language of Shakespeare . . . WYRMERIAN.

And yet, since the Prime Minister mandated that only English is permitted when speaking with dragons – and since the mass departure of dragons from the nation's capital – Wyrmerian is barely more than a whisper on the wind. It is a ghost language destined, if we cannot free ourselves from the ignorant rulership of Adrienne Wyvernmire, to be interred in the same graveyard as Sanskrit or Aramaic, or to become what scholars call a classical language; a museum trophy, admired and studied alongside Latin and Ancient Greek, but nonetheless returned to its display case at the end of the day, never to be spoken aloud.

Part of the North Sea Germanic branch of languages that includes Old English – languages which are therefore older than our modern English itself – Wyrmerian is not merely the dragon tongue of Britannia but its beating, Dragonese heart. Wyrmerian is the language of negotiation and commerce at the Royal Victoria Docks. It is the language of British aviation, the Wyrmerian word finn – used to designate the flight feathers of a dragon's tail – having been borrowed by the English language to specify a part of an aircraft's empennage. It is the tongue spoken by Queen Beatrice's Royal Dragon Advisor (who resigned upon the breaking of the Peace Agreement). It is the lullaby once whispered to the Western Drake dragonlings that used to nest along the Thames, back when dragons were respected members of British society. These dragonlings were referred to as fersc, the word for new in Wyrmerian. It designates newness in a way that only babies can be new, and was borrowed from Old English, where it meant fresh and pure.

But there is no place for such purity, such innocence, in Wyvernmire's Britannia. Not while it is home to species segregation, class inequalities and crimes against dragons.

Will you, the British people, stand by and watch the annihilation of our most refined dragon tongue, the forefather of Britannia's Dragonese? Or will you, in the name of patriotism and language preservation, rebel?

Three

CHUMANA'S STRAWBERRY SCALES SHINE IN THE lamplight, slick with a natural oil that protects the skin beneath from their rough edges. The sores that used to run up her legs, the result of years spent locked inside a dark library, are gone and her teeth are coated in blood. When I told Hollingsworth I wanted to live somewhere far from the First Class luxuries that reminded me of Bletchley Park, she insisted it be with Chumana. My eyes dart to the carcass of a young stag behind the pink dragon and my stomach lurches. So that's what the smell is.

I raise an eyebrow. 'Bon appétit.'

Chumana watches as I head to the makeshift parlour area in the corner of the warehouse and change into a nightdress. A wet wind blows in from the river, straight through the missing wall at the far end of the room. It was smashed away during a rebel attack before we moved in. We can't block it up because it's the only entrance to the building Chumana can fit through. A small fire burns within a metal barrel. I watch out of the corner of my eye as Chumana returns to her prey, holding it steady by an antler as she peels off strips of meat with her teeth. The scent of warm blood is overpowering. I pour myself a glass of water from the jug and sit down amid a pile of blankets to watch the Bulgarian dragon I live with crunch the stag's skull between her jaws.

'Chumana,' I say.

She stops chewing, blood trickling down her chin as her eyes flick lazily to me.

'Wyvernmire has appointed General Goranov as Dragon Chief of State.'

A low growl emanates from her throat. 'I know.'

My heart sinks. Of course she does.

So why am I the only one who didn't?

'Why would she do such a thing?'

Chumana licks her lips. 'She believes it will make her powerful on the world stage, to have a Bulgarian Bolgorith at her side.'

'And will it?'

'It will make her a threat,' she breathes. 'Britannia will be hated for allying with Bulgaria, but it will also be feared.'

'She's also made Slavidraneishá the country's national dragon tongue,' I say as Chumana eats.

'Are you surprised?'

'So British dragons cannot speak their own tongues, but the Bulgarian invaders can?'

A bone cracks loudly between Chumana's teeth. 'Wyvernmire will do whatever is necessary to keep control,' she hisses. 'Since she betrayed Queen Ignacia, no British dragon is required to be loyal to her. Ignacia may be refusing to ally with the rebels, but she still wants revenge against the government. As for the humans, the lower classes are joining the rebellion and the First Class is beginning to question her, too.'

'That's why she has Hollingsworth writing the Babel Decree articles,' I say bitterly. 'She wants to know what everyone is saying at all times.'

Chumana grunts. 'Assimilation through language is an age-old tactic among humans. Perhaps this war will be fought with tongues rather than talons or teeth. It is why Rita Hollingsworth chose you as her Swallow.'

'Her swallow?' I say.

'That is what she calls you. What the rebels call you.' Chumana looks up again, her grin full of blood. 'Don't you like it?'

'She wants me to be the face of the rebellion, but she doesn't bother to tell me anything,' I mutter. 'She still hasn't sent me to Canna. What's the point of learning to speak the tongue of the Hebridean Wyverns if I'm never actually going to use it?'

'So you assume you are ready to come face to face with a pack of wyverns?' Chumana breathes.

'I've read Clawtail's descriptions of them, of their behaviour and culture and environment, and I can speak basic Cannair now, so—'

'You forget that they are dragons, dragons with wings and teeth and a taste for flesh. And you are just a girl.'

'Just a girl?' I spit. 'Why is it that everyone has forgotten what I did at Bletchley Park, what Atlas and I . . .'

I stop as the memories unfurl again, threatening to wrap their cold hands around my throat and choke me.

'We could go to Canna together, couldn't we?' I continue. 'We could fly there tonight. And if I can't convince the wyverns to help us then maybe *you* can. They'll recognise you as one of their own.' I shrink beneath Chumana's fiery gaze. She stares at me, no trace of her meal left except for some shining white bones and a red stain on the floor.

'I will thank you,' she snarls, 'not to compare me to a wyvern. Obstinate, fickle, two-legged things.'

'*I* have two legs,' I say, swallowing the laugh in my throat. 'Does that mean I'm obstinate and fickle?'

'And yet,' she says, ignoring me, 'you would do well not to underestimate them. Wyverns are proud, prouder than any other species. They hoard knowledge like Bolgoriths hoard riches, as though they invented intelligence itself and should be rewarded for it. They hunt in packs, so swift and methodical that it is as if they are of one mind.' Her eyes fall on my face and I feel my smile disappear. 'You will not outsmart one, and you will not outrun one.'

'What's the difference between a wyvern and a dragon, apart from the number of legs?'

'Wyverns lack the solitary nature of dragons,' Chumana replies. 'They live by no maxim. They are an excitable, unpredictable species and their bodies are smaller, more pliable than those of dragons. I have seen one pass through the narrowest of gaps in search of its prey. I suspect that these particular wyverns—'

'The Hebrideans,' I say.

'—will only be found if they want to be.'

'Clawtail's journal says the Hebridean Wyverns only speak one language. Did you know that?'

Chumana growls.

'The only other species anywhere near as lazy about learning tongues are the Bulgarian Bolgoriths, and that's only because they communicate largely in echolocation.'

'Lazy. Such a compliment warms my heart,' Chumana says.

'You know I don't mean you,' I reply. 'Hollingsworth says that Goranov's army places troops in family groups because their strong emotional bond allows them to communicate effectively over long distances.' I steal a glance at Chumana. 'You were wise to tell us, you know. That the Koinamens is more than just language. You know I won't try to translate it ever again.'

When she doesn't reply, I push the pile of pamphlets Edward gave me towards her.

'Will you deliver these for me? Tonight?'

She sniffs. 'No one told me that living with you would involve becoming a giant dracovol.'

'Well, you're the most inconspicuous dragon-sized dracovol I know.' I nod towards the silver piece of metal lying in the corner. Chumana begrudgingly sticks her snout under the crown and tosses it on to her head. With the silver peak between her eyes, she looks just like one of Wyvernmire's dragons. I found it dented in the street in the aftermath of a rebel attack and after dragging it back here, Chumana used her flame to weld it back into shape. I'm surprised Hollingsworth didn't have one made for her, as it makes her night-time flights even less noticeable. Whether she likes it or not, Chumana is crucial to Hollingsworth, because only she can listen to the Bulgarians using her Koinamens. She can only understand their most simple calls, as she's not bonded with any of them, but it's enough to know where they're stationing patrols or where they'll attack next.

She takes the pamphlets in her mouth and lumbers over to the missing wall. I follow, the wind whipping my nightdress around my legs. I peer over the edge at the dark street below, then up into the starry sky. Chumana transfers the bundle to her talon.

'Keep back,' she growls. 'Do you remember how to listen for a Bolgorith?'

'Your wings beat slower,' I say, nodding. 'Two beats, not three.'

'Good. Extinguish the lamp.'

Chumana steps off the ledge and into the air. I gasp as she swoops low, her wings barely fitting between the rows of buildings, then lifts with such a force that the bushes lining the street bow in her wake. I go back to the blankets on the floor and pull them aside. Hidden beneath them are five more pamphlets. I slide them into my satchel. Tomorrow, I'll show them to Hollingsworth. She'll be angry at first, but they'll make her realise how dedicated I am to the rebel cause. They'll make her realise that I'm ready to go to Canna. I tuck them inside my satchel, then blow out the lamp and lie down.

The wind blows humid across the room, threatening to pull my covers away. I burrow down the way I used to do as a child in my bed, back when I slept on cotton sheets instead of floorboards. But I'm not frightened in the sugar house. I know I'm safer here than anywhere else in London. When Chumana and I first took up residence, both still wounded from the Battle of Bletchley, my body reacted to every creak and groan. Atlas's voice haunted my dreams and looking at Chumana, so bloody and beaten, was an unbearable reminder of how I felt. We kept to opposite sides of the building, me freezing beneath my damp blankets, until one night the floor beneath me shook and a hot wing dropped over my body.

'You can't sleep like this forever,' I had hissed bitterly into the dark. 'I'll just be an inconvenience to you.'

'You'll inconvenience me more if you're dead,' came the reply.

I lie still, listening to the sound of my own beating heart and the distant swish of wings outside. I wait for Chumana to return, for her presence to banish the thoughts that slip back into my mind every time I'm alone, those that remind me that the war still isn't won, that my parents are still imprisoned and that Atlas is still dead.

Dragon Chief of State . . . how will Britannia ever escape this mess?

I clutch the swallow around my neck and think of the pamphlets again. All I want is to make up for my mistakes: betraying Sophie, believing lies about the Third Class, taking so long to join the rebels. All I want is to live out the second chance Chumana promised me, to honour Atlas's memory by helping the Coalition. But writing about dragon tongues isn't going to achieve that. I remember what Chumana called me earlier and cringe.

The Swallow?

What would the rebels think if they knew the Swallow is hiding in a house in London while they fight dragons? And now Goranov is leading the country and Slavidraneishá is the only dragon tongue allowed. I bury my face into a cushion and scream. I have to do *something*.

Something dark slips into the sugar house as my eyes grow heavy, a desolation I haven't felt this keenly since Atlas died. Working for Hollingsworth – having a purpose – has been the only thing keeping it at bay. But now I let it flood the empty space around me, licking up the wooden beams like a cold, shadowy flame. Atlas's face appears in front of me, blood droplets spattered across his white collar. I see a silver revolver. Smoke. A motorcar hurtling through the trees.

The terrible memories engulf my dreams and I hear myself cry out just as a scaly warmth settles beside me.

There is the soft whoosh of flames.

A bird flies through my mind and scatters the nightmares, light trailing from its forked tail.

*

When I wake, Chumana is asleep beside me and smoky tendrils are spiralling above the cold barrel fire. The pink sunrise falls across the blankets and my heart jolts. I've overslept. I throw on my clothes as the morning light grows brighter. Hollingsworth will be furious with me for travelling after daybreak. Chumana snores as I step over her tail and run down the metal stairs. My despair at yesterday's events has formed a tight knot in my stomach that won't go away and I keep my head down as I come out of the Tube station and walk towards Claridge House. As long as I continue to play my role as Penelope Hollingsworth convincingly, surely the Chancellor will forgive my lateness.

I falter as I almost tread on a white sheet of paper, then spot more littered across the pavement ahead. It's only when a woman stoops to pick one up that I realise what they are. My pamphlets, scattered across several quarters. Chumana did well.

A man in a suit walks past, his coat looped over his arm and a pamphlet pressed to his nose. I feel my heart flutter. Guardians are collecting them into canvas sacks, but the people who walk by them have already picked up their copies and are reading, too. A Guardian tries to snatch one from an elderly man who lets out an angry sigh. 'Is it illegal to read now, too?'

Two girls in traditional Bulgarian dress gather pamphlets from the ground, giggling together. They remind me of characters from a Bulgarian storybook of Mama's. She translated it into English for me when I was small, setting the stories in London instead of Sofia. With Mama's copy lost and all the books in Bulgaria burned, the original Bulgarian stories are surely lost forever.

'This is England!' a man leers at the girls as they talk. 'So speak English, or go home!'

One of the girls opens her mouth to retort, but a Bolgorith lands on a nearby rooftop and they both scurry away. I pull my scarf over my hair as I cross the road. Has Wyvernmire forgotten that a portion of the British population is made up of Bulgarian refugees and their children, survivors of the Massacre of Bulgaria? These are the Bolgoriths that murdered Mama's family: *my* family. For all I know, the dragon that just landed could have burned my grandmother alive.

I walk past a building whose front wall has been blown apart, bricks scattered across the street. Inside, a registrar is officiating a wedding, the bride's white veil billowing in the open air. A high-pitched squeal makes me look away. On the corner of Grosvenor Square, a crowd is gathering. Guardians and civilians line the street, smoke rising above their heads. I freeze as the squeal sounds again and before I know it I'm heading towards the crowd. A dragonling, no bigger than a Yorkshire terrier, is flapping around on the pavement. Its blue scales glint in the sunlight, drawing attention to its twisted talon. It stumbles as a Guardian prods it with his baton and black smoke streams from its nostrils, a sign of distress. My mouth turns dry. Like the people around me, my instinct is to look up. The dragonling's parent must be nearby. As the Guardian prods the dragonling again and his colleagues laugh, some of the people hurry away. Anger bubbles beneath my skin. The dragonling will die of shock if they don't kill it first. I take a step towards them, my satchel full of pamphlets banging heavily on my thigh. The knot in my stomach pulls taut, begging for release. This is my chance to do *something*.

The dragonling cries out pitifully.

'Leave it alone!' I shout.

Faces turn towards me and a couple of the helmeted

Guardians reach for their batons. The Guardian prodding the dragonling does it again, and this time it curls up into a ball on the pavement, eyes closed and tail quivering. I spring forward and snatch the baton from the Guardian's hand.

'What do you think you're doing?' he shouts.

They all move towards me simultaneously, but their angry yells are muffled as an ear-splitting roar fills the air. My hands reach instinctively to protect my head as people scream. I dart for the cover of a nearby doorway, only for the Guardian to pull me backwards by the hood of my mackintosh.

'Let go of me!' I scream as fire licks along the street.

He drags me beneath an arch that leads into a private courtyard just as a Western Drake swoops low and catches the dragonling in her talons. She deposits it into the gaping pouch in her underbelly, then breathes another stream of fire that engulfs every human being on the opposite side of the road. I gasp as hot air fills my lungs and the Guardian beside me chokes, my hood still twisted in his fist. Bullets deflect off the dragon's scales as Guardians shoot helplessly and more flames rain down, the loud crackle of burning motorcars blocking out the screams.

'This is your fault,' I spit at the Guardian. 'You provoked her.'

I try to escape his grasp but my satchel catches on a rusty hook sticking out of the wall. There's a ripping sound, and then the pamphlets spill out on to the cobblestones. The Guardian looks down at them, then back at me. Horror pricks my skin.

'You're a rebel,' he barks. 'Who are you working for?'

'No one!' I say into the black visor. 'I was—'

A siren whirrs – the attack alarm. Any minute now the street will fill with people running to the bomb shelters we used back in the first war. The Guardian pushes me against the wall. Familiar screeches sound in the air.

A Bulgarian patrol is descending.

The archway above us shakes, dust falling on to our heads, and a leg the width of a tree trunk appears in the entrance. The black talons are encrusted with blood and dirt. Slowly, the Western Drake lowers her head until her face is level with us.

I don't have time to think. I just speak.

'I tried to save your child,' I tell her in Wyrmerian. 'Please, warn my friend that I'm being arrested. She's a rebel Bolgorith living in the sugar house on Sweet Street. She'll tell my boss that—'

The Guardian rams his hands over my mouth so hard that I taste blood between my teeth. The ground vibrates as several dragons land and the Western Drake lets out a hiss. Her eye winks once. Then her giant legs move out of view and I hear the whoosh of wings as she launches into the air with a warning cry.

'What did you say to her?' the Guardian shouts.

I twist in his grip and bite down on to his hand until he screams.

'The Bolgoriths will kill her anyway,' he spits. 'And her deformed offspring.'

He kicks my legs out from under me and pain radiates through my spine as he cuffs my hands. He pushes me out on to the street, which is teeming with fire engines and Bulgarian dragons. The park on Grosvenor Square is on fire, the trees awash with flames that send a greenish smoke spiralling into the air. Opposite, hoses are being used to douse the Academy in water, to prevent it catching alight. My stomach drops. What have I done? One look at my class pass and the Guardian will have Hollingsworth arrested for harbouring a rebel niece. And if he finds out who I really am, it won't take long to work out that Hollingsworth is with the Coalition, too. Dread fills me as a motorcar slows beside us, clanging noisily as it drives over a drain cover. The Guardian leans inwards to speak to the driver, his hand still tight on my arm. My fingers reach for my class pass beneath my jumper and tug until the delicate chain breaks. Then I toss the whole thing down the drain.

The Guardian wrenches the car door open and pushes me into the back seat.

'Identification?' he says, holding out his hand.

'I have none,' I say brazenly. 'I'm a rebel, remember?'

He doesn't move, and with his visor covering his face it's impossible to tell what he's going to do next. Then he slams the door shut. 'Croydon Airfield,' he orders.

The car drives through the familiar streets, then past Claridge House. I blink back tears as I stare up at the window of Hollingsworth's office. She must be wondering where I am. A pair of dragons fly behind distant clouds as we drive further out of London. Soon, the car slows. The driver shows a badge and two sets of military gates open for us.

The airfield is small but full of planes. I see them up close as we cruise past and realise I've seen planes like these before. They're identical to the one we used to escape Bletchley

Park, the plane Marquis, Serena and Karim built under Mr Knott's supervision. And I'm willing to bet they all breathe fire. Marquis would be devastated if he knew.

The car comes to a stop in front of a giant warehouse, patrolled by Guardians and several species of dragons: I spot Western Drakes and a whole group of Ddraig Gochs among the Bulgarian Bolgoriths. These must be the few British dragons that have chosen Wyvernmire over Ignacia, and over the rebels. We step out into the damp air. All I can think of is Chumana, who will expect me home this evening.

More shiny new planes fill the open warehouse on the other side of the airfield, and towering over them are two Bulgarian dragons. The first is low in rank, judging by its lack of jewels. The second is black with a diamond the size of my fist melted into his left shoulder. I feel a pang as I recognise him.

General Goranov.

What is he doing here? I hide my trembling hands in my coat pockets. There is nothing of Chumana's begrudging gentleness in these dragons. Behind them is a plane that is bigger than the others and maintenance workers climb up and down its steps, preparing for something.

The Guardian who drove me here lifts his visor. 'Go on, then. Tell them who you work for.'

I blink. 'Tell who?'

He nods his head in the direction of the dragons and I gape at him. If General Goranov sees me, he'll recognise me from Bletchley Park. The Guardian's hand flutters over his gun. Behind us, the gates slam closed.

'But they'll kill me,' I say hoarsely.

The Guardian stares at me, unblinking. I steel myself as I discard my torn satchel and turn towards the dragons. It's time to be impressive again. Impress the Bulgarian dragons, or die. I begin the walk across the airfield. Goranov's dark eyes narrow as I approach.

'Vivien Featherswallow, captured?' he growls, his accent hard and biting. 'How?'

'I was writing pamphlets,' I reply shakily. 'About Britannia's dragon tongues.'

'Wyvernmire's little translator. You were part of her feeble attempt at winning the war against her own people. And yet here you are, working to undermine her.'

I force myself to breathe. With my class pass gone, the Guardians won't be able to connect me to Hollingsworth. She and the rebel movement are safe, for now. But I'm not.

'What is a *pamphlet?*' the low-ranking dragon says, mispronouncing the word.

He can't have known English for long. He waits for me to reply, his huge head looming.

'The humans and dragons of Britannia have the right to speak their native languages,' I say. 'The pamphlets are . . . they're like a call to arms.'

A low hissing sound comes from the dragons. Laughter. My cheeks burn, but I don't flinch. Somehow, I have to convince Goranov that I'm not afraid of him. I have to convince him not to kill me.

'You have a Bulgarian Bolgorith who follows in your wake,' Goranov says. 'My brother was fascinated when I told him. However did you manage it?'

'Brother?' I say.

'The Regal Krasimir.'

I remember Hollingsworth's sketch of the Bulgarian trio.

'Well?' Goranov snarls.

'She doesn't *follow in my wake*,' I reply. 'But you certainly followed in Wyvernmire's, back in the forest at Bletchley Park. I saw it with my own eyes.'

Another growl comes from Goranov's throat.

'You think to provoke me? I will rip your head from your shoulders, you *kurtapàla*.'

The word is derogatory, an insult in Slavidraneishá.

'I speak only the truth,' I reply in the same language.

Goranov hisses at the sound of his mother tongue.

'I'm a polyglot. I speak with both humans and dragons in the languages they understand. That is how I help the rebels. And if you kill me, their greatest asset,' I lie, 'then they'll double down on London in revenge.'

I may be what Hollingsworth calls the face of the rebellion, but I'm not foolish enough to believe the Human-Dragon Coalition would be able to intensify the attacks if I were murdered. They're barely holding their own against Wyvernmire's army as it is.

'An enchantress,' the low-ranking dragon breathes in English.

'A brasstongue,' Goranov says.

His jaws part slightly to reveal a red, flickering tongue. I remember how he marched through the woods in Bletchley, camouflaged by the black smoke, a witness to my last moments with Atlas. The memory distracts me for a moment, until I hear a clicking sound. I feel the sudden, primal urge to run.

It's the sound of flame igniting in Goranov's chest.

He takes a breath and I see the fire swirl in his mouth. I stare in petrified awe.

This is how I die.

What will it feel like to burn?

'Stop!'

A strident voice echoes through the warehouse. The flames at Goranov's lips flicker into nothing. I turn my head. A woman is stepping down off the big plane behind the dragons, shrouded in a long black coat. Her red hair gleams in the morning sunlight and when our eyes meet in the shocked silence, she almost lifts a hand as if in greeting.

Blood rushes in my ears.

What is *she* doing *here*?

'Stop?' Goranov snarls. 'This human is a—'

'Passenger,' Wyvernmire says. 'On the prime-ministerial plane.' A smug satisfaction sits in the lines of her face. 'You can board now, Vivien.'

I feel my lip curl. The last time I saw her, she had just let Atlas bleed out on to the forest floor. Hatred bubbles inside me, snaking through my veins like poison. Nobody moves. The maintenance workers are cowering beneath the plane, their eyes on the smoke escaping Goranov's nostrils. I glance up at the cockpit. I don't have a choice. I know it and Wyvernmire knows it too. I can board the plane with her or be burned up by Goranov.

I walk calmly towards her, even though the heat

smouldering off Goranov's scales warns me to run. Because I have to convince her, too. Wyvernmire might not be a dragon, but she's a monster, nonetheless. When I reach her, she gestures a bony hand up the steps. I hold her gaze.

'Where will it take me?' I ask coldly. 'Bulgaria?'

'I've seen enough Bolgoriths for one day, haven't you?' Wyvernmire replies with a smirk. 'Besides . . . I think the Swallow will be of far more use to me on Canna.'

Four

THE PLANE RATTLES AS IT HURTLES down the runway. I stare out of the window at Goranov's hulking figure and marvel at the fact that I'm still alive.

And that I'm aboard a plane to Canna.

Wyvernmire sits in the row of seats across the aisle, watching me. 'I'll admit I'm surprised to see you.'

I feel my face flush hot as the sound of her voice brings more flashbacks – the dragon blood across her face, Atlas's hand in mine, the cool orders she gave as he lay dying. I want to close my eyes and forget but I can't, because here she is in front of me, her face like porcelain, that vulgar dragon's talon brooch pinned to her breast.

'Likewise.' I glower. 'Shouldn't you and Goranov be off building a nest somewhere?'

I sound like a petulant child, but I can't help it. I hate her.

'You've joined the rebellion,' she says flatly.

I don't reply. The plane vibrates as it lifts into the air.

'What use have they for *you*?' she asks. 'Aside from having you author those silly pamphlets?'

'Recruiting,' I lie. 'Rallying sympathisers for the cause.'

'And who do you take orders from? Serge Hammond in North London? Ava Richmond in Kent? Tommy Coin in Manchester?'

'I – I don't know,' I stutter. 'There was a long chain of command. They never told me who was at the top.'

Wyvernmire glances out of the window. 'The rebel leaders are unanimous in their determination to keep secret the identity of their faceless patriarch.' She lets out a bitter sigh. 'Such a waste of talent you are.'

'Why are we going to Canna?' I ask.

'I plan to finish the war there. Mainland Scotland still belongs to the rebels, and the neighbouring island of Eigg is home to the headquarters of the Human-Dragon Coalition.' Wyvernmire smiles. 'The female Grey Wyvern often lies with her enemies before killing them. Did you know that?'

I jump at the mention of wyverns. All this time I've been desperate for Hollingsworth to send me to Canna, but now Wyvernmire is the one taking me there. Does she know about the Hebridean Wyverns? Does she know the rebels are looking for them?

'Don't flatter yourself,' I say coolly. 'You're not worthy of your dragon-descended name.'

She smiles again. 'General Goranov disagrees.'

'You think you're in power,' I say slowly, 'setting up camp near Eigg so you can defeat the rebels, but what if Goranov is letting you fly to Canna because the Bolgoriths want you out of the capital?'

'Letting me?' Wyvernmire gives a girlish laugh. 'I know you believe that the Bulgarian dragons only came to my aid in order to tempt and entrap me, Vivien. And Bulgaria is powerful, of course, but the rest of Europe is human-run. If the Bulgarian Bolgoriths want to regain respect and legitimacy in the eyes of their neighbouring countries, they need the support of powerful humans. The support of the Empire.'

My heart sinks.

'Besides,' Wyvernmire says as clouds gather at the windows. 'If Goranov *is* plotting against me, then you might prove useful indeed.'

I frown.

What does she mean?

'It is outlandishly fortunate that you appeared on the airfield at the very moment I was preparing to fly to Canna. Some might call it suspiciously convenient. But I know the rebels would never have sent you to me. Like you told Goranov . . . you are their greatest asset.'

Her green eyes flash dangerously.

'Perhaps it's divine intervention. Atlas believed in that sort of thing, didn't he?'

A visceral rush of grief shoots through me, like air on an exposed nerve. Wyvernmire sees it and lifts her chin, triumphant. I almost gasp at her cruelty, at the boldness with which she pronounces his name. I could double over from the pain of it.

'Fuck you,' I whisper.

A radio crackles to life. It's coming from a duffel bag in

one of the overhead luggage nets.

'The battle for Britannia has begun, and on it depends the birth of her new age, free of corrupt Peace Agreements and political lies,' says a muffled voice.

I freeze as I recognise it.

Serena?

'Bulgarian Bolgoriths terrorise London and the nation's dragons are being silenced. Wyrmerian and Harpentesa are now illegal languages, as are the regional human dialects that built the United Kingdom. Prime Minister Wyvernmire would have you believe that dragons want to rule us, would have our kinds segregated, while she invites a massacring species into our midst! She would have you believe that friendship with dragons is perverse or dangerous. But we, the Human-Dragon Coalition, tell you otherwise.'

Serena's voice is that of an educated First Class girl, smooth and reassuring. It's not the voice one would expect of a rebel, and the Coalition knows it.

Language is a weapon, Vivien.

'And so does our Swallow. She is working with you, rebels of Britannia! The girl who broke the Peace Agreement, who began the Battle of Bletchley, is resisting as we speak. If we can stand up to our Bulgarian enemy then our country will be reborn. But fail, and the whole of Europe will fall into its jaws. As you read the Academy's newest Babel Decree article, remember this: banning languages will do more damage to our country than the fiercest Bolgorith.'

Serena's voice disappears into a long crackle.

'How touching,' Wyvernmire says. 'They broadcast almost

every day. It's often the girl talking, although I've heard your cousin on there too.'

My heart jumps.

'Marquis?' I say.

'Broadcasting from Eigg, no doubt, with the same arrogance found in your pamphlets.'

The thought of Marquis and Serena joining me in this small act of rebellion makes me want to weep.

A beetle crawls along the floor and I keep my eyes on it as it rubs its wings together. They're spotted like those of a Sandveld Sator, an African dragon I've only seen in sketches. I don't look up until the plane begins its descent. A vast, sloping land stretches below us, glowing green and gold beneath grey, moody clouds. It's broken up by stretches of dark blue water and as the plane flies lower, we veer past tall black stones that reach up to touch the sky.

'We're landing in Bualintur, on the Isle of Skye,' Wyvernmire says as my gaze falls on a small cluster of white houses in the distance. 'I will need you to move quickly, do you understand?'

I nod, refusing to ask why. All that matters now is that I get to Canna. From there, I can only hope that I'll be able to escape and find the wyverns. If that's even possible without Clawtail's journal.

The plane races downwards and we return to our seats as turbulence hits, the Scottish wind threatening to toss the aircraft, hitting the sides so hard it feels like a dragon is barrelling into us. I clutch the handle above me. The plane lands.

'I thought Scotland was rebel territory,' I say as the engine rumbles to a stop.

'Hence the need to move fast,' Wyvernmire replies, pulling her duffel bag down.

I climb down the steps into the cold highland air. The long grass of the sand-filled field swishes against my legs. Black mountains frame the horizon and beyond the field is a huge body of water. I can see a small boat bobbing on it and at its edge, standing in the thin, drizzling rain, is a small figure and a dragon. We hasten towards them, our boots kicking up sand. The man turns to us first. He's old with white hair sprouting out of his ears and large hands that smooth out the front of his waxed overcoat as he watches us approach.

'Prime Minister Wyvernmire,' he says with a Scottish accent. 'Welcome to Loch Brittle. We only have a few minutes.'

He works quickly, pushing a small motorboat through the shallows into deeper water. Wyvernmire watches from the shore and I hear her questioning him. The dragon still hasn't moved. She's a Bulgarian Bolgorith, a reddish pink almost the same shade as Chumana.

Several small blue jewels, embedded above the talons of her left foot, glisten in the light. She's young, I can tell by counting the white-tipped spikes on her face. I cast a nervous glance up at her as she stares out across the loch.

'My condolences,' she says.

Is she speaking to me?

'Condolences?'

'You're a prisoner, are you not? Isn't that what people here say, when something goes wrong?'

Her Slavic accent is strong, her pronunciation tentative and slow.

'Commiserations, maybe,' I say. 'Condolences are for when someone has died.'

I immediately regret it. What if I anger her? The yellow canines protruding from the sides of her mouth are a clear indicator of what could happen if I do.

'I thought you were a prisoner because you rebelled against your government,' the Bolgorith says. 'Am I wrong?'

I wonder how she knows I'm a prisoner.

'No,' I reply.

'Then I am sure many of your own have died.'

I open my mouth and close it, then nod as Atlas's still face fills my mind.

'My condolences,' she says again.

I stare at the old man, knee-deep in the water, as he climbs on to the boat and pulls the cord on the motor. It bursts into life with a whine.

'I don't know why we didn't just fly to Canna,' I mutter.

'And risk attack from Eigg or the dragons of Rùm?' the Bolgorith says. 'Britannia's dragons will bring down any plane that goes near their nesting space. Eggs need quiet, you know.'

'I *do* know, actually,' I retort.

I feel a sudden rush of anger at this invader, who has decided to lecture me on the practices of British dragons while collaborating in my arrest and kidnapping.

'But,' I say, 'you'd think the government and its Bulgarian friends would have more resources at their disposal than a dismal motorboat.'

A low rumble sounds from the dragon's throat. 'The government possesses plenty of superior boats in Mallaig, but it is rebel territory now. It is the closest part of the mainland to Eigg, where the rebel headquarters are, so of course it is armed with both human weapons and dragons.'

I have never even heard of Mallaig.

'You seem to know a lot for a dragon who only got here a few months ago,' I say dryly.

It's meant to be sarcasm, but the dragon's mouth immediately stretches into a grin so wide it looks menacing. I almost stumble backwards in surprise. The Bulgarian Bolgorith is smiling.

'Thank you,' she says. 'I did my research.'

It feels unnatural, comical even. I don't think I've ever seen Chumana smile.

'You know you're not here for a friendly visit, don't you?' I say.

The Bolgorith snaps at a fly. 'I was conscripted here at the orders of the Regal Krasimir, but I have my own reasons for coming to Britannia.'

I frown. Why is this dragon being so talkative? Bolgoriths are meant to be hostile and aggressive, and yet this one is as cordial as a diplomat.

'What's a regal?'

'Bulgaria is divided up between the great dragon regals,' she replies, her voice deep and warm. 'They are the strongest, most respected dragons, those who glitter in the jewels that make up their vast hoards.' She looks at me from beneath impossibly long eyelashes. 'What is your name?'

Does she not realise that we are enemies? That she is part of a foreign army threatening to turn my country into a new Bulgaria? My eyes run along the length of her body, which is solid and strong, her scales slick and shiny without a single one missing. I doubt she has ever seen battle. From the shore, Wyvernmire beckons me towards the boat.

I don't move. 'Vivien,' I reply. 'What's yours?'

'Daria.'

'I wish I could say it's a pleasure to meet you,' I say in Slavidraneishá. 'But it's not.'

Making a sudden switch to a different language is a way to test people, to gauge what they think of you by disarming them, catching them unawares. But Daria doesn't even flinch.

'They sent word about you,' she says. She watches a gull soar across the sky.

Goranov has echolocated to other Bolgoriths about my arrival? But we're miles from London. How could the Koinamens have stretched so far?

'You're the brasstongue from Bletchley Park, the place where the Bulgarian-British alliance was made.'

There's that word again.

Brasstongue.

'What does that mean?'

The old man waves frantically from the boat and I see Wyvernmire's face grow taut with impatience.

'A human who speaks many dragon tongues. Sometimes you can be useful. But most of the time you are . . . dangerous. In my country, there is not a single one left.'

'That's because you murdered everyone,' I spit.

Daria's amber eyes blink twice and I think she's about to reply when the old man bellows across the sand. 'Come on!'

Daria flicks her tail towards him. 'Go. The rebel dragons are almost here.'

She must be hearing their echolocation calls.

'You would do well to cooperate with your Prime Minister until you reach the island,' she continues. 'But then you must escape. If you wait until you are under Bulgarian guard, it will be too late.'

I turn to her. 'Why would you tell me that? I'm a rebel human. You're a Bulgarian dragon.'

Her red tongue flickers inside her mouth. 'You remind me of a survivor I once met in the motherland. I quite liked him.'

A survivor? In Bulgaria?

I walk towards the water. 'Bye.'

'Goodbye, brasstongue.'

My feet squelch into the algae-covered mud of the shallows. The old man helps Wyvernmire into the boat before offering me his hand. 'Do ye' want to be food for the dragons, wean?'

The boat is long and wooden, heavily varnished with leather seats and a steering wheel. It's the type used for pleasure-sailing, not war.

'Welcome aboard,' the old man says. 'I'm Craig.'

I take a seat. 'Are you a turncoat, Craig?' I ask calmly.

He laughs as Wyvernmire sits down next to me, her lip curling at the mud and water we have trailed across the deck.

'What makes ye' say that?'

'Mainland Scotland is controlled by rebels, but this piece of Skye that sits just across from the Small Isles is conveniently unguarded.' I look across the water at Daria, who is still watching us. 'So my guess is that *you* are the guard, and you've turned your station into another access route for the Prime Minister's Guardians.'

Craig raises an eyebrow at Wyvernmire. 'Clever little thing, isn't she?'

'The rebels will realise what you're doing soon,' I say.

'Course they will,' Craig replies. 'Scotland's PM is a right dragon-lover. But in the meantime—'

'You support *her* because you don't like dragons?' I interrupt, gesturing to Wyvernmire. 'You know we've only seen a fraction of the Bulgarian dragons about to invade Britannia, don't you?'

Craig sniffs. 'They only *think* they're in power. Prime Minister Wyvernmire will bide her time, use them to put the country back to rights, then send them on their way.'

'Right you are, Craig,' Wyvernmire says softly. 'Now . . . to Canna?'

I sit back in disbelief. What is it about politics that make people believe only what they want to believe? The boat speeds off across the water and I watch Daria get smaller until she is just a black pinprick in the distance.

The sun is high in the sky by the time Craig says we're near the archipelago of islands I read about in the library at Bletchley Park, the one I first saw from Marquis's plane. I hear the roaring before I see the first island.

'Sound travels faster across water than it does land,' Craig calls out, and I'm reminded of the way ultrasound travels more easily through glass.

A few moments later, he points to Rùm. It appears on the left side of the boat, a mountainous, barren island made of rock and black sand. I know from the maps I've studied that this dragon nesting ground is sandwiched between two other islands: Canna, controlled by Wyvernmire, and Eigg, home to the rebels. I instinctively shrink back from the sheer size of it, and at the sight of several Sand Dragons basking on a small beach. They could well be Ignacia's, and I am travelling with the woman who betrayed her.

Craig cuts the motor and lets the boat drift, steering it quietly around the island so that we come so close to the rock I could reach out and touch it. A creeping fear tingles across the back of my neck. With the Peace Agreement broken, a dragon could kill us now and get away with it. Stones and hot ash fall down into the boat and when I look up, I see what must be the edge of a nest built halfway up a cliff. Craig veers the boat back towards open waters and starts the motor again, and we glide through a cloud of afternoon mist until I spot another land mass, this one a long, horizontal stretch across the water.

'Welcome to Wean Island,' Craig says.

'Wean?'

'A Scots word for child,' he says with a wink.

Child Island.

Craig is referring to the Peace Agreement's imprisonment of so-called criminal children on Canna, left there as food for Ignacia's dragons as part of a secret clause.

'That's barbaric,' I spit.

'It's the concept that's barbaric, lass, not the name for it.'

I stare across the water at Canna. It's flatter and greener than Rùm and covered in white dots which, as we get closer, I realise are grazing sheep. It looks idyllic, far safer than Rùm, but I know the opposite is true. I feel a lurch of dread in my stomach. How long have I been begging Hollingsworth to send me here, desperate to finally set foot on the land where Clawtail once walked, to see the home of the Hebridean Wyverns with my own eyes? But now I'm here, I suddenly want to be back in London. Because at least if Hollingsworth had deemed me ready, she would have sent me to Canna with a pack of supplies. A team for protection. And, crucially, with more information than I currently have on the wyverns, like *why* they are the key to winning the war. I shrink back in my seat, smoothing down the thin material of my office trousers, as I realise how woefully unprepared I am.

We sail around one side of the island, keeping to the edges of the cliff faces. Someone has scrawled across them with a black liquid, the words half-painted, half-smeared.

LUCY WAS HERE.
CORALINE AND JACK FOREVER
EAT DUNG WYVERNMIRE

The rebels were supposed to liberate the children left on Canna. Have they done so already? As we skim the shoreline I begin to recognise the shape of the island from the descriptions in Clawtail's journal. Attached to Canna is what looks like a second expanse of land, sprawling across the water as if Canna has sprouted a wing. It's a tidal island called Sanday, linked to Canna by sandbanks and only accessible at low tide. We approach a small bay that embraces a body of water and to its right is a circle of rocks where boats are docked. I stare out across the rolling hills beyond and spot several Guardians marching through the fields towards us. They reach us as I'm stepping out of the boat.

'Prime Minister Wyvernmire,' one of them says as they all raise their visors. 'We have come to escort you to the camp.'

He takes the Prime Minister's bag and pushes it into the arms of another Guardian before reaching out a hand to help Wyvernmire out of the boat.

'Wonderful. As you can see,' she says with a glance at me, 'I have unfortunately been forced to play the role of prison warden.'

'Ma'am, we would have sent someone—'

'Please ensure *she* is escorted at *all* times.'

The Guardians eye me suspiciously as the motorboat sputters to life again. I turn to watch Craig speed away.

Rùm looms just across the water, closer to Canna than I thought it would be. I think of the children sent here to be eaten by the dragons nesting on Rùm and feel sick. It would take a dragon about a minute to fly the distance between the two islands. Back when I was staying on Eigg, sharing a guesthouse room with Ursa, Rùm was so much further away – a distant, abstract threat. I look for the rebel headquarters now, hoping to catch a glimpse of the island where I left my sister, but it's concealed behind Rùm's mountains of rock.

'This way, miss,' says the Guardian holding Wyvernmire's bag.

The face behind the white helmet is young and almost

apologetic. I wonder if he knows who I am. I follow him up a winding chalk pathway. I can hear the steady sound of birdsong I don't recognise, a constant squeaking that Clawtail must have heard each day when he lived here, and realise they must be the oyster-catchers he described. I find the thought vaguely comforting as I follow the Guardians in their white suits. We climb over a wooden fence and walk down a steep path, treading carefully around twisted tree roots and across sloping ground. Below us is a beach, completely invisible from the direction in which we approached the island. It's formed of dark, damp sand and is covered in green army tents, stacked up as close to the cliff face as possible to stay dry from the incoming tide. I can see Rùm from here, too, and the far end of Sanday. We walk across the compact sand and come to a stop outside the biggest tent. It's guarded by a Bulgarian dragon with a tattered wing. It leers at me, and I'm suddenly reminded of Daria's words.

If you wait until you are under Bulgarian guard, it will be too late.

Wyvernmire disappears into the tent and a moment later I'm being pushed through the same flap. I almost scream as a dragon's head appears at my shoulder, its black eyes staring, its yellow teeth caked in glue. There are a dozen of them, ancient, taxidermy heads that hang down from the high ceiling, sewn up at the neck and suspended by long strings. They're all wyverns, I realise. The wyverns that decorated the office at 10 Downing Street a mere few months ago, the ones I hoped Chumana's fire would burn.

'Familiar surroundings. How thoughtful of you.'

It takes me a moment to realise who Wyvernmire is talking to. The dim light from the oil lamp illuminates a small table and behind it, two people are waiting. The first is a tall man with olive skin and long, dark curls. When my eyes land on the second, horror settles in my bones.

His face seems to pale at the sight of me. I take him in – shiny Guardian uniform and smooth, white hands. They hover over something on the desk, trembling as if the object is too precious to touch. I feel a nervous swoop in my stomach. The contraption is small and made of steel, with a few more dials than I'm used to. But I know what it is. Just like the face of Atlas's murderer, I could recognise one anywhere.

Ralph Wyvernmire has a loquisonus machine.

Five

WHERE DID HE GET IT?

'Prime Minister,' the first man says. 'It is an honour to see you again.'

'You have the girl,' Ralph says, his gaze flitting from me to his aunt. 'How?'

Wyvernmire's eyes narrow. 'She was arrested in London. See that you don't lose her this time, Ralph.'

Two red spots appear on Ralph's cheeks at Wyvernmire's reference to how I escaped him in the glasshouse last year. Marquis knocked him unconscious before Atlas insisted we drag him to safety when Chumana set the glasshouse alight. Being the Prime Minister's nephew never got Ralph the special treatment he craved. Neither did shooting Atlas dead. A wave of grief knocks the breath from me.

The two men step aside as Wyvernmire takes a seat at the table. I glance around the tent, trying to ignore the staring eyes of the wyvern heads. One has long white fur – the last remnants of an extinct species dismembered and passed down in the Wyvernmire family. The furnishings are worn; a lumpy armchair and a small cooking stove. A faded, flowery curtain, perhaps stolen from a nearby house, sections off a private living space. I see the edge of a camp bed poking out, the bedspread turned down.

Wyvernmire pulls the loquisonus machine towards her and glances up at me. 'You know what this is, of course?'

I give her a curt nod.

'A gift,' she says, 'from my dear friend Andronikos Svetoslav, the last descendant of Tsar Theodore Svetoslav of the fourteenth century.'

The man next to Ralph looks up and smiles, flashing yellow teeth. I suddenly picture him in a tuxedo and hear the vibrant singing of violins.

'You were at the Bletchley Ball,' I say to him. 'The last Bulgarian prince. Why are you supporting a woman who has allied with the dragons that killed your own people?'

Andronikos takes a step towards me. 'In massacring my country, the Bulgarian dragons originally sought to liberate themselves from Ottoman rule.' His voice is woody and seductive. 'Then the probing of linguistic experts into their secret, telepathic language added fuel to the fire. The misfortune was that they didn't differentiate between their foreign human oppressors and their fellow native Bulgarians.'

'So after *liberating* their occupied country, the Bulgarian dragons are now occupying mine?' I say.

'Since your Prime Minister extended her generous invitation to me, I have conversed with many Bulgarian dragons. It is my belief that they would have spared the true Bulgarian people, had they been able to separate them from the Turkish oppressors.'

I roll my eyes and Andronikos smiles.

'One day, Bulgaria will thrive with human life again. And when it does, the British and Bulgarian humans will be armed with a protection we didn't have before.' He nods towards the loquisonus machine. 'It is one of the originals from Bulgaria, smuggled out with me when I fled. It has seen a few improvements since then and is fully functional—'

'But what do you need it for?' I interrupt, looking to Wyvernmire.

She inhales through her nose as she studies me. 'You will be glad to know, Vivien, that I am not as impulsive as you think. When you destroyed the last loquisonus machine at Bletchley Park I immediately sought another. A mere precaution, of course, in the event our new Bulgarian friends stray out of line.'

I blink.

The Bulgarian humans created the first loquisonus machine almost a century ago and were massacred by their dragons for it. Dr Seymour, a rebel spy who taught me how to use the machine in Bletchley Park's glasshouse, was able to make two, more advanced replicas, which Atlas and I destroyed. Anyone else with the knowledge of how to build another is dead.

'Andronikos knows how to use this one, but he cannot translate the calls. I was pondering a solution to that problem when it walked straight up to me in an airfield in Croydon.' The Prime Minister's serene smile stretches so wide I see her teeth.

I shake my head. 'Echolocation is impossible to translate. The Bulgarian humans failed and so did we, when we attempted it in the glasshouse.'

'That's not what you said back when you informed me you had cracked the dragon code,' Wyvernmire tells me coldly.

Wyvernmire doesn't know that the dragons' telepathic language, the Koinamens, is dependent on a bond. That it's impossible to accurately translate into a written or spoken language. I can only understand the simpler calls between dragons, and my human brain is still unable to comprehend the deeper meaning behind each one, transmitted between dragons through emotions and mental images.

'I was wrong,' I reply. 'It's too complex for the human mind and even if we *could* translate it, it would endanger dragons everywhere. Humans would use it to control them.' I raise an eyebrow at her. 'You already know that, of course. It's the reason there were loquisonus machines at Bletchley Park in the first place.'

'Indeed,' Wyvernmire says. 'And you told me yourself that I would need an understanding of echolocation to keep the Bulgarian dragons in check. You offered to be my translator, or don't you remember?'

I remember how desperate I was to stop the Bulgarian invasion back at Bletchley Park. I remember Atlas's face when I told him translating for Wyvernmire could be the only way of stopping the Bolgoriths from gaining full control. But that was before I knew what echolocation is to the dragons and before I smashed what I thought was the last loquisonus machine to exist.

'If you want to stop the Bolgoriths plotting against you, ally with the rebels,' I tell Wyvernmire. 'It's not too late. We can still turn this war around, seek the help of Ignacia and get rid of—'

'The rebels will arrest the Prime Minister as soon as she attempts surrender,' Ralph argues. 'Their dragon numbers are growing, and there are rumours that they have procured aid from France. If they drive the Bulgarian dragons from the country and Prime Minister Wyvernmire is incapacitated, then their politics will drag our country down into the dust. And let us not forget that their spies have infiltrated every institution in Britannia.'

Our eyes meet and I feel my heart race. He couldn't possibly know that Hollingsworth is the Academy's biggest in-house spy.

'You will translate the Bulgarian echolocation for me, Vivien Featherswallow,' Wyvernmire says. 'You will spy on the Bolgoriths, to ensure they are not attempting to overthrow me as you say, and you will listen to the conversations of both Ignacia's dragons and the rebels, too. If you do not, I won't simply take Eigg. I will torch it.'

Eigg, the rebel headquarters where I left Ursa and Marquis and Sophie. If Wyvernmire asks the Bulgarian dragons to attack now, when the rebels are still gathering forces, they won't stand a chance defending it. Perhaps the only reason she has left it untouched is that she planned to use it as leverage in case she ever found me.

I stare at her. An accurate translation of the Koinamens is impossible, but I'm going to have to pretend to try, at least until I can escape and find the wyverns. Wyvernmire pushes the loquisonus machine across the table towards Andronikos, who begins packing it into a leather case with straps. Ralph's eyes linger on it as Andronikos hands it to me. It hangs heavy on my shoulder, full of dangerous potential.

A Guardian walks into the tent. He leans across the table and whispers something to Wyvernmire, who turns towards me sharply.

'Rebel uniforms have been spotted not far from this camp, but heading in the opposite direction. What do they want with Canna, if it is not to spy on me?'

'I – I don't know,' I stutter in surprise.

Surely the rebels Hollingsworth sent to find the wyverns will be further inland by now?

'Take the loquisonus machine and go,' she snaps. 'Ralph will escort you to your tent.'

I nod at her brooch. 'Why do you still wear it? It's a symbol of the Peace Agreement, of your alliance with Britannia's dragons.'

'And *now*,' Wyvernmire replies calmly, 'it is the symbol of a superior alliance.'

Ralph gestures to me to step outside the tent. Sunlight bathes the beach, turning the sea turquoise. Guardians are gathered in groups, sharing food and cigarettes, and black and red dragons are poised on the sand and the surrounding cliffs. I'm under Bulgarian guard now. How will I ever escape?

'This one,' Ralph says, gesturing to a small tent.

I duck to enter, then spin around. 'What are you doing? You're not coming in with me.'

His eyes darken. 'I need to talk to you.'

I gape at him as bile rises in my stomach. 'I have nothing to say to you,' I spit. 'Murderer.'

I enter the tent. It's just tall enough to stand and contains a camp bed and a chamber pot. A change of clothes has been laid out on the bed – a white shirt, a jumper, thick khaki trousers with plenty of pockets and a heavy wool coat. Ralph follows me inside.

'Get out.'

He grabs my wrist, pulling me around to face him. I scream.

'Shut up!' he says, his hand covering my mouth.

I push him as hard as I can and the force of my rage causes me to fall back on to the camp bed. The loquisonus machine hits the ground with a thump and Ralph drops down beside it. He pulls it from the case and turns it over in his hands.

'What are you doing?' I say.

I scramble to my feet as he stands up, then places the loquisonus machine on the bed.

'I'm going to help you escape.'

'Sorry?'

Ralph glances towards the entrance to the tent, then back at me. 'Where do you want to go? Eigg? Or back to London? I'll get you there.'

I shake my head in disbelief. What kind of a trap is this?

He points at the loquisonus machine. 'But first, I need you to do something for me.'

I feel a sense of revulsion. *Do something* for the man who stole Atlas away from me? Who let him die in my arms?

I'm gripped by a sudden, furious desire to dash the machine against his head.

'I don't think so,' I snarl. 'You killed . . .'

I breathe in sharply. I can't bring myself to say his name out loud.

Ralph's smile disappears. 'That was an accident.'

I shake my head, my eyes filling with tears. 'You pulled the trigger. You shot him.'

'He was going to get away.' Ralph lights a cigarette and the tent slowly fills with smoke. 'Just listen, will you? The Bulgarian Bolgoriths have seen the benefit of collaborating with a few high-achieving humans. Myself. And perhaps you, if you're willing.'

I laugh in pure surprise.

'There is no alliance,' he says. 'When the time is right, the Bolgoriths will turn on the Prime Minister.'

My stomach drops. I suddenly remember how in Bletchley Dr Seymour begged Deputy Prime Minister Ravensloe to oppose the so-called collaboration, how she begged the government not to put Britannia under foreign rule.

'How do you know this?' I ask.

'Goranov,' Ralph says. He drags on the cigarette. 'We're a pair.'

'A . . . pair?'

'You haven't heard of such a thing?' Ralph says. 'Ah. Of course you haven't. You're too young. Too . . .' His eyes linger on my face. 'Inexperienced. Bulgarian dragons and humans have been known to pair up. It's a rare practice, but it happens more often during war. Each has something the other wants, and the pairing allows for an interspecies exchange, one that surpasses any social or cultural codes.'

'What could Goranov possibly want from you?' I glower.

Ralph smiles. 'Never you mind. The point is, I want to check the sincerity of the pairing on his side.'

'Are you telling me you had some sort of wedding ceremony with a dragon?'

'They'll wipe us out if we don't cooperate, you know.' Ralph bites a hangnail. 'Or herd us like cattle to be butchered at will. Or keep us as bargaining chips as they expand their regime across the globe.'

The smoke is burning my nose. 'Their regime?'

'The Bulgarian dragons have turned Bulgaria into a fully-functioning dragon kingdom, without a trace of humanity left. Their genius is on a par with that of the Roman Empire.'

'And does your . . . pairing mean that you want to help them take over?'

'Like I said,' he replies, 'they'll keep some of us. Involve us, train us, let us be part of the *new world*.'

I've never been to Bulgaria and they never taught us at school what it became after the Bulgarian dragons wiped out the human population. I find myself morbidly curious to find out.

'And Wyvernmire has no idea?'

Ralph laughs quietly. 'Of course not. She still believes in her so-called alliance. But if she can't regain control of the country, of those who no longer want to be governed by her, then the Bulgarian dragons won't see a need for her. That's why the rebels must be stopped. She's the only thing standing between us and a full-blown massacre.'

I don't know which scenario is worse. Ralph's, in which the Bulgarian dragons colonise and maybe eat the whole of Britannia, or Wyvernmire's, in which she helps them occupy the country *and* gain political immunity in the eyes of Europe. I look from Ralph to the loquisonus machine. I don't want to help him, but he might be my only way out of Wyvernmire's camp.

He flicks his cigarette into the chamber pot. 'Goranov will arrive tomorrow. I want you to listen to what he's saying. See if you hear anything about me.'

If I didn't hate him so much, I might almost feel sorry for Ralph.

'Are you really so desperate,' I say coldly, 'that you would believe anything that comes out of the mouths of one of those . . . monsters? If you've gone and made some sort of promise to a Bolgorith, then what does it matter if Goranov is lying? If you try to get out of it, he'll just kill you.'

'He needs me,' Ralph says stonily.

I laugh as I pull the loquisonus machine towards me. 'Yeah, right.'

'Just do it,' Ralph says as he opens the flap of the tent. He looks over his shoulder at me. 'Otherwise, my finger might just slip on the trigger a second time.'

I stare at the entrance long after he leaves, trying to control the anger that threatens to make me vomit. Wyvernmire and Ralph have both tried to recruit me to spy on the Bulgarian dragons, but both refuse to see that echolocation is an untranslatable language. There's no call for Ralph's name in the Bolgoriths' Koinamens. And even if I am able to catch Goranov talking about him, I'll barely be able to understand what he's saying.

I change out of my singed trousers and blouse and curl up under the itchy military-grade blanket. Hollingsworth and Chumana will be looking for me now, but there's no way for them to know I'm on Canna. I doze until someone brings me food – bacon, eggs and buttered bread – and I wolf it down. Then I sit cross-legged on the bed and pull the loquisonus machine on to my lap. I have no intention of translating the Koinamens for Wyvernmire – or Ralph, if I can avoid it. But perhaps listening in on the Bulgarians will give me some information that will help me escape without him.

I study the loquisonus machine, suddenly nervous. Didn't I promise Chumana I wouldn't touch one again? This machine is smaller than the ones I worked with at Bletchley Park, with a short, primitive-looking speaker. The dials are marked in Bulgarian as frequency and volume. But there is no switch for input and output, meaning that while this machine can listen to echolocation, it cannot attempt to speak it. I feel a sweep of relief. Wyvernmire won't be able to use it to send out recordings that could confuse or exploit the dragons, meaning that it cannot be used as a weapon against them. This loquisonus is *far* less dangerous than the ones we used at Bletchley.

I pull the headphones on, start the machine and twist the dial. I hear crackles, awful scratching sounds that slowly smooth out as I find the right frequency. And then . . .

Goosebumps rise on my skin as my ears fill with the familiar clicks and calls, long trills and loud pitches. I instinctively look skywards, forgetting I'm inside a tent. Canna is a cacophony of conversation. Where are all these dragons I'm hearing? Some of the calls are distant but the loudest ones come from close by. Are there dragons flying above the beach? Or am I listening to the inhabitants of Rùm across the water? A thrill shoots through me and I immediately feel guilty. I shouldn't be listening at all, Chumana made that abundantly clear. The Koinamens is a sacred language, one so deeply rooted in dragons' psyche that without it they cannot hatch their eggs. To live without it would be like humans living without touch or eye contact.

As I twist the dial again and focus on the loudest calls, translations come flooding back to me: *land, stranger, tomorrow*. I used to believe these calls belonged to separate dragon dialects, when actually their meanings differ depending on the emotional bond of the dragons communicating. I move the dial ever so slightly and an even louder transmission comes through, so loud that I almost pull the headphones off. The dragon must be right above my head. The calls are a Skrill-type06 followed by a Trill-type15 and a Pitch-type3. A slow shock fills me.

Impossible.

My translations must be wrong. I listen again, but the calls remain in my mind as if the time I spent in the glasshouse has permanently etched them there. How could I ever forget the encounter that changed everything? I string the translations together and feel my head spin.

Greetings, human girl.

I stand up so fast that the loquisonus falls with a clatter to the floor. With shaking hands, I push the tent flap aside and run out on to the sand. The black beach stretches out before me, frothy waves rising up to kiss the shoreline to my left. Seabirds whirl through the air and the taste of salt settles on my tongue. Across the bay I see green fields full of sheep and behind them, hills blanketed with trees. The pale smoke of a fire rises on the horizon but the sky is empty.

Where is she?

'You're supposed to stay in the tent!' Ralph hisses, surging out of nowhere. 'I'm not—'

A rush of flame pours down the cliffside, licking across the tops of the tents like a fiery snake. Screams sounds as Guardians run to put the fire out and Bulgarian dragons lurch from the sand towards the cliff. Ralph pulls me backwards as the tent next to us bursts into flames and I shake him off as a flash of pink streaks by. A dragon swoops low on to the beach in another whoosh of flame and my heart skips a beat.

Chumana.

I dart back into the tent and stuff the loquisonus machine into its case. Then I'm back out on the sand, running through the camp as Chumana circles above, snarling at the Bulgarian dragons closing in on her. My eyes water as I stare through the smoke. Why haven't the Bolgoriths attacked? Do they think she's one of their own? I need to get somewhere higher, somewhere she can reach me. I race towards the cliffs, my heart bursting. Chumana has come for me. I'm about to escape. Wyvernmire emerges from her tent amid a swarm of Guardians who push her further up the beach. The air is too hot to breathe. I run, almost tripping in the heavy sand, as screeches sound in the sky. When I look up, Chumana and the Bulgarian dragons attacking her have disappeared. My stomach drops.

No. No. No.

I'm too late.

I look over my shoulder. Ralph is running behind me, his expression furious. The fires are being extinguished and the Guardians are regrouping. One of them points at me. I scramble on to the path that leads up the cliffside as panic overwhelms me. Have the Bulgarians killed Chumana? My boots slip on tiny rocks and I skid downwards on to the beach, barely managing to keep a grip on the loquisonus machine.

'Recruit!' Ralph screams at me.

He's just a few footsteps away, his white helmet glinting.

A low whistle.

The world slows as it sounds again, then a third time. My eyes frantically search the cliff face, blinded by the sunlight. I'd know that signal anywhere. And then I see it between the rocks. A familiar face. I could cry with joy.

Marquis.

Chumana appears again, two Bulgarian dragons on her tail, her roars filling the air as fire and blood rain down on to the tents. The flames draw circles across the sand, keeping the other Guardians from reaching me. Marquis is gesticulating, his face frantic as he points urgently to something behind me. I hear a loud stamping and turn around as a tall figure emerges from the smoke. Not a dragon, but a horse. Its rider looks down at me, the sun shining behind his head. Terror ices my veins and I feel my knees buckle as I reach for the swallow around my neck. Because what I'm seeing just isn't possible. The figure slides from the horse and comes towards me, his arms pulling me upwards. I try to shake him off as tears blind me, because surely he must be a vision, a ghost. But he's as solid as I am, his hands warm on my waist. The smoke envelops us like it did in his final moments, but I see him as clear as day. The crooked smile, the smell of peppermint, those deep brown eyes. His voice is soft as he cups my face in his hands.

'Hello, Featherswallow.'

From the private papers of Patrick Clawtail

June 1862

We have been with the Hebridean Wyverns for six months, since we fled the government's forced eviction of Canna. There were whispers that the Prime Minister intends to make the island into a prison, and now every person we ever knew here is gone. June and I are slowly learning the wyvern tongue, aided only slightly by the fact that we speak Scottish Gaelic, from which it is descended. I have taken the liberty of naming it Cannair, and little Marguerite is already fluent. She is young enough to learn straight from the wyverns' mouths, deciphering the meaning of words from context like small children do, whereas we possess the tiresomely ingrained habit of translating inside our heads. I remind our daughter that as with any language, the dictionaries never reflect its entire flavour. To truly taste a new Draconic tongue, one must live among its dragons.

September 1863

In spending time with the wyverns and coming to know their intelligent, inquisitive spirit, I find myself seeking reason for it in their physical stature. It is peculiar that God has given such wild attributes to creatures who ponder the arts as deeply as any human, whose understanding of language is on an almost spiritual plane and whose traditions could bring order and peace to any civilisation or society.

Their wings are used, of course, for flying. Each day little Marguerite and I seek a sunny spot on the hillside to watch them soar through the air, accompanied by swarms of Grayling butterflies and trailing clouds like a stage magician might utilise smoke for a magic show. They have a strange command of the air, an ability to bring a water-soaked fog down upon us, or to clear an overcast morning with the sweep of a sun-kissed tail. Their tails are a tool used for balance and impressive speed, which must have put the Roman scourge to shame. I have also seen one sever the life from a fleeing sheep. Their huge eyes give them night vision, as many a ceremony takes place after dark in Canna's cool, salty starlight.

But what is the purpose of the long index claw? I

have watched them use it to dig in the dirt for materials — clay for sculpting, minerals for medicine. I have seen them use it to shear the wool from the sheep they hunt, ready to be wound on to the loom. But does that mean God intended for them to be creatures of artistic pursuit? And if that is the case, why did he not give humans pens in the place of fingers or the ability to paint landscapes with our eyes? Are we not the most artistic of all species, called to create like our creator?

It is a curious mystery.

June 1866

Government ships have been sighted. The wyverns are taking June and Marguerite to a hideout, but I await my accusers in a cave on the shore. It is my intention to argue with them, to defend my right to record the wyvern tongue and share it with the world. Britannia has already relegated Scottish Gaelic to the corners of the most tenacious Third Class homes, hoping that it will die out. And so it comes as no surprise to me that they do not wish to hear of its Draconic descendant, Cannair, which Abelio

Six

ATLAS CLIMBS BACK ON TO THE horse, then reaches down to me. I take his hand, my limbs moving of their own accord despite the blind ricocheting of my mind between two images. Atlas, blood seeping through his blue Bletchley uniform. Atlas, galloping towards me, the sun like gold on his skin. Suddenly I'm on a horse, its body hot beneath me as it snorts in panic. My hand curls around its wiry mane. Atlas's arms encircle me as he takes the reins. Thick smoke clouds the sky. I can't see Marquis or Chumana, but when the horse barrels through the smog and up the cliffside, a voice screams from behind us.

'Fuck!'

I turn to look over Atlas's shoulder. Ralph is staring up at me from the beach, pointing his gun. Our horse gallops up the path, foaming at the mouth as bullets whir past. I lower my head, pressing my face into its neck, and inhale its musky smell. It's the only thing tethering me to this moment, reminding me that I'm not in some sort of hallucination.

Dragonfire streaks past us and the horse rears, sending rocks skittering down on to the beach below. I hear Atlas's voice soothing it, calling it by its name. I look up as we reach the top of the hill. Below, flames are eating their way through the tents again. A Bolgorith lies across the sand in a gush of blood. Then we're streaking down the hill, the wind stealing my breath, and I see another horse galloping across the fields ahead, a tall, lanky figure on its back.

Since when does my cousin ride?

I close my eyes, clinging to the horse until finally we slow. It whinnies as we come to a stop outside a low flint wall. Behind it is a field of wheat, dotted with huts and backed by a huge forest.

'About bloody time,' says a voice.

The sound has me slipping from my horse and then I see him, holding the reins of a black mare and looking at me with a sheepish grin.

'Marquis,' I gasp.

We reach for each other and I hug him fiercely, my fingers grasping the back of his jacket. His hair is longer and he's wearing an army uniform and combat boots. When we come apart I see a black armband on his bicep, decorated with the outline of a swallow. I linger on it, not daring to turn around. I hear the soft whip of reins, the clink of the bit in a horse's mouth and then a thump as feet hit the ground. But still I can't look at him.

'He's dead,' I whisper to Marquis. 'I saw him die.'

Marquis rests his hands on my shoulders.

'He's not,' he says gently. 'We only thought he was.'

The oyster-catchers continue their squeaking amid the rush of the wind in the trees. Buttercups sprout up around my boots and I stare at them as I concentrate on breathing in and out. I turn to face Atlas. He has one hand on the reins and the other is stroking his horse's nose. His face is smeared with soot and his hair drenched in sweat. This is the first time I've seen him without his seminarian's collar – he's wearing the same clothes and armband as Marquis. And his eyes are searching mine, imploring me to . . . what? What do you do when the person you love dies and comes back to life?

He lets go of the horse and takes a step towards me. His hands are open, palms upturned, as if in prayer. I drink him in: the ruddy glow of his cheeks, the stubble on his chin, the bright hope in his eyes.

'After I was shot—'

'Get out of here!'

A voice interrupts Atlas and I turn to see a boy charging through the wheat field towards us. He's tall and slim and shirtless, with wild brown hair and a long, freckled nose. He stares at me with a sour expression. 'She can't be here,' he says. 'I told you, Wyvernmire will come looking for her.'

'All right, keep your hair on,' Marquis says. 'We weren't going to bring her back to camp.'

'You're already too close,' the boy says.

Several small children appear behind him, watching us from a distance.

'Jasper,' Atlas says, 'surely you can let her rest for a while?' He looks back over his shoulder. 'There will be dragons out searching for her, so let her hide here until nightfall. Then we'll go. You have my word.'

Jasper shakes his head. 'Sorry. Too dangerous.'

I jump as a hand slips into mine. 'Are you Viv?'

The girl is about ten years old, wearing a pair of trousers and a shirt several sizes too big for her. She grins at me and Marquis sighs.

'Yes, Philippa, that's Viv.'

'Jasper said Marquis and Atlas could go down to the Guardian camp to get you, and now you're here and they said you're a rebel from London and they said –' she gasps for breath – 'that you can talk to dragons.'

My heart races. Why did Marquis and Atlas need permission? Why are they living with Canna kids? What are they doing on the island in the first place? I nod at the girl, unsure how to reply. The warmth of her small hand in mine reminds me of Ursa. She turns to Jasper and sticks out her chin.

'Let her stay,' she says. 'I want to hear about the dragons.'

Over the top of Philippa's head, Atlas and Jasper are glaring at each other. Then Atlas points to Philippa.

'I saved yours,' he tells Jasper quietly. 'Now you save mine.'

Mine.

I don't know what he's talking about, but I see the hardness in Jasper's eyes soften.

'Fine,' he mutters, casting a look at the sky. 'But quickly.'

Philippa flashes me a grin that reveals several missing milk teeth.

Marquis leans towards me. 'Go across the fields and into

the forest with Philippa.' Then he nods at Atlas and Jasper. 'We'll straighten things out here.'

'You're joking,' I say. 'I don't even know—'

'We'll explain everything, cousin,' Marquis says. 'But for now, you have to stay out of sight.'

My gaze flits to Atlas again. He's watching me. I feel my breath quicken. I remember the last time I saw him, how his chest rose and fell and didn't rise again. He wasn't breathing. I was so sure of it. He offers me a small smile but I can't bring myself to return it. I spent three months in that sugar house, crying myself to sleep.

'Come on, Viv,' Philippa says as if she's known me her whole life.

I let her lead me across the field towards the huts. They're made of driftwood and sheets of iron nailed together, any gaps stuffed with what looks like grass and sheep's wool. Philippa slips between them, across paths pre-trodden in the wheat, and it's like walking through a village. Children stare out at us when we pass. They're all at work: repairing the huts, grinding the contents of huge clay mortars, gutting fish. A boy sits on a stool outside one of them, plucking a bird. No one I've seen so far can be older than sixteen. Philippa skips ahead, then comes to a stop in front of a long line of trees. She smiles and takes my hand again. The air is cool and damp as we climb up a dirt bank. She doesn't speak, her long hair swaying across her back, until we reach the top.

'You made it,' she squeaks, gesturing down the other side. 'Camp Jasper.'

The other side of the bank slopes down into a valley, a

natural crater in the earth surrounded by trees. They tower over us, their shadows enveloping everything in a green hue. I see more children, sun-kissed and long-limbed, running up and down the slope, stacking wood, stirring hot liquid in big pots. An older girl shouts at a group of younger ones and they scatter, shrieking like gulls. They're either wearing clothes that are too big for them or no clothes at all and I notice small, felt pouches hanging around their necks. Philippa has one too, tucked beneath her shirt.

'This way,' Philippa says, sliding down into the valley. 'I'll take you to your friends.'

'Friends?' I reply.

Philippa streaks ahead and I try to keep up, slipping awkwardly down the slope. I feel myself blushing as children stop their games to stare at me open-mouthed, like I'm some sort of exhibit in a zoo.

'Another new one?' a girl says.

'No,' a boy replies loudly. 'She's too old.'

Philippa circles back to me and tugs impatiently on my hand. 'Your friends,' she says again.

On the other side of the valley is a group of teenagers. Most have tools and knives made of flint strapped to their bodies, except for two, who are carrying guns and wearing black armbands. They look ridiculously out of place and when they stop their conversation to stare at me, I realise why.

'Serena?' I say incredulously. 'Gideon?'

Serena gives me a cool look. 'The rescue attempt was a success, then.'

Her hair is braided tightly to her head and the apples of

her cheeks are flushed and weatherworn. She's wearing the same uniform as the boys and a handkerchief, embroidered with dragons, around her neck.

Gideon stands beside her, looking at me reproachfully. A few months ago, he was so afraid of me cracking the dragon code before he did that he tried to kill me. I discovered afterwards that losing to me would mean he would be sent back to Canna, where he was originally recruited. He was desperate never to set foot on this island again, and yet here he is. Why?

'What are you doing here?' I ask. 'And how did you know I was on the beach?'

'Chumana turned up here looking for you,' Gideon says, glancing nervously at the sky. 'Said you'd been arrested.'

'We thought she was bringing you to Canna when we saw her,' Serena says. 'We've been waiting long enough. When we realised you weren't with her, Marquis and Atlas panicked.'

'What do you mean, you've been waiting?'

Serena and Gideon glance at each other.

'You weren't the only one given a mission,' Serena says. 'Once we completed our training we were sent here to look for a group of wyverns. Apparently, they're important.'

I stare up at the sky. *This* is who Hollingsworth sent to find the wyverns? The Bletchley recruits? Why didn't she send me with them?

'Have you found them?' I say. 'The wyverns?'

Serena purses her lips. 'Not yet. We've been a bit distracted by the military presence on the island, not to mention the Bulgarian dragons trying to eat us.'

Gideon raises his eyes to the sky again.

'This is Henry, Martha and John,' Philippa says, pointing to the other teenagers.

They nod at me in greeting but don't smile.

'I'd say they'll warm up to you, but they won't,' Serena mutters.

'They don't trust outsiders,' Gideon says. 'Can you blame them?'

'Viv!'

Marquis is walking into the camp, followed by Atlas and Jasper. 'You can stay the night.' He glances at the others. 'But we're to leave in the morning.'

'How did you convince him?' I ask with a nervous glance at Jasper.

'Atlas saved Philippa's life a few weeks ago,' Marquis says quietly. 'She's like a sister to Jasper.'

Jasper gives me a hostile look before marching past me into the camp.

'The dragons shouldn't be able to see you through the trees,' Atlas tells me as he joins us. 'But if they do, Jasper will hold me personally responsible. So stay put, Featherswallow.' His eyes shine playfully and I feel a swooping in my stomach.

What is going on? Atlas – *my* Atlas – is supposed to be buried in a churchyard of his mother's choosing. Who is this boy marching around camp as if he was born here?

Shadows gather as we venture deeper into the forest. There are no huts here, but several campfires are burning, surrounded by an increasing number of children as they all return from various directions. Two girls walk past us, carrying a net full of brown shells, which they toss into a huge metal pot with a clatter. Atlas hands me a canvas sack stuffed with straw. As he raises his arms, the sleeves of his jacket bulge. Didn't Serena say something about training?

'Sit,' he says gently.

I watch as the children move like clockwork, slicing bread and carrying water. The sun is sinking in the sky, throwing streams of golden light across their faces.

'Who are they?'

'Criminal kids,' Atlas says as he lights a cigarette. 'The ones that refused the rebels' offer of evacuation. Only a handful left the island before Wyvernmire's army turned up.'

I raise my eyebrows in surprise as Marquis, Serena and Gideon sit down next to us. 'They would rather live *here*?'

'Makes sense, really,' Marquis replies, looking at the group of children and teenagers spread out in the grass. 'No one wears a class pass here.'

'I'd rather wear a class pass than be eaten,' Gideon says.

He folds his arms and I realise he's still casting frequent looks into the sky. There are bags under his eyes and his face is thinner than it used to be. He seems terrified, but now it makes sense that he's here. He knows this island better than any of us.

A girl approaches and I recoil in disgust as she drops a pile of dead birds in front of us. 'Jasper says you lot are to finish the plucking.'

'Jasper can get lost,' Marquis mutters.

Gideon pulls a small knife from his pocket and reaches for a bird.

'Pigeon squabs,' Atlas says as Gideon begins plucking the beautiful white feathers from the bird's skin. 'Full-grown they're as tough as leather, but the squabs are fat and tender.'

My eyes meet his. 'Atlas,' I say. 'Now would be a good time to tell me what the hell you're doing here.'

Gideon lets out a snort.

'And the rest of you, too,' I say, looking at the others. 'Why would the rebels send a few teenagers on such a crucial mission? Where's your coordination team, your supplies, your weapons?'

'We have guns,' Serena says defensively. 'And a radio.'

She gestures to a small radio sticking out of the pack next to her, as well as a transmitter on a wire.

'How many Bolgoriths do you plan on killing with that?' I say.

'It's for reporting back on *you*,' Serena replies coldly. 'We're rebelling via radio these days. Haven't you heard of *Blighty Against Bolgoriths*, the rebel radio programme? They do news reports, entertainment segments, that sort of thing. Hollingsworth thinks it's good for morale. Some Oxford professor does a segment too, and then there's me.' She rolls her eyes. 'Reporting on every movement of the beloved Swallow.'

'My movement?'

'Only the superfluous stuff, in case the channel is intercepted. Today, the Swallow is stalking across the Hebridean hills,' she says mockingly. 'Today, the Swallow is wearing—'

'All right, I get it,' I snap.

'We've been on Canna for three weeks,' Atlas says. 'We were briefed by the Coalition to venture further inland, but we've spent most of our time trying to survive.'

'We've been taught what the wyverns' tracks look like, where they're likely to nest and how to stay alive while we find them, but there's no sign of them so far,' Serena says. 'Please tell me you know more, Featherswallow.'

'I had a journal,' I say. 'With information on the wyverns but . . . I left it in London.'

'London,' Marquis repeats, plucking a lighter from Atlas's breast pocket. 'What were you doing there?'

'The Hebridean Wyverns speak a language called Cannair,' I say, a lump forming in my throat as I think of all the research I left behind. 'I've been learning to speak it. Hollingsworth thinks I can convince them to join the war.'

Marquis sucks the smoke through his teeth. 'In London. Did you go home?'

Our gazes meet and I catch the longing in his eyes.

'No,' I say. 'I lived in a safehouse.'

I glance at Atlas. His brown eyes are framed with thick lashes that sweep down on to his face.

I take a breath. 'Why did you let me believe you were dead?'

Marquis shifts awkwardly.

'We were told,' Atlas says slowly, 'that you were on a crucial mission. Hollingsworth gave strict orders for you not to be distracted.'

'*I* was told your body had been sent back to your mother,' I say.

The four of them stare at me with stricken faces.

All I can think of is Rita Hollingsworth's lipsticked, lying mouth.

Philippa appears behind us, holding several deep-fried squabs on sticks. She hands one to me, slick with oil. Suddenly, I'm ravenous. I take a bite, burning my lips as my teeth pull at the succulent, savoury meat and my tongue bursts with flavour.

'We can finish this later,' Atlas says.

Fifty or so children are dining around the campfires, devouring squabs and slurping hot white clams from an assortment of chipped plates and teacups. Jasper dips a slice of bread into a cracked china bowl, watching the camp with wary eyes. He's scared, I realise. And who can blame him, with dragons above and Wyvernmire's most wanted rebel in his camp? What crime did he commit to get himself sent to Canna? What supposedly terrible things have these children done to deserve being left on a dragon-infested island to die?

After the meal, I watch as they climb up into the trees. 'What are they doing?'

'What does it look like?' Serena says, sucking the juices from a pigeon bone. 'They sleep up there.'

'In the trees?'

'Apparently, a wingless dragon called a Lyndwyrm hunts these parts. It seems you either learn to sleep out of its reach, or you don't survive the night.'

'How are you still alive, then?' I retort.

She glares at me and I shrug. 'Does it surprise you that I can't imagine Serena Serpentine sleeping in a tree?'

Philippa appears again and I'm suddenly glad of her presence. If it wasn't for her, we'd be out on the hill in the cold dark instead of by the fire. Soon, she and several other children are teaching me to tie myself to one of the lower branches while inside a sleeping bag, their giggling echoing through the forest. When I finally climb down, my arms and legs aching, Atlas is waiting.

'I thought we could go for a walk,' he whispers.

I nod, but he lays a hand on my arm. 'I don't want Jasper to see us. Follow me in a few minutes, all right?'

'All right,' I agree.

My heart races as he turns and skulks back into the shadows. I wait, my eyes on Jasper as he sits around the fire with Gideon and some others. Then I follow.

'Featherswallow!' a voice whispers.

I jump as Atlas emerges from behind an oak, his eyes searching my face. I feel my body temperature rise.

Atlas King.

For the first time, I have the presence of mind to really look at him. He's washed since the beach: his hair is wet and curling behind his ears and he no longer smells of sweat and horse, but of something flowery. He holds out a hand and I take it, avoiding his gaze because meeting it might just cause me to implode. We walk through the moonlit forest until the noise of the camp begins to fade.

'Aren't they afraid their laughter will attract dragons?' I whisper. 'Bolgoriths hunt by night.'

Atlas shrugs. 'Where the trees grow close together like this, it's difficult for dragons to land. And the kids have designated hideout spots across the island in case of daytime attacks.'

I force myself to look at him. His eyes are on the swallow around my neck.

'You still wear it.'

'Of course I do.' My stomach is doing double-flips. 'Never took it off.'

A silence falls over us and I know we're both remembering our last moments together: smashing the loquisonus machine, losing each other in the smoke, me holding him in my arms.

How can he be here, alive?

'Ursa,' I say, thinking of my sister back on Eigg. 'How is she?'

Atlas smiles. 'She's well, living in a cottage with Dr Seymour and her new baby. A true little mother.'

My heart warms at the thought of Ursa safe with people who care for her. I suddenly ache to kiss her, to inhale the scent of her golden hair.

'And Sophie? Karim?'

'Sophie was training for her own mission when we left Eigg,' Atlas says. 'I couldn't tell you what it is; everything's classified. And Karim's permanently stationed on the island as a medic.'

I nod. 'So what sort of training did *you* do?'

'Combat, survival and tracking, courtesy of Cormac Mackenzie, a First Class rebel who used to work with British Intelligence and, more specifically, the Department for the Defence Against Dragons.'

I raise an eyebrow in surprise.

'He's in command on Eigg and likes to remind people of

the fact. Marquis says joining the rebellion only made him fancy himself more. But his rural Hebrides childhood makes him an excellent survivalist, and he's a good man. Even if he did have us running laps on the beach at dawn.' He pauses. 'But you still haven't asked me.'

'Asked you what?'

'Why I'm not dead.'

His eyes search my face again, like I'm a ticking timebomb and he's waiting for me to explode.

'I . . .'

Atlas is right. I haven't asked the question because just thinking about it sets hot flames of anger dancing along my skin.

Hollingsworth *knew* Atlas is alive.

'What's the armband for?' I ask.

'It's the Coalition's new symbol, a reminder of the swallow who keeps us – humans and dragons – together. You smashing the loquisonus machine and your knowledge of dragon tongues has recruited more dragons to the cause than ever before.'

I reach out and touch the armband, remembering how Hollingsworth called me the face of the rebellion. It feels ridiculous to have been given such a role just because I cracked the so-called dragon code and then refused to give it to Wyvernmire. I know the Swallow is just a symbol, meant to keep the rebels fighting. And Hollingsworth is a liar . . . but what if she's right?

Could my being a translator, being a *brasstongue*, help us win this war?

'The swallow was my idea,' Atlas says. 'Remember the legend?'

I nod. 'Swallows were once dragons who could speak every language in the world,' I say softly, 'but it meant they carried the burden of being able to empathise. So they asked God to make them light and carefree. He turned them into birds, giving them tails forked like a dragon's tongue, to remind them of what they once were.'

Suddenly, my anger at Hollingsworth is doused by excitement at the prospect of unlimited time with Atlas, with no classes or categories to keep us apart. Before I watched Ralph shoot him I had dared to imagine a future with him, fighting the rebels side by side, sharing strategies, a meal, a bed . . . I stare out into the dark, trying not to blush, but I can feel his gaze on me and with it a wave of anticipation.

His brown eyes find mine. He takes a step towards me.

'Viv . . .'

And somehow my feet carry me forward without my permission, crossing the short distance between us until I'm so close I can see the flecks of gold in his eyes. His gaze flits from my face to my short hair, lingers on my mouth. And then his lips are crushing mine. My skin is ablaze and as a dragon roars in the distance, it's like its fire is filling me, hot and hungry. My back meets the rough bark of a tree and my hands find Atlas's hair as his own drop to my waist. I gasp and I feel his smile.

He pulls away, but keeps his arms around me. 'I didn't know Second Class girls kissed like that,' he breathes.

'They don't,' I reply. 'Rebel girls, on the other hand . . .'

He laughs quietly and I rest my chin on his shoulder. We

stand still for a long moment, listening to the sounds of the dark forest.

'We should go back,' he says eventually.

I would rather eat dragon dung.

'Wait,' I whisper into his jacket. 'Why aren't you dead?'

'Fireblod,' he says.

My head swims. The illegal medicine made from the blood of dragons?

'Fireblod can't bring back the dead.'

His hands grip my waist tighter. 'I wasn't dead, Viv. I was still alive, still hanging on. The fireblod healed the gunshot wound.'

'Atlas?' I say slowly. 'Who gave it to you? The fireblod?'

He frowns. 'Chumana. She flew me out of Bletchley. She—'

I let go of him. 'Chumana?'

He gives me a confused smile. 'Yes. She flew me to a scholar she knew, an old acquaintance from her early days in her library prison. He extracted her blood and fed it to me. Why are you looking at me like that?'

'I lived with Chumana,' I say. 'In a safehouse in London.'

His face falls. 'She didn't tell you?'

I shake my head, blood pounding in my ears. Hollingsworth knew Atlas was alive, and in her arrogance and twisted reasoning decided not to tell me. I'm not even surprised. But Chumana? She let me grieve Atlas that first night in the sugar house, when mere days before she had saved his life. Humiliation and betrayal fill me as I step backwards.

'Viv?' Atlas says. 'I promise I didn't know.'

'You should have written to me!' I say.

'I wanted to, but sending post was against the rules on Eigg, in case of interception.'

'Fuck the rules,' I whisper through tears. 'Everyone knew except me. *Everyone.*'

I thought Chumana and I were friends. I thought I could trust her. My vision blurs as I turn to walk back through the forest, but Atlas catches me by the sleeve and spins me back around.

'I didn't know,' he says again.

I want to scream at him, to scream the humiliation and misplaced grief away. Instead, I bury my face into his jacket. How many times have I wished I'd spent the weeks at Bletchley Park laughing with him, kissing him, instead of arguing? How many times in the last three months have I resolved to be less of a hot-headed idiot than I was last year?

I swallow my pride.

'I'm sorry they lied,' he pleads with me.

'It's not your fault,' I reply hoarsely.

Marquis spots us coming back into the camp. 'Where have you two been? Three of Wyvernmire's dragons just flew over.' He points at me. 'They're looking for you.'

'Any Guardians?' Atlas asks.

Marquis shakes his head. 'Not yet. Too dark, I reckon. We should leave at dawn.'

I look from him to Atlas, my body faint with exhaustion. 'Do you have any idea at all where the Hebridean Wyverns might be?'

'No,' Marquis says. 'But I think Jasper might.'

I nod. That's enough for me, for now. 'I'm going to bed.'

Atlas kisses my cheek and I see Marquis trying to keep a straight face. I pull myself up on to one of the lower branches of a tree, where a sleeping bag is waiting. Others are settling in the branches above me, their lanterns glowing like golden stars in the dark. Leaves rustle against my face as I listen to the hushed voices and the crackle of Serena's radio. There's a distant roar and I wonder where Chumana is. She must be keeping out of sight too. I feel my anger rise again at the thought of her and Hollingsworth's lies, but the elation from the day's events is stronger. They may have betrayed me, but Atlas is alive. It's more than I could have hoped for.

Tomorrow, we'll start looking for the wyverns. As a team, which is the opposite of what we were at Bletchley Park. If the rebels dropped Atlas and the others off here it's because the Coalition believes in their ability to complete their mission. But what about me? I'm only here because I got myself arrested. Was Hollingsworth ever going to send me to Canna at all?

I close my eyes. I *have* to make sure the Third Class and Britannia's dragons know freedom. I *have* to succeed in using my languages to win the war.

I imagine my parents being liberated from Highfall, Ursa running towards me, Sophie forgiving me for the pain I caused her when I got her demoted.

This is my second chance.

Seven

MY EYES SNAP OPEN AS A low bellow sweeps across the forest. Daylight filters through the leaves and I remember where I am – halfway up an oak tree. The realisation startles me and I grab hold of a branch to stop myself slipping out of my sleeping bag. My eyes scan the ground for the source of the noise until I spot a boy below, blowing a horn.

'Everyone stay put!' Jasper shouts from the tree opposite mine.

Birds fly from their nests as children slip out of their sleeping bags to stand on the wide branches, their faces turned to the sky. My heart hammers as I peer up at the clouds and then I see it.

The red belly of a Bulgarian dragon.

Philippa begins to cry above me and I hear Marquis's voice soothing her. The dragon glides like a bird of prey as everyone watches in silence. It turns on its side, basking its pink scales in the morning glow. I step on to the branch below mine.

'Viv!' Marquis whispers loudly. 'What are you doing?'

I climb down, my feet finding branch after branch.

'Featherswallow!' Atlas hisses from somewhere. 'Do you have a death wish?'

'It's Chumana, Atlas,' I reply calmly.

I reach the ground and walk through the forest to the wheat field, where the storage huts sit outside of the protection of the trees. Chumana has landed, knocking over a pot of stinking clam shells. She shakes her head to rid herself of the dust and dirt swirling around her. We glare at each other, her bright, orb-like eyes reflecting my entire face.

'Getting arrested by Guardians seems to be becoming a habit of yours,' she snarls.

I feel a contemptuous smile on my lips. My fury has been simmering all night, and has almost reached boiling point.

'I'm glad it has,' I reply. 'Otherwise, how would I have come across the dead boy you brought back to life by feeding him your blood? Did you forget to mention that, back when we were nest-mates?'

Chumana swings her head down close to mine. 'I did not forget. I kept it a secret from you. Those were my orders.'

'Hollingsworth's orders?' I hiss. 'So you *both* lied to me. You both let me believe Atlas was dead, for your own gain.'

'For the gain of the cause,' Chumana says. 'Hollingsworth knew your desire for revenge would motivate you to do your duty, and that you'd abandon it to go looking for Atlas if you discovered he was alive.'

I let out a weak laugh. 'My duty? I did my duty at Bletchley Park by smashing the loquisonus machine and joining the rebels! And yet still the Chancellor keeps me in the dark, letting the teenagers do the work without giving us any of the information we need. Do you know she hasn't told me what I'm supposed to ask of the wyverns, *if* we even find them? If she were a true rebel—'

'Rita Hollingsworth has been a rebel since before you were born!' Chumana spits.

'It must be easy to be a rebel while living in the Prime Minister's pocket, enjoying a prestigious job and the advantages of being First Class. She sits there, day after day, writing those disgusting Babel Decree articles, while my friends consider themselves lucky if they don't get eaten by Canna's dragons! At least now I'm one step closer to finding the wyverns I'm supposed to communicate with. For all I know, Hollingsworth was never going to send me—'

'So you compromised her position and risked the entire rebel movement being dismantled in a day for your own ego,' Chumana snarls. 'Then she was right to keep secrets from you. You cannot be trusted.'

'*You* cannot be trusted!' I scream.

Birds streak from the trees, shrieking.

A hand lands on my arm. Atlas pulls me backwards, his eyes flashing with fear, as Marquis and Serena watch from the tree line. I shake him off and turn back to Chumana.

'You speak of duty,' I say, my voice laced with hatred. 'Was what you did during the Massacre of Bulgaria your *duty?*' Tears burn my eyes. 'Was that *following orders*, too, Chumana?'

My heart sinks as the words leave my mouth. Tension grows taut in the air as Chumana's eyes narrow. I've referred to what she confided to me back at Bletchley Park: how she helped the Bolgoriths massacre Bulgaria's human population on the orders of the British government.

Her most devastating regret.

The accusation hangs in the space between us, cheap and cruel. Her tail sways dangerously. The hairs on my arm stand on end. Slowly, I turn to look at Atlas.

'Run.'

We both jump into movement as Chumana's tail swipes into several food storage huts, sending them splintering to the ground in a spray of wood and feathers. Our boots slam the hard ground as we dart back towards the forest, but something makes me hesitate. I look over my shoulder.

'Human girl!' Chumana roars.

Terror fills me as I see the amber of her eyes turn a dark, cloudy brown. She takes a step towards me and snaps furiously at the air. I turn and flee, following in Atlas's footsteps as the forest fills with terrified screams. A gust of wind hits me as I reach the trees and I turn to see Chumana lift into the air. She flies off towards the sea and I collapse beside Atlas, gasping for breath.

'She's gone,' Marquis says in disbelief.

'So what?' I spit. 'We don't need her.'

'She could have helped us!' Serena says. 'Protected us!' She flings an accusatory glare in my direction. 'Do you have an *ounce* of self-control?'

'She told me Atlas was dead!'

Children stare down at us from the surrounding trees. I see Gideon, cowering on a high branch, and Jasper, pale-faced and mutinous.

Atlas is staring at me with a mix of curiosity and confusion.

'What did you mean about the Massacre of Bulgaria?' he asks.

I turn away, feeling my body flood with shame. I'm not about to admit how I crassly brought up Chumana's mistakes, when she was the one who first told me I could be forgiven for mine. But I don't have to reply, because Jasper has climbed down and is walking towards us, Philippa clinging to his hand.

'You brought a Bulgarian dragon to our camp?' he shouts, looking from Atlas to Marquis to me. 'Out, the lot of you. Now.'

I shoulder the loquisonus machine as the others gather their belongings. I don't know what I'm going to do with it, but I can't leave it here. The camp is basking in an orange sunrise, the air suddenly alive with the sounds of birds and dragons. Philippa stands mournfully beside Marquis, pressing loaves of bread and a gourd of water into his hands. She cries as Jasper escorts us out of the camp and he whispers comfortingly to her.

'Why don't you find us some strawberries?' he says as we walk uphill in stony silence. 'The plants have white flowers, see?'

He points to a patch of small red berries, glowing like jewels in the morning dew.

'Here,' Marquis says, handing me a black armband. 'Hollingsworth's orders are to keep them on at all times.'

More orders.

'Why?' I say, taking the armband and glancing awkwardly at the swallow meant to represent me.

'To identify our bodies in case of dragonfire,' he replies, avoiding my gaze. 'They're made of dragonhide. Flameproof.'

'Wow,' I say dryly. 'How generous of her.'

We come to a stop on the edge of a cliff and Jasper points out to the sea. 'Over there is Sanday,' he says. His finger traces the curve of Canna's shore and then the length of land that juts out across the water directly ahead of us, a stretch of green that lies between us and Rùm.

'At low tide, you can walk from here to there across the sands.' Jasper glances at Philippa, whose mouth is full of strawberries. 'I shouldn't be telling you this, but Ruth's girls might be able to help you with those wyverns you're looking for.'

'Ruth's girls?' I say.

Jasper hands me a pair of binoculars and I direct them towards Sanday. The first thing I spot is a group of pigs, grazing in a pen. Then I see a girl, wearing white furs. My fingers fiddle with the focus thumbwheel. She has blonde hair, chopped lopsidedly above her shoulders. She's looking directly at me with her own pair of binoculars. Slowly, she lifts her hand high and raises her middle finger.

'Ruth used to be with us, back before the groups started fighting.'

'There are more of you?' I ask.

'Three clans, these days,' Jasper replies as he shoves his hands into his pockets and stares out at Sanday. 'Ruth attacked a boy from the other group. I don't blame her. He never told anyone what he got sent to Wean Island for, but it wasn't hard to guess. When it came to girls, he liked to take . . . liberties.'

'Let me guess,' Serena says. 'Ruth told him where to go?'

'She killed him,' Jasper says. 'In self-defence, but still . . . we had to banish her. For breaking our most important law. Enough of us die by dragon as it is, without us killing each other.'

I hand the binoculars back to him.

'What we didn't expect was for the majority of the girls to go with her.'

'Really?' Marquis snorts.

'When was this?' I ask.

'Years ago,' Jasper says. 'But now, Ruth can't set foot on Canna and we don't go to Sanday. Couldn't, even if we wanted to. Their defences are impressive.'

'No surprise there,' Atlas says darkly.

I glance at the boys, then gesture to myself and Serena. 'You'll have to let *us* do the talking.'

'We'll leave you here, then,' Jasper says. 'If Wyvernmire comes looking for you, we'll tell her what we did last time, that we've never heard of you. But don't come back. If she finds you with us, we'll wish we'd left Canna when we had the chance.'

With that, he takes Philippa's strawberry-stained hand and leads her away. We bask in the morning sun, sharing some of the bread as we wait for low tide. I watch Atlas as he sits on a rock, a small leather notebook sticking out of his pocket. He's loading his gun, humming quietly as he recites what sounds like a prayer.

I had almost forgotten that part of him, the priesthood part. Has *he*, I wonder? Did that part of him die when he did back at Bletchley Park? When he exchanged his white collar for a rebel uniform? Or is it still there somewhere, residing quietly even as he kisses me? I look at the others, Marquis and Gideon smoking as they watch the sky and Serena fiddling with the radio. It felt shamefully good to release my anger on to Chumana, but my skin prickles again when I remember how the other recruits were together on Eigg for three months, knowing that I was alone in London thinking Atlas was dead. I sneak another glance at Marquis. Even he kept the truth from me. I feel a distance between me and them, a cold remoteness that I can't shake.

'And you're back with Sandy and Drake on your daily broadcast of *Blighty Against Bolgoriths.*'

Serena stops twisting the radio dial.

'Our pitiful excuse for a Prime Minister sank her claws into her own capital yet again last night, with Bulgarian Bolgoriths destroying an entire South London quarter in search of rebels. But reports coming in tell us our Swallow has officially flown the nest on a mission that will soon deliver us from Wyvernmire's raptors.'

'Who are Sandy and Drake?' I say quickly.

Serena shrugs. 'There are rumours that they're a pair of Second Class university students who were banned from studying dragon tongues when the Babel Decree was instated, but who knows?'

'Today we're live with fellow rebel Drogo, somewhat of an expert in linguistics. What do you say, Drogo, to Wyvernmire's statement that the dragons of Britannia must abandon their tongues in favour of Slavidraneishá?'

'It is language assimilation,' hisses a voice. 'A group is forced to abandon its mother tongue, thereby severing its cultural roots.'

I look up from the radio in surprise. That voice belongs to a dragon.

'Tide's out,' Gideon says.

Serena turns the radio off and we walk down on to the now-visible sandbanks that stretch across to Sanday. Everyone except me has a pack and a gun similar to those the Guardians carry. I can't help but think that if I hadn't got myself arrested, I would have my own set of supplies. Gideon jumps whenever he sees a shadow on the waves, mistaking every seagull for a dragon. Sanday's huge, granite cliffs lean menacingly over us, taking the brunt of the chilling wind that blows in from the sea.

'Where is everyone?'

'They're pretending no one's home,' Marquis says as we walk around one of the cliff faces, staring up at the seaweed and barnacles clinging to it. The ground is full of small holes, rockpools that will fill with water at high tide, but for now are bursting with shells and edible treasures – mussels, starfish and tiny snails I don't know the name of. Our boots sink into the wet sand as we circle the mammoth rock, searching for a way up. Atlas's hand grazes against mine and I eye his gun again.

'Do you know how to use that thing properly?' I ask.

'Better than Ralph Wyvernmire, I'd say,' he replies with a smirk. 'I don't think any of his bullets got anywhere near us back on the beach, do you?'

'Hmm,' I agree absentmindedly as my eyes land on a footpath in the rock.

'Why was he so desperate to get you back?' Atlas asks. 'I'm guessing it has something to do with *that*?' He gestures to the loquisonus machine on my shoulder as if it's as lethal as the weapon on his.

'He thinks he has some sort of partnership with Goranov,' I say, 'and he wanted me to use the loquisonus machine to check Goranov isn't double-crossing him.'

Atlas frowns. 'A partnership?'

A bolt shaped like an arrow lands in the sand by my foot and I jump backwards, knocking into Atlas.

'Crossbow,' he breathes.

Ahead of us the others have frozen, more arrows at their feet. I look up. A girl appears on the clifftop above us, long hair billowing in the wind. She points the crossbow at us.

'We're part of the Human-Dragon coalition, rebelling against Prime Minister Wyvernmire and her Bulgarian dragons,' Atlas calls out. 'We've come to ask you what you know about the Hebridean Wyverns.'

The girl doesn't move.

'Jasper sent us,' I shout.

'What did you tell her that for?' Serena hisses. 'She probably hates him.'

'Leave your weapons on the sand,' the girl shouts.

We do as she asks and she hesitates for a moment before lowering her bow.

Two more girls appear behind her and when she nods at them, they run along the clifftop. Moments later they're walking across the sand, beckoning to us.

'I don't like this,' Gideon says quietly. 'Too easy.'

We follow the girls, who remain a safe distance ahead, to the far side of Sanday where the low tide has pulled back to reveal a semi-circular bay, invisible from Canna. Standing in it, weapons raised high, are at least twenty girls.

'Told you,' Gideon says.

The youngest wear tattered dresses or long trousers held up by braces, but the older ones are swathed in sheepskin. Their weapons aren't handmade like Jasper's. Instead they carry crossbows, revolvers and what looks like the rifles used by the Guardians of Peace. But that isn't what shocks me.

It's the dracovols.

The miniature dragons are everywhere, perched on the girls' shoulders, nesting in the cliffs around us and circling in the air in a way that makes them look like birds. The girl with the crossbow comes forward. She's about my age, with tangled golden hair and a sheepskin cloak that reveals long, brown limbs and bare feet. A purple dracovol chirrups on her shoulder. There's something ethereal about her, about all of them. With their flowing hair and hard faces, they look like something out of a Greek painting.

'Ruth?' I ask the girl. 'I'm Vivien Featherswallow.'

She glares at me. 'Jasper sent you?'

I nod. She considers me for a moment, then strokes the tiny head of the dracovol.

'Yes, I'm Ruth. What do you want?'

'We thought it might be more fun to hang around here rather than with Jasper's dreary lot,' Marquis says with a grin.

'We heard you're a murderer.'

I glare at him.

'Only in self-defence, of course,' he adds hurriedly.

Ruth doesn't reply, but a small smile plays on her lips.

'That's *not* why we're here,' I say. 'We're looking for the—'

'Hebridean Wyverns,' Marquis says, leaning against the cliff. 'We're wondering if you know where we might find them? And then we'll be on our merry way.'

I shake my head in despair and Serena lets out a long sigh. Marquis raises his arms above his head and Ruth's smile disappears. She reaches for her crossbow, and the other girls are just as quick as she is.

'Steady on,' he says, pulling a loaf of bread from his pack. He holds it out to the girls. 'A gift. Doesn't look like you have much wheat growing around here.'

Ruth reaches out slowly, takes the bread, sniffs it. She hands it to someone behind her and soon the loaf is being passed around like a trophy.

'Only you can come in,' Ruth says, pointing to me and Serena.

I resist the urge to give Marquis a smug smile.

'In?' Marquis says politely.

Ruth glances back at the cliff face that braces against the sea and I glimpse an entrance in the wet stone, a small crack just wide enough for a person to fit through. Marquis bows, causing several girls to giggle, then pulls a cigarette out from behind his ear and lights it. Atlas takes a seat on a rock as Gideon stares out to sea and mutters something about women.

'You can help us, then?' I ask Ruth. 'With the wyverns?'

She gives me a cool look. 'Might.'

I follow her into the bay with Serena, leaving the boys behind.

'*Might?*' Serena says. 'I've had enough cryptic messages to last a lifetime, haven't you?'

I smirk. Ruth leads us through the gap in the rock. It's dark and wet, the passage so narrow that it feels like the walls are closing in on us. I keep as near to Ruth as I can as water submerges my feet. There's a faint fluttering in the air above me and I muffle a shriek as a long tail tickles the top of my head.

'Dracovols, not rats,' I hear Serena muttering to herself repeatedly.

We take a sudden left. Further down the tunnel, I see a light burning. Beneath it is a circular staircase, cut into the rock and lit by candlelight. I glance back at Serena and she gives me a look of disbelief. We follow Ruth up the steps until we reach a long stone hallway with archways leading off into chambers.

'Who built this place?' I ask.

'Old islanders, probably,' Ruth replies.

'You have the best spot on Canna,' Serena says. 'Does Jasper know about this?'

'Don't be stupid,' Ruth replies sharply. Her hair glows almost ghostly in the candlelight. 'And you 'ent to tell him. Not him, not any of them men you've got outside. Their lot like to take what 'ent theirs.'

She stares at us, expectant, and I give her a hurried nod.

'I never suggested I'd tell anyone,' Serena replies sullenly.

Ruth leads us through an archway. The floor of the chamber is lined with sheep's wool, the ceiling studded with stones that twinkle like orange crystal. More tunnels lead off into other rooms. I wonder how far this home for girls stretches, imagining the tunnels snaking through the entire land mass that is Sanday. There's a table made of smooth wood, so long and sturdy that it must have been built in this room, and several wooden crates full of canned food. Mirrors and other trinkets decorate the walls – polished shells and faded illustrations of elegant women wearing ballgowns, ripped from a magazine.

Ruth sits on the table, her legs crossed beneath her. 'So,' she says. 'Wyverns.'

'Hebridean Wyverns,' I say. 'Have you ever seen one? I'd wager you've got a good view of Canna from the top of Sanday?'

'Last time I saw a Hebridean Wyvern was a few years ago. There are plenty of Greens about, but the Hebrideans are different.'

'So you *have* seen one?' I say, trying to keep the disbelief out of my voice. 'Was this before you were banished by Jasper?'

Ruth shrugs. 'Sure.'

'Different, how?' Serena asks. 'And what's a Green?'

'Green-Spotted Wyvern,' I say. 'But I was told the Hebridean Wyverns haven't been sighted at all since 1866.'

'And the person who told you that lives on the island, do they?' Ruth says.

'No,' I reply. 'But—'

'It's true that the Hebrideans keep to themselves. They nest way across the island – the Skye side, not the Rùm side. But those of us who actually live here sometimes see 'em. Rare as fairies, but they exist.'

I want to ask Ruth how she could possibly have seen wyverns that live on the other side of the island when she can't leave Sanday, but I remember the way she handled that crossbow as if it were an extra limb and decide against it.

'We've seen maps that show where the wyverns *could* be nesting,' Serena says flatly, looking Ruth in the eye. 'You haven't told us anything they haven't.'

'If you have maps, why did you come to me?'

'The maps are old,' I say quickly, before Serena can fit in another snarky reply. I think of the maps in Clawtail's journal. 'The landscape has probably changed since they were drawn, or the wyverns might have moved.'

'Course they've moved,' Ruth says.

I blink.

'The wyverns are tunnellers.'

Serena sighs. 'And that's supposed to mean *what*, exactly?'

'Don't they teach you about dragons on the mainland?' Ruth says.

I bite my lip and fight the urge to snap at her. Ruth runs a finger along her thigh, joining up the many freckles there with an invisible line. She's enjoying knowing what we don't. Beside me, Serena bristles.

'All wyverns are tunnellers,' Ruth finally says, 'but Hebridean Wyverns have a particular knack for it.'

I shake my head. 'Clawtail – he's the author of a journal

about the wyverns – never wrote anything about tunnels.'

'Cormac didn't mention tunnels, either,' Serena says.

'Have you been to Canna House?' Ruth asks.

I look up.

'It's hard to miss – the grandest house on the island. Ransacked a hundred times over, course, but none of the kids here are interested in what you're looking for.'

'We haven't got time to be visiting old houses,' Serena says through gritted teeth. She looks at me. 'We should have found the wyverns weeks ago.'

'They used to study dragons there,' Ruth says. 'I've seen sketches of wyverns.'

My heart leaps. If people used to study dragons in Canna House, then we might find information about where exactly the wyverns live. Ruth slips across to the far side of the room, to a small alcove.

'Look,' she says.

There's a small hole in the wall, a perfect circle, intentionally made but inconspicuous. Cool air flows through and when I press my eye to it I see the wet beach we crossed to get here. Beyond it is Canna, glowing green beneath a brewing storm cloud.

'Find the bay where the Guardian boats come in, then the flag with Wyvernmire's crest,' Ruth instructs.

I spot the famous W entangled in a wyvern's tail.

'Now look up. Do you see it?'

I do.

A tall house nestled between the trees, only a couple of miles from the coastline.

'Thank you, Ruth.'

Ruth accompanies us back outside. A group of girls are sprawled out on the grass, their noses buried in some very tattered, watermarked books. Every so often one of them sneaks a look towards the boys, who are all watching the cave entrance as they smoke.

'Jealous that you couldn't come in?' Serena smirks.

'Not exactly,' Marquis says.

Gideon puffs on his cigarette, his ears red, staring pointedly away from the shrieks coming from the beach below. I peer out at the distant tide. Slender, brown bodies are jumping around in the frothing waves, all delighted shrieks and whipping, wet hair.

'Are they . . . naked?' I ask.

'As the day they were born,' Atlas says.

His eyes don't move from the cave.

The girls reach down into the water, then bring their arms over their heads like ballerinas, pulling up nets full of purple, oval-shaped shells.

'Mussels,' Ruth says. 'They're delic—'

Her eyes fill with horror as she stares at the horizon. Marquis jumps up, reaching for his gun. Down in the water, the girls begin to scream. I follow Ruth's gaze, scanning the cloudy shoreline until I see it. A silvery shadow on the sea.

Eight

MY HEART STOPS.

'Release the bait!'

The shout comes from further along the cliff line. I see several girls running towards us and behind them, squealing, come a herd of brown pigs. Ruth's camp surges with movement, books dropping to the ground as the girls rise in a practised choreography.

'Back to the tunnels!' Ruth shouts.

A shadow falls across us, blocking out the sun. Horror prickles at my scalp. The dragon's belly is a bright yellow and dripping with water. Its wings span the entire clifftop, the soft undersides a deep brown. It shudders mid-air and flames fill the sky. Atlas's hand grabs mine and I feel the heat scorch my skin as we run towards the entrance of Ruth's tunnel system, our footsteps hammering the dirt as the mass of girls carries us along. I'm aware of Marquis and Serena beside me, but I don't know where Gideon is. And what of the girls down on the beach? My head spins as we reach the cliff face and a scream fills my ears. I look over my shoulder. The dragon is flying low behind us, its head so close it blocks out my view of the sea. Long, fine tendrils sprout out of its nose – a Sand Dragon. And it's found its prey. A lone girl, her face red and her sheepskin singed. She's still running up the cliff from the beach, but as her eyes meet mine she slows and reaches for something around her neck. A pouch, the same as the ones worn by the kids at Jasper's camp. Her fingers tease it open and she wrenches her head back, then pours the contents into her mouth.

I stop.

The dragons jaws open behind her and—

Its left eye explodes in a spray of blood and tissue. Agonised screeches echo across the clifftop as the dragon rolls mid-flight. I see a bolt drop to the ground.

'Viv!' Atlas screams.

Behind him is the entrance in the cliff face, the entrance to safety. Ruth is standing there, crossbow in hand. She shoots a second bolt. The dragon drops below the cliff edge, disappearing from view. At the same time, Atlas grabs me by my coat and pulls me into the dark.

We wait silently, the only sound the distant calling of seagulls.

'Is it gone?' I whisper.

I peer out from behind Ruth.

'It's gone,' she says.

Slowly, she puts her crossbow down and walks towards the girl who was almost eaten. She has sunk to the ground, her shoulders heaving with sobs. I watch as Ruth lays a hand on her shoulder, a reassuring gesture. But then she jerks the girl backwards and sticks her fingers down her throat.

I recoil as Atlas swears.

'What the—'

The girl retches, then vomits on to the grass. Ruth beckons for us to come out.

'That wasn't a Bulgarian dragon,' Atlas says as girls crowd around, hugging and crooning over the dragon's would-be prey.

'No,' Ruth replies. 'We call him Sargo. He's one of Ignacia's and he likes the taste of us. 'Cept he's out of practice.'

'What was that you ate?' I ask the girl, gesturing to the pouch around her neck.

'Juniper berries,' she says shakily.

'Poison pouches,' Ruth says. 'A full one can kill a grown British dragon as swift as wind if ingested by its prey. Juniper 'ent toxic to humans but it'll make us ill for several days. The pouches are meant as a deterrent. Lots of 'em have realised that killing *us* kills *them*, but Sargo isn't the brightest spark.'

'The pouches will only kill a British dragon?'

Ruth casts a nervous look at the sky. 'They haven't been working on the Bulgarians. They make 'em sick and confused, but they don't kill 'em. I think they're too big.'

A small pig, covered in coarse brown hair, digs at a root near my foot.

'And those,' I say. 'Deterrents, too?'

Ruth nods. 'It's how we've survived so far. Most dragons will settle for pork if it means they don't have to lie in wait for us.'

'They're the bait that keeps us safe,' the other girl says. 'Just like we keep the mainland safe.'

I feel a wave of revulsion for the secret clause in the Peace Agreement, for how Wyvernmire agreed to feed the children on Canna to Britannia's dragons so that they wouldn't be tempted to eat the rest of us.

'Is that yours?' Ruth asks.

She's pointing to something glinting in the grass.

The loquisonus machine.

My hand reaches for the empty leather case. I must have dropped it when I was running. Marquis's eyes darken when he sees it.

'What do you still have that for?' he says.

'I couldn't leave it with Jasper, could I?' I say. I lower my voice. 'If Ralph or Wyvernmire get their hands on it, they could listen in on the rebel dragons – the Bulgarian prince I met in Wyvernmire's tent says he's never tried to understand the calls, but I don't believe him.'

'What does it do?' Ruth asks.

'Nothing,' I say quickly. 'We should go.'

I doubt Andronikos would get far in an attempted translation of the Koinamens. But if a Bulgarian dragon were to see the loquisonus machine in Wyvernmire's tent, recognise it and realise she is trying to listen in on them . . . it would give them an even better reason to destroy Britannia in the same way they murdered the Bulgarian people for trying to exploit their telepathic language. I slip the machine back in the case and catch Atlas watching me curiously. Can he tell that a fleeting idea just flew through my mind, a brief but guilty truth?

A small part of me misses being able to listen to the dragons' thoughts.

'Take these,' Ruth says.

One of the girls appears at her elbow with a small box. Inside are six poison pouches.

A vague memory surfaces of myself at the Bletchley Ball, making small talk with a group of people who were marvelling about how the children on Canna had somehow learned to outsmart the dragons. And now we know how.

'If you're about to be eaten, swallow the berries,' Ruth says. 'If you can't save yourself, at least you can stop the dragon from feasting on your friends.'

*

Ruth was right: Canna House is hard to miss. It stands on one of the island's surviving roads, a lone, ghostly building that stares out to sea, hidden behind exterior walls climbing with bright green ivy. Daffodils and violets line the path that leads through the overgrown garden, having sprouted as they pleased for decades. I feel strangely nervous. Hollingsworth never mentioned Canna House to me, but Ruth said people used to study dragons here. It seems like a crucial piece of information to leave out. I had assumed the journal she gave me would have all the information I needed to know about the Hebridean Wyverns, but it doesn't even mention that they're tunnellers.

The red front door is hanging off its hinges. Atlas slips his gun off his shoulder and the others raise their own.

I remember them firing rifles in clumsy desperation as we escaped Bletchley Park. But now they all handle their weapons with expert precision. The past three months have changed them more than I thought. Do I even know them at all?

We enter a dilapidated hallway with a worn, cobwebbed carpet. Empty crates are piled up against the walls, likely raided by Canna's children years ago. Hanging against the peeling wallpaper is a portrait of a baby, and beside it in its cradle, a dragon egg.

'We're looking for an office,' I say quietly. 'Somewhere research might be kept.'

We wander from room to room, through several sitting areas and a kitchen covered in dracovol droppings.

'In here,' Marquis calls from down the hallway.

He pushes the door open with the end of his gun. A mahogany desk, littered with fishing rods and what looks like an old croquet set, stands in front of a marble fireplace. On the walls are cases full of pinned butterflies and beneath them, someone has left the remains of a meal – a rusting saucepan and a lump of mouldy cheese.

'Glass cases,' Serena says, following us in.

She nods to a line of display cabinets on the far side of the room. The glass is still intact, of no interest to any past raiders. Inside the cabinets are hundreds of drawings of dragons, each meticulously labelled. Some are rough sketches but others have been filled in with watercolours and my heart leaps at the sight of them. I see Canna's lush hills, its craggy cliffs and its blue-green sea, each environment depicted with the dragons that inhabit it – Western Drakes, Sand Dragons and knuckers. Marquis appears at my shoulder and gazes through the glass in a captivated silence. He's always been good at sketching.

'There,' Gideon says, reaching over my shoulder. 'Wyverns.'

The watercolours of the Hebridean Wyverns contain much more detail than the sketches in Clawtail's diary. I've met Green-Spotted Wyverns before, and Mama told me about the Spider Wyverns of East Asia, but I've never seen wyverns like these. They're a muted, blue-grey colour, standing on two legs, with wings where a dragon's forelegs would be. The wings are entirely feathered in shades of blue and white, making them resemble giant birds, but sprouting off the wings is a short pair of limbs with four curved talons, the index one triple the size of the others.

But it's the wyverns' faces that strike me. Their snouts are rounder than most dragons' and their eyes are surprisingly large and as blue as a robin's egg, giving them a soft, almost docile look.

'What are those?' Gideon says.

Sketched in at one of the wyverns' feet is a group of small objects. I peer closer and make out a smooth stone, an ink pen and a spool of coloured wool.

'Maybe they collect shiny things,' Serena says.

'Like you, you mean?' Gideon says, his eyes on the silver pin in Serena's hair.

She raises an eyebrow. 'Like magpies.'

'Like Bolgoriths,' I say. 'But none of this will help us find them.'

I walk over to the desk and begin rummaging through the

drawers, my frustration mounting. I pull out a paperweight, an old clockwork toy and a long-forgotten bottle of whisky.

'I'll have that, if you don't mind,' Marquis says, taking the bottle from me. He glances around the room. 'Where's Atlas?'

I shrug as I sit down in the desk chair. The journal describes the wyverns' flying practice, their hunting of sheep for meat and wool, their naming and funeral ceremonies. But all these things could be happening anywhere on the far side of the island.

There's a resounding boom as the floor vibrates beneath our feet. I jump up as the others look round in alarm. It's a sound we've all grown up with and it sends a chill through me now.

It's the sound of a dragon landing.

'Shit!' Gideon says, ducking away from the window. 'Guardians coming up the path.'

'The stairs,' I say, my voice barely a whisper. 'Quickly.'

I pause by the window, making sure to keep behind the curtain.

On the road beyond the garden, his black body stark against the sea, is Goranov. And with him is Ralph. I clutch the curtain as I peer closer. They're talking, standing close together, Goranov's huge head looming down above Ralph's. The dragon's flickering red tongue slides out from between his teeth and I recoil as the tip brushes across Ralph's forehead, his hair, his neck. Ralph stands stock still, his body rigid with fear. And yet he is allowing himself to be touched.

To be tasted.

I feel sick.

'Viv!'

Marquis is beckoning from the door and I run, scrambling up the staircase behind the others. Where is Atlas? I swear as my foot almost goes through the rotting wood of one of the steps. As we reach the first bedroom, I hear the Guardians kick away the remains of the front door. Marquis holds out one of the long, dusty curtains and gestures to Serena and Gideon to hide behind it.

'Viv, under the bed!' he orders me as he slips behind the door.

I creep as quietly as I can across the floorboards, then crouch down by the bed. The space beneath it is crammed with boxes. My stomach lurches as footsteps sound from the stairs.

'Viv!' Marquis whispers as I dart out on to the landing.

I push open the first door I see. Another bedroom, this one a nursery. There's no bed, just a tiny cot, a rocking horse and a wardrobe. I step into it, pulling it closed as the door to the nursery opens. I crouch awkwardly among the musty clothes, cobwebs sticking to my face. The floorboards creak gently and I breathe as slowly as I can as I peer through the crack in the door. Ralph is scanning the room, his brow furrowed. He takes a step towards the wardrobe. I lean backwards to hide behind the clothes. The hangers chink against the iron bar.

Shit.

Ralph smiles. He wrenches the door open and pulls me out.

'Found you, little swallow,' he sneers. 'Where is it?'

My eyes dart traitorously to the loquisonus still inside the wardrobe. Ralph keeps my coat tight in his fist as he rummages for it, then pulls it out. Heavy boots pace the landing.

'Nothing here,' someone shouts. 'They'll be halfway up the hillside by now.'

I glare at Ralph as the Guardians march back down the stairs. 'Aren't you going to call them?' I whisper.

'No.' He hands the loquisonus machine to me. 'Goranov is nearby. I want you to listen to him now.'

I hesitate and his lip curls.

'Do it.'

I take the loquisonus machine out of the case and place it on the ground, then kneel down beside it. 'You're right not to trust him, Ralph,' I say quietly. 'He'll kill you, when he no longer needs you.'

'You don't know what you're talking about,' Ralph says. 'Goranov will always have need of me.'

'Why?'

He lifts his gun and points it at me. 'Start the machine.'

I flick the switch, then put the headphones on. The clicks and trills of the Koinamens fill my ears. 'I can't tell which one is Goranov,' I say. 'What you're asking me to do is impossible.'

'Just listen for any calls you might recognise,' Ralph says. 'Tell me what you hear.'

'Something about prey,' I say as I concentrate on the sounds. 'There's a Trill-type42 . . . I think that means *unfamiliar* or maybe *foreign*. And then . . . something about forces or fliers or—'

The door behind Ralph slams open and he spins around, lifting his gun.

'Get away from her,' Atlas spits.

I rip the headphones off my ears.

'Take another step, King,' Ralph snarls, 'and I'll shoot you again.'

I feel the colour drain from my face. On either side of Atlas, Serena and Marquis are pointing their own weapons. I stand up with the loquisonus machine in my arms.

'Stay where you are,' Ralph barks at me, his eyes still on Atlas.

'Viv, walk towards me,' Atlas says.

Ralph swings his gun around and points it at me. Atlas's jaw tenses.

'Keep the machine, Wyvernmire,' Marquis says. 'We only want Viv.'

'It's useless without her,' Ralph snaps.

I can feel sweat beading on my skin. I know just how capable Ralph is of firing that gun.

I slip the machine into the case. 'Andronikos will help you,' I say, holding it out to him. 'Have it, and let us go.'

'No!' Atlas says. 'Don't give it to him.'

'What are you on about?' Marquis says. He looks at me. 'Leave the machine, we don't have time for this!'

I drop the loquisonus at Ralph's feet and walk slowly towards the others. Ralph won't shoot me if he thinks I'm the only one who can translate the Koinamens for him, but Marquis keeps his gun raised all the same.

'We're going to close the door now,' Serena tells Ralph as I reach them.

I back out into the hallway where Gideon is waiting.

'One,' she says.

Marquis keeps his gun on Ralph.

'Two.'

Ralph scowls.

'Three.'

Atlas dives through the door into the nursery with his arm outstretched. Ralph shouts and his gun goes off, the bullet burrowing a hole into the wall.

'Atlas!' Marquis screams.

Atlas stumbles back towards us, the loquisonus machine case flung over his shoulder. We run for the staircase and my feet barely skim the top step. I'm vaguely aware of the others behind me as Ralph shoots again and then there's grass beneath my feet. Guardians in white suits turn towards us as we race down the garden path into the fields and Serena shrieks as more bullets blow up pieces of grass around us. Sheep scatter as we run upwards, the land sloping invisibly beneath the thistles and ferns.

'We'll never outrun them,' Gideon wheezes.

Atlas's hand slips into mine as we charge past a second herd of sheep. When I look over my shoulder, the herd has moved so that the Guardians have to run straight through. They're forced to slow, to swerve between the grazing sheep. There's a flash of blue amid the woolly white coats.

Wings erupt from the herd and a juvenile Western Drake emerges from its hiding place, snapping up the first Guardian with one jerk of its head. I see his body break in the dragon's jaws, see its talons rake the back of another Guardian's suit, piercing his bulletproof vest as if it were made of gauze.

The ground drops out from beneath me and suddenly

we're falling, down the side of a ditch as Atlas's hand is tugged from mine. Pain radiates through my shoulders as I hit the bottom. I spit out a mouthful of leaves and look up. Atlas and Serena are beside me and Marquis and Gideon are scrambling down the slope and into the forest where we've landed. Up on the hillside, the Western Drake roars.

'A camouflaged Western Drake?' I breathe, getting to my feet. 'That was lucky.'

'Lucky?' Marquis snarls. 'It was downright miraculous.' He turns to Atlas. 'What the fuck were you thinking? Ralph was going to let us walk out of there.'

'We can't let the loquisonus get into the wrong hands,' Atlas says calmly.

'It wouldn't have mattered, Atlas,' I say gently. 'This loquisonus doesn't have an output switch, so Wyvernmire can't use it to—'

'Shut up, all of you,' Gideon says. He casts a glance up in the direction of the Western Drake. 'It might hear us.'

We fall into a nervous silence.

'All we know,' Marquis whispers, 'is that the wyverns are tunnellers. That means we'll find them, oh, I don't know, some time next year.'

A quiet groan comes from Serena. I hadn't noticed her still sitting on the ground, cradling her arm.

'Are you hurt?'

'Shot, I think.' She winces.

My stomach lurches as Marquis drops to the ground beside her. He pulls her sleeve away to reveal a small, circular wound, a split in the skin that looks deep enough to need stitches.

'Is the bullet still in there?' Atlas asks, pulling supplies out of his pack.

Marquis nods as he takes the bandages and the bottle of alcohol.

Serena grimaces. 'Don't I need surgery?'

'I've seen kids shoot at each other on this island,' Gideon says. 'Trust me, you don't want to go digging around for that bullet. It's better left where it is.'

'The wound will get infected if it isn't closed,' Atlas says. 'Serena, you're going to have to go back to Eigg, find a medic.'

Serena shrieks as Marquis pours alcohol over the wound, then begins to bandage it.

'No,' she says shakily. 'I'm not spending the most decisive weeks of the war in a hospital bed.' She reaches for her own pack and pulls out a small vial of orange liquid. 'Don't look at me like that, Marquis. We all have one.'

'Fireblod?' I say incredulously. 'The rebels gave you fireblod?'

Fireblod is the black-market medicine that saved Atlas's life. It was banned by the Peace Agreement as it's made from the blood of live dragons.

'It's stock from the First Class hospitals they raided,' Serena says. 'The rebels don't support the making of fireblod, but we can't let what has been made go to waste. It could save rebel lives.'

'I wonder how the rebel dragons feel about that,' I say.

Serena unstoppers the vials and drinks the liquid.

'Serena's right,' Atlas says grimly. 'We can't afford to lose her now, and with the fireblod that wound will be closed by tomorrow.'

'I'd rather be mauled by a dragon than ingest that stuff,' Marquis says.

'Well, if my arm doesn't heal, the Bolgoriths will smell the blood and then you will be,' Serena retorts.

'We'd have the protection of a Bolgorith if it wasn't for Viv's big mouth,' Gideon mutters.

'One look at Chumana causes you to lose your senses, Gideon,' Marquis says.

'Shut up,' I say. 'Look.'

Something black is streaking through the air towards us. It's the size of a large crow, except it has a long tail and is carrying something bulky in its claws.

'A dracovol.'

The creature doesn't land. Instead, it flies at Gideon, who shouts and bats at it with his hands.

'Stop it, you idiot!' I shout.

The dracovol drops a package at Gideon's feet before zipping away.

'What's wrong with you?' I hiss.

'I thought it was attacking me,' Gideon mutters.

'Do you often get attacked by postal workers, Gideon?' Marquis scoffs.

'Wait,' Atlas says as Gideon kneels down by the package. 'There could be anything inside.'

We all stare at it. It's large and wrapped in brown paper.

Gideon's eyes grow wide. 'You think it could be a bomb?'

'The person sending it would have to be in possession of something belonging to Gideon for the dracovol to scent,' I say. 'You haven't had tea with Wyvernmire lately, have you Gideon?'

He shakes his head and pulls the brown paper away. His shoulders slump. 'It's a book.'

I peer over his shoulder and feel a jump of recognition. It's not a book.

'It's a journal!' I say. 'Clawtail's journal. Hollingsworth must have sent it.'

Gideon frowns. 'But why did she send it to *me?*'

I flick through the journal, relief filling me. Hollingsworth, despite being a liar, hasn't abandoned me completely. A piece of paper pokes out of the top of the journal and I slip it out.

Some Eigg dragons inform me that Clawtail's friends have an interest in Skrill-type20. If you walk in a straight line from Trill-type30 with the colourful Screech-type2 to the Skye side of the island, you might find them.

Good luck,

Dr Seymour

'Dr Seymour?' I say.

Gideon shrugs. 'I had a room back on Eigg. She must have taken something for the dracovol to scent, as she didn't have any of your belongings.'

'How silly of me to think *the Chancellor* might be the one helping us,' I mutter under my breath. I look to Gideon. 'Can you remember what Skrill-type20 means?'

He bows his head, thinking, as the others watch us.

'She's using echolocation calls as a code?' Atlas says.

I nod as I try to recall our time in the glasshouse, before

we destroyed all the translations we made of the dragons' echolocation calls.

'Man-made affairs?' Gideon offers. 'The wyverns have an interest in man-made affairs?'

'Not affairs,' I say. 'Buildings. Don't you remember Soresten once ordering a patrol around all the buildings at Bletchley Park? He used a Skrill-type20, I'm sure of it.' I run my eyes down the note again. 'And Trill-type30 means *church*. Bletchley town had two.' I glance at Atlas. 'But are there churches on Canna?'

'Three, actually,' Gideon replies. 'Screech-type2 means *glass*. That's how the Bletchley dragons used to refer to the glasshouse. Only one of the Canna churches has stained glass. It's a few miles from here.'

I look at the pages the note was pressed between. Clawtail drew a map of Canna across them, one that I studied countless times back in London. I notice a tiny cross. Directly opposite it, on the Skye side of the island, is nothing but hills and rivers.

'That's the Stepstones,' Gideon says, pointing to the spot on the map. 'It's used as an alternative nesting spot to Rùm. It's quieter.'

'The wyverns could be there, then.'

He nods.

'That's a lot of dragon knowledge for a boy who's terrified of the things,' Serena says.

'Are you saying you're not?' I mutter at Serena. I stuff the journal into Marquis's pack and take the loquisonus machine from Atlas.

'Put your poison pouches on,' Serena snaps. 'If you sense

movement above, don't look up, just run.'

'She doesn't know what she's talking about,' Gideon says. 'If you sense movement above, then you're already dead.'

Transcript – BLIGHTY AGAINST BOLGORITHS

Sandy: Today we're live with fellow rebel Drogo, somewhat of an expert in linguistics. What do you say, Drogo, to Wyvernmire's statement that the dragons of Britannia must abandon their tongues in favour of Slavidraneishá?'

Drogo: It is language assimilation. A group is forced to abandon its mother tongue, thereby severing its cultural roots. Britannia is both a victim and a perpetrator of such a practice. Scotland once banned its own Gaelic, and the nation has imposed both English and Dragonese on the African continent. I saw it first-claw in Italy in the nineteenth century, when the Savoy government replaced Sardinian with Italian and Sardu-descended dragon tongues with what is now the country's national Draconic language, Retillese.

Drake: And to what end would you say our dear old Prime Minister is working, Drogo?

Drogo: She would have us adopt a new language and with it a new identity, a new government, a new way of life. That of the Bulgarian Bolgoriths. It is a one-way process. Members of British society, dragon and human, will acquire Slavidraneishá and abandon all dragon tongues, and eventually English itself, with the endpoint being Slavidraneishan monolingualism. The Bolgoriths only speak their own tongue, and how will we obey them if we cannot understand them?

Sandy: Now, be reasonable, good sir. Why would Wyvernmire advocate for such a thing?

Drake: Did you really just tell a dragon to be reasonable, Sandy?

Drogo: In her mind, Britannia would be all powerful. No human army would dare come against her Bulgarian alliance. The British Empire would be one on which the sun never sets. But it would also be one that the Bolgoriths control. And it is not only the humans they will force into submission. If the Bolgoriths win this war, they will not allow Britannia's dragons to stay.

Drake: You don't believe the British dragons are a match for the dragons of Bulgaria?

Drogo: Such a battle would require every pair of British wings and every British soldier. Only courage will bridge the gap between us and a victory. And where we lack courage, the Bolgoriths will reap it.

Sandy: Is that a quip directed at Ignacia, Drogo? Best not answer that. Instead, tell us what happened in Sardinia all those years ago.

Drogo: Sardu, its dialects and Sardinia's dragon tongues were repressed for centuries, by Savoy rule and the Spanish before that. When Italian was made the country's official language, some Sardu dialects changed, shaping themselves around the predominant language. But Sardu, like Scottish Gaelic, had the heart of a dragon.

Drake: It went down fighting, then?

Drogo: On the contrary. It refused to die.

Nine

WE EXIT THE FOREST IN THE direction Gideon gives us, continuing our walk across Canna's sloping fields to reach the other side of the island.

'The Swallow is on the move, armed with the best of the Coalition's arsenal and the spirit of rebellion.'

My cheeks burn as I stare at Serena, who grins into her transmitter.

'The battlefield is ever-changing – a war-torn capital one day and a sheet of ciphers the next. This is a war of languages and what are languages if not a secret code? Rest assured, people of Britannia, that every cipher has a weakness. And to the Swallow and the Bletchley Park recruits, Wyvernmire's war is simply another code to be cracked.' She turns the microphone off and winks. 'Spirits need uplifting, Featherswallow, and I'm hardly going to give you *all* the credit.'

She stalks off towards the others.

'I bet she was thrilled when Hollingsworth gave her that radio,' I mutter.

Atlas glances at me. 'Be gentle with her, Viv. She's doing her best, despite everything.'

I frown. 'Despite what?'

'Her parents,' Atlas says quietly. 'Wyvernmire had them killed.'

I stop walking.

'The Prime Minister will hurt the rebels any way she can,' he says grimly.

I stare at Serena's back. She failed her Examination and refused to marry the First Class man her parents found for her, so they sent her to Bletchley Park. She won't even have had the chance to tell them goodbye.

A flock of tiny birds twist and twirl above our heads, basking in the last of the day's light.

'They come back every spring, but they're late this year,' I hear Gideon tell Marquis.

I see the birds' forked tails and know what they are.

'Only you could bring the swallows back,' Atlas says softly.

My heart skips as he takes my hand, not to pull me out of the way of a dragon or a Guardian of Peace, but just because he wants to. We trail behind the others and my hand grows hot in his.

'Can you believe we're here?' I say. 'Chasing dragons together?'

He kisses me, his lips like warm silk. How many times did I dream of doing this again, back in the cold, dark sugar house? I remember how his voice used to haunt my dreams, how my body ached to be held by him one last time. I kiss him back, my arms encircling his neck as the swallows dive above us, and feel him tense.

'What is it?' I whisper.

He shakes his head, rubbing a hand across his face and giving me a weary smile. 'Nothing.'

'It's the priesthood, isn't it?' I say. 'It's okay if you're having doubts, Atlas. Back at Bletchley Park, when you said you weren't sure about being a priest any more . . .' My eyes drop to my boots. 'People say all sorts of things when they're on the brink of war.'

His hand cups my face and lifts my chin up. 'I meant what I said.' A flash of hesitation crosses his face. 'But you're right that it's not a decision to take lightly. And I can't be a priest *and* kiss you like I did back at Jasper's camp.'

I blush at the memory. I'm sure he mentioned it to lighten the mood, but I don't even try to force a smile. I just got Atlas back and now something is threatening to take him away *again*. Up ahead, the others have stopped walking. Beyond them is a field, surrounded by green hills. Gideon drops to the ground and I see what he's hiding from.

Eight large dragons.

'Oh,' I breathe as Atlas goes still.

Marquis is frozen to the spot. He glances back at us, eyes wide with panic. There's nothing but a tree between us and them.

'Go back,' I squeak. 'Go—'

'No,' Atlas whispers. 'They'll see us.'

'Then to that tree,' I say, adrenaline tensing every muscle in my body.

I have to force myself not to run. The time it takes to cross the space left between us and the tree feels like an eternity. We reach the others and I press myself up against the trunk, breathing as quietly as I can.

'What are they doing?' Serena whispers.

There are three Western Drakes, two Sand Dragons, two Ddraig Gochs and a Silver Drake. We're so close I can see the gleam of their scales in the bronze twilight.

'Ignacia continues to hide away,' the Silver Drake says in Wyrmerian. 'Between ourselves, the rebels and the Bulgarians, we have burned London to the ground. And still she has not taken flight.'

He's a young male, probably no more than fifty years old.

'Her Majesty is biding her time,' growls one of the Ddraig Gochs. 'No alliance will be amenable to her.'

'That is because she wants true peace,' a Sand Dragon snarls. 'And no one in this war can offer it to her.'

'Not true,' I say under my breath. 'The rebels want peace.'

'Not the kind she's looking for,' Gideon says.

I glance at him. I didn't know he spoke Wyrmerian.

'The Queen is reluctant to give up the secret privileges she has always enjoyed,' says a scarred Western Drake in a husky voice. 'She wants to keep her freedoms, her collusions, her feasting quota of human younglings.'

'Then her peace does not extend to all,' the Silver Drake says.

The two Ddraig Gochs let out bone-chilling roars.

'Treason!' one of them spits. 'It was the humans that betrayed her Majesty, and now—'

A high-pitched screech pierces the air. It must be on high frequency because I am certain I feel it in my body, in my bones. An immense dragon appears in the sky above the treetops, as black as dragonsmoke. Behind it, Bolgoriths in shades of black and red fly in formation.

'Goranov?' Serena whispers.

A sheer, boundless horror is building in my chest. This dragon is bigger than Goranov. I shake my head. 'Krasimir.'

Goranov's brother circles above, flying around the field as the other dragons stare up at it. Rabbits flee past us in the long grass. Only when one of the British dragons lets out a warning bellow does Krasimir begin his descent.

'Run!'

Every instinct in my body recoils with Gideon's scream. I grow hot with panic as I turn towards his petrified face. He's going to get us seen.

'Run, run!' he screams again.

He sprints out from behind the tree and in my shock I almost follow. The Bulgarian regal is gliding closer. Gideon is going to die. My legs buckle.

But Krasimir approaches calmly, drifting through the air on wings like black sails. Gideon has disappeared into the undergrowth before Goranov's brother even attempts to land. Krasimir must have seen him. His lack of interest is chilling.

'What's that on his body?' Marquis croaks.

I stare, transfixed. 'Jewels. Bulgarian dragons wear . . .'

I trail off. What I'm looking at doesn't resemble a jewel. Krasimir is almost to the ground, and I can see it's not a precious stone embedded in his chest. It's something else. I press my hand to my mouth. The scales on Krasimir's chest have been sliced away and replaced with iron rings that hold the severed talon of a dragon and a human foot. Swinging from another is a chain strung with pointed, yellow canines.

And several of his spikes are adorned with the empty poison pouches of Canna's children.

Marquis sinks down next to me. 'See those woods over there?'

I can't tear my eyes from Krasimir, but I hear the anguish in my cousin's voice.

'Run towards them and don't look back.'

But I can no longer control my limbs. I sway in front of the gruesome display as Krasimir extends his talons. Flames erupt from the dragons' mouths as they turn to face their attacker, but he doesn't land. Instead Krasimir swerves abruptly, re-angling so that he can strike from behind. His fangs bite through the head of the Silver Drake. It doesn't even scream. The other dragons rise in retaliation, a terrible roaring filling the air. Krasimir's army stays at a distance as he turns to face them. The two Sand Dragons attack, but the first is struck from the air with a crack by Krasimir's tail. The second jerks as Krasimir's jaws close around its foreleg and dislocate its shoulder and as the other dragons advance, he ploughs through them as if they were as light as birds.

I turn to face the others, my movements sluggish like I've been drugged. All the dragons are dead, but Krasimir doesn't stop. He turns, blood dripping from his mouth like some awful caricature monster, and lunges for a Bolgorith. They fight for what feels like seconds until he snaps its neck, then advances on the others like a rabid dog.

'He's . . . he's killing his own troops?' Serena says.

'Run,' Atlas cries. 'Now!'

I run, so terrified that my neck won't turn so I can look over my shoulder. Krasimir could be just behind me, about to sink his talons into my back, but there's no room in my mind to hold the thought. Everything in me is screaming at me to survive.

We find Gideon in a nearby graveyard, vomiting up the contents of his poison pouch. No one talks as we sit among the headstones beneath the trailing leaves of a weeping willow.

'I heard rumours about him being insane,' I say into the approaching dark.

'It was like he couldn't be stopped, once he'd tasted blood,' Atlas says grimly.

'I bet there are more like him,' Marquis says. 'There would have to be, to make the Bolgoriths capable of massacring their own humans. Perhaps they're all insane.'

A knot of anxiety twists in my stomach. Even if we find the wyverns – even if I can communicate with them – how can they possibly defeat the Bolgoriths? And what will happen to Britannia if they don't?

I stare around at the headstones and uneven mounds of earth where extra graves have been dug. They're marked with shells or small rocks and one even has a soaking wet felt doll.

I glance at Gideon. 'These look recent.'

He shrugs. 'We used to bury the kids, for a time, when there was a body left to bury.'

'We?'

'The group I was with. But the deaths got too frequent, so we started burning them instead.'

Jasper only mentioned three Canna groups: his own, Ruth's and another. So Gideon's must have been the one whose leader attacked Ruth.

'How long were you on Canna before you went to Bletchley Park?' I ask him.

'I lost track of the time,' he says quietly. 'But I was just a boy when they sent me here.'

I hear the quiet peeping of nesting birds.

'We should start walking,' I say.

'See the church?' Gideon says. He points to the left, where an old stone church stands in the moonlight. 'The Stepstones are on the other side of those hills.' He gestures in the opposite direction. 'We can't cross them in the dark.'

'You mean we're supposed to wait here for Krasimir to pick us off one by one?' Serena whispers.

'Would you rather fall to your death?' Gideon replies.

'Quite frankly, yes.'

I shift uncomfortably in the wet grass, shivering. 'We'll go as soon as it's light.'

Serena turns on her radio and soon, a monotone voice, listing off names, fills my ears.

'Lucy Cartwright. James Fowler. Rebecca Swiftalon. Joshua Bennett.'

'Missing rebels?' I ask her quietly.

'Dead rebels,' she says. 'This is the daily death toll. See why Hollingsworth thinks spirits need lifting?'

We lie still in the night, staring up at the countless stars.

As the sounds of breathing slow, I wonder how any of them can sleep with Krasimir nearby. Atlas's hand finds mine and I roll over so that I'm closer to him. The moon disappears behind a cloud, turning the darkness pitch black. I reach up to his face and trace the shape of his high cheekbones, his nose, his jaw prickling with stubble. Would I be able to recognise him blind, with nothing but touch? I don't think I would, and it occurs to me that a month at Bletchley Park is not enough time to get to know a person. There are still so many questions I don't know the answer to. Why he trained to be a priest. Why he became a rebel. Why he chose me.

Will he make the same choice this time round?

Is it selfish of me to want him to?

He catches my fingers. 'What are you doing?'

'Trying to decipher who you are.'

'I'm a code to be cracked too, am I?' he says.

'A true enigma,' I reply.

He buries his face in my hair and I close my eyes. Screeches sound across the island as I try to work out my feelings for Atlas. Is this love? Or infatuation? Or do I merely crave someone to cling to beneath dragon-filled skies?

The cold morning air wakes me, creeping into the collar of my coat and stiffening my joints. Atlas is gone. I sit up and scan the graveyard until I see him in another field, sitting by a small stream. He's staring up into the sky, seemingly lost in thought.

The first sunlight streams over the horizon as we climb into the hills with rumbling stomachs.

'What were you doing out in the field by yourself this morning?' I ask Atlas.

'Praying,' he says. 'Why?'

I feign a casual shrug. 'I thought you'd chosen not to be a priest.'

Atlas snorts. 'You don't have to be a man of the cloth to have a relationship with God, Viv.'

'Good,' I say, glancing at him from beneath my eyelashes. 'Because the swallow on your arm suits you much better than a white collar.'

He smiles, but it doesn't reach his eyes. My attempt to flirt suddenly seems ridiculous. I feel my cheeks burn. What's happening to me?

There's a flash of white as a bird plummets towards us.

'Bloody skuas!' Gideon shouts, waving his arms as it attacks him.

'Skuas?'

The bird dives again as Gideon plunges his hands into a nest in the grass and pulls out an egg.

'Breakfast,' he says, passing it to me.

I stare at the brown egg in my palm.

'Only the cold ones,' Gideon tells Marquis as he reaches into another nest. 'If they're warm, there are likely chicks inside.'

The nests of the great white birds litter the hillside.

'I'm not eating a raw egg,' Serena says.

'Starve, then,' Gideon replies.

He cracks the egg on a rock and tips the fat, viscous yolk into his mouth. I hand my egg to Atlas and shake my head in disgust. We keep walking, climbing with the sun, until the hill flattens out into a cliff that looms over the sea. I see merlins and orchid flowers and Grayling butterflies, wildlife I only know the names of thanks to Clawtail's journal.

'Are those puffins?' Atlas asks.

The black and white birds zip to and fro between the cliff edge and the sea, their orange beaks stuffed with tiny, silver fish.

'Clawtail wrote that the Hebridean Wyverns feast on puffins,' I say. 'Maybe that means we're getting close.'

Soon, the landscape changes again. The cliffs begin to slope downwards so that we're closer to the sea and I see something circling in the frothy white waves.

'A wyrm,' I tell Atlas.

'I once heard that the Loch Ness Monster is actually a wyrm that got fed up dealing with the bad-tempered Scots and retreated to the water forever,' he says quietly.

'Aren't the Scots known for being friendly and honest?' Serena says. 'There's a reason theirs is the country with the most rebels.'

'I'd say so,' Marquis says. 'Just look at Karim.'

I give him a sad smile. Marquis's Scottish boyfriend is the gentlest boy I know.

'The Stepstones,' Gideon says.

The slopes lead into a vast valley, miles of green hills shot through by streams and dotted with the remnants of ancient stone walls and volcanic rock. Canna would be beautiful if it wasn't a feeding ground.

'How are we supposed to find wyvern tunnels from up here?' Marquis says as he puffs on a cigarette. 'Chumana could have done a bit of echolocating for us, but I'd say you've thrown a bit of a spanner in the works when it comes to asking her for favours, wouldn't you, cousin?' He winks at me.

A bit of echolocating.

I feel a burst of energy as I pull the loquisonus machine out of its case.

'The wyverns must echolocate underground, no? If we take the loquisonus down to the Stepstones, I can listen and determine where the calls are loudest. We might be able to follow the sound until we find them.'

'Brilliant,' Atlas says. His face lights up. '*You're* brilliant.'

I flush with pleasure. It feels addictive, having his eyes on me.

'There'll be interference,' Gideon says. 'From the other dragons on Canna.'

I nod. 'We can try to avoid that by going to the lowest point of the valley.'

'Look for a river, then,' Marquis says. 'The bottom of a valley usually has one, or at least an active stream.'

'There,' says Serena, pointing to a long, blue line of water.

We venture down towards it, the sun warm on our backs.

'Let me help you,' Atlas says.

He doesn't wait for my reply before reaching for the loquisonus machine, his fingers brushing mine. I count the moles on his face as he sets the machine on the ground by the river, then crouches over it to plug the headphones in. *What if he does decide to be a priest?* I think suddenly. He could still change his mind, and what would we be then? Strangers? Lovers? Friends who kiss against a tree from time to time? Of course not.

No. He wouldn't allow it.

Atlas King would never agree to loving my body but not my soul.

I take the headphones from him and sit by the water to listen. My ears fill with the clicks and trills of echolocating dragons, each one as loud as the next. I shake my head and stand up with the machine, moving further along the stream. My heartbeat slows as I close my eyes. I let my mind search for the calls it recognises, then follow the ones it doesn't. The ones I haven't heard before.

'What does it feel like?' Atlas says. 'To understand them?'

I don't open my eyes. 'It feels like . . . like listening to an unintelligible stream of sound, except that one day the sound becomes several distinct sounds, imbued with enough meaning that suddenly the stream is replaced with words and phrases that make sense. And you can never hear them as gibberish again, no matter how hard you try.'

But the calls of Canna's dragons are almost impossible to differentiate. I didn't study these in the glasshouse. They probably refer to the hunting of puffins or the rising tide rather than the comings and goings of life at Bletchley Park. It's like learning a new language.

I step over another small stream as one of the calls gets louder, then quieter. The clear, oscillating vibration of them stops me in my tracks. This echolocation sounds strange. I step back over the stream and the volume increases again.

'There,' I say, nodding to the spot where I was just standing. I glance up into the sky but see no dragon. 'Maybe there's something below.'

'There's no feathers or fur or dragon dung,' Marquis says.

Gideon shakes his head. 'No tracks or discarded prey.'

I keep listening, the calls still loud in my ears as I walk along the stream. Something glints in the grass. I turn it over with the toe of my boot. It's a piece of transparent, orange rock, the size of a pebble. As I kick the grass back I see more of them, tiny treasures buried in the ground. My boot meets Serena's.

'Someone's turned up the earth here,' she says.

We follow the stream for another half-mile, deeper into the valley as I try to concentrate on not losing the clearest calls I'm hearing among all the others. They vibrate in my ears, then die, then stutter to life again. They sound like a faint yet persistent music. The valley is as still and crisp as the untouched landscape of a fairy tale, yet the ultrasonic sound bursting in my ears tells me it's full of life.

But where is that life hiding?

'Stop,' Serena says.

The stream snakes into a small pool of water surrounded by trees. At the far end is a tall cliff face with a waterfall crashing down from above it. We pause, hot and breathless, as Atlas walks around the pool and lays a hand on the wet wall of the cliff.

'There's no tunnel here,' he says.

'Behind the waterfall?' I say hopefully.

Atlas edges along the cliff and sticks his head behind the curtain of water.

'Nothing,' he calls out.

I put the loquisonus down and sit on the grass.

Serena holds out her hand for the headphones. 'Can you still hear it?'

I nod as she sets them on her ears and her eyes light up.

'If there's an entrance around here, a wyvern is bound to come out at some point, right?' Marquis says.

'You do understand the concept of *underground tunnels*, don't you, Featherswallow?' Gideon snorts.

'Wyverns still have to fly,' I snap.

'And so the Swallow waits. Again,' Serena mutters, handing me back the headphones. 'Our radio listeners might just die of boredom.'

'You were the ones supposed to track and find the wyverns, Serena,' I say. 'I'm just here to master the language.'

'Ah yes, we forgot we are merely your footmen,' she replies. 'The meagre enablers of your higher translation powers.'

Marquis grins and I turn my back on them both, closing my eyes in the sun. We wait, listening to the birds and the calls from the loquisonus machine. I pull a thick blade of grass from the ground and suck the sweet sap from the end as my stomach gurgles. Marquis leans back against a tree, his eyes on the cliff face.

'How was Karim when you last saw him?' I ask quietly.

'Furious.'

'I can't imagine Karim furious.'

Marquis snorts. 'He couldn't believe we were being sent to Canna without Cormac or any of the adult rebels. He called it a suicide mission.'

I nod, thinking of Krasimir. 'He's not wrong.'

'Hollingsworth is willing to risk our lives to find these

wyverns, so why hasn't she told us how they're supposed to help us?' He raises an eyebrow. 'Do you think, maybe, she doesn't know?'

I shake my head. 'You said it yourself: she's risking our lives. She wouldn't do that unless she had a bloody good reason to.'

'Then why hasn't she . . .' Marquis trails off as he bolts upright. 'I saw something. In the water.'

We all peer into the pool. Its surface ripples in the centre.

'A shadow,' Serena says lazily.

'Or a fish,' I offer.

'*No*,' Marquis insists. 'It was bigger than that.'

I stare at the water, willing myself to see a shape. A dark shadow blooms beneath the surface as if summoned. I clutch Marquis's arm. The shadow is huge, taking up the whole pool, but in the blink of an eye it's gone.

We've found the wyvern tunnels.

'The entrance is beneath the water,' Serena says.

'One of them must have seen us and gone back inside,' Atlas replies.

'So how do we get in?' I ask.

'I . . . are you sure we want to go in there?' Gideon says. 'Underground tunnels full of wyverns, and only an underwater exit?'

'Stay here if you want,' I say. 'But this is what we came for.'

I hide the loquisonus and the journal with our packs behind the waterfall, then turn back towards the pool.

'Time for a swim, recruits,' Marquis says.

He steps out of his trousers first.

I look pointedly at the water as I shrug off my coat and pull my jumper over my head. The air is cold on my bare skin and I realise I'm standing in the most regrettable underwear possible, taken from a donation package provided by Hollingsworth back in London. I look anywhere but at Atlas. At the line of white birch-rod scars on my naked arm, and then at Serena, infuriatingly chic in the white brassiere she's been hiding beneath her military uniform. The wound in her arm is almost healed.

We line up by the pool and as Atlas steps into the freezing water I sneak a glance at him. He's skinnier than I thought he'd be, a lump of scar tissue knotted across his left shoulder. I study the curve of his bare arms and the dark hair at his navel. Serena is staring too. She catches my eye and smirks. I step into the pool. The glacial temperature cuts my breath short and my feet begin to burn.

'Too cold,' I hear Gideon gasp.

I force myself further into the water until I'm waist-deep, my body trembling uncontrollably.

Serena shivers beside me. 'I don't think I can.'

Gideon swears as Marquis dives suddenly, disappearing beneath the surface. We wait in silence until he re-emerges and takes several deep, desperate gasps.

'There's an entrance,' he says, his teeth chattering.

Atlas wades in next to me. The tops of his thighs are bright red.

'I'll go first,' Marquis says.

'I'll go with you,' Serena says, wincing. 'Someone needs to

be able to pull you out if you start to drown.'

I swallow. They dive one after the other and it's just me, Atlas and Gideon left, standing in our underwear on the most dangerous island in Britannia.

'What's taking them so long?' Gideon says.

'It hasn't even been a minute.'

'And what's the plan when we get in there? Provided we don't get eaten.'

I blink. I hadn't thought that far ahead. Before anyone can answer, Marquis surfaces and Serena emerges next to him.

'You only have to swim for a few seconds before the tunnel gets higher than the waterline,' Marquis says, gasping again. 'We'll be able to breathe down there.'

'All right,' I say, feeling a swoop of dread. 'Once we're inside, I'll try to convince the wyverns to let us stay. Then we have to get to know them. Whatever secret weapon Hollingsworth thinks they have should soon become clear if we befriend them.'

Atlas is nodding. 'Once we have it, we get out. The rebels won't be able to hold off the Bulgarians forever and the information we uncover could be crucial.'

I look around at them. 'See you inside, then.'

I dip beneath the water. The cold freezes my brain and everything in me begs me to return to the surface. I open my eyes. The water is clear and Atlas's face is in front of me, his cheeks bulging with air. I gesture at him to hold on to me and he nods, his hands settling on my waist. Then I follow Serena downwards towards a patch of dark water. Tiny silver fish trailing algae dart in and out of the cave entrance. I don't want to go in, but if I hesitate we'll run out of breath. I grip the rocky edge of the entrance and push us inside. I swim upwards, looking for the place where the ceiling gets higher, but my head hits solid rock. I immediately go dizzy with panic, but when Atlas's feet meet the bottom of the tunnel, he pushes us forward. I can just make out Serena's shape in front of me as she reaches out a hand and pulls me towards her. We surface, gulping air. The water is up to our necks, but at least we can breathe.

I feel for Atlas in the dark. 'Are you all right?'

My hand meets with his ear and when he replies I feel his breath on my cheek.

'Now I am,' he pants, his voice echoing through the dark.

We move along the tunnel as Marquis surfaces behind us, followed by Gideon. I use my arms to pull myself through the water until the ceiling above us disappears at the same time as the floor drops out.

'This is the most stupid thing we've ever done,' I hear Gideon say.

'For once, Gideon,' Marquis whispers, 'I agree.'

I tread water as my eyes adjust to the light streaming in through small gaps in the walls. We're in another pool that sits inside a cave. And directly opposite us, staring out from beneath the overhanging rocks, are a hundred pairs of eyes.

Ten

HORROR CREEPS UP MY SPINE. AS the light pierces the gloom, I see the shapes of a crowd. The creatures are at least a head taller than Marquis and standing on their hind legs, frozen except for their swaying tails, like cats about to pounce on their prey. And I've never felt as much like prey as I do now, half-naked in front of a pack of dragons whose canines are longer than my finger. The wyverns don't look as harmless as the watercolours at Canna House suggested. They have doe-like eyes and rounded snouts, but their bodies are nimble and they have enormous foretalons, the index curved and longer than the others. One of them bats its feathered wings together and lets out an unwelcoming screech. How do we show them we're not a threat?

'Featherswallow?' Serena hisses.

I suddenly remember we don't have to rely on body language to communicate.

'*Nà foin*,' I try to say, wincing at my pronunciation. 'We are sorry to intrude.'

I must have said it wrong, because a low growl sounds from the wyvern's throat. Its foretalons snap together like a pair of monstrous scissors.

The others follow suit, emitting shrieks that echo through the cave. I tread water and see the alarm on Marquis's face. There's nowhere to escape to. These wyverns could tear us to pieces here in this pool and no one would ever know. Explorers will find our skeletons years from now, buried in the rock, and think we were looking for food or shelter.

'*Fasgadh*!' I shout. 'We need *fasgadh*.'

The wyverns fall silent.

I remember the word from Clawtail's journal. It's Gaelic, but borrowed by the wyverns as part of their tongue, and means *shelter*. And they take it seriously. Immediately, their wings drop and their heads bow.

'*Hva thu tha?*' the wyvern snarls. 'Who are you?'

When I hear Cannair spoken out loud for the first time, the puzzle pieces click together inside my head. It's like hearing sheet music played by a virtuoso on a fine-tuned instrument, when you've only ever heard the notes stabbed at on a broken piano. It's as melodious as Gaelic and as smooth as whisky.

'Tell it we're not invading,' Marquis whispers.

'I . . . We are . . . friends,' I stutter in Cannair, my mind grasping at the vocabulary I learned from the journal.

The wyverns blink.

'Gideon,' Atlas says quietly. 'You're a polyglot, too. Don't you speak Scottish? Maybe it's similar.'

'Cannair is descended from Scottish Gaelic, not Scots,' I snap. 'They're two different languages.'

'And yet somehow neither of you speak either of them,' Serena whispers shrilly.

I steady my breathing and try to block out their voices as I picture Clawtail's writings on linguistics.

'We are . . . friends of Patrick Clawtail,' I say.

The first wyvern takes a step forward and the scant daylight illuminates the white scars across his face. Most of his wing feathers are white, but some are a luminescent, royal blue.

'Patrick Clawtail is dead,' he snarls in Cannair.

Relief crashes over me. The wyvern understood what I said. I smile smugly at Serena. Does she not realise what an important moment this is?

'Yes,' I say with a shiver. 'But we have the journal he wrote when he sought *fasgadh* with you. That is where I learned Cannair.'

A second wyvern comes forward, this one younger with silver mottling on her blue scales.

'You learned it,' she says tentatively, 'from . . . paper?'

I nod.

The second wyvern says something to the first, who has smoke rising from his nostrils. He glances at the tunnel entrance hidden beneath the water, then back at me.

'You lie,' he says. 'Patrick would never have written of our location.'

This wyvern looks old. Did he know Clawtail personally?

'No,' I say quickly. 'We found your tunnels with a . . . machine.'

'A machine?' he says slowly. 'A human-built machine that detects *skugvels*?'

I don't know the word *skugvels*, but I'm willing to bet it means *tunnels*.

'Yes,' I say. 'I left it outside, with the journal. I can show you if you like.'

The other wyverns begin leaving the cave, creeping away down various tunnels while casting curious looks behind them, as if summoned by an inaudible call.

'From what do you seek shelter?' the first wyvern growls.

I hesitate, wishing I had discussed this with the others before we entered the tunnel.

'War,' I say simply.

'War?' he says. 'What war?'

I cast a look back at the others.

'He's asking what war I'm talking about,' I tell them.

Their expressions echo my own confusion.

'The war between Prime Minister Wyvernmire and her Bulgarian dragons, and the Human-Dragon Coalition,' I say.

'We are not aware of such a war,' he says.

'And we are not interested in participating in it,' the female wyvern adds.

I grab hold of the ledge of the pool, my legs tired from treading water. 'But you must go above ground sometimes?' I say slowly.

'Have you not seen the Bulgarian dragons flying above?'

'We do not occupy ourselves with the affairs of other species,' the first says.

I nod, trying to process what I'm hearing. The wyverns

we're supposed to seek an alliance with don't even know there's a war going on. I feel a rush of despair.

'Canna is dangerous for us,' I say. 'We are being hunted. We ask that you let us stay.' I hesitate. 'Like you did for Patrick and his family.'

'No,' he replies. 'Wyverns have lived in concealment, far from all humans, for half a century. We cannot help you.'

'They invoked *fasgadh*, Abelio!' the female wyvern says.

Abelio.

I remember the name from Clawtail's last journal entry, the sentence he never finished.

The two wyverns stare at each other, communicating silently. Then Abelio lets out a low hiss.

'Cindra insists we award you the shelter you claim,' Abelio says finally. 'But you must prove yourselves to be amenable to our own requests.'

'Of course,' I reply. 'What are they?'

His talons twitch. 'All in good time.'

We step out of the water and follow the wyverns down a tunnel. The air is stiflingly warm and steam rises off our bodies as we walk. I stare at the wyverns' backs, studying the way they walk on their hind legs, how they gesture with the scaly limbs attached to their great wings. They're much smaller than dragons, though they still tower over humans by several feet. They move quickly, their gestures fluid and sinuous, and their wings quiver every so often as though lifted by a breeze. They are like silent, blue phantoms in the dark tunnels, which grow lighter the deeper they wind. The path ahead is lit by lanterns filled with what seems to be oil-soaked sheep's wool.

The stone walls drip with condensation and glitter with flecks of tiny orange rock like the ones we found in the dirt by the stream. Soon my skin and hair are completely dry, but I feel like I'm suffocating from the overpowering heat.

'They accepted us rather easily, don't you think?' says Atlas's voice in my ear.

I startle, not having realised he was so close. He walks next to me, his hair a sweep of humid curls. Sweat glistens on his bare shoulders and I see him snatch a glance at me before dropping his eyes to the ground. I avert my own.

'They want something from us, too,' I whisper.

We turn a corner into a wider passageway. I see the flames of a roaring fire flickering in a chamber further along. Tapestries stitched with blue and emerald-green thread cover the walls, depicting wyverns flying across the sea, wyverns hunting in forests, wyverns lighting fires beneath white, oval eggs. As we walk, we peer into chambers with high ceilings, carpeted with thickly woven rugs. Each has a fire in its centre, the smoke exiting through a small hole in the ceiling, the same one that lets the light in. In one of the chambers, I see a wyvern standing as still as a statue, its white wings folded peacefully on its back as it reads a human-size book by the fire, moving only to turn the pages with a long talon. In another, several wyverns are crowded around what seems to be a metal sculpture of a human boy. To see such gentle domesticity in these feral, screeching creatures is strange, almost unsettling.

Abelio and Cindra say nothing as they lead us further into the maze of tunnels, maintaining their silence even as other curious inhabitants peer out to look at us with blue, glassy eyes.

At the entrance to another tunnel to my left, two wyvernlings the size of human toddlers chase after a frog, taking turns to attempt to scald it with small puffs of flame. I stumble, tripping over Cindra's tail as she halts without warning.

'Your living quarters,' she says, gesturing into a large cave with her longest talon.

A small fire is burning in the centre hearth.

There are no tapestries or rugs, but I see several alcoves in the walls containing tweed blankets and books. A small stream trickles around the edge of the room, pooling into a stagnant puddle in the corner.

'You will wait here until somebody arrives to collect you for the Twilight Meal.'

I nod to show her I've understood – at least I think I have – and she backs out of the cave. Abelio gives us a last glare before following her down the passageway.

I turn around to face the others. 'They want us to dine with them tonight.'

Serena's hair has doubled in size with the humidity and Gideon's face is a furious red.

'Well, shit,' Marquis says, picking up a book from an alcove before flinging it down again. 'Are they even dragons?'

'Of course they're dragons,' I say. 'Have you never seen a dragon read before?'

'Have I ever seen a dragon read *Gulliver's Travels*, you mean?' Marquis says, glancing at the discarded book. 'I can't say I have.'

Gideon slurps loudly from the stream, then wipes his mouth with the back of his hand. 'Why all the tweed? The rugs, the tapestries, the blankets . . .'

'So they like tweed,' I say impatiently. 'What's wrong with that?'

'It's all a bit tame, isn't it?' Serena says, wrapping a tweed blanket around her shoulders. 'They're hardly a match for a Bulgarian dragon.'

My heart sinks, perhaps because a small part of me has been thinking the same thing. 'There's nothing tame about their talons,' I argue, as much with myself as with Serena. I give them all a steely look. 'Chumana told me not to underestimate the Hebridean Wyverns. If we do, we'll never win their trust, and they'll never help us.'

'Make the wyverns who almost ate us, like us,' Serena jeers. 'Easy.'

'I admit that might be hard for you, Serena, seeing how unlikeable you really are,' I snap.

'Let's find out what we can about them at this Twilight Meal, then reconvene afterwards to decide what it is we can offer them,' Atlas says. He looks around at the others. 'This is the mission you've been given by the Coalition. Did you think it was going to be easy?'

We pull out more tweed blankets to rest on, my legs aching from the many miles of hill-climbing. I wrap one around me despite the heat and think about my own mission: to speak enough Cannair to make these wyverns trust me, and to understand what it is about them that can help us. A while later, another wyvern enters the cave. He's smaller than Abelio and Cindra, with white rings around his huge eyes. He bows to us in the archway, our clothes clutched in his talons.

'It is an honour to host you, friends of the great Clawtail,' he says in English. 'I am utterly delighted that you have invoked *fasgadh*.'

'You speak our language?' Marquis says.

'Indeed. Only a rare few of us do, although some wyverns have begun learning the human tongue Gaelic. My name is Aodahn – bringer of fire. I have come to escort you to the Twilight Meal.'

I stand up as he sets our clothes down. The wyverns have been outside to collect them, but he hasn't brought the journal or the loquisonus.

'Where did you learn it?' I ask him as I pull on my shirt. 'I thought the Hebridean Wyverns hadn't seen any humans in years.'

'Patrick,' Aodahn says. 'And human books. They are the reason many of us are applying ourselves to learning –' he lowers his voice – 'human tongues. We like to wander the paths of human literature.'

He beckons us out into the passageway and walks at a leisurely pace, the tip of his wing unfurling to point into more chambers.

'I call this cave here King's Cross,' Aodahn says.

'Come again?' says Marquis.

'King's Cross,' the wyvern repeats. 'It is where we design our travel routes, with several new tunnels built each year. I believe it is a place in London, is it not?'

'Uh, yes,' I say quickly.

I exchange a look with Marquis, who is trying desperately not to laugh. We move on to the next cave, which slopes downwards, deep into the earth. The only illumination comes from two flaming torches, which give enough light to see the shapes of hundreds of twisted metal hearts stuck in the ground.

'Bleeding Heart Yard,' Aodahn says. 'Where we burn and mourn our dead.'

We pass by another cave but Aodahn doesn't stop. I glance inside it anyway. The ground is a bed of smouldering feathers, kept alight by several wyverns hovering above and breathing fire. Nestled among the feathers are rows of eggs, and I watch as a wyvern on the ground carefully turns one of them.

'What's in here?' Atlas asks, peering into another cave.

'Take heed!' Aodahn cries.

Atlas stops abruptly before he falls off the ledge of the cave entrance. I look in from over his shoulder. It's a great open space, lit by streams of white light. It must be several miles wide and is so deep that I cannot see the bottom. Ledges jut out from the walls and wyverns perch on them.

'Wuthering Heights,' Aodahn says. 'This is where our wyvernlings partake of flying practice.'

'Wuthering Heights?' Serena says. 'I've heard of that book. It's a novel. The daughter of one of my mother's friends was reading it.'

'His English is certainly straight out of a novel,' Gideon mutters.

The heat becomes stifling as we walk deeper into the tunnel system and when Aodahn brings us to a stop I see why. We are in a huge cavern with a giant bonfire burning in the middle. A hundred or so wyverns are gathered around it, basking in the orange glow created by the reflection of the flames in the huge chunks of amber rock in the ceiling.

'Welcome to the Amber Court,' Aodahn says.

Every inch of the walls is covered in tweed tapestries, with white scrolls of paper tucked inside. I peer closer, trying to work out what they could be. As Aodahn leads us inside, wyverns turn to look at us. Abelio and Cindra are closest to the fire, sitting with a group of wyverns whose heads are bent in concentration. When Abelio sees us he stands up and I realise what the wyverns are looking at.

The loquisonus machine.

They're peering at it in great fascination, examining the dials and the speaker with their snouts and talons. I imagine their great claws scratching at the metal or spinning the dial off its mechanism and resist the urge to shout at them to stop. Clawtail's journal lies open on the ground. Cindra's eyes narrow as she sees me watching.

'Greetings to our human guests,' Abelio bellows in Cannair.

The cave goes silent as wyverns turn to listen, but Abelio is speaking too fast for me to make sense of what he is saying. I'm reminded of what it was like when I was a small child learning dragon tongues for the first time, and of the frustration I felt when I was able to understand certain words, only to lose track of them once they were strung together in conversation.

Serena prods me in the back. 'What's he saying?'

'I don't know,' I say. 'I . . . I think something about learning. And a challenge.'

'Brilliant,' she mutters.

Abelio must see the confusion on my face because suddenly his speech slows and becomes easier to understand.

'Today we have the opportunity to offer shelter to a group of humans,' he says. 'Some of you have never heard *fasgadh* called upon before. But there is nothing the Hebridean Wyverns do better than hospitality.' His eyes land on mine. 'Our knowledge and tradition lend themselves well to entertaining guests. Indeed, we wyverns are learned creatures, the most erudite and progressive of dragons.'

Aodahn is whispering a translation of Abelio's speech to the others and Marquis raises his eyebrows.

'He's changed his tune.'

Abelio's manner of speaking is hard to describe, the sound of it jaunty and fluctuating in pitch and tone.

'Cultivated in the arts, the sciences and the ways of life of our ancestors, we have the ability to shelter these humans from the ills that threaten them. They could walk these tunnels for an eternity without ever wanting for food, water or intellectual stimulation because everything they need is within. We ask only that each human thus protected pays their dues.'

My mind races as I try to keep up and I glance at Atlas. 'I think he's about to tell us what he wants in exchange for letting us stay.'

'Who gave you Patrick Clawtail's journal?' Cindra asks.

The question is directed at me.

'The Academy for Draconic Linguistics,' I reply in English, before switching back to Cannair. 'It was founded only –' I pause, trying to remember any wyvern words for numbers – 'thirty years ago. No . . . equivalent word –' I shake my head – 'in your –' I point around at them – 'language. It's an institution dedicated to recording and –' I ponder the sentence – 'translating dragon tongues.'

Abelio's eyes narrow. 'And who controls it?'

'The British government,' I say.

'Then you are foes,' Cindra snarls. 'Patrick was no friend of the government's.'

'Neither are we,' I say calmly. 'We are part of the resistance against it. Prime Minister's Wyvernmire's government is at war with the rest of Britannia.'

Abelio picks up Clawtail's journal. 'But how can one learn an entire tongue from a book?'

I hesitate. 'I'm a polyglot. Learning languages is something I'm good at. But I'm not fluent, as you can probably hear.'

Cindra's nostrils twitch.

'We would like to offer you what we can, in exchange for your *fasgadh*,' I say.

'And you will,' Abelio growls. 'You, *an nighean leis an inneal òir*.'

What did he call me?

'It's Gaelic. Such a name does not exist in Cannair,' Aodahn whispers, his eyes wide as moons. 'Girl with the golden machine.'

'You will teach us how your tunnel detector works, giving us a detailed explanation of its inner body and a demonstration above ground.' He blinks. 'Such an invention could lead to new, wyvern-originated ideas.'

I find myself nodding vigorously, but my mind is whirring, trying to figure out how to pretend the loquisonus is a tunnel detector while hiding its true purpose. The wyverns may be different to dragons, but they share their ultrasonic language, and I don't think they'll appreciate the fact that my *golden machine* was made to listen to it.

Abelio points his longest claw at Atlas. 'What can he offer us?'

I feel Atlas tense beside me. He doesn't need to speak Cannair to understand the demand.

'I can whittle wood,' he says. 'Craft shapes from tree bark and driftwood, 'weapons—'

I shake my head, lacking the vocabulary to translate what he said, so Aodahn does it for me.

'We are well-practised in the art of carpentry,' Abelio replies.

The wyverns stare at him expectantly, the only sound the roaring of the fire. I count the beads of sweat on Atlas's brow. It hits me once again that we're surrounded by dragons. Dragons with teeth and flame who are under no obligation to keep us alive.

'Why don't you offer to give them Bible readings,' Marquis hisses from behind.

Serena snorts and I turn around and glare at them, but it does nothing to wipe the grin off Marquis's face.

'Atlas is a soldier,' I tell Abelio. 'He's been rebelling against the government for years. He knows all there is to know about the war and those inflicting it on us.'

'We have no interest in your war,' Abelio growls.

'Forgive me,' I say. 'Only, I thought you said you were *progressive* dragons. But how can you possibly be progressive if you don't know where progress is needed?' I pause, preparing my next sentence. 'You've been isolated from human and dragon society for years, but Atlas can teach you about its politics. Starting with the breaking of the Peace Agreement and the Academy for Draconic Linguistics.'

Cindra's eyes gleam like molten silver and Abelio lets out a satisfied grunt.

Atlas grabs me by the elbow. 'Translate, *please.*'

'You're to be their Professor of Politics,' I say.

Marquis bursts into fits of laughter behind us, hastily covering up the sound with a cough. Atlas gives me a bewildered look.

'And this one?' Cindra says, taking a step towards Serena.

Serena smiles sweetly. 'The feminine arts.'

I raise my eyebrows and try to translate, but I don't think the wyverns have the same concept of *feminine* as we do.

'What is this art that is carried out by females?' Cindra asks.

Serena lists off her achievements. 'If you want to learn needlework, embroidery, decoupage, flower-arranging, drawing, oil-painting or the pianoforte, then I'm your girl.'

'I don't see many pianofortes around here, do you?' I tell her, but she watches Cindra with a lazy confidence as Aodahn attempts to relay the information.

'An artist,' Abelio says solemnly. 'There are many among us, but we will gladly learn from this one.' His gaze flicks to Marquis.

'Oh, I dunno,' Marquis says, stuffing his hands in his pockets. 'I studied dragon anatomy, before. The dragon body and how it works, inside and out.'

'A healer?' Abelio ask hopefully.

'That's right,' I reply quickly.

The old wyvern nods.

Aodahn translates Marquis's job description to him as Abelio stares Gideon down.

'Human tongues,' Gideon says. 'I know five.'

A surprised warble comes from Aodahn, but as I relay the information Abelio shakes his head.

'We need not know the tongues of man. Only our own tongue, Cannair, matters. On the contrary, it is men who should learn to speak our language, the most superior of—'

'You would deny us such a resource?' Cindra hisses to Abelio. 'Are not all languages linked? This boy could help us learn more about our beautiful Cannair, about its roots.' She rounds on Gideon. 'Do you speak Scots? Gaelic?'

'Scots,' Gideon tells Aodahn, who is still translating.

Abelio stares at him and his jaw chatters like a cat on a hunt. 'Very well.' Then he turns to the other wyverns, who are still watching the spectacle. 'Our cultural exchange will begin at dawn. But now, the Twilight Meal.'

Several wyverns appear in the entrance to the Amber Court, pulling wooden trolleys attached to the base of their wings by harnesses made of dried, twisted seaweed. On the trolleys are clay pots of all shapes and sizes and Aodahn reaches for one and sets it down in front of us.

'Gather, eat!' he tells us, leaning back on his hind legs.

Is it their short front limbs, which serve as arms, that allow the Hebridean Wyverns to act more human than dragon, to read books and weave tweed and serve food? We sit in a circle around the pot, imitating the wyverns, and I see Aodahn cock his head as he observes the way I cross my legs. Marquis lifts the lift of the pot eagerly, then recoils. It's full of large chunks of glistening, raw meat, scattered with some sort of green herb. I glance around as the wyverns the next pot over use small stone bowls to scoop out a serving of meat each, then clink their bowls together before burying their snouts in the food.

'Manners,' Serena says incredulously. 'They're using their manners to consume a bowl of blood.'

'Oh, I do beg your pardon,' Aodahn says.

He has a fascinating way of speaking, using sentence structures that could only have been learned from Britannia's First Class. Where did he get it from?

He returns the lid to the pot, then breathes fire on to the clay. When he removes it again, the meat is cooked and steaming. We scoop it up into bowls and eat. The meat is coated in salty juices, as if the herb used to season it has just been fished from the sea. For a moment there is only the sound of chewing and slurping as we fill our stomachs for the first time in days.

'Hungry, are you?' Atlas mutters with a sly smile.

I lower the bowl, feeling myself blush.

'I was joking, Viv. Don't stop on my account.'

He slurps so loudly from his bowl that Aodahn looks up in astonishment and I burst into laughter.

'Do you think it would be rude to go back for more?'

'Featherswallow, you've gone from a comfortable Second Class existence to Bletchley Park to rebel life in London to a secluded island with the boy you thought was dead, but here you are worrying about wyvern social codes.'

I snort.

'Have you noticed how they're barely speaking?' he says.

I glance around at the wyverns. They're eating in quiet groups, but they have an energy, and mannerisms, like the twitch of a tail or the flare of nostrils, that suggest they're communicating in silence.

'Echolocation?' Atlas says in a hushed voice.

I nod.

'Aodahn,' Serena says, adopting a soft, high-society voice. 'Have you read *Wuthering Heights?*'

Aodahn's eyes light up. 'Yes. I have my very own copy. Would it please you to borrow it?'

'I'd love to,' Serena says. She leans forward, her empty bowl still clutched in her hand. 'But where did you get it?'

Aodahn's own bowl of cooked meat is untouched. 'From the old human smuggling caves,' he breathes. 'They were used back when people lived on the island. The wyverns came across them when tunnelling and Cindra allows us to visit it to retrieve books. The caves are still being used, you see.'

'Used?' I say. 'By who?'

'Perhaps by the humanlings on Canna, or by merchants from a neighbouring island. Every so often they fill with objects – food, clothing, literature.' He suddenly looks apologetic. 'I only take books, and never more than I can carry.'

I catch Atlas's eyes and know we're both asking ourselves the same question. Who is sending supplies to Canna?

'What are those?' Gideon asks.

He's pointing to the tweed tapestries containing scrolls of paper.

'Memory tapestries,' Aodahn replies. 'Made of the most durable textile known to wyverns. Our memories deserve to be preserved in our old age. The wyvern tradition is to record them on paper and keep them inside the tweed, so that we never forget.'

He stands to pull a scroll from the wall and begins to translate the writing aloud.

It is Edin who teaches Aodahn to weave his first piece of tweed. She sings to him about how the loom has a mind of its own, about how no two tweeds are the same, about how a wyvern must weave just as he must breathe. Aodahn watches his mother's tweed appear on the loom, the wool bright white, and decides she must have mixed it with moonlight.

'My favourite memory of her,' he says, tucking the scroll back inside the tweed.

I point to another tapestry, this one embroidered with hundreds of wyverns flying like a flock of birds above the sea. On the water are several huge ships.

'Is that a memory too?' I ask.

'The wyverns are a peaceful species, but there were times before we came underground that we had to be formidable fighters. And we were. We commanded the respect of all Canna's dragons.'

Marquis raises an eyebrow.

'But when the British government came for Patrick Clawtail and killed him despite our defences,' Aodahn says in a hushed voice, 'it shook Abelio to his core. We didn't know that human battleships can shoot a wyvern out of the sky.' His wings flutter gently on his back. 'We lost many.'

'They sent battleships for one man?' Gideon asks. 'What was so special about Clawtail?'

'He was the first person to suggest that dragon tongues should be recorded and recognised as official languages,' I say. 'The government was on the verge of signing the Peace Agreement with Queen Ignacia, secretly hoping to use it to subdue dragons. But what Clawtail was proposing would have empowered them.'

I yawn, my eyelids growing heavy. The heat of the fire envelops us and throughout the cave, wyverns are basking lazily in the flickering shadows of the flames. Aodahn moves next to me, so close that the silky feathers of his wings press against my bare arm. I can feel the heat rising from his scales. They're a pearly blue, the colour of a dragonfly.

'You will not be asked to explain the golden machine tonight, dear one. You could retire to your chamber, if you so wish.'

Dear one.

Chumana is not as gentle, and yet the closeness of Aodahn and the way he calls me something other than my name makes me miss her. I suddenly long to hear the words 'human girl' growled at me. I wonder where she is now and what possessed me to be so unkind to her.

I nod, mumbling goodnight.

'You're going to bed?' Marquis says incredulously. 'This is the first time in our lives that we've socialised with dragons.'

He jumps as a wyvernling appears at his side, wearing a

harness made to carry glasses filled with a golden liquid. His wings flutter beneath the weight of it and he rises just above the ground.

'A honeyed wine, for erudite dreams,' Aodahn says. His tail intertwines with the wyvernling's and gently tugs him back down to the ground. He lets out a purr as Aodahn gestures to Marquis to take a glass.

'Th-thank you,' he stutters to the wyvernling.

Atlas and I walk back to the chamber together, hand in hand down the hot tunnels.

'These are the oddest dragons I've ever met,' I say. 'My mama would be fascinated. I wish she could see them. Their tapestries, their memory scrolls, their *wine*. Dragons who make art, it's . . . What's wrong?'

Atlas is walking with his eyes on the ground, his mouth set in a tight line. 'Sorry?' he says, as if I've woken him from sleep. 'Nothing, I'm fine.' He looks up and gives me what he must mean to be a reassuring smile. 'It's a lot to take in.'

We curl up beneath tweed blankets and the feeling of lying in his arms is so strange that my body responds to his slightest movement. His face is buried in my hair, his hands placed firmly above the blankets. But as my mind begins to drift and my breathing slows, I feel him slip away, gently extracting his arm from under me, to sit by the fire. He feels uncomfortable lying next to me, I think as my heart hammers silently inside my chest. There's something different about him. An inwardness – a turmoil – that has replaced the confidence he had back at Bletchley. He isn't sure about us, not any more. We've never really defined what *we* are, after all. We've not even spoken about all that happened between us when we were Wyvernmire's prisoners.

I think of the reckless abandon with which he kissed me back in the forest, of how natural it felt to walk across the island hand in hand. But if those things were real, then why do I get the impression that Atlas is more of a stranger to me than I thought?

Eleven

'HOW DID YOU BRING THE LOQUISONUS machine inside without getting it wet?' I ask Abelio.

His request to show him how it works came at the crack of dawn, and Cindra barely has time to nudge a cup of herbal tea towards me before Abelio is leading me through the tunnels.

'We have several tunnel entrances,' Abelio says. 'One thing you will learn about wyverns is that we are resourceful.'

He has a spring in his step and I realise that our cultural exchange has officially begun. My dread rises as I follow him, the loquisonus machine in my arms. The time has come to lie, to pretend that the loquisonus is a tunnel detector that I can teach Abelio to use, while somehow convincing him to help me win this war. I catch a glimpse of Gideon inside a chamber, looking pale as Aodahn animatedly interrogates him on his knowledge of French. Abelio leads me past the cave with the pool entrance and down another tunnel. We climb up a steep slope towards a tall, vertical line of light.

'Here.'

Abelio creeps through a gap in the rocks, the same sort of entrance that led to Ruth's tunnels, and I press the loquisonus machine to my chest as we climb through. We're standing on top of a grassy sand dune and behind us is what looks like a cave entrance blocked by a rockfall. You'd never guess it leads to an intricate underground tunnel system.

'Where are we?' I ask.

'The north side of the island still, but facing west,' Abelio says.

I stare out across the island in the direction of Wyvernmire's camp, but the view is blocked by hills and mist. Is she still sending her Guardians and dragons out to look for me? Does she know we're searching for the Hebridean Wyverns on this side of the island? Will she come this far?

'A demonstration?' Abelio says politely.

It's not a suggestion.

I set the loquisonus on the ground, keeping an eye out for dragon-shaped shadows.

'Did you always live on this part of the island?' I ask him. 'Even before you went underground?'

'Yes,' Abelio replies. 'We have always been private creatures and the proximity of the opposite side of Canna to the other islands does not appeal to us, especially during the nesting season, when Rùm is overflowing.'

'So when Clawtail lived with you, it was here?'

I fiddle with the dial on the loquisonus, waiting for his answer.

'Of course,' he replies.

The government has been here before, then. This must be where they killed him. I hand Abelio the headphones.

They're much too small for his head.

'You can press these to your ear,' I tell him. 'They're for listening.'

He gives me a curious look as he takes them. I flick the switch and the loquisonus machine whirrs. Abelio recoils as the crackling noise fills the headphones, but it's quickly replaced by the steady musicality of the Koinamens as I find the correct frequency. The machine is designed to convert echolocation into a series of sounds audible to the human ear, and so while Abelio can hear the sounds through the headphones, they in no way resemble what he, an echolocating dragon, hears when communicating telepathically.

He has no idea he's listening to a transmuted version of the dragons' most sacred tongue.

I pick the machine up and gesture to him to walk with me towards the cave entrance.

'The closer we get to any tunnels, the louder the alarm will sound,' I lie.

I know the sound will grow louder as we approach the tunnels because the wyverns are echolocating there. Then I turn and lead him away again, down the dune in the direction of the sea, where there are no wyverns.

'The noise is quieter here,' Abelio murmurs.

I nod, counting my luck. If there had been a dragon flying over the water, the sound of their echolocation would have come through the headphones and what I've just told Abelio wouldn't have made sense.

'It is odd,' he murmurs, 'that the tunnels sound like the strings of a musical instrument.

How does the machine work?'

'I didn't invent it,' I say slowly.

My heart races. What can I make up on the spot? I need Abelio to believe that I have some knowledge to offer him, so that he will allow me to stay long enough to figure out how the wyverns can help the rebels win the war. My eyes dart to more of the amber-coloured crystals in the grass. 'But I think it has something to do with . . . the presence of minerals in the earth, which are closer to the surface where tunnels have been made.'

I am a better liar in Cannair than I am in English.

Two dragons swoop across the sky and I see Abelio startle. The noise in the headphones is changing. I stumble back in the direction of the cave, but I can tell by his expression as he follows me that he's noticed.

'Why did the noise start again back there, if there are no tunnels?'

I shake my head. 'It started again because we came back this way,' I say, gesturing to accompany my stilted speech.

I watch as the dragons fly over us. Slowly, Abelio reaches for the loquisonus machine and carries it back to the spot where we were standing a moment ago. With the dragons overhead gone, it is no longer detecting their echolocation and I let out a small sigh of relief. His lower jaw quivers, revealing small, sharp teeth. Does he know I'm lying?

'Perhaps,' he says slowly, 'the machine was detecting old tunnels in the cliffs. In the past, when our passageways have been discovered, we were forced to fill in the entrances and abandon them.'

My head spins as I grasp at his words, mentally translating at a snail's pace. 'That must be it,' I reply.

'Fascinating,' he says with a wide-lipped smile.

'What use might you have for a tunnel detector?' I ask him tentatively. 'If you made the tunnels, then surely you know where each is located.'

'It is always useful to know which weapons one's enemy might have in their arsenal,' he replies.

'And your enemy is who, exactly?'

'We have lived underground since the British government came looking for Patrick Clawtail. We lost many of our own in the fight to protect him. After that, we decided to keep to ourselves.'

'This is the only tunnel detector known to exist,' I say. 'So you don't have to worry about—'

'I thought you said Britannia was at war,' he interrupts.

'It is.'

'Then what makes you think the same government that attacked us once before won't have more machines like this one at its disposal?'

'What makes you think Britannia's government is interested in detecting wyvern tunnels?' I reply.

I'm pleased with my quick retort. Perhaps mastering Cannair won't be so hard, after all. And *perhaps* this is the information I need. Perhaps Abelio is about to tell me what Hollingsworth didn't.

'Because we shielded a rebel the government wanted,' he murmurs. 'And now it seems we are doing so again.'

His blue tongue hisses between his teeth.

'So you know from first-hand experience how ruthless Britannia's government is,' I say. 'The Peace Agreement was corrupt, allowing dragons to feed on human children abandoned on Canna after the people here were forced from their homes. And now that same government is trying to ban any languages that aren't English or the Slavidraneishá of the Bulgarian Bolgoriths. Languages like your beautiful Cannair.'

'Prohibit a language they do not even know?' Abelio hisses. 'Shielding our wyvernlings from such ignorance, from such cultural decline, is paramount. Do you see why we live the way we live? Why your mere presence is unnerving?' His eyes flash. 'You are a link between us and the terrible government you speak of, girl with the golden machine. After you have used our *fasgadh*, I am not sorry to have to ask you . . .'

'Yes?' I prompt.

If there's anything I can do to make Abelio more willing to help us in the war against Wyvernmire, I will.

'. . . to never return.'

I feel my shoulders slump as Abelio holds my gaze. His scales are a deep blue against the roiling grey sea in the background. They are alike, Abelio and the sea. Wild and passionate on the surface. yet unmoving beneath the waves.

He will never agree to fight in a war.

'You may stop your machine,' Abelio says.

I flick the switch and follow him back inside the cave. As we walk through the tunnels, I hear a loud thumping.

'To the left,' Abelio says.

I follow the source of the noise into one of the chambers. Serena is standing at a large wooden table with Cindra and several other wyverns. A length of thick grey material is spread out on the table, with three wyverns on each side and Serena at the head. They are beating the cloth with their long index talons.

Cindra lets out a low, hissing whisper and Serena looks up in surprise as the other wyverns copy her.

'What are they doing?' I ask quietly.

'They are waulking the tweed,' Abelio replies. 'It is an ancient Gaelic tradition, shared by humans and wyverns. Once the wool is removed from the loom it is drenched in urine and beaten to shrink the fibres, to ensure that the cold and damp of the Hebrides cannot pass through.'

I recognise the word for *loom*. It appears in Clawtail's journal at least a dozen times. I watch Serena, but the expression on her face is imperceptible. Is she going to dip her hands in urine in the name of the feminine arts?

'Where are the looms?' I ask Abelio.

'In the weaving chamber,' he replies.

Of course.

'The tweed,' I say. 'It holds your memories, doesn't it? And you use it to make rugs and—'

The soft whispers become low, haunting chants. Serena presses her hands into the tweed as I try to understand the sung Cannair, but I don't recognise any of the words. The rhythmic thumping of the cloth on the table, accompanied by the wailing song, is almost hypnotic.

'The waulking of the cloth serves many purposes, but one is to tell stories and express emotion. It is a tradition that wyverns and humans once undertook together, a way to communicate.'

'Did the humans of Canna speak Cannair?'

'It is said they did in centuries past, but certainly not in my lifetime,' Abelio replies.

'What are they saying?' I ask as I stare at Cindra and the other wyverns.

Abelio attempts to explain but I don't understand the words he uses, so I just look quizzically at him. It's odd, being able to understand only when he uses the simplest of sentence structures and vocabulary I remember from the journal.

'It is the story of a wyvern with a *brotnacroí*.'

I understand part of the word – *croí*, which means heart and is pronounced *kree* – but not the rest. A big heart? A broken heart? I can only guess. Instead, I content myself with listening, relaxing now the first demonstration of the fake tunnel detector is over, and as the singing echoes through the tunnels I almost forget Abelio and the other wyverns are there. The beauty of the chanted words was unknown to me back when I was studying Cannair in Hollingsworth's office with just the journal for reference. Studying this language on paper was like feeling around in the dark, Clawtail's notes revealing only a muted chink of a much brighter, fuller light. And yet I still feel blind. Afterwards, I go looking for Aodahn. I find him still at work with Gideon.

'No,' I hear Gideon say as I enter the cave. 'In French, the *n* of *dragon* is silent.'

Aodahn re-attempts his pronunciation.

'Better,' Gideon says.

Aodahn's cave is smaller than the one we sleep in, the

ground littered with so many piles of books that I don't know where to stand. The walls are painted the colours of the rainbow and wooden shelves hold all sorts of trinkets: colourful stones, seashells, an arrowhead and a pair of reading glasses. Aodahn gestures for us to sit around his central fire.

'Have you been at this since this morning?' I ask Gideon.

Gideon nods as Aodahn scurries across the room to retrieve a pile of papers, then lowers his voice. 'I think he's going to drive me mad.'

'Gideon, speaker of tongues, is a dedicated teacher,' Aodahn exclaims. 'Look at all the words he has taught me!'

He gestures to a list of vocabulary, his long talon dripping with ink.

'Aodahn, would you help me with something?' I ask.

Gideon gives me a look of grateful relief.

'The word *brotnacroi*. What does it mean?'

Aodahn pauses thoughtfully. 'It is like . . . a heartbreak, but stronger than that. It is irremediable, a heart that is not simply broken, but broken forever.' He lets out a surprised yelp that makes me jump. 'It is like Gideon, speaker of tongues taught me with the French word *Adieu*! It does not only mean goodbye, but goodbye forever. A definitive farewell.'

I'm nodding. Explained like that, it makes sense. I've deciphered a word that doesn't even appear in Clawtail's journal and the sensation it gives me takes me straight back to the glasshouse. I can almost smell the citrus freshness of Dr Seymour's plants around me. It's the feeling of not just translating a language, but recording it for the first time. When I look up at Aodahn again, his huge eyes are shining.

'Patrick Clawtail showed the same enthusiasm for Cannair as you, Vivien Featherswallow. But it only brought us closer to our own forever farewell.'

Aodahn stirs the pot that sits in the fire with a wooden spoon the length of my arm. Then he ladles the liquid into three earthenware cups so large that I have to hold mine in both hands. It's a hot, savoury broth, coating my tongue and warming my body.

'Abelio talks as though he is closed to any form of interaction with humans, but that can't be true, can it, if he was letting Clawtail learn Cannair with the aim of promoting it?'

'Abelio has changed since Patrick died. Now, his priority is protecting Cannair from outside influence, preserving its pure, undiluted form.'

'No language is pure,' I reply. 'It's a living thing, changed by those who speak it and other languages it comes into contact with. If Patrick had been given the chance to share Cannair with other humans, he would have passed on mispronunciations, tiny mistakes. It's inevitable.'

Aodahn buries his snout into the cup and slurps the broth. 'Patrick had an almost perfect mastery of Cannair. And his little daughter spoke it as if she were born to the Hebridean Wyverns.'

'But he never finished translating it,' I say. 'I've seen the journal. He stopped recording the language two years after he joined you.'

Aodahn sets his cup down, his milky eyes swimming again. 'Cannair is a complex language, dear one.'

'You knew Clawtail well,' I say softly. 'Perhaps better than we think?'

Slowly, Aodahn goes to a shelf.

'This is all I have left of Patrick,' he says, unwrapping a piece of cloth and bringing it to the fire.

Gideon and I peer closer at a gold ring, wound in a piece of yellow thread. It's tiny in Aodahn's talons.

'A wedding band?' Gideon said.

Aodahn nods. 'We wrap our dead in tweed before we burn them, to preserve their memory. But we never found Patrick's body, so this is the best I could do.' He sniffs, a puff of black smoke escaping his nostrils. 'The other is with his wife, no doubt.'

I think of Clawtail's journal, seeing the careful handwriting in my mind. Back in London he was just a piece of history, a faceless figure unknown to everyone but Hollingsworth and me. But now, he's Aodahn's friend.

'I'm sorry for your loss,' I say.

Aodahn places the ring back on the shelf and I know I have to take advantage of the moment to ask him what he knows.

'Some humans claim that the Hebridean Wyverns could help them win the war against the government,' I say slowly. 'The government that killed Patrick. Do you know how that might be?'

Aodahn blinks. 'If they have weapons like they did before, then there are too few of us wyverns to withstand an attack.'

I catch Gideon's eye as Aodahn shakes his head. 'I am afraid that the humans are mistaken. Be it by teeth or by talon, the wyverns cannot help you.'

*

Our own cave is quiet during the hours that the others are busy with the wyverns. Atlas is teaching about how the dragon industry of metallurgy influenced the British rebel movement and Marquis is shadowing one of the healers. I sit by the ever-burning fire, turning Cannair words over in my mind. So far, the three months I spent studying the language have done me little good. If what Aodahn said is true then Abelio considers my learning Cannair a dilution, a weakening of the language rather than a respectful attempt to master it. He's made it clear that he has no interest in the war, which makes our presence here pointless. In fact, I suspect that his fascination with the loquisonus machine is the only reason he is tolerating our request for shelter at all.

I pull my jumper off in the sweltering heat of the cave. Perhaps we should call this mission off and return to the rebels on Eigg, then get word to Hollingsworth that the war will have to be won without the wyverns. I try to imagine the look on her face when I tell her I've failed and my skin crawls. Surely she has a Plan B? I look up as Atlas walks in, tucking his notebook into the pocket of his jacket.

He smiles. 'Did you find any tunnels, girl with the golden machine?'

I roll my eyes. 'No. But Abelio wants nothing to do with the government, or with bringing it down. He's waiting for us to leave.'

Atlas nods. 'The wyverns coming to my classes on the Peace Agreement and the rebellion seem nervous to be there. They're all so intrigued by human-dragon relations, but

Abelio is the opposite.'

'At least you're doing something. I'm useless here, and *I* was supposed to be the one using Cannair to convince the wyverns to join the rebels. Half the time I can't even understand what they're saying.' I can barely keep the bitterness out of my voice. 'Now I'm here, I'm realising that I've barely scratched the surface of the language. Maybe we should leave. I could go back to Hollingsworth and—'

'What if we use the loquisonus?'

Atlas's eyes are on the wooden swallow around my neck. I frown. 'What for?'

'You already know the basics of echolocation. It would take a lot less time to learn the wyverns' Koinamens than to become fluent in Cannair. You've done it before, haven't you?'

When I don't reply, he continues, 'You could listen to it to know what they say to each other. Maybe, from that, you could figure out how they can help us.'

I shake my head. 'That would be spying. And the Koinamens is—'

'Sacred, I know,' Atlas says. 'But this is *war* we're talking about. And we wouldn't be hurting the wyverns. When we leave here with them we'll destroy the machine, like we did with the other two. No one will ever be able to listen to echolocation again.'

I hesitate. 'A few months ago you would never have suggested such a plan.'

Atlas shrugs his jacket off, a weary frown on his face. But I remember perfectly well what Chumana told me back at

Bletchley Park – that the Koinamens is a sacred language of dragons that gets more complex depending on the bond, that it's made up of emotions so strong it can make tiny dragonlings grow inside their eggs. If my work in the glasshouse taught me anything, it's that the Koinamens is not to be tampered with.

I shake my head. 'I don't know what I was thinking. What Hollingsworth was thinking. It takes years of study to learn a new language, let alone communicate effectively in it. This task is impossible. Almost as impossible as understanding the deeper meaning of echolocation calls.'

'But—'

'No, Atlas.' I stare at him until he meets my gaze. 'You know the Koinamens is more than just a set of audible noises. I couldn't make any use of it even if I wanted to, because I'm not a dragon. And anyone who has told you otherwise—'

Atlas stands up abruptly, his jacket falling from his lap. 'No one has told me otherwise,' he says quickly. 'I'm not stupid.'

I gape at him. 'I didn't say you were.'

'I'll see you at the Twilight Meal.'

I watch as he leaves the room without a backward glance, my cheeks burning with humiliation. It's not like Atlas to sulk. My eyes fall to the jacket on the floor, the notebook sticking out of the pocket. I pull it out. It's bound in marbled leather, with a small pencil tucked into an elastic loop. I open it. I can tell from the printed dates that it's a diary. One quick look could tell me what's going on in his head.

The pages are covered in Atlas's small, untidy handwriting and the sight takes me back to a time when we exchanged secret notes. I glance at the last sentence he has written and my heart freezes.

This mission is a sin.

An uneasy feeling creeps over me. What mission is he referring to? Finding the wyverns? Why would that be a sin? My heart hammers as I flick through the pages.

What I'm being asked to do goes against my every instinct. And yet I know that its fruits will be good. If I refuse, or fail . . . the consequences don't bear thinking about.

I jump when I hear clattering in the passageway. I close the diary and slip it back into the pocket of Atlas's jacket, where a piece of green cloth has been cut away from the lining. Atlas just tried to persuade me against leaving the wyverns, so this can't be the mission he's referring to. Dread floods my body. Has he been entrusted with another? And if so, why is he keeping it a secret?

THE DAILY TELEGRAPH
LONDON. WEDNESDAY, APRIL 16, 1924

LINGUISTIC ANARCHY: IS IT ALL PUN AND GAMES?

Guardians of Peace have made several arrests on the London Underground this week following reports that entire cars of commuters were conducting conversations in Scouse. The *Telegraph's* undercover reporter, Susan Barnhill, confirmed the allegations after being offered a 'bevvy' of Scale Ale, an alcoholic beverage brewed in Liverpool and used by dragons to polish their scales.

Further breaches of the Babel Decree have been uncovered among the First Class, after chemists and school nurses across Britannia were dumbfounded when presented with medical prescriptions written entirely in Dragonese. In Cornwall, the Call to Military Service by the British Armed Forces of all able-bodied men and dragons has been met with an influx of counterfeit class passes. Men are reporting for duty carrying documents labelled with the names of dragons: Hieronymus, Moondancer and Rebellius have been listed as some of the most popular. At the Royal Victoria Docks in London, a Western Drake collected his day's wages as 'John Smith'.

We spoke to two Third Class soldiers, who did not wish to be identified.

'Britannia used to be multilingual, with English spoken by the working class, Norman French by the aristocrats and Latin by the clergy. Nowadays, it's a shame that *multilingual* is a word only used to describe dragons. And if the Prime Minister had her way, she'd take that from them, too,' said the first.

The second disagreed. 'It's only right for a country to have one national language. If there's too many of them, the patriotism gets divided up. But speaking the language of the Bolgoriths in place of our own Wyrmerian? Now that's disloyalty to Crown and Country if I ever saw it.'

Twelve

THE WYVERNS ARE IN A CONSTANT state of creative pursuit. They read great piles of English and Gaelic books, sculpt with their curved foretalons and sketch with large pencils carved from tree bark. They sleep curled up together in large groups, hot scale upon hot scale, but the night is for hunting too and sometimes I see a select few drag in puffins and fish and entire sheep. Hunting is the only reason they leave the tunnels. With my loquisonus demonstration complete I wander aimlessly, but the others are much solicited: Serena for her ability to embroider a pretty pattern or sketch scenes from her First Class London upbringing and Atlas for his lectures on the Peace Agreement, the lives of London's dragons and the Babel Decree. Marquis rarely leaves the healing caves, which the rest of us are not permitted to enter. I am thoroughly bored, fit only to help Gideon and Aodahn with their lists of French verbs and German adjectives, and Atlas with his lectures.

'Remind me which Babel Decree articles were instated when you were in London with Chumana?' he asks me.

We're looking over his notes in the mostly empty Amber Court, the sunlight shining through the orange stones above us in a dappled, golden glow.

'The last one I heard was the instatement of Slavidraneishá as Britannia's national dragon tongue,' I tell him.

He nods, the warm light flickering against his dark skin. He's serious, business-like in his manner and when he reaches towards me to take the pen from my hand, I lean in to kiss him.

He pulls away.

'What is it?' I ask, stinging from the rejection.

'Nothing,' he says, his eyes on his paper. 'I'm just trying to concentrate.'

I feel my heart flutter unpleasantly. 'Is this because I didn't agree with your plan to listen to the wyverns' echolocation?'

'Of course not,' he replies, still avoiding my gaze.

'You've been acting like a spoilt brat lately!' I burst out furiously. 'Admit to that at least.'

Atlas doesn't reply.

Is your secret mission bothering you? I want to say.

I bristle with anger, yet I'm still hungry for his touch, just a hand on my back or whisper in my ear, a sign that there's no bad feelings between us. But the past couple of days he's barely looked at me, and last night he didn't come into our cave until I was asleep. I wonder if he somehow knows that I read his diary. I glance around the cave, desperate to show him that I have something – anything – better to do. Cindra is standing beneath one of the memory tapestries, watching me. This is the third time I've caught her staring, her tail coiled around the books at her feet, her talons snapping in ... what? Trepidation? Anticipation? I glance at Atlas again, but he's busy scrawling something across the page.

'If you're not doing anything,' he says without looking up, 'could you take a look at my notes on Bolgorith battle weaknesses? There's a paragraph on family bonds that needs editing.'

The boredom and sense of uselessness smoulder gently, then combust.

'I'm not your bloody secretary,' I snap.

I stand up and cross the cave to Cindra.

'Cindra,' I say, forcing a smile. 'Is there something you want from me?'

I hear a clicking sound in her chest and expect anger, but she nods. Her eyes dart to the entrance, then back to me. 'But not here.' She gestures towards the left-hand passageway, which leads away past our sleeping cave and the pool entrance. I glance back at Atlas, who hasn't looked up, then follow Cindra out of the Amber Court. We walk quietly past more wyvern chambers and I hear running water. Cindra doesn't speak until we reach a small waterfall, crashing down from somewhere high up in the rock. The noise echoes so loudly that I can barely hear her talk.

'Cindra?' I say in Cannair. 'Is everything okay?'

'No, Vivien Featherswallow,' she replies in English. 'Everything is not okay.'

I reel in shock. 'You speak English?'

'Yes,' she hisses in reply. 'But Abelio must *not* know.'

'Why?'

She lets out a tutting noise. 'Because he believes it, and everything it stands for, will contaminate Cannair, and the wyvern way of life, and our . . . concealment.'

I think of Aodahn's English names for the different wyvern caves.

'You don't agree with it, then?' I say carefully. 'With the living underground?'

'Abelio laments that the wyverns harbour a strong interest in humans and claims that it began when Clawtail walked among us. But he is wrong. It is since he made us live away from the rest of the world that we have come to covet human ways.' She growls.

'The wyverns didn't always make art, then?' I say. 'But what about your tapestries, your tweed?'

'Wyverns have always been creatures of comfort and creation and ceremony. They are things we *do*, in the same way that bees build hives. But since we have lived underground, unable to fly except for the purpose of hunting, our minds no longer travel. Our souls are tethered. Our art forms have changed. Weaving can still be practised underground, but glass-blowing, flame-throwing, cloud-spinning . . . these are all but lost to us.' Cindra casts a glance back down the empty passageway. 'And so we have found solace in other pursuits, such as the consumption of human literature. This is why the wyverns sculpt human figures, write about humans, speak like humans. A bird will mimic human singing if caged for too long. Abelio is well-intentioned but misguided. In seeking to preserve our traditions and language, he fails to see that it is the sharing of them that would keep them alive.'

'If you were to come out of concealment, dragons and humans would witness the waulking of the tweed, see the memory tapestries, hear Cannair.'

Cindra is nodding. 'Some of us, those who lived before Clawtail, speak other tongues, too. We are not all monolingual.'

'You're the one who asked Clawtail to translate Cannair!' I say.

Her eyes gleam. 'Yes. And now I am asking you to continue Patrick's legacy by translating Cannair into English so that it can be recognised by your Academy as a dragon tongue.' She pauses. 'As things stand, if the Hebridean Wyverns were to perish, then Cannair would die with us.'

'Cindra,' I say gently. 'To record a new language would take me years.'

'You need not record the whole thing. Not to begin with.'

Her tail sways as she moves towards an alcove in the wall and pulls out a huge stack of papers covered in thin, inky lines of written Cannair, scratched by a talon dipped in ink. 'My writings on the Hebridean Wyverns,' she says. 'Our history, our traditions, our language. Patrick did not have this last time. You will not have to start with nothing, like he did. If you are able to translate merely a few of my writings, you will be making an English record of Cannair and of the wyvern way of life. This your Academy will accept, yes?'

I hesitate. It's true that the Academy only requires a small translation sample in order to award a language what it calls *pre-emptive official status*.

'And in exchange, the wyverns will fight in your war.'

My heart leaps. I'm getting close to the information Hollingsworth wants, I'm sure of it. 'Fight . . . how, exactly?'

The movement of Cindra's tail is a blur until it cracks against the stone wall above me, bringing down a rain of shards. I cover my head with my hands as she snarls.

'Do not trouble yourself with the fighting skills of the wyverns. I can assure you they are more than satisfactory.'

'That's not what I meant,' I say. 'I have been told you have an advantage over other dragons. Something that makes you different.'

Her eyes narrow into cat-like slits. 'Translate Cannair for us and you might just find out.'

I pore over Cindra's writings for the rest of the day as I wait for the others to finish their various activities. The pages are too big for me to carry around, so she leaves them in our cave. They contain far more complicated descriptions of the wyvern practices than those Clawtail recorded in his own journal. Cindra dedicates a hundred pages to the waulking of the tweed, full of information I don't understand. One section describes a young wyvern's first hunt. The wyverns have words for things that simply don't exist in English, like the very particular sensation the wind makes on the tertiary feathers of a wing, or an expression that refers to locating one's prey in the air which, translated literally, becomes *to taste a pulse on the back of a cloud*. When I ask Aodahn to explain certain terms to me, he lacks the English vocabulary to translate exactly what they mean.

'I have to talk to you,' I tell the others as they trail into the sleeping cave that evening, exhaustion on their faces.

'Can't stop,' Marquis mutters. 'I have to attend a flying lesson.'

I sigh. 'Then we'll come with you.'

As we follow Marquis through the tunnels, I tell them what Cindra has proposed. 'If we can't find out exactly what Hollingsworth thinks is so special about the wyverns, then this could be the next best thing. At least, if Cindra can convince Abelio to let the wyverns fight with the rebels, we will have achieved something.'

'But how are you going to translate an entire language?' Serena says.

'I'll start with some basic translations,' I reply. 'Eventually there'll be enough to get Cannair recognised officially, but in the meantime Cindra will ask the wyverns to ally with the rebels, and we'll win this war.' I feel a thrill of excitement. 'English is the language that sets the narrative of the world. The more obscure languages rarely get to add their perspective. Translating Cannair would be giving the wyverns the opportunity to write back. Some translators never get a chance like this in their whole careers.'

'But it won't help us discover *how* the wyverns are supposed to help us win this war,' Atlas says bluntly.

I stop walking as Serena raises an eyebrow.

'I asked Aodahn outright, Atlas. He didn't know what I was talking about.'

'What if they're lying?' Atlas says, his cheeks turning pink. 'What if they know how to help us, but they don't want to?'

'Translating Cannair might *make* them want to,' I argue.

He doesn't reply and I feel another pang of hurt. What has

gotten into him?

'I think this is the flying cave,' Marquis says.

When we enter the gloomy cavern, the one Aodahn calls Wuthering Heights, we're standing on a narrow ledge. I press my back against the wall so as not to risk toppling over the edge just as we're on the verge of progress. The vast space stretches out in front of us, a bottomless drop below and a ceiling so high that I think we must be directly beneath a hill. Ledges and perches jut out into the air and long vines snake across the walls, growing in the dark. The only moonlight comes from the small gaps in the rock, giving the cave a ghostly feel. It's cold without a fire burning. I hear water rushing below us and the sound merges with the flapping of wings.

'How can wyvernlings possibly learn to fly in the dark?' Gideon says.

'Wyverns have excellent eyesight, especially at night,' Aodahn replies. I hadn't noticed him standing at the far end of the ledge, watching Cindra and another wyvern lead a group of wyvernlings across a great slab of rock that juts out into the vast drop below us.

'That's more than can be said for the Bolgoriths,' Marquis says, winking at me.

He's right. It's an advantage the wyverns have over our enemies. But it's the only one I can think of.

'Why are you attending a flying lesson, anyway?' I whisper to Marquis.

He points to the silvery blue wyvern standing with Cindra, so old he's missing half his scales.

'I'm supposed to be shadowing Dòmhnall,' he replies. 'A

healer is always required during lessons in case of accidents.'

Across the cave, Cindra, Dòmhnall and three wyvernlings perch on the ledge. As they beat out their wings and turn to her for instruction, their white-blue feathers glow in the dark. Cindra throws back her head and I see the authoritative flick of her tail. I know she is talking to the wyvernlings in echolocation and yet I'm surprised. Surely the tricky act of flying requires more detailed instructions, an intimate understanding of each other's more complex echolocation calls which is only possible through a close bond? As far as I know, none of these wyvernlings are part of Cindra's family. So how is it that they know when to lift up their left wing, to spread out the tips of their feathers for better balance as I see them do now, when these instructions are all given in silence by a teacher who surely doesn't share much of a bond with any of them?

'Do you often have accidents?' I hear Marquis ask Aodahn as the flying begins.

'No,' Aodahn replies. 'But they have become more frequent as of late. Our wyvernlings don't have the strength they used to. Abelio believes it is because food is scarcer, with the influx of Bulgarian dragons, but . . .'

He trails off, tapping his talons together nervously.

'I know a dragon who spent years locked inside a library,' I say quietly. 'She didn't see much sunlight and you could tell from the colour of her scales—'

'A library?' Aodahn squeaks. 'I would very much like—'

He's interrupted by a loud screech. I see Marquis drop to his knees, leaning over the rim of the ledge to peer down at something. I follow his gaze. One of the wyvernlings is stuck, its wing caught in the gap between two rocks it has attempted to fly through. Cindra soars down to examine it, beating her wings fiercely but unable to hold the hover for long. She circles, then dives again, like a frantic bird trying to reach a fallen chick.

'We must help them,' Aodahn says.

He takes to the air, swiftly followed by Dòmhnall. We watch as they join Cindra and the other two wyvernlings land again, black smoke trailing from their jaws.

'If dragons can heal each other with the Koinamens,' I say quietly, 'then what do the wyverns need healers for?'

'They have a herb for just about everything in the apothecary cave,' Marquis says. 'The Koinamens heals wounds, but I don't think it can do anything for illness.'

I watch as the adult wyverns attempt to dislodge the shrieking wyvernling, and Atlas appears at my side. He's holding the loquisonus machine.

'What's that for?' I say coldly, still sulking after his behaviour in the Amber Court.

'I think you should listen to it,' he says, his eyes pleading. 'See if you can understand something.'

His suggestion from the other day rings in my ears as I glance nervously at the wyverns. *Listen to the wyverns' Koinamens to know what they say to each other.*

'All right,' I say quietly. 'Just to hear what it sounds like.'

I place the loquisonus on the ground, then put the headphones on my ears and turn the dials as Serena and Gideon watch. I find the frequency almost immediately. The same melodious notes I heard back when we were searching for the wyvern tunnels fill my ears.

'It's like a . . . like whispering,' I say.

Atlas holds his hand out for the headphones. When he puts them on his eyes grow wide.

'Like a whispered music,' he says. 'Is that normal?'

'All the dragon echolocation I've heard sounds a bit like birdsong, or at least the social calls do. But nothing like this.'

He passes the headphones to Gideon, who listens and then hands them back to me. I stare from Aodahn, Cindra and Dòmhnall to the other two wyvernlings as their ultrasonic communication sounds loudly, reverberating in different rhythms, like several murmured voices, yet all of them playing together like an orchestra.

'I think they need help,' Marquis says.

The wyvernling's squeaking is growing more frantic and at the same time, the echolocation in my ears is more erratic. It dangles by its wing from the rocky crevice and Cindra lets out a frustrated roar as she attempts to pull it free with her mouth.

'She'll never manage,' Marquis says as he peers towards them. 'The wyvernling is stuck tight.'

I'm about to reply when he shrugs off his jacket.

'Where are you going?'

'To teach a dragon to fly.'

Marquis jumps from our ledge to the one below, dropping lower and lower until he reaches the perch above where the wyvernling is stuck. The wyverns continue to soar above it as Marquis seizes the root of the wyvernling's wing in one firm hand and uses the fingers of the other to pull at the stones that have lodged around it. Suddenly, the wyvern is free. It drops from Marquis's grip and I cry out as it plummets into the dark.

'He killed it,' Gideon cries in panic. 'He's gone and—'

The wyvernling surges up from beneath us, a flash of midnight blue, and flies to join its peers as Marquis lets out a triumphant whoop. All six wyverns meet in the centre of the cave, flying through the shafts of silvery moonlight, then diving down beneath a waterfall before twisting in the air on themselves.

'See how they move?' I murmur to Atlas, unable to tear my eyes away as their bodies rise and fall in a victorious dance. 'They're completely in sync.'

'Like birds,' Gideon says.

'Like swallows,' I reply. 'But how can they be this in tune with each other if they're not related, not bonded?'

'Put it away,' Serena says sharply as the wyverns begin their flight up towards us. 'They're coming back.'

Atlas hides the machine behind his back as the wyverns land on our ledge.

Marquis takes longer to climb back up and as we wait, Cindra doesn't take her eyes off him. The wyvernlings crowd the edge, their long tails intertwined, and they part as Marquis's hand grabs the bottom of the ledge and Gideon pulls him up. He flexes his fingers, cut and bleeding from his climb, and kneels to catch his breath.

'You have done us a great service, Marquis, healer of wyverns,' Cindra says in Cannair.

She glances at Aodahn with impatient eyes and he quickly

translates.

'You will have the honour of attending our egg-choosing ceremony,' Cindra continues.

Marquis bows his head. 'Thank you,' he manages to reply in Cannair.

A low warbling comes from Cindra's chest and I realise it's a sign of pleasure. I roll my eyes as Marquis pushes his hair off his sweaty forehead and joins Dòmhnall in inspecting the wyvernling's wing. Of course he has earned Cindra's acceptance with a few daredevil moves. If I didn't admire his audacity I might be jealous.

'What's the egg-choosing ceremony?' Gideon asks Aodahn as we return through the tunnels, leaving Marquis to the healing of the wyvernling.

'The most sacred of our practices,' Aodahn replies.

'I've seen the eggs,' I say. 'In that giant nest?'

'The nursery,' he says with a nod.

'Why do you keep them all together like that, instead of in individual nests with their parents?'

'Hebridean Wyverns share everything, including our wyvernlings,' Aodahn replies.

I think of the wyverns in the nursery, turning the eggs and breathing flames across their shells.

'Eggs need specific conditions in order to thrive,' I say. 'Surely it would be easier to raise yours above ground, in your natural habitat?'

'It is true that fewer of our eggs survive these days,' he says quietly. 'But to raise our eggs above ground we would need to leave our concealment, and Abelio . . .'

Cindra slinks past us, her long tail trailing behind, and he falls silent. She glances back at me and I see something in her eyes that reminds me, bizarrely, of Hollingsworth. It's a mix of expectation and intimidation and – dare I say it – hope.

*

I begin to live and breathe Cannair, immersing myself in Cindra's writings while the others grow restless.

'The wyverns have been asking all sorts of questions about the war,' Atlas says. 'Abelio heard them yesterday and shut my class down.'

'Mine too,' Serena says. 'He said I've taught enough human-made practices to last a lifetime.'

'Look,' Gideon says. 'Why don't we call it a day? We haven't found the information Hollingsworth wanted, so let's just admit defeat and stop wasting our time larking around down here when we could be winning the war up there.'

'No,' I say. 'Cindra asked me to translate Cannair and that's what I'm doing. I might still discover what Hollingsworth wants to know in Cindra's writings. And if I don't, then at least we'll have the wyverns on our side.'

'A fat lot of difference tweed-spinning wyverns will make,' Gideon snaps.

'Gideon has a point,' Serena says. 'We have no idea how the war's going. I can barely get any radio signal down here. For all we know, the rebels could be—'

'The egg-choosing ceremony is in a few days,' Marquis says. 'Let's stay until then.' He looks at me. 'That will give you time to translate enough of Cindra's Cannair, right? And like you say, you might just find something out in the process.'

I nod gratefully but avoid his gaze. I don't dare tell them the truth. That part of me has already realised that translating Cannair is a thankless task. Putting it into English makes the language sound stilted and monotone, losing the melodious quality of the words and the meaning of the wyverns' expression. But I have to let Cindra see me try. Is it possible, I wonder, that there are languages you can have deeper thoughts in? Languages that allow you to think about things differently, because they have more words, more meanings for ideas that don't exist in others? If so, Cannair is one of those languages.

I don't go to the Twilight Meal, choosing to stay with my studies instead. I take out the photograph of Ursa and trace the outline of her little face. What will happen to her if the wyverns don't help us and we lose this war? I jump as Atlas walks into the cave. He sits down next to me, tucking his feet under my tweed blanket.

'You're supposed to be at the Twilight Meal,' I say with a glare. 'Don't tell me you suddenly have time for me again? Is that because Abelio put a stop to your classes?'

'You're right,' he says softly. 'I've been distracted. I'm sorry.'

He elbows me playfully, but I don't smile. 'It's my turn to be distracted,' I mutter. '*Sorry.*'

He picks at the blanket and when I steal a glance at him, his eyes are on the loquisonus machine.

'The wyverns' echolocation sounds different to the

dragons', doesn't it?'

'Hmm,' I reply.

'Could that . . . mean something?'

'Like what?' I say. 'These wyverns are different to dragons in every way imaginable. The only similarity they have is to Bolgoriths, because many only speak one tongue.' I pause. 'I thought you knew that Bolgoriths communicate so frequently in echolocation that they organise their fighting groups by family, because their Koinamens bond means that they can literally see into each other's minds?'

Atlas is nodding. 'I do. But these wyverns don't have that. Most of them have never fought another dragon in their lives.'

Everything I learned about echolocation suddenly catches up with me.

'But what if whatever Hollingsworth knows about them, what she wants with them, has something to do with their echolocation?'

Atlas leans closer. 'Do you have something in mind?'

My shoulders slump. 'No. I wish I'd just bloody waited for her to tell me, instead of trying to save that dragonling and getting myself arrested.'

Atlas's arms encircle me and he kisses my cheek. 'It was *very* rebellious of you,' he whispers in my ear.

I lean back into him and he kisses me again, on the mouth this time, and my mind drifts between the delicious softness of his lips and echolocation, the sweet smell of his hair and the wyvern tongue . . .

'Wait,' I say, pulling away. 'What if the reason I'm struggling to translate the wyvern tongue is because I'm trying to be too faithful to the source text?'

Atlas raises an eyebrow, his hands still on my waist.

'At university, I learned about language subordination and domination,' I say. 'The Academy considers a good translation to be one that is subordinate to the target language, meaning the translation of the dragon tongue into English is so fluid, so natural that it's like it was never even translated at all. It conforms to its target language and the translator becomes invisible, but the original style, the peculiarities of the dragon tongue, get lost.'

Atlas's fingers find the bare skin of my hip beneath my jumper. 'And language domination?'

I think of the lines and lines of Cannair written by Cindra.

'Language domination is when the translation dominates the target language, preserving the source language's original rhythm, its word order, its idiosyncrasies, so that when we read it we remember that we're reading a translation.'

'But doesn't that make the English translation hard to understand?' Atlas asks.

'Yes, which is why the Academy won't accept it,' I say. 'But some Draconic translators argue that subordination gives us a purely instrumental view of language. They say that when we focus on the outward beauty of the translation, we neglect to imitate its true form.'

'And that's what you're doing with the wyvern tongue?'

I nod. 'I've been so focused on making Cannair sound perfect in English, but perhaps that's impossible. Perhaps it doesn't matter if the translation sounds bad, as long as I'm not betraying the original meaning.'

'But how will the original meaning be conveyed if the English makes no sense? How will anyone ever be able to learn the tongue if they don't understand what they're saying?' I bite my lip. I don't know the answer to that question. And yet, I know the Academy won't ever accept my translation of Cannair unless it makes sense in English.

'I think you were right, earlier,' Atlas says. 'Your willingness to translate Cannair is what will get Cindra to fight with us. And perhaps when the wyverns see the Bulgarian dragons in action, they'll use whatever secret weapon they have. We've just got to get them above ground.'

I smile. Despite the distance that has been building between us, despite the fact that he is keeping some sort of secret mission from me, I still feel drawn to him like a moth to light. Atlas saw the good in me when I hated myself. He listened as I confessed my darkest secret, and didn't let it change a thing. In doing so, he became the light at the end of every dark tunnel in my mind. The desire to kiss him again, to continue the conversation about language that brought him back to me, is relentless. Maybe he hasn't told me about the mission because he can't. Atlas is the best rebel I know. He'd die for the cause. No wonder he's distracted, if he's been tasked with something the rest of us can't help him with.

'Translating Cannair was the thing that got us into these *skugvels*,' I say quietly. 'So perhaps it's the thing that will get us out.'

Thirteen

THE EGG-CHOOSING CEREMONY TAKES PLACE IN the Amber Court, when the night's first moonlight shines through the gemstones in the ceiling. The usual orange hue surrounds the wyverns as they gather around the great central fire and amid the flickering flames I catch a glimpse of the white, oval eggs.

'Why have they been moved here, do you think?' I whisper to Atlas.

'And why are they *in* the fire?' he mutters back.

'Shhh!' Marquis hisses.

He's sitting cross-legged behind us, with Cindra at his side, the picture of reverence and respect. Serena, Gideon and Aodahn join us and I stare at the eggs, their shells maintaining their bluish sheen despite the direct contact with the flames. Wings shiver in anticipation as Abelio approaches the fire and begins to speak. So many of the words of his introductory speech are new to me, but I recognise some from Cindra's written descriptions of the wyvern hatching process.

'For the last phase of incubation, the eggs must be kept as hot as possible, so that the wyvernlings inside can develop their flame,' Aodahn whispers to us.

'How does each wyvern know which egg is her own?' I whisper back.

At the same time, several wyverns creep silently towards the fire. These must be the mothers. I watch as they tread carefully, without any sense of urgency or excitement. A male wyvern joins one of the females and they approach the fire together, the air around them still and silent except for the crackle of flames. I count the eggs. There are ten of them, more than the number of wyverns approaching to collect one. So where are the other parents? I feel a crackle of electricity in the air, and I can tell by the others' faces that they feel it too. Aodahn is deep in concentration, a far-off look in his eyes. The wyverns observe the clutch of eggs, their huge eyes fixed on them as if they're saying a silent prayer or incantation. Every so often, the eggs tremble. Abelio breathes more fire on to the bed of feathers and wool beneath them, then resumes his position patiently. The pair of wyverns press their snouts to a flaming egg. They pause as if to consider, then look at each other. The female – I think her name is Aberdine – takes the egg in her mouth.

But how can you be sure it's yours? I want to call to her.

Is the wyvernling inside the egg communicating with its parents through echolocation? Does the egg release a pheromone that attracts its biological mother? Surely Aberdine cannot differentiate this egg from its identical nest-mates by its appearance alone? I lean forward in fascination as she and her partner leave the fireside and sense someone move beside me.

'Aodahn?' Atlas whispers.

I stare in surprise as Aodahn circles the central fire. He moves slowly from egg to egg, reaching down to press his face to one before continuing to walk. The others watch, unperturbed.

'But he lives alone, doesn't he?' I say to Atlas. 'He doesn't have a partner?'

Aodahn opens his jaws and carefully takes an egg in his mouth. He walks proudly back towards us and sets it down in front of me and Atlas. Smoke rises from its base and beneath its thin shell I see the shadow of a movement. Aodahn told us that the wyverns share everything, including their eggs. But I didn't realise he meant this, a communal nest from which to take an egg they didn't even lay. No other dragons do *this*.

I see my awe reflected in Atlas's eyes as the orange light bounces off the eggshell. Aodahn and the other wyverns around us cast loving looks towards it. This is more than just a ceremony. There is something almost religious about what we are witnessing, a spirituality I will never be able to put into words. At least not any words I know. The wyverns are communicating telepathically, experiencing the ceremony on a level we humans will never understand, on a plane our minds will never reach.

'Aodahn,' Atlas says quietly. 'What made you choose this egg?'

'How do you know it's the right one?' I add.

'I do not know,' Aodahn says. 'I simply chose.'

I frown.

'But we saw you deliberating,' Atlas says. 'You took your time, stopped by each egg.'

Aodahn's eyes grow wide like moons. 'I made a choice that had to be made. It is the choice, the choice of wyvernling, the choice to commit to it for the rest of my life, that makes it *the right one*.' He pulls the egg towards him with his curved talon and shelters it beneath the feathers of his wing. '*That* is what makes it mine.'

I find the response profound, but Atlas gets to his feet.

'Where are you going?' I ask him.

It's like he hasn't heard me and he leaves the Amber Court without a word. As the ceremony comes to an end, I linger with the others. The wyverns gather in small groups around various eggs, sipping honeyed wine as they watch the movement of the wyvernlings inside the eggs and glance at each other with knowing looks. When they talk in hushed voices I listen, trying to hang on to the threads of the different conversations, and when they talk silently in their heads I sit back and watch how their body language tells the story of what they're saying instead. I get the sense that I have seen something that I will never again witness, and the thought makes me feel like I could fly. Beside me, Aodahn gazes at his own egg.

'When will it hatch?' Marquis asks him.

He and Gideon are passing a cigarette between them, the last of Marquis's stash. Serena dozes, stretched out between them, her third glass of wine still full.

'Within the next week, I hope,' Aodahn says, blowing another burst of flame on to the egg.

I'm thinking of the parts of Cindra's writings that mention the egg-choosing ceremony. No wonder I haven't understood them. There are no words in English to translate the gentleness with which each wyvern approached the fiery nest, the wholehearted awe with which Aodahn chose his egg, as if he had been enlightened by some supernatural source.

I glance at the brand-new father next to me.

'Aodahn,' I say. 'If I were to try and write about the egg-choosing ceremony in another language, so much of its meaning would be lost.' I glance over at Cindra, who is admiring Aberdine's egg, and lower my voice. 'And it's the same for Cannair. Some of it just doesn't work in English at all.'

'Ah, the curse of translation,' Aodahn says softly.

I swallow. 'Curse?'

'Translation translates, but does not necessarily preserve.'

'What do you mean? Translation is a tool for preserving ideas, information.'

'But not always meaning,' Aodahn replies, his eyes unblinking. 'And not always the language the ideas come from.'

'Sometimes, meaning gets lost,' I say, nodding. 'But every act of translation requires sacrifice, no?'

'Why should we sacrifice?' Aodahn says, his tail flicking. 'So that the wyvern tongue can fit into the confines of English? Of – and I mean no offence – one singular, limited human tongue?'

Language subordination.

'In India there's no great translation tradition,' Gideon interjects. 'The people and dragons simply speak each other's languages. Monolingualism is very rare there.'

'But . . . but translation is a noble pursuit,' I say. 'It brings voices that might otherwise be lost to—'

'No one said it wasn't noble, dear one. But is it enough? You yourself admit to being at a loss for words. What will happen once you've translated Cannair – *if* you succeed? Your translation might move some to attempt to learn Cannair, but most will content themselves with the English version of Cindra's texts.' Aodahn breathes another small flame on to his egg and my head spins.

He's right. What good is a translation if it transforms one language into another, only to let the original die?

I think of Cindra's writing, the pages gathering dust, her careful choice of words and sharp wit lost forever.

Aodahn gives me a sad smile. 'Cindra believes that translating Cannair will save it. But does translating a French text for British readers keep the French language alive? Of course not. It merely rewrites the author's words into English.'

I'm suddenly reminded of the Bulgarian storybook of my childhood, the one that doesn't exist in its original language any more – not even inside my head – because Mama translated it into English for me instead. The translation didn't preserve the Bulgarian language, its sound or rhythm, nor the style of the Bulgarian author. It turned it into something an English reader could understand and relate to, exchanging *Petar* for *Peter*, *Sofia* for *London*, the Bulgarian Bolgoriths for Western Drakes . . . until there was nothing left of the original story.

Translation translates, but does not necessarily preserve.

'Then what do you suggest?' I say more sharply than I intended.

'What if sacrifice isn't necessary?' Aodahn blinks. 'Patrick had the solution.'

'Did he?' My hands reach for the journal, but it's back in the sleeping cave.

'Why do you think he stopped translating Cannair?' the wyvern says.

I hesitate. 'Are you saying Clawtail *chose* to put an end to his study of the wyvern tongue?'

Aodahn nods. 'To learn Cannair in its fullness, one must hear it from a native speaker. Patrick could not preserve Cannair through written translation, but he made sure his daughter spoke the language. Perhaps, wherever she is now, she has passed it down.'

Could there be a family somewhere in Britannia speaking Cannair?

'So, you're saying that you think the wyvern tongue is untranslatable, at least into English?' Gideon says.

Aodahn glances nervously at me. 'No language is entirely translatable. Like you said, Vivien, there is always sacrifice.'

Untranslatable.

I can hear my pulse beating, like a rushing in my ears, as my mind swims with panic. If that's true, then I have not only failed to translate Cindra's writing and therefore failed to solicit the wyverns' help. It means my whole career is a lie. What do I have, if not languages? Who am I, if not a translator?

I set down my glass with a trembling hand.

'Courage, dear one,' Aodahn tells me. 'You should perhaps—'

'Viv?' Atlas strides back into the Amber Court. 'When did you last see the loquisonus machine?'

I frown. 'This morning. Why?'

'It's broken,' Atlas says.

I tense, my heart pounding.

Broken?

'The tunnel-detecting machine?' Aodahn says.

Across the court, I see Abelio watching us.

Cindra approaches. 'Show me,' she tells Atlas.

The five of us follow Cindra and Aodahn to our sleeping cave. We find the loquisonus machine still in its case, but when Atlas pulls it out, broken parts rattle inside.

'You found it like this?' I ask Atlas.

He nods. I glance at Cindra.

'Do you think one of the wyverns was curious, and accidentally . . .'

Abelio slinks into the cave. When he sees the loquisonus machine hanging from Atlas's hand, his turquoise eyes flash. 'You have vandalised it,' he hisses.

'It wasn't Atlas,' I say sharply.

'You want to ensure we cannot use your tunnel-detecting machine!' Abelio continues. 'This is sabotage.'

I feel my eyes narrow. 'Sabotage? Or perhaps,' I say slowly, 'you wish to dissuade the wyverns from escaping the concealment you have forced on them.'

Cindra gives me a sharp look as Abelio recoils. 'Without this machine, you cannot keep your side of our agreement,' he snarls at me. 'You must leave immediately.'

'*Fasgadh* is freely given, Abelio,' Aodahn stutters.

'Five dawns of *fasgadh* is generosity enough,' Abelio snarls.

'*He* did it,' Marquis says quietly.

My cousin glares in the wyvern's direction and I know he's right.

'Did *you* break the machine, Abelio?' I ask.

He lets out a bird-like screech that sends a chill through me. I sense the others tense.

'Abelio,' Cindra says sharply. 'If we banish the humans after nightfall, they will be hunted.'

'So be it!' Abelio shrieks, his eyes wide. 'The wyverns owe them nothing.'

'What's he saying?' Gideon whispers.

Abelio bares his teeth and I see the flicker of flame in his throat. A threatening clicking comes from his chest. The sound of fire.

'Cindra, please!' Serena shouts.

'Tell him the Bulgarian dragons will kill us, then sniff out the wyvern tunnels looking for more food,' Atlas tells me.

I translate and Abelio's snarl growls louder. 'We are a match for any dragon, we are Hebridean—'

'Tell him the machine isn't a tunnel detector.'

I freeze. 'What? No.'

'Tell him we lied,' Atlas says.

I shake my head, then glance at Aodahn and Cindra, who are staring at him in stunned silence.

'We need your help, Aodahn,' Atlas says gently. 'That's why we came here. The machine doesn't detect tunnels, but echolocation.'

'Bloody hell,' Marquis mutters.

'Dragons call it the Koinamens, in English,' Atlas says quietly. 'The language you speak – not Cannair, the other one. The one you keep inside your heads.'

Cindra is translating for Abelio and growls erupt from the wyverns, even Aodahn. My gaze lands on his gentle face as his eyes cloud with confusion.

'*An Smuainswel?*' he whispers.

Smuainswel.

The word for the Koinamens in the wyvern tongue. I recognise the Scottish Gaelic word for thought, *Smuain*, and the Cannair word for a sea wave, *Swel*.

It's beautiful.

I see Gideon shrink against the wall as Abelio seems to grow, his wings unfolding behind him as a high-pitched howl erupts from his throat.

'We can listen to it, but we can't understand it!' I say. 'We found your tunnels by following the sound of it with the machine, but that's all. I've heard your Koinamens and it's the most beautiful sound in the world. I would never do anything to—'

Cindra lets out a warning screech and I fall silent.

'How many humans can listen to the *Smuainswel?*'

'We have the only machine,' I say quickly. 'But I can't use it, can't translate—'

'Translate?' Cindra chokes, taking a step towards me. 'You speak of translation?'

Atlas steps in front of me, his arms outstretched. 'We

know that the Koinamens is sacred, used to heal and grow. Viv respects that. But we resorted to using the machine to listen to it because we were desperate to find you. Because we need your help.'

'Do you see, now, the entitlement of these humans?' Abelio snarls to Cindra. 'They bring nothing but danger.'

'What sort of help, dear one?' says Aodahn.

'Dr Hollingsworth, leader of the Human-Dragon Coalition, believes that you could be instrumental to us winning the war,' Atlas says calmly.

'But we are so small in number compared to Queen Ignacia's dragons, to these Bulgarian Bolgoriths joining our skies,' Aodahn says. 'How can *we* help you?'

I shake my head. 'We don't know.'

The admission is mortifying.

'Cindra,' Aodahn says, gesturing to Marquis. 'He saved the life of our wyvernling. You cannot sentence him to death.'

Cindra growls, then looks at me. I know what she's thinking. I've only just started translating her writing and if she banishes me now, her hope of sharing Cannair with the world will be lost. Her eyes flick from side to side and her lower jaw shudders menacingly. 'You will keep your *fasgadh*, temporarily.'

'They will leave us now!' Abelio roars.

Cindra snaps at him, catching the side of his snout in her teeth, and the two dragons spit and scream in a stand-off than makes my blood run cold. Abelio glares at her, his eyes rabid, but she doesn't back down. He turns, his head swinging side to side, a performance meant to ward off a threat. Then he lets out a low hiss and lurches from the room. Cindra's eyes flash at me again before she follows.

'What did you do that for?' Marquis spits at Atlas.

'He was going to kill one of us!' Atlas retorts. 'And we can't leave here with nothing.' He looks at me and the hardness in his eyes is unsettling. 'We *need* the wyverns.'

I crouch down on the tweed blankets as the water from the stream trickles into the silence. In front of me are the broken loquisonus, Cindra's writings and Clawtail's journal. Each are an attempt to understand the Hebridean Wyverns and yet I'm no closer to achieving the mission Hollingsworth set me than when I arrived on the island. All this time, I've been trying to learn Cannair to find out how the wyverns can help the rebels win the war, only for it to be untranslatable.

It's the glasshouse and the Koinamens all over again.

'Hollingsworth was counting on the success of this mission,' I whisper. 'But Cindra will hardly agree to fight with us now. What if we've just lost the war?'

'She can't have based her entire victory plan on the off chance we find a lost group of wyverns,' Serena says.

'But what if she did?' I reply. 'Wyvernmire has *Bulgarian dragons* on her side. Hollingsworth must have realised she needed more than just the average teeth and claws.' I look to Atlas. 'I think you're right. The wyvern echolocation must be the answer.'

He nods, his eyes shining.

'It is truly the *Smuainswel* that interests you?' Aodahn

says. 'Well, then. Your dishonesty is poor repayment for our *fasgadh* indeed.'

His eyes flick from me to Gideon, shining with sorrow, before he scurries from the room.

'Great,' Gideon seethes. 'The only dragon I ever actually liked hates us.'

We undress for bed in silence. I lie back on the blankets beneath the muted moonlight that shines in through the ceiling. Atlas's hand finds mine and he turns towards me.

'We haven't failed yet, Viv,' he whispers.

He's still full of hope, despite everything. But he and the others have achieved their mission, to find the wyverns.

Only mine remains unfulfilled. I'm supposed to be Vivien Featherswallow, Draconic Translator. Except I still haven't succeeded in translating Cannair. If Cindra makes us leave tomorrow, our deal will be off. What use will I be to the rebels then? Who am I, if I'm just Viv?

My eyes fly open in the shadows.

I don't even know who *Viv* is.

A newspaper sketch of my own face dances before my eyes, turning into Hollingsworth's before transforming into Abelio's. He breathes out a foul-smelling flame that chokes the air I breathe.

An acidic scent burns the rims of my nostrils, pulling me from sleep. I sense Atlas stir next to me and as I gaze across the murky room, I see Marquis sitting up. He starts to cough and at the same time, something seizes my throat. Atlas jumps to his feet. He lights a lantern and it fizzes to life, bathing the cave in light. Smoke coats everything around us in a green haze that clings to the walls.

'Poisonous gas,' Marquis croaks, his arm over his face. 'Humans.'

Fourteen

I STUMBLE TO MY FEET, COUGHING, as my head begins to spin. Serena seizes a second lantern from the wall and we run out into the tunnels. Screeches sound from the other caves as wyverns burst from their chambers.

'That way,' Atlas gasps, grasping my arm and pushing me in the direction of the fleeing wyverns.

'Wait!' I choke. 'Whoever sent in the gas will be waiting by the exits. We have to use the waterfall one.' I gasp for air. 'It's invisible.'

Atlas nods, his eyes streaming with tears. We turn and run back through a crowd of wyverns surging against us. 'Turn around!' Marquis screams at them, but the gas distorts his voice.

He collapses without warning and I stop myself from crying out, from breathing in more of the poisoned air. I take short, sharp breaths as I drop down next to him and hook my arm under his. His eyes roll as more of the green smoke skims his face, but someone appears at his other shoulder and lifts him. It's Gideon, a handkerchief tied over his mouth. He heaves Marquis forward and I stumble with them as Atlas and Serena drive a path for us. Some of the wyverns have had the same realisation and as they begin to change direction, others follow. I see several carrying heavy rolls of tweed, scrolls of paper dropping to the ground to be trampled underfoot. The memory tapestries.

'Leave them!' I try to shout, but the inhalation of air burns my throat.

A group of wyvernlings fly by us and I watch them race ahead down the tunnel. Then, several drop from the air with a thud. And suddenly they're at my feet, dead wyvernlings with green liquid oozing from the corners of their mouths. My head aches, a deep pulsing that threatens to implode my brain as hands push me into freezing water and I swim, with nothing to follow but the blue-white sheen of wyvern scale. I flail, my eyes scrunched tight as the pain in my head and the burning in my lungs paralyse me, until I feel a long, slick body beneath mine.

I emerge from the pool gasping for breath and suck in the cold, fresh air. Aberdine slips out from beneath me, her egg in her mouth, but the thank-you on my lips gets stuck in my hot, raw throat. I stare at the trees around me as my vision clears, the pain receding with each breath of pure air. Wyverns are still bursting from the water and on the banks of the pool I see Marquis, lying on his back in the sunrise and taking long steady breaths as Gideon and Serena lean over him. Atlas emerges on the back of another wyvern, his eyes red and burning. I wade towards him and when we reach each other he clings to me.

'I can't see,' he mutters.

I splash more water on his eyes as Cindra drags a lifeless wyvernling out of the pool and bites its tail until it takes a tiny, raspy breath

She looks up and her eyes meet mine. Gunshots sound over the crashing of the waterfall.

'Guardians,' Atlas says. 'We have to move.'

There's a roar as more shots sound. In the distance, I see the wyverns who have been ambushed at the other exits fill the sky with flame.

'Your Prime Minister did this?' Cindra snarls at me. 'She will go to such lengths to find you?'

'They're looking for us, Viv,' Atlas says, climbing out of the water.

I stare around at the wyverns. 'Where are the others? There are barely fifty wyverns here.'

Another slick body bursts from the water.

Aodahn.

He thrashes in the pool, his tail lashing as he struggles to see through swollen eyes. Atlas staggers back into the water, narrowly avoiding the spiked tail.

'Aodahn!' he shouts. 'Calm yourself.'

Slowly, Atlas and Aberdine guide Aodahn from the water. He lies on the bank next to Marquis, breathing heavily, as Serena wipes his eyes clean with her handkerchief. As he turns to his side, I see the bulging pouch of his underbelly and something dark beneath the skin. It rolls out on to the grass, a black, cracked oval. I recoil. Aodahn opens his eyes and lets out a strangled sound.

'My egg,' he rasps.

I drop to my knees beside the egg, but Cindra is already there. She nudges it with her nose and part of the outer shell falls away. For a moment she rests her face on it, listening. Then she gives a small, trembling nod.

'It's dead,' Aodahn says. 'My child is dead.'

An agonised howl comes from his chest.

Around us the other wyverns begin to echo it, and the forest fills with one simultaneous wail.

Goosebumps erupt on my skin as Serena's eyes fill with tears. The egg, so beautiful and pearly just a few hours ago, when Aodahn was echolocating with the wyvernling inside, is turning a chemical green colour. I swallow the sob in my throat, unable to bring myself to offer Aodahn any comfort. His loss is too great for words.

'We can't stay,' Marquis hisses from behind me.

He glances at Abelio, who is perched on a rock with his wings outstretched, staring at the wyverns in the sky across the hills. They are still raining fire down on to the Guardians shooting at them, and I think of the wyvernlings that went the wrong way, and the ones that never made it out of the tunnels.

I nod. We brought the Guardians here. It only took them a few days to find us.

And Abelio isn't going to forget that.

My failed translation of Cindra's writings is inside, as are Clawtail's journal and the loquisonus machine. The only trace of the wyverns' Cannair, lost to the tunnels. I'll never see them again. Anger fills me. I couldn't translate the wyvern tongue fast enough, and now here we are, under attack with countless wyverns dead. For the first time in my life, my languages have failed me.

'We need Chumana's protection,' Atlas whispers. 'If the Bulgarians and Guardians are on this side of the island, we won't survive long.'

I nod. Gideon and Marquis are already standing, holding our packs and backing away into the trees. I see Serena deposit a tearful kiss on Aodahn's wing as she leaves him. But Cindra has seen us. Her eyes dart to Abelio, who seems frozen in shock, then back to me.

'I wish you dead,' she croaks slowly. 'I wish you devoured.'

I feel my legs shake as her threat takes my breath away. The same talons used to waulk the tweed snap ominously. Cindra's tail flicks from side to side, quick as a whip.

'We will embark towards the Northern tunnels, near the coast,' Abelio calls out.

'Can you not see what these years of concealment have done to us, Abelio?' Cindra snarls. 'We thought we were safe underground, when in truth an unknown enemy lurked just above. Concealment has made us weak, ill-prepared.'

'How dare you insult—'

'And now our wyvernlings have paid the price!'

Aodahn casts an exhausted look in our direction. He dreamed of an end to the wyverns' concealment, but not like this. I begin to cry. The sight of him is too much devastation to bear.

'Courage, dear one,' I hear myself murmur.

I don't think he hears me.

Cindra and Abelio's snarling can be heard even after we have retreated into the forest. Serena weeps quietly as we walk and I see Marquis reach for her hand.

'How long were we underground for, do you reckon?' he mutters.

'No more than a week. We need to find Chumana,' Atlas says again.

His eyes are red-rimmed and he's holding my hand so tight it hurts.

Serena reaches for her radio and begins turning the dial. 'We need an update on how the war has progressed.'

'If Wyvernmire gassed the tunnels it's because she knew we were in them,' I say. 'That means she's still looking for me. And the loquisonus machine.'

'Then she's still wary of her own alliance with the Bolgoriths,' Atlas says. 'Which means she must be uncomfortable with the amount of power they're wielding.'

A cheery voice crackles from the radio. '—and as the search for our rebel soldiers continues, Sandy and Drake would like to remind you that swallows always return to the nest. So, if our flighty Swallow can hear us now, then please, do us all a favour and give us a wave. We will repeat this message every hour.'

'The rebels in London must think you've abandoned them, if Sandy and Drake are using their show to send you cryptic messages,' Serena says. 'What if Hollingsworth believes we're dead?'

'She couldn't know the wyverns were living underground,' I say. 'So maybe she does.'

'Chumana will spread the news that we're okay, and she can tell us how many battles we've won and lost,' Atlas says.

I cringe at the thought of seeing Chumana again. She saved me from Wyvernmire's camp only for me to throw the ugliest of words in her face. And I have nothing but bad news to give her. Hollingsworth believed our victory depended on an alliance with the wyverns and now most of them will never want to see us again.

We walk back the way we came in silence. If I'd been able to translate Cindra's writings, I might have won her favour before Wyvernmire gassed the tunnels. The wyverns would be flying into battle against the Bulgarian dragons, armed with whatever secret advantage Hollingsworth believes they have. My heart races as I watch the others climb over twisted tree roots. What kind of translator fails to translate a language she's been studying for months? What is the point of me if I can't use the one thing I'm good at to help us win the war?

We walk back through the valley in the pink sunrise. Birdsong keeps me from falling too deep into my thoughts, instilling a strange calm as my legs burn with a satisfying ache. We climb back up the hills and the physical effort and the birds and the fresh air soothe my senses. I had forgotten how bright the sunrise is.

A small gasp.

Serena has reached the top of the hill before me. I stride up after her and my stomach drops. Dead dragons litter the hilltop. Their huge bodies are still as we walk between them, each lying on a patch of blood-soaked earth. They are Western Drakes and Sand Dragons, Ddraig Gochs and Silver Drakes.

'British dragons,' Marquis croaks.

A piece of black cloth is tied round one of the dragons' talons, the white swallow stained red. 'Rebels,' I say, blinking back tears.

We cross the rest of the hilltop in silence, occasionally glancing at each other in wordless horror as we walk past dragons missing a limb, or whose entrails are spilling out on to the ground. The smell of blood is metallic.

'Krasimir's gone rogue,' Marquis says.

I shake my head. 'He can't have done this alone. If the rebels launched an attack on Canna, it means they have no other choice. The Bolgoriths aren't biding their time any more.'

'You mean you think they've overthrown Wyvernmire?' Atlas says.

I nod, feeling sick. 'Sending her Guardians to attack the wyvern tunnels must have been a last attempt at finding me and keeping a sense of control.' I lay a hand on the cool scales of a Silver Drake. She's young – too young to be dead. 'But meanwhile, the Bulgarians were doing this.'

I jump as a loud groan sounds beside me. The Silver Drake moves her head and her huge eyes meet mine, pleading.

'She's alive!' Marquis says, dropping to his knees beside the dragon. 'We have to help her.'

My eyes flit to the huge gash in her stomach and I shake my head. It's too late. I press my lips to her ear. 'You fought bravely,' I whisper in Harpentesa, the mother tongue of her species. 'Rest now.'

The Silver Drake lets out another heavy breath, then goes still. I move to the next dragon, a Western Drake, and whisper in Wyrmerian. He's already dead, but at least the last words spoken over him will be his own tongue. I feel eyes on me as I move to a Ddraig Goch. I don't speak Talwynn, the national dragon tongue of Wales, but I do know one word.

'*Gadvalen,*' I murmur, my breath catching in my throat.
Farewell.

'The Swallow is alive and well. I repeat, the Swallow is in flight.' Serena is speaking into her radio transmitter. Her eyes meet mine and her lip curls. 'And she has a message for Wyvernmire's Bolgoriths.'

I stand up.

'Britannia may be burning, reduced to smoke and embers, but embers are as hot as the fire that created them. And every fire starts with a single spark.'

'Shit. Look,' Gideon says quietly.

My heart jolts when I see what he's pointing at. A black Bulgarian dragon standing among the trees. And at his side, a human.

'Goranov and Ralph.'

'Viv!' Marquis says as I stalk across the field towards them.

I ignore him. I have to find out what they're saying before they leave again. How many losses have the rebels suffered since we went underground? I feel an awful pang of dread. As I get closer to the forest, I can hear Goranov talking in a low, rasping voice that sets my teeth on edge. Ralph replies, but I can't make out what they are discussing. The others are following silently behind me. I glance back at them, then drop into the long grass. I crawl to the treeline on my stomach and a stench like stale urine and burnt leather hits me.

'Three days of battle,' I hear Goranov snarl in English. 'We did not expect such numbers.'

'The rebel movement has grown,' Ralph replies softly. 'But you won. We won.'

Goranov lets out a grunt and they both fall silent. I hear the rustling of leaves as Goranov's tail moves across the ground, but I can see nothing but the back of the dragon's head and the line of spikes along his spine. Are they whispering now, too quietly for me to hear? I move closer, dragging myself through the dirt. Then, as I pull myself around a bush, I catch a glimpse of Ralph's hair. He's lying in the shadow of the tree trunk, both his arms extended in a spread-eagled position. A numb horror floods me.

Goranov has killed Ralph.

He's eating him.

No. Something here doesn't make sense. I see Goranov's blood-covered snout, pinning Ralph to the ground by his arm. But he's not dead. Ralph's sleeves are rolled up to the elbows, revealing the white crooks of his arms. On the ground beside him is a small knife, responsible for the neat gashes that are pooling with blood. And Goranov is licking it from Ralph's skin, sucking and swallowing like a baby at its mother's breast. I don't dare exhale. Something taps at my foot. Atlas is behind me, crawling on his stomach. When he reaches my side and sees what I'm seeing, he pales. Ralph's head lolls to the side and his eyelids flicker as he lets out an involuntary, 'Oh.'

I shudder. Whatever we're watching is perverse. Unholy.

Atlas begins backing away and I do the same, not standing up until we're in the field. Then we all bolt, running in silence until we're back among the dead dragons.

'He was *drinking* his blood,' Serena whispers as we duck behind the body of a Sand Dragon.

I struggle to find the words to describe what I've just seen.

'Is this what Ralph meant when he said Goranov needed him?' I say.

'But why would a dragon need to drink a human's blood?' Atlas replies. 'Have you ever seen this, Gideon?'

Gideon shakes his head, pale-faced.

'But why would Goranov drink Ralph's blood when he could just eat him?' I say slowly.

The birds are singing in the trees.

'What if it's like fireblod,' Marquis says slowly, 'but in reverse?'

'In reverse?'

'Fireblod has to be taken from a live donor. That's why the dragons had it banned in the Peace Agreement. Atlas, the fireblod that saved you was made from Chumana's blood, and that's what Ralph is giving Goranov.'

'Do you think Goranov is injured?' I say hopefully.

Marquis shrugs. 'Maybe the blood strengthens him.'

'Why not suck Ralph dry, then?' Gideon says.

I wrinkle my nose in disgust.

'Because Ralph is a replenishing source,' Serena says slowly.

'Canna isn't exactly bursting with humans to eat,' I say. 'The children here have too many tactics to avoid the dragons now. And like Marquis said, perhaps there's something about human blood that makes it stronger when it's taken from someone who's still alive.'

I remember the way Goranov licked Ralph back at Canna House. Now it makes sense.

'But why would Ralph give his blood to—'

'Because Goranov has promised Ralph everything,' I say. 'His life when the Bulgarian dragons eventually destroy Wyvernmire and her government; power when they imprison or eat any human who opposes them; and status when they eventually run Britannia the same way they do Bulgaria.'

I try to imagine a country where humans are not only a dead food source but a live one. We keep walking and I can't ignore the twinge I feel at leaving the massacred rebels behind. They – the dragons – are the strength of the rebel army. How can so many of them be dead? I wonder what their names were, where they were hatched. How many more are we going to lose? My heart sinks. We were supposed to stop this.

It rains as we reach the graveyard where we hid from Krasimir. I stuff my cold hands into my pockets, glancing at the names etched into the small rocks left in place of headstones for Canna's children.

John, Peter, Josie . . .

Ivy grows across them, stretching its leaves out over the ground so that I almost miss the flash of emerald green beneath them. I stop. Lying on one of the graves is a long, stiff piece of cloth woven in threads of green and gold. It's tweed, worn from age or the elements and stuffed with several large, browning scrolls of paper.

As Marquis and Serena tread a path in the grass and Gideon and Atlas wander from grave to grave, I kneel by the tapestry and pull the ivy away. A shock shoots down my spine as I read the words stitched across the tweed. How did I miss this last time?

Patrick Clawtail, 1827–1866.

'But . . . he's not supposed to be buried here.'

Gideon turns to look at me. 'Who?'

I gesture to the grave.

'Aodahn said the government never left a body. So what's he doing here?'

Atlas's eyes widen. 'That's Clawtail?'

'With a memory tapestry on his grave?' says Marquis.

I look at him, then back at the grave. 'But how . . . ? The wyverns couldn't possibly . . .'

'They must know he's buried here,' Serena says.

'But why would Aodahn lie?' says Gideon.

'The grave is probably empty like the rest of them,' Marquis says.

I crouch and run a finger down one of the scrolls. The paper is thin and brittle. When I try to unfold it, to read a memory of Clawtail's life, it disintegrates in my hand. I reach for the one that is fresher, still white, and begin to read.

'It's written in English, not Cannair,' I say.

Beneath a sky taut with stars and bullets, Patrick cradles his daughter Marguerite, who has been shot. He begs the wyverns to help her. He has discovered their secret and knows what it can do. It is the last thing he will ask of them, as government Guardians storm the island, and they know it. So they gather en masse, wing-to-wing, around the girl and let Patrick witness what no human has seen before: the healing of a child through an ultrasonic dragon language. On the day Patrick dies, Marguerite lives. This is how he will be remembered: a linguist who trusted in the power of language, even the kind he would never understand, until the very end.

I stare at the memory scroll. This is impossible. I scan the words again.

An ultrasonic dragon language.

'This was written by a human, not a wyvern,' I say slowly.

Marquis takes the note from me and looks up with a frown. 'Dragons can't heal humans with the Koinamens. That's why Chumana had to give Atlas her blood to save him.'

'So the note's a lie,' I say.

'Whoever wrote it must know we were looking for the wyverns,' Serena says. 'Maybe Wyvernmire is trying to confuse us.'

'Or,' Atlas says quietly, 'what you suspected back in the tunnels is true.' He looks at me with determination in his eyes. 'There's something very different about the echolocation of the Hebridean Wyverns.'

'*What?*' says Marquis.

I turn to my cousin. 'Their echolocation sounds different.'

Marquis's jaw clenches. 'You've listened to the wyverns' Koinamens?'

I nod. 'And they're ... they're not like other dragons. What if this is what Hollingsworth wanted me to know?'

'You two and that fucking loquisonus machine.'

Marquis spits the words so hard that I recoil.

'You're obsessed, the pair of you. Was this your plan the whole time? Is that why you insisted we bring it with us?'

'I only listened once!'

'We would never have found the tunnels without the machine,' says Atlas.

'What happened to the Koinamens being sacred?' Marquis says, his eyes flashing. 'You promised Chumana you'd leave it alone, but now it's distracting you from what's important.'

'*This* is important!' Atlas says.

'It's not if it doesn't help us win the war!' Marquis roars.

A crow flees from a tree branch with a caw.

'Cousin,' I say calmly, 'what if their echolocation is *how* we win the war?'

Atlas's gaze softens. 'She's right,' he says, his eyes still on me. 'The wyverns *are* different.'

It's like a veil has been lifted from my mind, revealing, finally, the path we must take.

'Maybe wyvern echolocation can heal humans,' I say, standing up from the grave. 'Maybe it has hidden strengths.'

'Viv,' Marquis says in a warning tone.

'Strengths that can win the war!'

'We don't even know if what's written on that memory scroll is true,' Serena says.

'And if it is, and Hollingsworth knows about the wyvern echolocation, she would have just told you back in London,' says Gideon.

'Maybe she was going to,' I say breathlessly, 'except I was arrested.'

I turn to Atlas. He's looking at me in a thoughtful silence, his eyes willing me on. I flush beneath his gaze. He believes what I'm saying and that fills me with confidence. I brandish the memory scroll at them.

'Back during the egg-choosing ceremony, when the wyverns were echolocating with the eggs, I felt something like electricity in the air. I thought I was imagining it, but I wasn't. I felt it because their Koinamens is so strong that it can touch even human minds. This must be the information we've been looking for,' I say excitedly. 'Hollingsworth wants the wyverns to use their unique echolocation to help the rebels win the war . . .' I trail off.

Wait.

'So her grand idea,' Marquis says icily, 'is to exploit the wyverns' Koinamens to help the Coalition? The same Coalition that agreed never to touch dragon echolocation because of what it could be used for, what *Wyvernmire* wants to use it for?'

I feel myself deflating at Marquis's words.

'If humans were to learn of the existence of echolocation – of the loquisonus machines – they could use it to control and oppress dragons,' Marquis says through gritted teeth. He looks from me to Atlas. 'You both *know* this. So what the hell's got into you?'

I hang my head, feeling sick. He's right. Chumana told me to keep the Koinamens a secret for that very reason.

'If the wyverns agree to help us – which they won't – and we win the war, then the whole world will want to know *how*. The existence of dragon echolocation would become common knowledge,' Gideon says. 'Why would the leader of the Human-Dragon Coalition want that?'

'It must be more complicated than that,' Atlas says quietly. 'Hollingsworth must have a plan.'

I shake my head. 'Atlas, they're right, this can't be it. Hollingsworth would never exploit the dragons to win the war. That would make her as bad as Wyvernmire.'

'But what if, somehow,' Atlas says, 'she could protect the wyverns?'

'She can't,' Marquis says bluntly. 'So we stick to the plan, find Chumana.'

'What if, when they use their Koinamens, the rebels could ensure their safety?' Atlas stares at me, ignoring Marquis completely.

'That's impossible, Atlas.'

'How do you know?' he bursts. 'God dammit, Featherswallow, why don't you listen for once?'

A deathly silence fills the graveyard.

I sway inwardly. His words cut a wound and I fill it with fire.

'Why don't *you* listen?' I spit. 'Or is that not necessary for your secret mission?'

Atlas's face is stony. It's almost like he hasn't heard me, except I know from the tremble of his lip that he has.

'Secret mission?' Marquis repeats.

They all stare at Atlas as his face grows hot.

'The rebels gave you a mission,' I say slowly. 'One you've been keeping from us. I read it in your diary.'

A thunderous expression passes across his face. 'You *read* my *diary*?'

'Yes.'

I meet his eye, too angry to feel ashamed. A gust of rain-filled wind blows across the graveyard and the bushes around us rustle.

'The echolocation,' Atlas says. 'I think it's key.'

'You sound awfully sure,' Gideon says. 'So what do you know that we don't?'

'Is that what this extra mission has to do with?' Serena says. 'The Koinamens?'

'I . . . I can't tell you,' Atlas replies with a scowl. 'You've just got to trust me.'

'How can we trust you if you're keeping secrets?' I say.

His eyes fill with hurt. 'Viv . . .'

A long whistles sounds.

I feel a rush of dread.

'That wasn't a bird,' Marquis says in a low voice.

My eyes lift to the sky as my body screams at me to run, but I see no dragon. A figure erupts from the bushes and in his hand I see the flash of a knife. Gideon flinches.

'Don't run into the forest—' he shouts, but the rest of his sentence is drowned out as I dart instinctively towards the trees.

I hear the slap of boots behind me, Marquis's ragged breath at my shoulder.

'Viv, on your left!' Atlas screams from somewhere unseen.

My head snaps to the left just as a group of people storm out from behind a tree and I'm slammed to the ground.

Fifteen

I HEAR SERENA SCREAM AS MY face grazes the forest floor, before the person on top of me pulls me roughly to my feet. I blink dirt from my eyes. Marquis and Gideon are on their knees, their captors standing over them in brown clothes and odd-looking masks made of tree bark and leaves. Serena writhes in the arms of another, spitting insults.

Where is Atlas?

'Do what they tell you,' Gideon says, his eyes on the ground.

Ten people surround us, their faces hidden, poison pouches hanging around their necks.

'Search their packs,' someone barks.

A couple of them take our packs and begin rifling through the contents, pulling out medicine and spare socks and ammunition. One takes a step towards Gideon. The person is broad-shouldered with long, blond curls tied back with a piece of cloth. Their hands are small, fingernails bitten down to their beds.

'I don't believe my eyes.'

The voice behind the mask is low and gravely, but young. I hear a London accent, probably Third Class. Its owner removes their disguise and behind it is a boy our age. He has a round, bullish face and a sneer that means nothing good. His green eyes watch us hungrily.

'Gideon?' he says.

'It is!' one of them laughs. 'Thought they took you back to the mainland.'

The first grabs Gideon by the hair and stares into his face. 'Giddy, my boy. Is it really you?'

Gideon scowls, his arms still pinned to his sides by the person holding him.

'Hello, Freddie,' he mutters.

Freddie lets out an incredulous laugh. 'We just get luckier and luckier, don't we boys?'

The boys surrounding us let out loud jeers as they remove their masks.

'Gideon?' I say. 'Who is this?'

Freddie's head jerks towards me. He comes so close his nose almost touches mine and as I breathe in the hot, dirty smell of him, I see Marquis tense in my peripheral vision.

'Viv, right?' he says. 'Pretty. You can stay.'

Freddie moves to Serena. 'Nice accent,' he says with a coy smile. 'Could have listened to you all day. But what's a First Class girl like you doing so far from home?'

Serena doesn't flinch as she meets his gaze. 'We're here as part of the Human-Dragon Coalition.'

Freddie snorts. 'So that's what you call it. And what's your name?'

'Serena Serpentine,' she replies, lifting her chin.

Freddie's eyes linger on Serena's face as two more boys burst through the bushes.

'The other one took off,' the first mutters.

I blink back tears as I stare at my boots. Did Atlas really just abandon us? Freddie doesn't seem to care that he has escaped. His eyes narrow in Gideon's direction. 'But how can Giddy be a rebel, when he was taken from us months ago by order of the very Prime Minister the rebels are fighting? Turncoat, are you?'

I look at Gideon. 'This is the group you were with on Canna?'

Gideon nods miserably.

'*This* is the group that the boy who attacked Ruth was from?' says Marquis.

Freddie's eyes light up when they land on Marquis. 'Look at you!' he says. 'You're even prettier than the girls are.'

He looks around and is rewarded by a few laughs, then turns back and punches Marquis in the stomach. Marquis drops face first in the dirt, wheezing as he clutches his sides.

'Marquis!' I shout.

I fly at Freddie, escaping the grip of the boy holding me, and when my nails meet with the back of his neck I dig them in hard. He screams and twists arounds, catching me by the collar of my coat and flinging me away so that I land next to my cousin. Freddie breathes heavily as he stares at me in astonishment. His hand goes to his neck and when it comes away it's smeared in blood. A slow grin spreads across his face.

'Maybe they are rebels, after all.'

I reach over to Marquis and pull him into a seated position. Our eyes meet.

'Are you all right?'

He's gasping for breath, his lungs, still struggling from the poisonous gas, desperately drawing in air. But he manages to nod.

'Now,' Freddie says. 'Who's Ruth?'

'The one that offed my cousin Sinclair,' says another boy, pulling his camouflage away. He has a shaved head and small, sharp teeth. 'His frigid girlfriend. Perhaps I should pay her a visit. Show her a good time.'

'I'd like to see you try,' Marquis croaks.

'Shut up, Roy,' Freddie says. He turns to me. 'You'll have to excuse Roy. Living out here has caused him to lose his manners.'

'And you yours,' Serena spits.

His lip curls. 'We'll finish this back at camp,' he says. 'It's almost feeding time and that Bulgarian ain't caught anyone in weeks.'

The boys haul us to our feet.

'What do you want with us?' I say as they push us deeper into the forest.

'Speerspitzes, mostly,' Freddie replies. 'But we'll take what we can get.'

The boy pinning my arms to my sides grips them tighter, as if my question might allow me to escape again. I twist around and look him in the face. He's skinny with brown hair and huge, dark eyes.

'What's your name?' I ask.

He blushes and pushes me onwards. 'Pascal.'

'What's a Speerspitze, Pascal?'

We reach the edge of the forest and through the trees I see an old stone church. Its spire is blackened and falling apart. In the place of the door is a dirty curtain, blowing in the wind.

'The Speerspitze is the key to our hunt,' Freddie says. 'We had pretty much mitigated the threat of death by dragon until these Bulgarians came along. They hunt in packs, appearing out of nowhere so we don't even have time to use those.' He nods at the poison pouch around my neck. 'Since the start of spring, we've lost a third of our number. The Speerspitzes'll change that.'

'Jasper's group has barely lost anyone,' Serena says as we reach the church. 'So perhaps you're just slow.'

'It's because the Bulgarians prefer to hunt on this side of the island, smart arse,' says Roy. His fingers dig into Serena's shoulder. 'We must taste sweeter.'

'Ain't nothing sweet about you, Roy.'

Freddie and Roy snicker and when I catch Serena's eye I feel a sense of unease.

'So . . . what?' I say. 'You think you're going to hunt Bulgarian dragons?'

'It's about time the tables turned, ain't it?' Freddie says.

Freddie lifts the curtain in the church doorway but doesn't move from beneath it, so when Pascal pushes me through we brush against each other. I'm close enough to see the peeling skin on Freddie's dry lips, and then I notice the dragon scales beneath the string of his poison pouch. They're sewn together in a long strip and wound around his neck so that he looks like he's slowly turning into a reptile. He catches me looking and leans forward.

'The Bolgoriths like to go for the throat.'

The church is bare and cold, but light filters in through the stained-glass windows, casting the pews in a purple glow. The blue sky peers in through a hole burned in the ceiling. Blankets and old mattresses litter the space and at the back are long tables covered in an assortment of scavenged weapons: knives, a few guns and several fire pokers. There's a pungent, overpowering smell in the air. Above the old church organ, tens of pheasants and rabbits have been strung up, a few feathers occasionally floating down. I feel my face pale. Surely they must attract dragons?

More boys, of various ages, look down at us from the balconies, all wearing the same hostile look. Pascal lets me go. I sit down on one of the pews next to Serena. There's a busyness to the boys, a feeling of movement that we've just interrupted. Through the wooden balcony railings I see food being sorted and packed. They're preparing for something.

'Lads,' Freddie calls out. 'I've brought you something none of us have seen in a while. Girls!'

Cheers and laughter ring out, echoing through the church. I see a smaller boy sitting on the balcony, his legs swinging down and his face smeared with jam, watching us with a grin.

Freddie jumps up on to one of the pews. 'Here we have the sophisticated Serena,' he says with a mock bow, 'and Viv, a true vixen.' His eyes flash. 'And this maiden here is Marquis.'

Marquis glares at Freddie as the air rings with more whoops and jeers.

'And of course, our very own snivelling, spineless sissy, Gideon, still as terrified of dragons as he always was. Who remembers him pissing himself?'

The boys stamp their feet as Gideon hangs his head, dust pouring down from the rafters into his hair.

'Give it a rest, Freddie,' says a familiar voice.

I frown as a tall boy emerges from behind the altar.

'Jasper?'

Jasper skulks towards us, hands in his pockets. He's wearing more clothes than when I last saw him, but his feet are still bare.

'What are you doing here?'

He glances at the boy next to him, also from his camp. I remember that his name is Henry.

'Allying,' Jasper replies. 'Wyvernmire's Guardians destroyed our camp.'

My face falls as Marquis swears. 'Was anyone hurt?'

'No,' Jasper says. 'The rest of the group is sheltering not far from here.'

'You know these lot, Jasper?' Freddie asks.

'I wish I didn't.' Jasper glowers.

'There's a war on, Jasper,' Serena says. 'Wyvernmire would have come for your camp with or without us.'

'The Bulgarians just murdered dozens of rebel dragons a few miles from here,' I say. 'You should all be hiding.'

'We won't need to hide when we have the Speerspitzes,' Freddie says.

'What,' I ask again, 'are Speerspitzes?'

'Guns that kill dragons!' the small boy on the balcony shouts.

Freddie sees our confusion. 'You really ain't heard of them?'

I glance at the others, then shake my head.

'Bulgarian Bolgoriths, fire-breathing planes and Speerspitzes,' he says. 'Wyvernmire has the full set.'

'Imported from Germany,' Pascal says in a gentle voice, 'and named after a snake, a lancehead.'

'Spearhead,' Gideon says. 'The German translates to *spearhead*.'

'Whatever,' Pascal says. 'She's using them against her enemy dragons. They're being set up right now, along the coast.'

'The *Bolgoriths* are using them,' I correct him. 'They're in control of Wyvernmire and her government now. And if you don't let us go, they'll kill the rebels and seize the whole of the United Kingdom.'

'How do you reckon you'll be getting your hands on these guns?' Marquis snorts.

'There's a stash hidden behind the sand dunes near our camp,' Jasper says.

'Have any of you ever been trained to shoot a dragon from the sky?' I say coldly. 'The Bolgoriths are stronger than British dragons. That's why the poison pouches don't kill them. Even with a hundred Speerspitzes, they'll still be the predator and you the prey.' I glare at Jasper. 'Krasimir is like a rabid dog. If you don't give up on this ridiculous idea, you'll have children's blood on your hands. Philippa's blood.'

His expression darkens.

'Go to Sanday,' I say. 'Beg Ruth to take you in. You'll be safe there.'

'And risk getting shot by a crossbow?' Freddie says.

'Better than getting mauled by a dragon, you great prat.'

In one swift movement, Roy grabs Marquis by the throat. I jump from my seat as they stand nose to nose, Roy's shirt caught in Marquis's fist.

'Go on, then,' Marquis snarls. 'Let's see what you've got.'

I take a step towards Roy and a hand grabs my sleeve.

'Don't,' Gideon warns me.

Roy presses his face up against Marquis's, his eyes bulging.

'Not this one, Roy,' Freddie says slowly.

Roy's lip curls and for a minute I think he isn't going to listen. But then he lets Marquis go. Neither boy lowers his eyes.

'Send a group for the Speerspitzes in the dunes, if you must,' I say quietly as I sit back down. 'And then go to Sanday. Ruth has the best view of the island. You'll be able to shoot whatever you want from there.'

A shadow falls across the pews as a dragon flies over the church. Everyone tenses. When the light bursts back in, we wait in silence to be sure it isn't about to return.

'That's if you make it that far,' Marquis mutters.

'Why should we let you go?' Freddie says.

I lean forward, resting my elbows on my knees. 'You heard us arguing in the graveyard, didn't you? We're part of a rebel military operation against the Bolgoriths, and if you don't let us get on with it, I promise you, not all the Speerspitzes in the world will save you.'

Freddie stares at me, then nods.

'Where will you go?' Jasper asks.

'To find Chumana.'

And Atlas, I add silently. He's not in the fields around the church and when we traipse back through the forest, there's nothing among the trees but a salty breeze.

'I reckon they're all barking mad,' Marquis says, rubbing the spot where Freddie punched him.

'That Roy certainly is,' Serena mutters. 'Do you think they'll go to Sanday?'

'Probably. Jasper lost his pig-headed nerve when Viv mentioned Philippa,' Marquis replies. 'Where the hell is Atlas?'

I bite my lip. If Atlas managed to escape Freddie's group, then why didn't he wait for us nearby? I think back to our argument and feel a sinking sense of dread. What if he's right and the wyvern echolocation *is* the key to winning the war?

We walk for hours, until the sun is high in the sky and we can see the sea. Below us is Canna House and then the bay with the footpath that leads to Wyvernmire's camp. A huge tent has been erected on the beach, so tall that the top of it is higher than the cliffs.

'Get down,' Marquis says, pulling me into the grass as a dragon flies overhead.

We crouch in the purple heather as more of them soar over the beach and back again. Across the fields, at the same height we're currently at, is the top of Compass Hill. I stare out to sea. Big clouds of black smoke are rising off Rùm.

No.

Horror pricks my skin.

The smoke is further back, coming not from Rùm but from somewhere else.

'Eigg,' I say. 'The Bolgoriths have attacked Eigg.'

Sixteen

I TAKE SMALL, PANICKED BREATHS AS I think of Ursa, of Dr Seymour and her baby, of Sophie and Karim. We only spent a few days down in the tunnels, yet somehow, the fighting has already started.

And the people we love most are in the middle of it.

'We need a boat, or a dragon,' I say.

Hot panic courses through my body. When was the attack? Who has been killed? I imagine the shadow of a Bulgarian dragon cast over a fleeing Ursa and swallow a sob. Every second standing here is a second wasted.

'Look,' Serena says.

A group of dragons is flying across the water towards Canna. They attempt to avoid Wyvernmire's camp by keeping close to Sanday, but they've already been spotted. Bulgarian dragons rise up to meet them.

'I recognise that one,' Marquis says. 'It's Soresten.'

'Soresten? From Bletchley?' I reply.

He nods. We watch as the Bulgarian Bolgoriths advance towards the incoming dragons. Before they even reach them, a burst of flame comes from Soresten. There's a sound like metal tearing as the dragons clash in the air.

'Right,' Serena breathes. 'It seems the next battle is now.'

'Let's go,' Marquis says. 'If Chumana is with those rebels then she can fly us to Eigg. We'll do what we can to help the Coalition and find out what Hollingsworth's back-up plan is.'

I nod, refusing to consider the possibility that there is no back-up plan. All that matters to me now is seeing Ursa unharmed. We run for Compass Hill, tearing across the fields and past the low stone wall that leads to Jasper's empty camp. We reach the top drenched in sweat and crawl through the grass on our stomachs. Across the water, Soresten is still fighting. We peer over the cliff's edge at Wyvernmire's camp. The tide is out, making it even bigger. Hundreds of dragons stand on the black sand, white Guardians of Peace milling between them. They're setting up what look like small cannons along the shore, pointing the heavy barrels skywards.

Speerspitzes.

The guns are slimmer than I imagined but the weight of them sinks deep gouges into the sand. Hostile screams carry in from the waves as the survivors of Soresten's group begin to retreat and the Bulgarian dragons circle back, not even bothering to follow them.

'Look at Wyvernmire's tent,' Gideon says quietly.

My eyes skim over the Guardian helmets and scaly dragon bodies, just in time to see a figure slip into the back of the tent.

Atlas.

I feel the pit of my stomach drop.

'What's he doing?'

'God knows,' Serena says, rolling her eyes.

Marquis snorts.

The minutes pass torturously slowly as we wait for Atlas to emerge from the tent. I stare at the fabric billowing in the breeze, at the dragons on the other side, and pray that he's alone in there. Maybe Wyvernmire has been imprisoned somewhere else. Maybe she's dead.

'The secret mission I read about in his diary,' I say, my cheeks warming at the admission. 'Are we just going to pretend it doesn't exist?'

I feel Marquis turn towards me, but keep my eyes on the tent.

'I think he's a fool to be chasing after that ridiculous echolocation theory,' he says. 'But it *is* possible that the Coalition entrusted him with something else, and why punish him for that? Things have to be classified during a war, that's just the way it is.'

I bite my lip. Then – movement.

Atlas slips out of the tent, his hands full of paperwork. He stuffs it into his jacket pockets.

'*That's* what he went in for?' Serena says.

Atlas looks up, scans the clifftops, stops. He's seen us. As our eyes meet, an agonised screech comes from the beach. Atlas ducks for cover, but none of the dragons or Guardians on the sand seem to take notice. The screech sounds again.

'It sounds like a tortured animal,' I whisper.

Marquis points across to the other side of the beach. 'How much do you want to bet it's coming from inside that giant tent?'

The tent is surrounded by armed Guardians.

'What do you think's in there?' Gideon says. 'A dragon prisoner?'

We stare at it in horrified silence.

'What if,' Serena says quietly, 'it's a wyvern?'

My skin crawls. 'We have to go and look.'

'And do what?' Marquis says.

'I don't know,' I reply impatiently. 'But what if it's Cindra? Aberdine? Aodahn?'

Marquis sinks back into the grass. 'Are you proposing we free an imprisoned dragon from right under the enemy's nose?'

'I've done it before, haven't I?'

He rolls his eyes, then points to the beach. 'Looks like he's as mad as you are.'

Atlas is running along the edge of the beach towards the big tent, zigzagging between the cliff faces that jut out across the sand. I bite back a smile.

'He's going to get caught,' Serena breathes.

We watch as he almost runs into the path of a Guardian, diving behind another army tent just as the Guardian turns around.

'Come on,' I say.

We slip down the side of a cliff on the opposite end of the beach. Gorse and thorns catch at my trousers as I keep close to the cliff face and out of view of the camp. I spot a crowd of people over on Sanday.

Jasper actually listened to me.

We creep across the sand to where Atlas is waiting, crouched among the rockpools. Our eyes meet.

'Well, that was a bright idea,' I snap. 'What on earth did you go into Wyvernmire's tent for? And why did you go off without us?'

'Because there's no time to waste.' He pulls the papers out of his pocket and hands two sheets to me. The first is a newspaper article, dated six days ago.

ESPIONAGE UNVEILED:
CHANCELLOR HOLLINGSWORTH A REBEL ON THE RUN

My breath catches in my throat.

'She's been found out,' Marquis croaks.

'But not arrested,' Atlas says quickly.

I glance at the second document, which sports a government stamp.

17th April, 1924

Hebridean Wyverns are rarely seen on Canna but their presence has been confirmed by the Royal Observatory of Dragons and Dragonlings. They have no dealings with other species and are not well-liked by Canna's dragons, on account of their fickle, snobbish nature. The Hebridean Wyverns speak only one language: their own unrecorded tongue. Researchers claim that even this may be redundant as large groups are able to understand each other simply, from, the source claims, 'instinctive mannerisms which act as a sort of sign language'.

– Information procured through enhanced interrogation techniques from the source Arabesqua, a Sand Dragon detained by the D D A D, whose offspring is currently a ward of Dr Arthur Burke.

'Do you think Wyvernmire always knew the rebels were searching for the wyverns?' I ask hoarsely. 'Do you think she knows why?'

'I doubt it,' Atlas says.

'Unless . . .' says Marquis.

He doesn't need to finish his sentence.

My eyes fall on the words *enhanced interrogation techniques*. Unless Hollingsworth has been arrested since the newspaper article was published, and had the information tortured out of her. I feel a wave of nausea as I imagine the Chancellor at Highfall, her fur coat and rings replaced by undignified prison clothes, cowering as Guardians force her to give up rebel plans, identities, locations.

I hand the papers back to Atlas. 'We can't win,' I hear myself say in a small voice. 'Not if the Bolgoriths have gained control of the rebel headquarters. Not if there's no other plan but the wyverns—'

He turns to me abruptly, grabbing me by the shoulders, and plants a kiss on my mouth. Marquis lets out a disgusted groan. Atlas smells of peppermint. I push him away.

'What are you doing?' I mutter impatiently. 'Didn't you say I never listen? Didn't you—'

'If we haven't lost then we can still win, Featherswallow,' Atlas says with a wink. 'Did you see Soresten in the sky earlier?

If he's flying free, then Eigg hasn't fallen yet. This isn't over.'

I think of Ursa and feel a flicker of hope. 'We go to Eigg, then. But first, we need to make sure the Guardians aren't torturing a wyvern inside that tent.'

Atlas nods. 'Except we can't just walk in there.'

'Yes, we can,' Serena says.

We look at her. She leans one arm on the cliff face and points at the entrance to the tent. Ralph is standing guard, looking smug.

'Featherswallow,' Serena says sharply. 'Ralph wants you and your loquisonus machine. So you're going to walk out there and let him think he can have both.'

'No!' Atlas and Marquis exclaim together.

'Yes,' I say, nodding. 'I'll distract him so you can get into the tent.'

'And then what?' Marquis says. 'How the bloody hell will we get you back again?'

Another loud roar comes from inside the tent.

'The only way to control a dragon is to insert a detonator under its skin,' I say. 'So you cut it out, like I did last year with Chumana, and whichever dragon is in there will burst from that tent so fast that the whole camp will go up in flames. I'll run and then we'll escape to Eigg.'

'That's a stupid idea,' Marquis snaps.

Serena rolls her eyes. 'No more stupid than hanging around here talking about it.'

'Viv is my cousin, Serena! And while you might not give a damn what happens to her, I can't—'

'We've all got skin in the game, Marquis,' Serena spits.

'Did you know Wyvernmire made sure my parents died by dragonfire? She forced an imprisoned rebel dragon to set our estate alight, just to add insult to injury.'

Marquis falls silent, his cheeks burning as she turns her icy stare to me.

'I'm sure cousin Vivvy will be *fine*.'

Atlas's hand comes down on my wrist. 'You make a good rebel, Featherswallow, but there's a fine line between being good and being reckless.'

'Yet another insult, King. I'm beginning to think you don't like me.' I meet his gaze. 'I'm doing it. And you're not going to stop me.'

He glares back at me, his mouth twitching.

'It's the best idea we have, Atlas,' Gideon says.

Marquis swears and Atlas turns back to the beach, but his hand is still on mine.

'Fine, but there's no point all of us getting caught. I'll sneak into the tent once Viv has distracted Ralph. You three –' Atlas glances at Marquis, Serena and Gideon – 'should go and find Soresten or Chumana, so we can fly to Eigg as soon as we've released the dragon in the tent.'

'You agree, then?' I say. 'That there *must* be a back-up plan? That Hollingsworth's intention was never to exploit the wyvern echolocation?'

'Whatever her plan was, all that matters now is that the rebels are ready for the next battle. Have you seen how many Bulgarian dragons are on the beach? If we can't pull out all the stops, things are going to get bad.' He grimaces and points to another newspaper sticking out of his pocket.

'The Bolgoriths have taken London. A portion of the French dragon army came to the rebels' aid in the battle for the city, but we lost. And Ignacia's troops have retreated. More than half of Britannia's dragon population is in hiding.'

I reel like I've been slapped.

'Half?' Marquis echoes.

'Fancy being the Dragon Queen and failing to fight for your own country,' Gideon says. 'If she joined the rebels, we might stand a chance.'

'The wyverns would never have been able to help us, then,' I say. 'There aren't enough of them, not if they can't use their . . .'

I trail off as Atlas's eyes dart to mine. I see the truth staring back at me and my heart sinks. He still believes the answer has something to do with echolocation. He's still going to try and convince me. That's why he's sending the others away.

'Go,' I tell Marquis.

He nods, then pulls my head towards him and plants a kiss on my hair.

'Don't get caught, cousin,' he says. He glances at Atlas. 'And don't die this time, King.'

Atlas grins. 'I wouldn't dream of it.'

Serena winks at me and the three of them climb back up the cliff and disappear across the top. I return my gaze to Ralph, who is picking at his nails in front of the tent.

'I should go.'

'Wait,' Atlas says.

I turn to look at him.

'I'm sorry about what I said in the graveyard. And for

being so . . . distant.'

'You mean cold,' I say.

'Distracted,' Atlas says.

'Uninterested,' I correct. 'Inattentive, agitated, completely unlike yourself.'

'Since we left Bletchley, I've been questioning everything,' Atlas says. 'My role in this war, on this island, in this life.'

'This is about the priesthood, isn't it?'

Atlas hesitates, his brown eyes searching mine. 'Yes.'

'Well, go on, King,' I say, folding my arms. 'I'm listening.'

'You know I've always thought that priesthood is my vocation. The thing I'm called to?'

I nod.

'Well, sometimes I wonder if I'm drawn to it so much because it's a way of hiding away – with my books and my prayers – and of loving quietly. Priests say Mass, counsel people, pray for them. They get to be good without necessarily being called to anything dangerous, like, say, soldiers are. Being sent to Bletchley Park ripped me away from that quietness, forced me into the rebellion in a new way, no longer on the sidelines but in the middle of the battle.' He swallows. 'And then I met you. And no amount of prayer could help me work out what that meant. Now, I can't imagine going back to seminarian school, or staying a rebel soldier.'

'No?' I breathe.

'No,' he replies. 'Every future I imagine, Viv, is with you.'

We're still kneeling among the rockpools when he kisses me. I sink against the cliff face as he leans in, my fists full of sand. His hands cup either side of my face and his mouth trails fiery kisses from my lips to my neck and back again. He tastes of salt and tobacco.

'*Vocare*,' I whisper.

'Hmm?' Atlas murmurs against my mouth.

'Vocation is from the Latin *vocare*. And *vocare* doesn't just mean *calling*, Atlas. It means to *designate*. To *choose*.'

He nods. 'It means I can decide. I realised that down in the tunnels. Aodahn's egg was his because he *chose* it, and God wants me to choose my vocation. It's—'

A spine-tingling roar erupts from the tent. We jump apart.

'I have to go,' I say, scrambling to my feet. I brush the sand from my trousers. 'When you cut out the detonator, whatever you do, do not drop it.'

Atlas rubs his rosy face and gives me a hurried nod. I take one more look at him, at his glistening lips and the swallow on his arm, then step out on to the sand. Ralph drops his helmet when he sees me. He blinks and scans the beach.

'I'm alone,' I say.

His eyes narrow suspiciously. 'What are you doing here?'

'The rebels have lost,' I reply. 'Wyvernmire has seized London and soon the Bulgarian dragons will discard her to take the rest of the country, just like you said they would. So I'm here to make the best of the situation. To help you listen to Goranov using the loquisonus machine, in exchange for a place in the new world. I'd rather see my family enslaved than dead.'

A smile spreads across Ralph's lips. 'You said echolocation was untranslatable.'

'It is. But you don't always need to translate a language to understand it. Sometimes, you just need a few lessons from the source. And I happen to be friends with a Bulgarian dragon.'

Ralph's smirk grows wider. 'Where's the machine?'

'I've hidden it,' I reply. 'I'll go and get it, if you promise to let me go once you have the information you need.'

Guardian voices sound from the other side of the tent. Ralph pulls the flap of the tent open for me. 'Inside, quickly.'

I hesitate. This wasn't part of the plan, but I don't dare glance back at where Atlas is hiding. Instead, I step inside. The light is disorienting, extending in great, blinding beams from giant, battery-powered torches that only a ship could have brought in. Ralph follows me in as my eyes adjust. The tent's sides rise up to a singular point, like a teepee or a circus tent, and thick, metal chains dangle down from the top.

I blink, trying to comprehend what I'm seeing. Ralph steps in behind me and I feel his hand land assuredly on the small of my back. The hairs on my neck rise as his lips brush against my ear.

'Say hello to your friend.'

I sway, nausea rising in my stomach.

Caught in the chains, her wings stretched out like a crucifixion, is Chumana.

THE RADIO TIMES
THE OFFICIAL ORGAN OF THE B.B.C.
EVERY FRIDAY

Headlines:

WYVERNMIRE'S CONSCRIPTION DRAFT NOW IN EFFECT : 300,000 MEN EXPECTED

FRANCE AND ITALY DECLARE WAR ON BULGARIA

REBEL RAID ON ACADEMY FOR DRACONIC LINGUISTICS UNCOVERS SEVENTY 'MISSING' DRAGONLINGS

DEBUTANTE HYACINTH GOLDWING ARRESTED FOR OPERATING CLANDESTINE SCHOOL FOR DRAGON TONGUES

SURRENDER OF HUMAN-DRAGON COALITION IS 'IMMINENT', CLAIMS DEPUTY PRIME MINISTER RAVENSLOE

COMMUNISTS URGE MUNITIONS WORKERS TO STRIKE, DECLARING 'WORKERS HOLD THE KEY TO BRITANNIA'S SURVIVAL'

ESPIONAGE UNVEILED: CHANCELLOR HOLLINGSWORTH A REBEL ON THE RUN

Seventeen

THE TENT IS SILENT EXCEPT FOR the sound of the waves and my own sobs. I stare up at Chumana, bound to the iron structure of the tent, her tail dangling lifelessly behind her. Blood drips from her face, a steady plink that sets my teeth on edge.

'Is she dead?' I whisper.

'Not yet,' Ralph replies.

His hand rises to settle on the back of my neck. He squeezes. 'No more negotiating,' he says softly. 'Here's how this is going to go. I will tell the Prime Minister that I arrested you trying to break into this tent. She'll hold you prisoner, to use as a bargaining chip for the rebels' immediate surrender, because she's still too oblivious to realise that the Bulgarians will have disposed of her in a few days' time. I'll come to you tonight and take you to Goranov and his brother. I want to know what they are saying to each other – and if what he has promised me is true.'

I breathe through my tears, staring at the wooden platform up by Chumana's head. It's suspended by more chains and accessed by a portable stairlift.

'Why aren't you with Goranov now?' I say shakily.

'He prefers to fly without me,' Ralph replies, a hint of bitterness in his voice. 'When we reach him, you're to stay hidden with the machine. If you can find out what I want to know, I'll make sure he sees your value when Britannia falls to the Bolgoriths. Understand?'

I nod. 'What happened on Eigg?'

'The Prime Minister attacked, but the rebels defended it well. Most escaped on dragonback. She's furious.'

Thank goodness.

'Not as furious as she was when she found out the Chancellor is an undercover rebel.' He looks at me. 'Of course, she's guessed that's who you were working for.'

'Did a rebel betray her? I mean Hollingsworth.'

'A dragon,' Ralph nods. 'In exchange for her dragonlings' lives.'

I close my eyes, thinking of the newspaper report Atlas found. When I open them, I see a tiny pulse in Chumana's throat. Atlas won't be able to free her from those chains and if I set one foot out of line, Wyvernmire will have her killed. My only way out of this is to give Ralph what he wants. I feel the barrel of his gun between my shoulder blades.

'On your knees, Featherswallow.'

I sink to the ground.

Shouts sound from outside. Ralph swears and we both go

still, listening. Then I hear the unmistakeable whoosh of flame.

'Fuck!' Ralph cries.

He seizes the collar of my coat and pulls me to my feet, then presses his nose to mine.

'Stay here,' he snarls, a fleck of saliva landing on my face. 'Don't try to escape – you'll only be burned alive.'

He dips out of the tent and I wipe my cheek with my sleeve, listening as someone starts to scream. My feet carry me to the stairlift as gunshots sound outside. It creaks as I climb, until the sound is drowned out by the sudden boom of a cannon. The Speerspitzes.

My breath catches in my throat as I reach Chumana's head. It hangs down on to her chest, blood dripping from a deep gash below her eye. I see the white glint of bone. I reach out, my arms wide, and gently cradle her hot, spiked face in my arms.

'Chumana,' I whisper. 'It's me. It's Viv.'

She lets out a long, slow breath.

'How long have you been here?'

'Three days,' she replies, her voice weak. 'You must leave.'

A Speerspitze fires again.

'I'm not going anywhere without you,' I reply.

'Then you are a fool.'

A laugh bursts from my throat, turning into more sobs.

Chumana's head moves slightly so that one of her amber eyes is looking into mine.

'Wyvernmire still wants you and that loquisonus machine,' she growls. 'She hasn't been able to get your location out of me, so now she leaves me here in the hope you will be drawn to the bait. And you have walked straight into her trap, you stupid, stupid child.'

I shake my head, the scales of her face burning hot through the sleeves of my coat. Three are missing from above her eye, leaving gaping, bloody craters. I know who's responsible. Back when he worked in Germany, Ralph learned how to slice off a dragon's scales one by one.

'I didn't know you were here. But I'm going to get you out.'

I stare up at the chains holding Chumana, wishing it was just a question of cutting out a detonator.

'Viv?'

Atlas's voice calls out from below.

'I'm up here.'

Atlas stares up, shielding his eyes from the light, and I see his expression turn to one of horror as he realises what he's looking at.

'We need the keys,' I call down to him. 'Or some tools.'

But he's already crashing up the stairs behind me. 'How did they get you in here, Chumana?'

'Bulgarian dragons,' Chumana mutters weakly. 'They built the tent around me.'

I turn to him, feeling the terror seep into my bones. 'What are we going to do?' I say, my voice barely a whisper.

'You must leave!' Chumana roars.

Atlas stares at me with wide, shining eyes. I have no idea what he's thinking.

'The rebels are attacking,' he says. 'What if we—'

A slicing sound fills the tent, so loud that I jump, causing the stairlift to sway. Atlas grabs me as I let go of Chumana and we cling to each other, swinging mid-air. There's a second slash, the sound of fabric ripping, and I scream as a dragon's open jaws bite through the tent at our backs. We lurch against the side of the stairlift and I close my eyes, waiting for the hot sting of teeth on my skin. But it doesn't come. An eye is staring through the hole in the tent. It disappears and is replaced by a red snout. The face of a Bulgarian dragon pushes through the gap and I feel the fear chase the breath from my body and Atlas's arms tighten around me. The dragon snarls and I gasp in recognition.

'Daria?'

The sound of battle – roaring and clashing and the gnashing of teeth – rings outside.

'This contraption is about to come down,' Daria growls. 'Get out.'

I shake my head. 'I'm not leaving her, she's my—'

'I know who she is, human girl!' Daria growls.

Human girl.

But only Chumana calls me that.

'Do you have a knife?' I gasp at Atlas.

He pulls one from his pocket and hands it to me.

'Keep me steady,' I tell him.

I turn to Chumana and reach over the top of her head. The stairlift sways again and Atlas's hands come down on my waist, holding me still. My fingers search the back of her neck, where the scales were removed many years ago. I find the tough ridge of an old scar and, beneath it, a fresh cut.

'I'm sorry, Chumana,' I whisper to her as I slip the blade

into the wound until it touches metal.

I angle the knife and push upwards, my other hand catching the bloody metal box. She doesn't even growl.

Ralph bursts into the tent. 'Intruders!' he screams. 'Rebel Number One has breached the prison!'

I duck as hot flames scorch the top of my hair. Ralph dives and the fire hits the front of the tent instead, engulfing it hungrily. I press the detonator to my chest and cling to Atlas as we stumble down the stairs, shying away from the heat devouring the fabric around us. Daria has disappeared and Chumana is still hanging from her chains. The dragonfire spreads across the tent, reaching up into the canopy and closing in on Chumana. I carry the detonator to the far side of the tent and gently place it in the sand. Through the smoke I see Ralph crawl outside.

'Over there,' I gasp at Atlas, pulling him towards the gap before we lose sight of it.

Daria crashes into the tent. Metal shatters and chain links fall as her tail collides with Chumana, knocking her sideways with a metallic screech. For a second she is suspended by one wing, but then she drops to the ground with a boom that I feel beneath my feet. Atlas pulls me out on to the beach. A Bulgarian dragon lies across the sand, its belly slashed open, purple entrails spilling out. We duck behind the body as bullets spray. The sky is full of dragons, so many that the beach is cast into dark shadow. It's impossible to tell rebel from Bolgorith.

'Towards the cliff!' Atlas cries.

Guardians charge at us as we stumble back across the

rockpools. I drop into a crouch as a Bulgarian dragon swoops down on to our path, swinging its head in our direction. 'Surrender to Krasimir,' it snarls at me, 'and he may show mercy to your comrades.'

I recoil. Atlas steps out in front of me and suddenly, a huge, tawny body descends on us, its talons reaching for the Bolgorith's face. It screams as a claw pierces its eye and its body is lifted from the ground, suspended for a few seconds before slamming back heavily on to the sand. It lets out a lethal screech and launches itself into the air in retaliation, hot blood droplets raining down. Another Bolgorith joins it in its attack and suddenly the beach opens up, a clear path stretching out in front of us, the pale cliff a beacon in the salty smog. We're running, our feet dragging in the sand, smoke filling our throats as we reach the cliff path. I turn my head to Atlas as I grasp at the long grass to pull myself up the steep slope.

'Chumana, did she—'

'That's Soresten!' Atlas cries. 'And his sister, Addax.'

The tawny dragon that attacked the Bulgarian has been joined by another, with the same sandy colouring and zigzag markings.

The Bletchley dragons are back.

The prison tent erupts from the ground like a cork from a bottle and Chumana bursts from its trappings, broken chains trailing from her wings. She soars upwards, higher than I can see, then streams back down like a shooting star, a slash of ruby against the grey sky. When she opens her mouth, twenty Guardians are engulfed in flames. Daria appears at her side, smaller and slimmer but the same triumphant shade of pink.

'Why did she release Chumana?' Atlas shouts.

I shake my head. I have no idea why this Bulgarian Bolgorith has defied orders and released a prisoner. My foot misses a dip in the ground and my ankle twists painfully, but Atlas drags me forward, away from the battle.

'Listen!' I shout at him.

We stop near the top of the hill, gasping for breath.

'Do you hear that?' I say.

Atlas's eyes widen. It's the sound of hooves. Horses appear on the path behind us, galloping up the hill at twice our speed with Guardians on their backs. We run, reaching the top, but Atlas's hand is ripped from mine. I turn as the silver flash of a baton knocks him to the ground and trip, my nose slamming into the dirt. A horse screams, rearing as dragons circle above us. I roll over and stare up into the helmet of a Guardian, looking down at me from his horse with his baton raised high. Atlas crawls towards me, blood pouring down the back of his neck on to his jacket, and I grab his arm tightly.

We drag ourselves backwards on our elbows, fingers deep in the mud as the Guardian and his horse walk calmly beside us. He lifts his helmet.

Ralph.

'No new world for you, little Swallow,' he spits.

'You think your partnership with Goranov is going to give you a future,' I shout, 'but to him you're nothing but a live source of fireblod.'

Ralph's face twists in anger.

'You're disposable to him, just like you are to your aunt.

Wyvernmire didn't want you in the glasshouse and Goranov won't even let you fly with him That's why you've sided with the Bulgarian dragons. Because you're desperate to feel needed.'

The other Guardians are holding back, looking to Ralph for direction as he sneers down from his horse. 'And what about you, *recruit*? You've sold yourself to the highest bidder, to whoever will let you play at being a *Draconic translator.*' He laughs. 'You jumped at the chance to use that loquisonus machine. You're just as desperate as I am.'

Did I not feel a prick of excitement when I laid eyes on the machine after I thought they'd all been destroyed? Did I not sit smugly in Hollingsworth's office, proud to be using my languages to help the rebel cause? Did I not waste time trying to translate an untranslatable language, because I couldn't bear to fail?

'You're right. I've built my life around translation, thinking languages were the answer to all my problems. And now, without them, I don't even know who I am. It's like being on a boat you thought could never sink, except it's already wrecked. I can't save the rebels. I can't save myself.' I stare up into Ralph's bloodshot eyes as smoke wafts around us and the air fills with more screeches. 'But being Goranov's pet won't save you, either.'

Atlas pulls me closer to the cliff edge as Ralph jumps off his horse, the glint of his baton suddenly more menacing than any dragon in the sky. We crawl backwards through the grass and as one of my hands find Atlas's, the other meets with thin air.

I look at him, my eyes shining, and he nods.

Ralph points the baton in my direction. A smile spreads across his face. As the other Guardians close in, he moves the baton to his other hand and raises it over Atlas's head instead.

'I'll kill him this time,' he whispers.

I roll sideways, Atlas's jacket tight in my fist. His body rolls with mine, crushing me momentarily so that stones and tree roots dig into my back, and then suddenly they're gone.

I bury my face into his neck as we plunge, tangled together like two warring dragons, into the sea.

Eighteen

MY BONES SCREAM. ICY COLD BURNS my skin and my mouth fills with saltwater. I take an instinctive breath and the water floods my lungs. My eyes fly open in panic.

Atlas is gone.

The sea is a dark blue-grey. It propels me forward with a gigantic force and I raise my hands in front of my face just as it flings me against a solid shape. My cheek grazes the side of the rock but I feel no pain. I choke, the pressure in my head so strong that my eyes feel like they might burst from their sockets. The swirl gathers me again, the wool of my coat unravelling around me in a pale line, like the trail of a fish. I shake the heavy material from my shoulders and swim upwards, kicking my aching legs with the last energy I can muster. My lungs burn, threatening to explode, and my head breaks the surface just as dots begin to dance before my eyes. I gasp, inhaling cold air, as a wave crashes me back towards the cliff face.

The evening sky is on fire.

I flail, turning my body to face the cliff. It towers above the water, its sprawling smoothness unforgiving, its grey rock polished flat by centuries of waves. There's nothing to hold on to, no way of pulling myself out of the water.

I'm going to drown.

I stare out at the white current coming towards me.

'Atlas! Where are you?' I scream.

I take another breath as the waves hit, sending me spinning, then burst out of the water as they roll over my head. I see a small, dark circle ahead.

The waves pull back, taking Atlas with them, before pushing him towards me and sending us both under the foamy swirl again. When we surface, he grabs me by the arms. I want to cling to him but that could kill us both. The cold is like a blade on my skin.

'Where—' I gasp, but I can't finish my sentence.

I stare out at the churning sea.

'There,' Atlas chokes.

He's pointing to the columns of basalt rock that jut out from the cliff face, forming narrow ledges too high for us to reach. But the waves push us up against the cliffs, hoisting us higher, and we let them toss us until Atlas is close enough. As we're pushed flat against the grey surface he stretches his body out of the water, reaching up to a ledge. I draw in a breath as the waves steal me away.

They pull me towards the deep but I force myself to stay still, knowing that they'll bring me back again in a dance of rise and fall. When they spit me out I set my eyes on Atlas, who has pulled himself up on to the ledge. I reach him and flail for his hand, my legs treading nothing. He catches me by my wrists and pulls me upwards. My shoulders pop in protest, the muscles in my sides pulling painfully as I hang in the void. Then he grabs the back of my jumper and lifts me, scraping my stomach against the jagged rock.

I don't dare move, lying still with my face against Atlas's leg as we both catch our breath, the lower half of my body still hanging over the edge. The ledge, barely wider than a baby's cradle, can't hold us both. I lift a leg to grip the side and Atlas's hand comes around the top of my thigh, holding it there. I stare at the swirling depths below. The air is sharp and smoky, stinging the salty cuts that smart beneath the gashes in my trousers. Atlas's teeth chatter.

I stare at him, still crouching with his hair plastered to his forehead and the soggy papers stolen from the tent sticking out of his pockets. Watery blood drips from the back of his neck and when he turns his head I spot the wound made by Ralph's baton, a small, red gash on the back of his skull.

'Sti – stitches,' I say with a shiver.

A Speerspitze explodes and a Ddraig Goch drops into the sea with a crash. Atlas's hand tightens around my leg as the ripple effect sends water surging up to meet us, spilling over me. I can only see the far side of Wyvernmire's camp from here, the closer half hidden by the cliffs that stretch across the sand. There is no sign of Guardians or the Prime Minister, no human presence at all. Only the sky, dark but alight with flame, is in battle. The rebels must be sending the dragons in first. Ash, still glowing orange, floats towards us, extinguishing as soon as it touches our wet skin.

'I thought it would burn,' I say hoarsely as my limbs begin to tremble.

'I wish it would,' Atlas mutters.

My legs are aching, the rim of the ledge digging into my ribs, my toes turning numb. But there's nowhere to climb up or down to and if Atlas tries to move, we could both fall. He hooks his arm under mine as we wait hopefully, as if a dragon we know might just fly by and spot us. I think of Marquis, Serena and Gideon, looking for Chumana when all along she was in the tent.

'I don't think I can stay like this for much longer,' I shout over a series of roars.

Atlas nods in agreement. 'I'm going to have to let go of you so I can sit down. All right?'

I grip the ledge with stiff, bone-white fingers. Atlas lets go of my leg and slowly moves from his crouching position so that he's sitting down, dangling his legs over the edge. Then one of his hands reaches over me and grabs the back of my belt. He pulls me up and across his lap.

'Now sit up and turn around slowly,' he says, 'and wrap your legs around my waist.'

'Around your what?' I splutter.

'Just do it, Viv.'

I pull my knees in and use the rock behind Atlas to twist myself round to face him, then slide my legs on either side of his waist.

'Careful not to crush my paperwork,' he murmurs.

'I don't think it's the paperwork I'm crushing,' I reply.

'Now put your arms around me.'

'Why do I get the impression you're enjoying this?'

Atlas snorts. 'Do you want to fall back in?'

I wrap my arms around him, my fingertips barely touching as they stretch across his back to meet each other.

'Atlas?' I say.

'Hmm?'

'If you're still the praying type, now would be a good time to, you know . . . pull some strings.'

He bursts into laughter, his lips grazing my shoulder. Then his voice changes.

'If we survive this,' he says, 'we have to convince Cindra to help us. We can't give up, Viv. The alternative is—'

His voice breaks as his fingers press into my skin, clutching me tightly. Tears spring to my eyes at the emotion in his voice.

'I know,' I soothe.

This is how we stay, our frozen bodies slowly warming each other, until the fire and the fighting stop. At some point, the tip of his cold nose on my neck makes me jump and for a second I panic, thinking he's fallen asleep and we're about to go over. But his hand rests on my back, his fingers drumming the rhythm of a tune I can't hear. A seagull flies past, settling on the grassy clifftop above, and looks down at us with a beady eye. I feel oddly vulnerable.

'We're going to have to get back in the water,' I say, my voice thick with cold. 'We can't climb, so we'll have to swim. So much for asking God for help. He could have at least sent a—'

'Boat?' Atlas says. He nods towards the water. 'Look.'

I turn slowly to look over my shoulder. A small rowing boat is coming towards us, surrounded by the cool morning mist. I squint in the sombre light and see two figures.

'Who *is* that?'

'I think it's Ruth,' Atlas says.

Ruth and the girl rowing behind her angle the boat as close to the cliff as they can and gesture up to us. Atlas helps me turn around and I take a deep breath before jumping into the sea.

The freezing cold makes my body cry out but hands grab me before I can choke on water, pulling me on to the boat. I gasp in shock as I sit on one of the benches and watch the girls pull Atlas on board.

'Here,' Ruth says, throwing a sheepskin shawl at me.

I mutter my gratitude and wrap it around my shoulders.

'Thanks,' Atlas says as he pulls his own on. 'Things were starting to look—'

'Bleak?' Ruth says with a smirk. A dracovol scurries out of her furs and comes to sit on her shoulder. It lets out a loud screech.

'Our night watch spotted you, but it wasn't safe to come out until now.'

She picks up her oars.

'Did Jasper reach you?' I ask her.

'Yes,' she says, a little indignantly. 'And Freddie's group. I almost shot them dead. You weren't supposed to tell them about the tunnels.'

'I didn't mention the tunnels *specifically*,' I say. 'You didn't turn them away, did you?'

Ruth shakes her head as she begins to row. 'I 'ent in the

business of letting innocent kids die, although I haven't decided about that Roy yet.'

'Let Sargo have him,' I whisper through chattering teeth.

Ruth grins. She looks at Atlas, then points to the dracovol. 'I found this fellow on the other side of the island. He 'ent one of ours.'

On the other side of the island?

'But Ruth, aren't you banished?'

'He's been looking for you,' she tells Atlas.

For a moment I think she must be joking, but then I see Atlas's face. He freezes, his cheeks red.

'Me?' he says, his voice tinny and forced.

Then I see it. The slip of paper clasped in the dracovol's left talon.

'He was carrying this,' Ruth says.

She opens her palm to reveal a small piece of green wool fabric, the same material that Atlas's Coalition-issued uniform is made from. I remember the square cut from the inside of his jacket pocket. The dracovol jostles its leg and slowly Atlas's eyes come to meet mine. He takes the folded paper. His surname is scrawled on the front in a looping handwriting I recognise.

My heart sinks.

'Open it,' I tell him. 'And read it to me.'

K.

I know you will do everything it takes to ensure we succeed. By the time you reach me, I am sure minds will have been changed. I am waiting where the sketches are.

H

He looks up, his eyes smarting with shame.

'H,' I say coldly. 'Not . . . *the* H?'

His silence tells me all I need to know. As the girls row in silence, casting curious glances between us, I let the shock settle. Atlas is communicating with Hollingsworth. All this time, we were trying to figure out what she wanted us to ask of the wyverns and if the rebels had a back-up plan . . . and he never once said he could reach her. He knew she hadn't been arrested or tortured, but he let us believe she might have been. Cool realisation dawns on me.

Who else would have ordered him on a secret mission?

'I take it she *does* want to use the wyvern echolocation to fight the Bolgoriths?' I say to him. 'That's all you've been able to talk about these past few days.'

'Viv,' Atlas says miserably. 'If you come with me to Canna House, she'll—'

'Canna House?' I erupt. 'Hollingsworth is on the island? What was the point of going for Chumana, if the answers to our questions are waiting in the bay?'

'She wants to see you,' Atlas says. 'And all this will be explained. You think you've failed in your mission, Viv, but you haven't. Not yet.'

'My plan to translate Cannair to convince the wyverns to help us was doomed from the start,' I say. 'So if we can't win without them, then—'

'Come with me to see her,' Atlas says. 'Please!'

He clutches the crumpled piece of paper to his chest and for a moment I think he might cry.

'Otherwise . . .'

His fists clench as he swallows the rest of his words. I frown, alarm building in the pit of my stomach.

'Otherwise what, Atlas?'

'Just . . . just say you'll come,' he pleads shakily.

I stare at him, the waves lapping ominously against the boat. Where is the boy who was joking with me earlier?

'Fine,' I say. 'We'll go there now.'

Ruth rows us to a small cove further along the coast, away from Wyvernmire's camp. I turn to her as Atlas steps out of the boat. 'Ruth, if the rebels lose the war then Canna will be overrun with Bulgarian dragons. You and the other kids will need to leave, sail back to the mainland.'

She laughs and shakes her head. 'Don't fret, Featherswallow. Where we're going, not even a dragon will be able to sniff us out.'

I want to ask her what her plan is but the girl behind Ruth is tugging on her furs, casting anxious glances at the sky. They're exposed here, I realise, to both the dragons above and the Guardians on the ground. I nod.

'Thank you for saving us.'

Atlas reaches out a hand to help me off the boat but I ignore it and step out on to the wet sand. My clothes cling uncomfortably to my skin but I barely feel the cold any more. As we set out on foot, not saying a word to each other, my body is hot with both curiosity and dread.

What am I about to discover in Canna House?

When we reach it, the front door has been entirely kicked away. The first rays of sun caress the front garden and I steal a glance at Atlas.

'Are you sure she's here?' I whisper.

He looks at the slip of paper in his hand. 'It's dated four days ago.'

Glass crunches beneath our boots as we walk down the hallway, peering into each of the rooms.

'Empty,' I say, my voice echoing through the gloom.

Shadows loom across the floorboards in the slow sunrise and I try not to think about what they could be hiding. What if Guardians are waiting to ambush us? What if the dracovol post is fake?

'Atlas, I don't like this.'

'She must be up here,' he whispers, disappearing up the stairs.

I hesitate. Anyone could be waiting at the top. As I stare at Atlas's back a chill runs down my spine. He's been in contact with Hollingsworth and hiding it from me this whole time. What else is he keeping secret? Can I even trust him?

I shake myself and follow him. Things have to be classified in war, that's what Marquis said. Despite his dishonesty, Atlas is still a rebel and Hollingsworth is still the leader of the Human-Dragon Coalition.

We pause by the nursery where Ralph found me last time. It's empty, too. We continue down the hallway, scanning each room.

'She's not here,' I whisper. 'We should find the others, then wait for Chumana.'

'There's another staircase,' Atlas says.

He's right. At the end of the hallway is another set of stairs. I move aside and gesture him up them with a glare. There's a door at the top. Atlas pushes it open and candlelight falls over his shoulder on to the steps. A chemical smell fills my nose as I follow him inside. The curtains are tightly closed and the blue flame of a portable gas burner flickers in the corner. Food tins are stacked in neat piles and behind them is an armchair.

Someone is sitting in it.

I hear a match strike.

The person lights the lamp by the chair and the room fills with a yellow glare, illuminating a puff of hair and a creased, familiar face.

'Dr Hollingsworth,' Atlas says.

Hollingsworth gives him a weary smile, then looks at me. 'Hello, Vivien.'

I stare at her, heat blooming across my cheeks. I can't speak. If I do, I don't think I'll be able to keep myself from screaming. I look at the rebel uniform she is wearing in the place of her usual fur coat and feel like I'm part of a terrible trick. I haven't seen her since that last morning in her office, back when the wyverns were just a story in Clawtail's journal.

'What are you doing here?' I say.

'That's hardly a way to apologise for leaving me behind in London, isn't it?' she says with another smile.

'How about an apology for letting me believe Atlas was dead?' I spit. 'For never telling me what you wanted me to ask the wyverns for? For demanding that I learn an impossible language?'

As my voice gets louder, I see Atlas shift uncomfortably. And suddenly I hate him.

'How long have you two been conspiring together?' I say

shakily. 'You didn't think you could trust the rest of us, is that it? And why is that? Because you're Hollingsworth and King, the *original* Bletchley Park rebels?' I glare at them both, unable to keep the venom from my tone.

'Atlas,' Hollingsworth says with a raised eyebrow. 'Would you care to explain?'

Atlas blushes an even deeper shade of red. 'It's true that I had a secret mission,' he croaks. 'A mission to tell you what you didn't know about the Hebridean Wyverns, and why they were the key to winning the war.'

'Then why didn't you?' I say. I turn to Hollingsworth. 'Why didn't you send *me* a dracovol?'

'Because you needed the information fed to you slowly,' Hollingsworth says without flinching.

A low laugh escapes my lips. 'I'm sorry?'

Hollingsworth stands up. 'You know now that wyvern echolocation has the capacity to save us from the Prime Minister and her Bolgoriths, yes?'

'So Atlas keeps saying,' I reply. 'How? And why didn't you tell me that back in London, instead of telling him?'

'My plan was to inform you gradually, Vivien. That is why I didn't send you to Canna straight away, and why I was devastated when I found out you had been arrested and taken here.'

I frown and Hollingsworth folds her hands together, her silver rings glinting in the candlelight.

'What you went through at Bletchley Park was dreadful,' she says. 'I know the bravery it took to refuse to translate echolocation for the Prime Minister, how difficult it must have been to see the truth about who she is and change allegiances, so to speak. At the time I had recently confirmed what I had long suspected to be true – that the echolocation of a group of Scottish wyverns could help the Coalition. Except you had just learned from Chumana of the danger that the human exploitation of this hidden tongue poses to dragons. So how could I then ask you to do exactly that in the name of the rebels you only barely trusted?'

'I sure as hell didn't expect you to be the one advocating for it,' I say icily. 'I told Atlas that you would never endanger dragons in such a way. You, the leader of the Human-Dragon Coalition.' I look at Atlas, who is still staring at the floor. 'It seems I was wrong.'

Hollingsworth nods as if agreeing with me and I feel my mind spinning out of control. *What is going on?*

'I knew you wouldn't take kindly to the idea. So I had Atlas feed you the information piece by piece, so that you might come to a gentler realisation of why this unexpected new avenue is crucial to winning the war. Of why I sent you to communicate with the wyverns in the first place.'

I blink.

Feed me the information?

Atlas looks miserable.

'What . . . what do you mean?' I breathe.

'I told you, back in London, about how Bulgarian dragons communicate primarily in echolocation, did I not? That is why they speak fewer tongues than most dragons, why their fighters are sorted into bonded family groups. That sounds a lot like the Hebridean Wyverns, doesn't it? When my spies informed me Wyvernmire was in possession of a loquisonus machine and that you had escaped with it, I had Atlas suggest you use it to listen to the wyverns. And then I told him where Clawtail's grave was, so he could take you there.'

I stare at him, my whole body hot. He doesn't move, doesn't look at me.

'How did you communicate?'

'I assigned the secret mission to Atlas before he was sent to Canna,' Hollingsworth says.

'And she sent a dracovol telling me to keep the loquisonus machine close, which reached me when we were searching Canna House the first time,' Atlas says. 'Then I stole Serena's radio in the tunnels and got a signal—'

'Which is how you knew about the grave,' I finish weakly. I look at Hollingsworth. 'You're the one who wrote that memory scroll? How do you know the wyverns can heal humans?'

'When I received warning from Clementius that Guardians were on their way to my offices to arrest me, I was able to escape and begin the journey to Canna. I knew how angry you would be when you found out about Atlas's second mission. And I wanted to be the one to tell you the full truth myself.'

'The full truth?'

'Think, Vivien, about what you know about echolocation. What can it do?'

I hesitate. She doesn't deserve an answer from me, but I want to know. I want to know everything.

'It can heal,' I say angrily. I remember how Aodahn and Aberdine pressed their snouts to their eggs to talk to their wyvernlings. 'It can hatch. And—'

I think about what Chumana told me back at Bletchley Park.

Of course you didn't know that the Koinamens can kill, just as it can heal and grow.

'It can kill.'

Hollingsworth nods.

'Please don't say that's what you spent this whole time trying to tell me?' I spit. 'That's what you needed Atlas for? To lead me to the conclusion that the Koinamens can be used to kill? You think that helps us? It can kill dragonlings inside their eggs,' I say. 'Vulnerable, unborn dragons. The wyverns can't kill the Bulgarian dragons with their minds, you fool! If they could, dragons wouldn't need teeth or claws.'

'It is not dragonlings' physical weakness that allows them to be killed,' Hollingsworth interrupts. 'It is the *unbreakable bond* between dragon and dragonling that allows the kill call – so against a parent's natural instinct – to function. A dragon cannot kill an egg it hasn't bonded with, Vivien. But the Hebridean Wyverns, with their unique, multi-wyvern bond, can overcome any need for relationship, penetrate any mind, as long as they emit a call *together.* Together, their echolocation can heal a human. Together, it can kill a full-grown dragon.'

Multi-wyvern bond?

I feel like I'm falling, plunging headlong into a cold, obvious truth. I suddenly yearn for the web of confusion I felt in the wyvern tunnels, the one I thought Atlas and I were caught in together. Everything Hollingsworth has just told me makes sense, and I despise myself for not seeing it before.

'Then to exploit the Koinamens would be even more dangerous than we previously thought,' I say. 'If the wyverns can do what you say they can do – kill Bulgarian dragons with nothing but their bonded minds – then they are a danger to the whole world. And if they were to agree to help us, they would be hunted, murdered by humans and dragons alike.'

'Dr Hollingsworth can protect them,' Atlas interrupts, looking up for the first time. 'Otherwise I would never have agreed—'

'Even my six-year-old sister wouldn't have fallen for that lie,' I spit.

His face falls.

'At what stage of our relationship did you decide you were going to betray me?'

'I . . . Viv, I didn't want to,' he says. 'I only agreed because Dr Hollingsworth insisted, because the rebels *have* to win the war, because I knew that, once you understood that the wyverns would be protected, you'd want to do whatever it took to save Britannia from—'

'Not this,' I say, shaking my head. 'The Koinamens is a secret for a reason and now we know what the wyverns can do, there's all the more reason to hide it from the world. This is what we fought for at Bletchley Park, Atlas.' My voice breaks. '*Why* have you done this?'

He takes a step towards me and I flinch. He stops. 'You *have* to listen to her, Viv. You *have* to convince the wyverns. Otherwise, you'll lose everything. *I* will lose everything.'

I turn from him to Hollingsworth. 'So you didn't have me learn Cannair so I could find out how the wyverns could help us. You already knew how. You simply wanted me to gain their trust, so that I could make this unhinged demand of yours.' I shake my head. 'You know, for a moment I thought it might be possible. To translate Cannair into English and in exchange solicit an alliance that might reveal what you wanted to know. But what *I* didn't know was what Clawtail himself had discovered: that the wyvern tongue is untranslatable.'

Hollingsworth frowns. 'How so?'

'We don't have the words in English to accurately translate its meaning. And more importantly, no translation would preserve it, which is what the wyverns wanted all along.' I take a breath. 'A written transcript of a language can't capture an accent or a tone of voice or an idiom. It can't keep tradition like the waulking of the tweed or cloud-spinning alive, not if there are no words to explain how they work. I made a deal with one of the wyvern leaders, Cindra, to do that but I failed, because her language and mine are incompatible. Allowing others to learn Cannair through immersion, through first-hand experience of the wyvern culture and not from the dry pages of a book, is the only way to preserve it. The wyverns will need to come out of concealment, Dr Hollingsworth. Do you think they'll be able to do that, once the whole world knows about their echolocation?'

'The wyverns have an opportunity to play a crucial role in history and we will celebrate them for it, without revealing how it came about,' she replies. 'The Coalition is fine-tuning a wyvern protection plan and still advocates for the destruction of every single loquisonus machine in existence.' Hollingsworth stands up. 'Yes, we are asking the wyverns to use their echolocation, but we do not intend to touch it ourselves. The Koinamens should and will always be out of bounds to human interference. It is this promise that keeps the rebel dragons on our side.'

'They know, then?' I say. 'The rebel dragons know of this plan?'

'A select few.'

'Does Chumana?'

Hollingsworth sighs and shakes her head.

'You haven't told her,' I say in disbelief, 'because you know she will be against it.'

'Yes,' Hollingsworth admits. 'I was counting on you to explain to her why it must be done. Because I believe she will be able to see the truth, Vivien, like I believe you are able to. I believe you will be able to move her, just like you will be able to move the Hebridean Wyverns.'

'Because I'm a Draconic translator,' I say quickly. 'Except I've failed at translation, Dr Hollingsworth. I've built my whole life around a pursuit that is not the noble, infallible thing I thought it was. Translation doesn't always preserve. Sometimes, it only gives the illusion of preservation. So what's the point of it?' My eyes are treacherously wet. 'I don't think I want to be a translator any more.'

'You're worth more than just your languages, Viv,' Atlas says softly. 'It's just a job, it's not who you are.'

'Vivien, I didn't choose you for this mission simply because of your linguistic capabilities,' Hollingsworth snaps. 'Do you remember when we first met?'

I nod, remembering the meal at home in Fitzrovia before

my parents were arrested and my life changed forever.

'That night, I saw a young girl who was unsure of everything she said, who was desperate to please, who, despite her impressive academic achievements, showed a lack of confidence in herself. But just a few hours later you released a criminal dragon from the University of London, convinced her to set fire to Downing Street and negotiated a job for both you and your cousin that would save your entire family. That was when I knew what you were.'

A hot feeling comes over me.

'And then I saw what you did at Bletchley Park.'

'Studying the Koinamens for Wyvernmire,' I whisper, my skin prickling with shame.

'Not that,' Hollingsworth replies. 'Refusing to turn Dr Seymour in when you found out she was a rebel spy. Destroying the loquisonus machine. Trying to save Atlas despite knowing it would surely end with you getting caught. I believe in you, Vivien, not because you are a translator but because you are willing to move heaven and earth to make sure the right side wins this war, to make sure the dragons and the Third Class are free. That is why I made you the Swallow – because I believe in your capacity to succeed.'

'Sorry to disappoint,' I mutter.

'You haven't disappointed me. I know you still have it in you to convince the wyverns to help us. You possess more of an understanding of languages, of the expectations and emotions they carry, than most, because of the way bilingualism has been part of you since you were born.'

I think of how I speak English with Dad and Bulgarian with

Mama and a mix of the two with Ursa. How both languages hold different halves of me, how I'm not the same in each one. How, in a way, parts of me are untranslatable, too.

'You're the leader of the Human-Dragon Coalition,' I say quietly. 'Surely you have another plan, another weapon?'

'The Koinamens is a language and language *is* a weapon,' Hollingsworth says. 'I've told you that before.' She sighs. 'Will you ask the wyverns to help us, Vivien? Will you fight for the rebels, this one last time?'

I want to say *yes*. Yes, if you keep the wyverns safe. Yes, if I never have to see Atlas look at me this way again.

'No.'

Hollingsworth's mouth sets into a thin line.

'The wyverns have suffered enough,' I say. 'And even if they agree, you'll never be able to protect them, to hide what their echolocation can do. They've taught me more about translation than the Academy ever has and I'm not about to exploit their most precious, intrinsic language for our gain, Dr Hollingsworth. Not even to win this war.'

Slowly, Atlas sinks down into Hollingsworth's seat. My feet carry me down the stairs and it's as if my soul has left my body, preceding it out into the cold morning air as the realisation of everything – my failure, Hollingsworth's corruption, Atlas's betrayal – sinks deep into the sinew of my very being. It creates a dark cloud of anxiety that sits on my chest, restricting my breathing, as I remember how Hollingsworth let me talk about Atlas as if he was dead, how Atlas kissed me and told me he didn't see a future without me.

Both have used me.

I let out great, desperate sobs, howling in the dawn the way I did in those months after I thought Atlas had died, how I wanted to howl when I saw him upright and alive.

I lost him and found him only to lose him a second time. And this time, I know there's no going back.

Atlas King will never kiss me again.

Rain begins to fall. I stare up into the clouds and let it drench me, droplets coursing through my hair, breathing in the petrichor smell of Canna's water until it seeps into my clothes and chills my bones. And I sob some more for everything I've lost. Translation, Atlas and the war.

A shadow swoops across the sky.

I don't move as the dragon lands. I let her walk towards me, let her tail encircle me, let her giant head touch mine as her hot breath blows down my neck. All I can do is reach up like a child, my fingers finding the grooves of hot scales, my soul finding my body again as both collapse with grief and exhaustion.

Then Chumana wraps her wings around me and flies me into the sunrise.

Nineteen

WE LAND ON SANDAY. IT'S PEACEFUL in the morning light, the tidal island empty except for a huge dragon skin that lies on the grass in front of us.

'Yours?' I croak, my throat sore from crying.

'It was time to be rid of what the Wyvernmire boy did to me in that tent,' Chumana growls.

I nod, goosebumps rising on my arms. I don't want to know. I crawl down off her back and stand in the wet grass, my back to Ruth's tunnel system, staring out to sea.

'I can't be a translator any more,' I say.

'Please don't contaminate my air with your nonsense,' she replies.

Chumana's spiked tail curls around me, its heat a balm on my skin. I watch the waves roll like they did when they tossed me against the rocks.

'Atlas betrayed me, Chumana,' I whisper.

A low growl comes from her throat as her head swings

down to my level. The white rings around her eyes are made of tiny tufts of fur and the scales along her jaw are tinged with blood. We watch the sea in silence until voices sound. I peer down on to the beach. Marquis, Serena and Gideon are clambering off Daria's back.

'Why did she save you?' I ask as they begin climbing up towards us. 'Do you know her?'

'Chummie!' Marquis calls. 'Nice to see you again.'

'You will not call me that a second time,' Chumana snaps as he reaches us.

Marquis's grins widens until he notices my tearstained faced. 'What's wrong? Where's Atlas?'

'He's . . .' How do I even say it? 'Atlas has been in contact with Hollingsworth since before we got to Canna,' I whisper, my heart sinking as I remember the events of last night. 'She's here, in Canna House. She gave him a mission to lead me to realise what she didn't tell me back in London – that the way to win the war is to ask the wyverns to echolocate a kill call, which is so strong thanks to their bond.'

'What?' Serena says as Chumana snarls.

Marquis's jaw tightens. 'So Atlas was right? And he knew it the whole time?'

I nod, blinking tears from my eyes.

'But why didn't Hollingsworth tell you from the start?' Serena says.

'Because she knew I'd refuse to ask it of the wyverns,' I say. 'Chumana told me what the Koinamens is to dragons, why it can never be exploited, but Hollingsworth thought that with time, and with Atlas, I would agree.'

'This cannot be true!' Chumana explodes. 'Rita Hollingsworth has defended the Koinamens since she first discovered its existence.'

'She says it's the only way,' I reply. 'She thinks she can protect the wyverns, can make sure that the world doesn't find out what role they played, so that echolocation will stay hidden.'

'Impossible,' Daria breathes. 'Every nation will want to know how the British defeated Bulgaria's dragons.'

I stare up at the dragon I met on the beach on the Isle of Skye. She's smaller than Chumana, slighter in stature, but even fiercer, somehow, with an angular face and sharp, glinting scales.

'Who are you?' I ask her. 'Why are you here?'

'I told you the first time we met,' she purrs. 'I came to Britannia looking for a friend.'

'And did you find them?'

Daria looks at Chumana with bright eyes.

'Oh.'

I stare between the two dragons.

'We know each other from my time in Bulgaria,' Chumana growls.

'I see.'

Chumana only lived in Bulgaria briefly, when she was sent there by the British government to help the Bulgarian Bolgoriths massacre their countryhumans. It's the reason she was about to kill herself back in the library at the University of London on the day I appeared to set her free. So is Daria guilty of the same horrors?

'When Chumana returned to Britannia, circumstance prevented me from going with her,' Daria says. 'I haven't seen her in fifty-nine years. But when I was conscripted to your country at the beginning of this war, I knew it was the perfect excuse to find her.'

I look at Chumana. 'But isn't she the enemy?'

'No, human girl,' Chumana says. 'Daria is no supporter of Goranov or Wyvernmire. She is one of us.'

I nod, feeling sick at the irony of finding an ally in a Bulgarian invader when the rebel I trusted most has betrayed me.

'Krasimir, Goranov and I were fathered by the same dragon, many years apart,' Daria says quietly. 'But that is where our family ties end.'

'*You're* the third dragon in the Bulgarian trio?' I say, unable to keep the accusatory tone out of my voice.

But Daria just grins.

'I thought Bulgarian dragons didn't speak other languages?' Gideon says, eyeing Daria warily.

'They do when they learn them in secret,' Daria quips.

I turn to my cousin. 'What happened to you after you left Wyvernmire's camp?'

'We didn't find Chumana, obviously,' Marquis says, rolling his eyes. 'But we came across Jasper, on his way back to his camp to salvage any supplies before he holes up in there.' He points to the caves that house Ruth's tunnel system. 'He said he saw Ralph giving Goranov his blood.'

'Again?'

'Goranov was drinking Ralph Wyvernmire's blood?' Chumana says sharply.

Marquis nods and I see the two dragons exchange looks.

'We saw him do it after Wyvernmire gassed the wyvern tunnels, too,' I tell them.

'It's not making him stronger, though,' Marquis says. 'Jasper said Goranov was having trouble flying.'

'Then it *is* strengthening him,' Daria growls. 'Goranov is gravely ill. So if what you say is true, the Wyvernmire nephew's blood may be the only thing keeping him alive.'

'Ill?' I say.

Daria nods.

'The Bulgarian tradition of blood-perfuming was once a practice reserved for regals,' she says. 'But with so few humans left in Bulgaria, the Regal Vasil, head of the council of regals, claims the privilege for himself. No other dragon is permitted to partake in it.'

'What's a regal?' says Serena.

'Bulgarian dragon royalty,' I mutter, my eyes still on Daria.

'The practice involves taking on a human *protégé*, one that will willingly mutilate their own body to allow a dragon to drink their blood,' she says. 'The cells in the human blood create a chemical reaction in the dragon's body, causing its own cells to regenerate. If drunk every day by a healthy dragon, it can extend their lifetime by a century. Drunk by a dying dragon, it can tether him to this world for several more years.'

'So human blood heals dragons?' Marquis says.

'Yes,' Chumana hisses.

My skin crawls as I remember how Ralph described a Britannia in which humans are herded like cattle by the

Bulgarian dragons. How hard would it be to convince a person to offer up their blood to keep their family alive?

'Next time I see Ralph, I'm shooting him,' Marquis growls. 'We need Goranov weakened, not high on Wyvernmire hemoglobins.'

'Ruth's coming,' Serena says.

Ruth is walking out of the caves towards us, flanked by Jasper and Freddie. They hesitate when the dragons turn to look at them, but I lift up a hand and they don't stop.

'Back so soon?' Ruth says to me with a raised eyebrow. She doesn't mention Atlas.

'Fucking Bulgarian dragons?' Freddie murmurs to Jasper. 'I thought—'

'You thought they were the enemy,' I say, my eyes landing on him. 'These two are different, although I can't promise Chumana won't eat someone if Ruth asks her to, so make sure your lot behave.'

Ruth gives me a sly smile and hands me a pair of binoculars. 'Over there, above the hill.'

I level the binoculars in the direction she's pointing. Flying in the sky towards Compass Hill are the lithe blue bodies of the Hebridean Wyverns.

'That's Cindra,' I say as I focus on one. 'And Aberdine.'

'Can you see Aodahn?' Serena says hopefully.

I shake my head.

'Looks like they've decided to fight,' Marquis says. 'I wonder what Abelio thinks of that.'

'Hollingsworth wants me to ask them to use their echolocation to defeat the Bolgoriths,' I say, turning to look at everyone. 'But if they do, they'll have to live in hiding for the rest of their lives.'

'What's an echolocation?' Jasper says.

'Ultrasonic dragon language,' Marquis replies cheerfully. 'Don't tell anyone.'

Chumana growls.

'So I'm not going to ask them to,' I finish.

I look around at them, waiting for an objection, but none comes.

'So, we 'ent going to win this war?' Ruth asks.

I shake my head.

'We will fight anyway,' Chumana says, 'No dragon chooses surrender when they could die in flight.'

'And *you* need to hide,' I tell Ruth, Jasper and Freddie. 'As deep into the tunnels as you can go. You'll survive a few months down there if you pool your supplies.'

I think of Ursa, who will have escaped Eigg on dragonback with Dr Seymour. She'll have the sense to hide my little sister and her own baby. Perhaps they'll go underground, too.

Ruth is shaking her head. 'We changed our minds.' She glances at Chumana and Daria. 'He's got some dragon-killing guns –' she points to Freddie – 'and I want to try 'em.'

Freddie grins.

'No,' I almost shout. 'I can't ask that of you. You'll be killed!'

'We're not doing it for you,' Jasper scoffs. 'We *want* to fight.'

'You think this is *your* battle?' Ruth says to me, her eyes flashing. 'We were the ones abandoned on this island. Fed to the dragons as part of Wyvernmire's Peace Agreement. And

I'm going to make her pay for it. This is as much *our* war as it is the rebels'.'

'But—'

'Lay off, Viv,' Gideon says. He casts another nervous glance in Daria's direction. 'I *can't* be eaten by a Bolgorith, all right? The teeth, that awful clicking sound . . .' He pales. 'I think we should try those Speerspitzes.'

Freddie slaps him on the back. 'That's the spirit, Giddy.'

'We'll leave the littl'uns in the tunnels with the supplies,' Ruth says, turning to Freddie and Jasper. 'If we don't come back, they'll have enough food to survive down there until next spring, and I'll tell my girls to up the doses in their poison pouches.'

I turn away, my heart hammering as they all casually discuss their potential deaths.

Atlas's face appears in my mind. Is he still with Hollingsworth? Does he truly believe that the wyverns won't come to harm once the existence of their Koinamens is revealed to the world? I think about the efforts he put into teaching the wyverns about Britannia, of the horror on his face when Aodahn's egg died. The Atlas I know wouldn't be advocating for this if it meant hurting them, if he didn't believe it was the right thing. Hollingsworth must have tricked him.

He still betrayed you.

I remember our conversation on the beach before we found Chumana. Was any of that real? He let me believe his hesitation was about the priesthood. So were his plans to leave that all behind a lie, too? All this time I thought we were working as a team, but actually he was leading me by the hand like a gullible child.

'Viv?' Marquis says.

I turn around and they're all looking at me.

'We should join the wyverns.' He points at Ruth, Jasper and Freddie. 'They'll come to Compass Hill once they have the Speerspitzes. All right?'

I look at them, at these three underfed, determined teenagers, and nod.

'If any of you see a Guardian feeding his blood to Goranov, kill him,' Marquis says grimly.

'Our efforts should be concentrated on Krasimir,' Daria growls. 'He is the strongest.'

My stomach lurches. I can't imagine any number of Speerspitzes bringing him down and Chumana must agree.

'Only a dragon can kill him,' she says.

'But,' Daria adds quietly, 'a human could draw him out into the open.'

'Like bait?' Gideon says.

The Bolgorith nods, grinning again, and Ruth shrugs.

'We're good at being bait.'

I watch as Marquis, Gideon and Serena climb back up on to Daria's back, settling awkwardly between her spikes.

'We reconvene on Compass Hill,' she says, her eyes unblinking.

I nod and climb on to Chumana. 'It's the one above Jasper's Camp, where—'

'Where you took it upon yourself to remind me of my sins?' Chumana growls. 'We know where Compass Hill is, human girl.'

'Oh, yes, right.' I pause. 'I'm so sorry for what I said to you, Chumana.'

Her wings rise up on either side of me.

'Chumana?'

'Yes?'

'Why did you and Hollingsworth let me believe Atlas was dead?'

Chumana's wings fall.

'I told you. Rita wanted you ready for revenge.'

'And Atlas?' I say quietly. 'Why didn't he write to me, do you think?'

Chumana pauses as Ruth, Jasper and Freddie back away. 'I believe he was afraid he wouldn't survive. He wanted to spare you the heartbreak of losing him again.'

My knuckles turn white as my grip on her scales tightens. 'Too late for that.'

Chumana leans forward and then we are in the air once more, watching a flock of children emerge from the caves on Sanday. I welcome the cold, clean air, letting it blow the smoke from my hair and clothes. Peering over Chumana's hot scales I see the sea, with Rùm and Eigg behind it, and I feel a wave of dread. I hope that Ursa is somewhere far, far away.

We drop lower and I spot Compass Hill. I watch the wyverns land in disbelief. Why have they agreed to fight? Will it make a difference? Humans are joining them, climbing up the green slopes of the hill from both sides. I startle, my skin prickling with fear as a dragon appears beside us, but it's just Daria, stretched out like a majestic bird. The tip of her wing kisses Chumana's and butterflies dance in my stomach as the two Bulgarian Bolgoriths swoop across and beneath each other, their tails looping together in the air.

I flatten my body against Chumana's as she dives, then glides, only for Daria to reappear at our height, her mouth open to reveal her forked tongue. Gideon grimaces, letting out a scream I can't hear. Marquis and Serena double over in the wind, which blows so hard that I can't even gasp for breath. Clouds drift around us at the speed of motorcars. Up here there is no war, no winning or losing. There is nothing but the exhilarating, uncontrollable current of our own existence.

I lean in against Chumana and smile. We are no longer rebels or linguists or Bulgarians. We are simply a blur of pink in the sky. Four recruits and two dragons who are, in this brief, singular moment, as light and carefree as swallows.

Dragons are flying in over the bay with people on their backs. There are so many humans that they must have come from all over: Eigg, mainland Scotland, London. We hover over Wyvernmire's camp. It's empty except for a few Bolgoriths who are herding Guardians of Peace into the tents. It's happening just like Ralph said it would. The humans are being imprisoned. If Wyvernmire gassed the wyvern tunnels to get to me and the loquisonus machine, maybe she knew the Bulgarians were about to turn on her. Maybe she was trying to escape. That would explain why there's no sign of her on the beach.

Chumana roars as she reaches Compass Hill. 'Rita Hollingsworth! It seems not all rebels are party to the same secrets.'

The Hebridean Wyverns back away as Chumana and Daria

land. Cindra stands at the front of the group. It's smaller than before and I feel a rush of grief for the wyverns lost. Abelio isn't among them. We stand feet away from Hollingsworth, small but imposing in her green uniform and leather boots, her hair gathered by a black ribbon. Atlas is by her side and when I meet his pleading gaze, I feel both a reluctance to leave the warm shelter of Chumana's body and a rushing desire to be caught up in his arms. I ignore him as I climb to the ground.

'I am relieved to see you, Chumana,' Hollingsworth says.

'Do you greet me with more lies?' Chumana snarls.

'Not lies, Chumana. Just delayed truths.'

'The Koinamens will be left to the dragons, will not be tampered with, will not even be spoken of. Those were your words, uttered to the dragons that joined the Coalition,' Chumana says.

'And why did you join that Coalition?' Hollingsworth replies. She stands like a soldier at ease, staring up into Chumana's great, spiked face. 'To extinguish a corrupt Peace Agreement. To abolish an unjust Class System. To ensure that dragons and humans can live together peacefully, without one trying to dominate the other. We are a single battle away from achieving these things, Chumana, with the wyverns' help. But without it, the Coalition simply doesn't have the numbers for a victory.'

'So you begin your so-called peacetime with the exploitation of dragons,' Chumana hisses. 'History repeats itself.'

Hollingsworth glances at Cindra. 'It isn't exploitation if they agree. Vivien, would you care to introduce me?'

Dread floods my body. Chumana looks like she might be

about to breathe fire, or worse, abandon us altogether.

A flash of blue.

Aodahn has scuttled forward. He casts a nervous look up at Chumana and then his head turns to Atlas.

'This is about the *Smuainswel*, is it not, dear one?'

Atlas stares at Aodahn as if he's seen a ghost.

'Are you Abelio?' Hollingsworth asks.

Aodahn shakes his head. 'I – I am Aodahn,' he stutters. 'This is Cindra.' He gestures with his wing to Cindra, who takes a step forward.

'Abelio refuses to remain above ground,' she growls at Hollingsworth. 'Who are you?'

'Chancellor of the Academy for Draconic Linguistics and leader of the Human-Dragon Coalition,' Hollingsworth replies as Aodahn's eyes widen. 'You may not remember me. It was such a long time ago.' She reaches into her pocket and pulls out a silk handkerchief, which she unfolds. I crane my neck to see what's inside.

A ring.

'This belonged to June Clawtail. My mother.'

From the private papers of Patrick Clawtail

Marguerite is now seven, tall and grey-eyed and coltish, so different to the soft, supple baby we brought to live with the Hebridean Wyverns. She knows no human children, and does not understand what a strange sight it is, her playing with the wyvernlings. Yesterday, she told her mother and I that she was hatched from an egg. 'Neamroque' (my own spelling) was the word she used. I believe the Cannair for 'egg' translates literally to 'heavenly rock,' born from the Gaelic 'neamh' (Heaven) and the Anglo-Norman 'roque' (rock.)

I sometimes amuse myself with these small etymological games, reflecting on how the wyverns might spell certain words if they recorded their own grammar on paper. But what interests me a great deal more these days is the 'neamroques' themselves, and, well, the promise they hold. The eggs, with their pearly sheen, that sit in a great nest down on the beach, bathed in the heat of flame and sunlight, are a promise of a future on Canna. A future for Cannair and the Gaelic that cradled its beginnings.

I know how fortunate we are to be here, living secretly among dragons, when so many islanders were torn from their homes. I watch my wife and child, jumping the waves, Canna's sun settling like gold around the shape of their bodies and catching in the soft spirals of their hair as if to bind them here forever. The Hebridean dusk turns the sea lavender and the abandoned stone houses stark against the horizon. The music of oyster-catchers and crooning dragons mixes with the silence of a tongue that once told of sea and isles. The basalt columns reach up to kiss the heavens.

Neamroque.

Such a heavenly rock is Canna.

Twenty

I FORGET TO BREATHE.

'My father wore the other,' Hollingsworth says, 'but as his body was never found, I do not have it. It was I who set up the empty grave on Canna, with the memory tweed, as per wyvern tradition.' She smiles.

My head spins. Rita Hollingsworth is the little girl Clawtail writes about in his journal? She's his daughter?

'You are Marguerite?' Aodahn says.

'Yes,' she replies softly. 'My parents and I lived with you before you disappeared.'

'I remember!' Aodahn says delightedly. He glances at Cindra as she comes forward, sniffing the air as if searching for a lie. She turns to him, communicating silently.

'You've met these wyverns before?' I say to Hollingsworth, my voice shaking. 'You've lived on this island, you speak Cannair? And yet you sent me here blind?'

'You have lied to us all,' Chumana spits.

'You could have found the wyverns yourself!' I shout at her.

'Found the wyverns myself?' Hollingsworth says calmly. 'Vivien, I am sixty-five years old. I no longer have the strength to go traipsing across an uncharted island, no matter how much I wanted to return to the place of my earliest, sweetest memories. I cannot remember more than a few words of Cannair. And you forget who I am. If I had simply run off to Canna, our cover would have been blown.'

'So that's why you had Clawtail's diary,' I say. 'It didn't belong to the Academy. You got it from your family.'

'From my mother,' Hollingsworth says with a nod. 'After the government killed my father, we were relocated to England, forgiven for our family's *treason* as long as we assumed new identities. Of course, I never forgot our lives with the wyverns, even as their language began to fade from my young mind. There was barely a trace of our past left until I founded the Academy, secretly in honour of my father.'

Out of the corner of my eye I see Aodahn move. He reaches inside the pouch where his egg should be and pulls out a tiny, gold ring.

'Patrick's wedding band,' he says, holding it out in his large, clumsy talons.

Hollingsworth's eyebrows knit together in surprise as she takes the ring. It sits next to its partner in the palm of her hand.

'Then you were a friend of my father's?'

'Indeed, dear one,' Aodahn says. 'He taught me English and I taught him Cannair.' His eyes grow wide. 'It was with me that *you* learned to read.'

The apples of Hollingsworth's cheeks turn a rosy pink and

her lipsticked mouth trembles. I glance up at the sky as more dragons land around us, rebels I've never met jumping off their backs. But where are Goranov and Krasimir? Where are the Bolgoriths?

'Aodahn,' Hollingsworth says. 'My recruits have spoken to you of the war our country is fighting, of the invasion of the Bulgarian dragons, which you have now witnessed for yourselves.' She looks at the other wyverns and her eyes land on Cindra. 'I have come to ask you to use your Koinamens to help rid Britannia of these invaders. I know it is sacred to you, a secret best kept among dragons. We rebel humans have fought to protect it, but I come begging you to share it, once now in return for our eternal gratitude and respect, and then never again. Without it, our country is doomed to become the stomping ground of Bulgarian Bolgoriths, and our own humans and dragons mere food and slaves.'

'But how can our *Smuainswel* help you?' Aodahn asks.

'Together,' Hollingsworth says softly, 'the Hebridean Wyverns can echolocate a call strong enough to kill one of the Bulgarian leaders. He, in turn, is so intimately bonded to his two siblings, that I believe they will suffer the effects of the call through him, and perish also.'

Daria's tail curls like a snake.

'Patrick would never have asked this of us,' Cindra snaps in Cannair.

'You're right,' I reply in the same tongue. 'You *must* refuse, Cindra. If you use your *Smuainswel*, every human and dragon in the world will know who you are and what you can do.'

Hollingsworth opens her mouth to speak, but changes her

mind when Chumana takes a step forward.

'Humans will try to turn you into a weapon,' I continue, switching back to English. 'Dragons will try to kill you. You won't be respected, only feared. Fear breeds hatred, Cindra, and you will be the most hated dragons in Europe.'

'The *Bulgarian Bolgoriths* are the most hated dragons in Europe,' Hollingsworth cries. 'Is their power not respected? Our country will fall to them, just like their own country fell. We *must* fight them with a weapon they are not expecting us to use. And not only do you have such a weapon, but you have an optimised version. A version that will save us all. Cindra, I implore you.'

Chumana snaps at Hollingsworth and she jumps backwards, the colour draining from her face.

'The wyverns will fight alongside you, girl with the golden machine,' Cindra says. 'But with our teeth.' She glares at Hollingsworth. 'Not our minds.'

I nod, relief flooding me, and I see the tremble in Hollingsworth's hands as she turns away. She stalks across the grass, stopping only when she reaches the edge of the hill to stare at the horizon.

'Bolgoriths,' Serena says sharply.

A whole horde of them is flying towards us from inland and opposite, and soaring in from across the sea are yet more rebel dragons. Small black figures drop from their hulking backs into the shallows, carrying their weapons as bullets begin to spray.

'There are more of us than I expected,' I say quietly, hope brimming.

'I thought the rebels didn't have the numbers?' Marquis breathes.

On the beach, Guardians are loading a line of Speerspitzes under Bulgarian supervision, pointing them at the influx of British dragons. And from somewhere far off comes the distant hum of planes. A Sand Dragon lands next to me.

'Greetings, recruit,' Soresten says, bowing his head. 'We were told we would find the Swallow here.'

'It's good to see you, Soresten,' I say breathlessly.

Someone slides off Soresten's back. I recognise him only vaguely. He's the man I saw with Dr Seymour when we landed on Eigg after the Battle of Bletchley, the father of her child. As someone bellows orders and the rebels around us begin to organise themselves, I catch glimpses of other human faces behind folding wings. Arthur Burke from the Academy. Hollingsworth's driver, Johnstone. A greengrocer from Pimlico. My stomach lurches. George Beecham, who hosted the Pimlico party and . . . Edward? When did he join the Coalition? Is Hyacinth here too? My head snaps back towards the crowd, searching for her face, but someone grabs me by the arm. I spin around.

A skinny figure, long blonde hair and the flash of a red friendship bracelet.

Sophie.

I burst into tears.

'Viv!' she says, grinning. 'What's the plan?'

She looks different. Her face is rounder and there's an athletic curve to her body. I stare, slightly stunned, into her bright eyes.

'Why do you look happy to be here?' I say through tears.

She laughs as a Speerspitze explodes. 'Isn't this what we've been training for? Last year we were prisoners, Viv, but now, we're rebels!'

Her last words are muffled as Marquis pulls her into a hug. Serena turns to say something to me and a flicker of orange is reflected in her eyes.

'Get down!' Atlas screams.

Dragonfire rains down on us, so hot that the grass at my feet wilts. A pink veil descends on me as I fling myself to the ground. When I open my eyes I see the paper-thin leather of Chumana's wing and then Atlas's face next to mine, his eyes scrunched shut, his arm flung across my back.

'Serena?' I scream, and my voice is muffled behind the protective tent of Chumana's wing.

'Here,' Serena says weakly.

The wing lifts and I see her lying in the grass next to Hollingsworth, Sophie and Marquis. Fire rages across the grass, licking up the legs of the dragons and sending the humans running for cover.

'Where's Gideon?' Marquis says.

'With Aodahn,' I say as I get to my feet, spotting the wyvern towering over Gideon, his tailed curled protectively around him as a Bolgorith circles.

A hand slips into mine.

Atlas.

There's a boom as Guardians fire the Speerspitzes below. I look at him. He stares back.

He might as well be a stranger.

Chumana lets out a scream and she and Daria rise to meet the Bolgoriths as they attack. The sky is crammed with dragons and I stay low as I spot a massive black dragon flying over the hills in an erratic manner, rising high before swooping low, the left half of its body dragging on the wind.

'Is that Goranov?' Serena says.

'And Ralph,' Atlas says grimly.

As Goranov gets closer, I see Ralph on his back, nestled like a parasite between the dragon's wings. Guttural screams echo from the beach as Bolgoriths swoop down on the rebels. Metallic clangs ring out as scale meets scale. There's a flash of pink. Chumana and Daria crash back across the hillside, entangled with a third dragon. We duck again, pressing ourselves to the ground as the dragons tumble over the edge and into the air. I see Western Drakes, Sand Dragons, Ddraig Gochs and even several Silver Drakes battling the Bolgoriths.

'I can't see Krasimir,' I shout to the others. 'We need to draw him out here!'

Hollingsworth's eyes meet mine and she nods in silent agreement.

I take a deep breath.

So she hasn't given up, either.

'Krasimir?' Sophie says as we group together again. 'He's my mission. Cormac and I –' she points to a man in a kilt who is charging down towards the beach – 'have been tracking him with Daria's help.'

Sophie has been working with Daria?

She smirks at my surprise. 'They're bonded, so Daria can sense where he is.'

'Chumana said Daria hates her brothers,' I say.

'She does. But they raised her.'

I suddenly remember how Goranov echolocated my impending arrival to Daria on Bualintur, despite the miles between them. Krasimir must have been positioned somewhere between the two, bridging the distance.

'So where is he?' I say warily. 'Krasimir?'

Sophie eyes the sky. 'He's in the forest behind Canna House, letting his advance forces do the hard work.'

A group of wyverns streaks towards the beach and hooves thunder nearby. Ruth and Jasper are tearing towards us on horseback, a dragon behind them.

'That's Sargo,' I say, reaching instinctively for my poison pouch.

The dragon flies lower, closing in on Ruth, but she doesn't look back. She rides the horse bareback, her long hair catching in the wind. There's a whoosh as Sargo is blasted from the air, crashing into the hillside. My eyes search for the source of the force and I hear it before I see it.

A joyous whooping.

A line of Speerspitzes has been erected on Sanday, each manned by a young boy.

'See?' Ruth says breathlessly as she pulls her horse to a stop beside us. 'We're the bait that keeps you safe.'

I turn to the others. 'That's what we need to do with Krasimir.'

'There's Freddie,' Serena says.

Below, Freddie and a group of Ruth's girls are dragging more of the dragon-killing guns through the rockpools.

'Do you think you could fire one of those things?' Atlas asks Serena.

She snorts. 'How many times did I beat you at target practice, King?'

'You should go and help them,' I say, nodding. I glance at Marquis and Gideon. 'You too.'

'What about you?' Atlas says.

I don't look at him. 'I'll go with Sophie to be Krasimir's bait.'

'*You* can't be the bait.'

'Why not?'

He stutters. 'I don't want you to—'

'That's none of your business any more,' I snap.

I glance at him, an awful part of me hoping that my words will hurt him as much as his have hurt me, but he's glaring at me with no trace of the tortured, apologetic Atlas I saw last night.

'Forget it,' he says. 'You're not going.'

My eyes narrow. 'Shall we send someone else instead? Who do you suggest should take my place?'

'No one,' Atlas says. 'No more kids will be offering themselves up as food for dragons, all right?'

His defiant gaze lands on Hollingsworth and an understanding passes between them. Something else I'm not part of.

'King is correct,' Hollingsworth says.

She is still surveying the battle below, a cigarette smoking between her fingers. She turns to Sophie. 'Now, Miss Rundell. Please direct me to your mark.'

'*You* want to be the one to draw Krasimir out of hiding?' I say incredulously.

'Yes,' she replies with a smile. 'It's about time I saw some battle.'

We all gape at her and Sophie shakes her head. 'I – I don't think Cormac would allow it.'

'It's a good thing Cormac isn't the head of the Coalition, then.' Hollingsworth stamps out her cigarette under the sole of her shoe. 'Hop to it, recruit. We haven't got all day.'

'But why would Krasimir come out of his hiding place for you, Dr Hollingsworth?' I say.

She laughs. 'Do you think that, in the whole time the Bulgarian dragons have been occupying our country, they never once tried to contact me? They saw the weakness in Wyvernmire's ruthless ambition and used it to their advantage. But they found no trace of weakness in mine, so they tried to befriend me instead. I too have been offered a place in the new world,' she says, her eyes settling on me. 'And I'm going to let Krasimir think I want it. Perhaps we *do* still stand a chance, even without the wyvern Koinamens.' She glances down at the array of dragons, wyverns, humans and Speerspitzes on the beach. 'The bastard won't know what's hit him.'

I grin.

'I'll go with you, ma'am,' Gideon says, shouldering his gun as he looks to Sophie. 'Lead the way.'

'Gideon,' I say. 'There will be—'

'Bolgoriths?' he says weakly. 'If I'm not killed by one today, I'll never complain about dragons again.' He glances at Sophie and Hollingsworth. 'But if I keep them safe while they do what they need to do, then at least I can say I did something in this war.'

Sophie grabs my hand and squeezes, and the three of them start making their way down the hillside. Atlas's eyes linger on their backs.

'Right,' Serena says. 'Let's get on with it.'

'My group's almost ready,' Jasper says. 'The Guardians are their target.' He points further along the beach to where a big group of teenagers are hurriedly strapping all manner of flint-based weapons to their bodies. A wall of white fog surrounds them, keeping them hidden from the Bolgoriths fighting just a few feet away. I look up and see streaks of blue amid the rotating wall of cool mist.

'The wyvern art of cloud-spinning,' I say quietly.

I stare at Atlas and I know he knows what I'm thinking. I can't fight like the others. I can't track Krasimir or translate Cannair. There's nothing that I, Viv Featherswallow, can do to help win this war. He takes a step towards me.

'Just go,' I tell him. 'I'll stay out of the way, don't worry.'

I take in his tired face, the cuts on his hands from where he pulled me up on to the rocky ledge, the damp curls on his forehead. Right now, I don't even care that he lied to me. All I care about is the fact that if he goes down on to that beach, he might not come back.

His eyes search mine.

'I don't know where to start,' he says softly, 'except by saying I'm sorry.'

I suck in a breath. 'No time for that.'

'Viv, I want you to know. I . . . I –'

'Please,' I whisper. 'Don't say it. Not here. Not like this.'

He opens his mouth as if to protest, then gives a curt nod. Marquis is watching us, his eyes shining. I look at him and Serena and force a smile.

'Bletchley Park to the rescue again,' I joke as Marquis pulls me close.

I breathe in the smell of him, just in case it's the last time. One day, I hope, we'll eat pierogi from Mama's best china again. He pushes a small flint knife into my hand. Atlas gives me a long look and then the three of them dart down the hill towards the Speerspitzes on the beach.

I'm the only one left on Compass Hill.

I stand, painfully exposed, my eyes on the sky as the battle rises around me. How long until I'm spotted by a Bolgorith? I wish I could use a knife like Jasper's kids or ride a horse like Ruth. Instead, I have a head full of untranslatable Cannair words and nothing to show for it. What is there left for me to do, apart from hide with the children on Sanday? Every part of me is awash with terror as I see Atlas, Marquis and Serena reach the beach. What if they're killed in front of me? How can we stand a chance without the wyvern Koinamens?

I watch the patterns of battle emerge. The rebel dragons are fighting the Bolgoriths in the air while the humans take aim from below. The rebels seem to have assigned one dragon and three humans to every Bolgorith, working together to exploit the creatures' weaknesses. I watch as one rebel punctures a pouch around his neck, filled not with poison but with blood. Its target smells it immediately and changes course, while the other two rebel humans take aim. They're firing rifles, not Speerspitzes, but the Bolgorith's inattention causes it to display the soft undersides of its pouch. A rifle bullet slices through the skin and as the Bolgorith lets out a furious scream, the rebel dragon drags it to the ground.

Along the beach, someone emerges from one of the tents. Wyvernmire.

So she *is* still here. Two Bolgoriths walk on either side of her, but this is no prime ministerial envoy. Her right shoulder drags, dislocated, and her sleeve is drenched in blood from what can only have been a bite.

They're escorting her to another tent and just before she reaches the entrance, she lifts her face to the sky. Her mouth twists into a horrified grimace. What must it be like to know that the reason you cannot see the clouds through all the Bulgarian dragons is because you invited the enemy here? What must it feel like to have failed your country so spectacularly? She ducks into the tent, a prisoner of war.

The fighting lasts for hours, but it feels like minutes. I crouch, shielding my head, and planes rattle above. I can't tell if they're flown by rebels or by the Guardians being forced to fight for the Bolgoriths. More dragons reach the shoreline. They plough through the sky like airborne giants, but their wings beat and curl with the effortless elegance of butterflies, as if moved by invisible currents. My heart leaps at the sight of an immense Western Drake, so blue she's almost black.

'Bolgoriths?' she bellows. 'Bow!'

Dragons part as the solid mass of spikes and scales lands on the beach, her tail slashing the face of a Bolgorith that is battling two rebel Ddraig Gochs.

I stare in awe. So *that*'s where the rebel numbers have come from.

'You dare defy the Monarch of the Deep Sea Isles?' the Western Drakes snarls. 'Victor of the last dragoning, Raptor of Britannia, Mother of Dragons, the Blue Baroness, Terror of Beatrice? *Your* Queen?'

I sink to my knees in relief.

Ignacia has joined the Coalition.

Her voice is coarse and vicious and the other British dragons appear almost small beside her. She is the same size as the Bolgoriths that immediately launch an attack. A shadow falls across me and I recoil behind the rock as more Bulgarians flock towards the Dragon Queen. They descend on her like dogs and the battle suddenly shrinks to her perimeter as the rebels move to defend her.

I stare at the scene through the long grass. Sand swirls in great golden gusts, Canna abundant with countless British dragons. Children armed with knives and guns and crossbows dart between the huge scaly bodies and wyverns screech as they soar through the air like birds. I spot Atlas and Cormac loading a Speerspitze together while, beside them, two Guardians are helping Serena to point her own skywards. My body tingles. It's no longer Wyvernmire against the rebels, but Britannia against the Bolgoriths.

And we might just win.

A rush of black.

Goranov streaks past me, another dragon on his tail.

Krasimir.

I jump to my feet, looking for Sophie or Hollingsworth, but there's no sign of them. Body parts swing from the rings embedded in Krasimir's skin as he lunges at Ignacia, taking a bite out of her side. She screams in pain as her guards force Krasimir backwards, one of them ripping a lump of scales from the regal's face.

He springs towards the Queen again in a rush of blood and arrogance.

'He is demented!' snarls a voice.

Chumana flies over me. She glides through Ignacia's defence line, and she must be echolocating because none of them try to stop her. She whirls round to face Krasimir, her jaws an open grin as Ignacia's tail flicks in recognition. The Queen lets out a groan and then the two dragons launch themselves simultaneously towards Krasimir. The sunlight blinds me momentarily. All I see is a flare of blue and red on black.

'Death awaits you, oh great Regal,' Chumana snarls.

They fight him side by side, the dragon who signed the Peace Agreement and the dragon who broke it. Chumana bites down on Krasimir's leg and he roars in agony. Ignacia clamps her jaws around his tail and jerks him backwards, sending him spinning through the air. The fighting has resumed but it's almost half-hearted, every eye drawn to Chumana and Ignacia, the scene magnetising the attention of both rebels and Bolgoriths. My blood burns with energy. I'm witnessing history.

I'm witnessing the best of Britannia drive the Bulgarian invaders from our land.

Ignacia lets out a blood-curdling scream as Krasimir strikes from behind. Chumana's talons rake across his back, but not before his jaws close around Ignacia's head. Krasimir rolls in the air, twisting the Queen's neck. She is decapitated in one swift jerk. Blood sprays as her body falls. It collapses to the ground with a thump that reverberates beneath my feet.

As dragonfire erupts on the sand around her, Krasimir flies higher, parading Queen Ignacia's head through the smoky sky.

Twenty-One

ATLAS STUMBLES IN THE BLOOD-SOAKED SAND below, staring in horror at Ignacia's headless body as Cormac swings the Speerspitze around towards Krasimir. The sky fills with shrieks and movement as several dragons streak back towards the sea. For a moment I think they are flying out to meet another incoming Bolgorith assault, but that's not what is happening.

Ignacia's dragons are fleeing as fast as they arrived.

Krasimir drops the queen's head into the water with a splash. Where is Chumana?

Two Speerspitze shells almost find their target, but Krasimir deflects the first with his tail and the second ricochets off his scales. He hangs over the battle, a stark, gigantic shadow, and leers as his troops maul a rebel dragon, its lifeless body crushing several humans when it falls. I see Serena crawl out from behind it, dragging herself across the sand, a mere hair's breadth from death.

I can't breathe.

Marquis is loading a Speerspitze while Freddie fires. Atlas is still motionless, staring at the sky, his face red in the heat of the dragonfire. I follow his gaze. The clouds part suddenly, fat raindrops falling, and with them comes Chumana.

She's in freefall, as straight as a pin, her wings tucked against her body as she picks up speed. Krasimir doesn't have time to look up. Her wings erupt at the last minute and she seizes him by the neck, shaking him like a terrier shakes a rat. Three Bolgoriths attack her from the side and she's forced to let go. They grapple in the air.

I see a snare of wings stretched and entangled at unnatural angles.

Then comes the crack of bone.

'Chumana!' I scream.

My heart hammers in my chest as I stare, trying to see through the flashes of taut tendons and floating feathers.

They're going to rip her apart.

A screech.

The wyverns mob the Bolgoriths, diving like gulls. Blood streaks the sky as they bite into flesh and muscle and Aodahn's tail twitches like a whip, blinding its victim. Chumana is free and she pivots to face Krasimir again as he veers across the sky, this time with less ferocity.

I taste iron and realise my face is splattered with blood. Krasimir's neck is pulsing, the laceration left by Chumana's teeth a mess of white sinew and bone. He drops, then rises, then sinks towards the waves.

'Traitress,' he roars as Chumana glides towards him. 'You

desert your own motherland.'

Bulgarians breathe a flurry of flames that don't reach Chumana. Soresten and Addax are flying above, their own dragonfire redirecting the inferno.

'Such a mother deserves desertion,' Chumana snarls.

Krasimir lets out an enraged bellow as he drops even lower, his talons skimming the waves. His neck convulses, like a muscle spasming of its own accord, and he lets out an anguished scream as he forces his head round to face Chumana. She closes in on him, her jaws open, her tongue curled as if to administer a kiss of death.

A *coup de grace*.

A final blow.

'Brasstongue!'

A black dragon is hurtling towards me. I jump out of the way of Goranov's flame. The heat skims my face as it scorches the grass where I was standing.

'Up, up, you're nose-diving!' I hear Ralph scream.

Goranov swoops upwards and as he flies along the curve of the cliff I see Ralph still sitting astride his back, his feet dug between the black scales and a Speerspitze across his lap. Panic flares in my chest as I look out across the bare hilltop. No matter which direction I choose, I have too far to run. Another stream of fire will reach me before I find cover. I force my legs to move, crashing blindly down the hillside as Goranov rises from below, his body parallel with mine. I see Ralph's face, small and pale in the wind as he clings to his master's back. My feet leave the ground as I stumble several feet down the hill and land so hard the breath leaves my body. Someone pulls me to my feet.

'Dr Hollingsworth?' I say. 'I thought you went with Sophie?'

We both look up as Krasimir flies across the sea, still alive. Then Goranov veers, circling me.

Hollingsworth's hand tightens around my arm as she flings back her head. 'Take her!' she bellows into the sky. 'Take her now!'

What?

Time slows as Goranov's jaws open. Orange flickers between his teeth. I feel the skin on my face peel.

A screech like a motorcar braking slices through the air and a wave of heat shoots by me. Chumana's huge frame skims the top of my head as she lands with a snarl, her wings outstretched in front of me like a shield. Goranov is forced to double back and circle above us and as she reaches up her neck to snap at him, she lets out a deafening cry.

'Touch her and you'll burn,' she spits.

I catch a glimpse of Ralph's face, wincing as he struggles to keep his grasp on the Speerspitze. Goranov aims another blast of fire at me and Chumana deflects it with her tail.

'Son of a bitch,' I hear her mutter in Slavidraneishá.

She breathes her own cloud of fire, engulfing Goranov's wing. The edges singe, the flames dangerously close to Ralph, and Goranov is forced to plummet towards the sea to douse them.

'I cannot protect you here,' Chumana says, turning to me. 'You will have to fly.'

I nod, looking for Hollingsworth, but she's gone. I climb

Chumana's tail, using the spikes to pull myself upwards and on to her back. My feet find the familiar holds between her scales and as I lie flat against her body, my face flush on her hot skin, I'm reminded of the very first time.

'You should have killed Krasimir!' I shout.

'And let Goranov kill *you*?' she snarls.

We lift into the air. Chumana flies across the sea, scouting Goranov and Ralph from above. The wind steals the breath from me and makes my eyes water. Goranov is still flying erratically, lopsided, and he only picks up speed when he realises we are above him.

'What's wrong with him?' I scream.

We swerve sideways, Chumana on Goranov's tail. 'He has not drunk his fill,' she says.

I look down at the beach and my heart sinks. Krasimir is fighting on land, his teeth sunk into the back of another dragon's neck. I see Soresten and Addax attacking him from above, but his tail swipes Addax from the air, crushing her against the high cliffs.

'No!'

Then I see Hollingsworth, running down the hillside towards the beach. What happened back there? Who was she shouting at to take me? Chumana . . . or Goranov? Further along the shore, Marquis, Freddie and Serena are still fighting alongside Wyvernmire's Guardians and a shot brings another dragon down into the sea with a crash. Marquis is grinning, wielding the Speerspitze like he was born to it. This is what he wanted, where he's felt he should be ever since those protests broke out in Fitzroy Square in what feels like a lifetime ago. Marquis always knew which side he should be on and suddenly here he is, a trained rebel, making a difference in this war. And here *I* am, sitting between Chumana's wings as she fights, unable to help her. I came to this island thinking I, *the face of the rebellion*, was going to save everyone. But now, without my languages, without any sort of training, all I can do is hope to be saved.

'Where is Atlas—' I begin, but the breath is snatched from my lungs.

The cliffs fly by beneath us, each grey rock dotted with fire. Battle writhes across Canna's green arms and spills on to its beaches. Chumana's body seems to lengthen as she tucks in her wings and flies back along the coast, following Goranov's volatile path through the sky. She shoots towards the hillside, riding the wind like an arrow about to hit its mark. There is Atlas on the top of Compass Hill. Panic fills me. What is he doing up there? He must be looking for me. I grip Chumana with my thighs as she snaps at Goranov's tail, my hands frozen cold around her spikes. Goranov swings around, hurtling back towards the battle again.

'He knows he can't fight you,' I shout at Chumana. 'He wants you to tire, to land.'

Chumana laughs. 'I will land when I'm dead. But not while Bulgaria subjugates our skies.'

Goranov is dropping lower, shuddering mid-air.

'Up!' I hear Ralph scream as Goranov barrels through several warring dragons, then swoops upwards again, this time sluggishly slow. Chumana lets out a roar as she follows him and I lose sight of Atlas, but see more movement across neighbouring hills – people on horseback. Ruth sends her horse cantering down towards the beach, narrowly missing the snapping of jaws as she stoops to pick up an injured rebel. Gideon rides a second horse, Sophie behind him. I take a deep breath.

For now, everyone I love is still alive.

My eyes settle on the scars between Chumana's wings from where I cut two detonators out of her skin. Who was the girl who set a criminal dragon free from that library? I'm not her any more. And I'm not the girl who ventured into the wyvern tunnels, either.

As the sound of battle rings around me, the glacial wind strips me of everything else. My education, my reputation, every qualification and expectation and birch-rod scar. I'm not a Draconic translator or a codebreaker or the face of the rebellion.

Right now, flying free with Chumana, I'm a clean slate. As new as the day I took my first breath.

There's a jolt as Chumana's jaw closes on Goranov's haunch. His body curves round to retaliate as he snaps at her front legs, his yellow eyes suddenly on me.

'You have lost, brasstongue,' he snarls.

'She is no brasstongue, Goranov,' Chumana hisses. 'She is Vivien Featherswallow.'

Chumana pronounces the words with such finality, as if there is nothing more to me than my name. It feels terrifyingly ordinary. Mediocre.

Liberating.

I'm just Vivien Featherswallow.

And if that's enough for Chumana, then it's enough for me.

In the twist of wings and scales I see Ralph lift his arm.

'Chumana!' I scream.

The rounded end of the Speerspitze is loaded with a heavy metal sphere. I stand up, my arms encircling Chumana's head.

'Fly!'

Chumana clamps her mouth on to Goranov's back leg. With a strength that almost shakes me from her back, she pulls the limb away from his body, his flank splitting open to reveal thick, viscous blood. He lets out an enraged moan.

Chumana is propelled backwards with a loud boom that cracks open my skull.

She rolls.

Suddenly I'm blind, no longer able to tell the difference between sky and sea. And then we're falling, dropping through the cold air faster than I can think. Something sharp rips open my elbow as I feel Chumana turn beneath me, but when we hit the sand, no pain comes. I open my eyes to darkness.

'I can't see,' I whisper frantically. 'I can't . . .'

Chumana's wing drops from around my body, letting the sunlight and smoke in. I'm lying on her chest, the hard scales of her breastbone hot on my face, my arm sliced open by one of her spikes. I slide down her body carefully, then jump off her tail into the sand. The sound of fighting still hums in the air around us, but I can't see it from here. We're in a sheltered bay.

'Chumana,' I gasp. 'Are you all right?'

My eyes dart along the beach, but there's no sign of Ralph

or Goranov. I run around Chumana's body to her head and fling myself on to my knees next to her. She blinks and lets out a huff, and droplets of blood spray from her mouth. My stomach lurches. I scan her flank until I see it – a bullet the size of my fist buried above her left leg.

'It's nothing,' I say. 'It's nowhere near your heart, or anything.'

'Humiliating,' Chumana growls.

I climb back up on to her curled tail to reach the bullet. Its rough metal surface protrudes from the open flesh, leaking a shiny grey substance.

'It's nothing,' I tell her again. 'I'll get it out.'

'It has already reached my bloodstream, human girl.'

I sit back. 'Your bloodstream?'

'Canna's children aren't alone in their idea of using poison against dragons,' Chumana says.

'The bullets are poisoned?'

'How else do you think they bring a dragon down?' she tuts.

Imported from Germany and named after a snake.

I swallow.

Then I remove Marquis's knife from my belt and plunge it into the wound.

Chumana roars.

I seize the handle, dragging the blade through the skin around the bullet, trying desperately to dislodge the metal as more liquid seeps across the knife.

'Pointless, you fool!' Chumana screeches.

Her tail comes out of nowhere, launching me from her

body so I fall to the ground beside her, wheezing for breath.

'Fuck you!' I gasp angrily as I try to stand. 'Do you *want* to be poisoned? Hold still and let me—'

'Human girl!'

I freeze.

'Come here.'

I swear again, then kneel down by her head. Her amber eyes glow just as brightly in the sunlight as they do in the dark. She blinks as if tired. I reach down and wipe blood from the corner of her jaws.

'If you don't let me get that bullet out,' I tell her with a shaking, voice, 'then it will kill you.'

She sighs, and more blood speckles the sand.

'It already has,' Chumana replies softly.

My chest constricts as I let out an odd, unfamiliar noise. 'Why . . . why are you giving up so easily?'

Chumana chuckles. 'Do you call this giving up? Krasimir is injured and Goranov will bleed out before nightfall. He's as good as dead.'

'What if he's not?' I say. 'Besides, there are hundreds more Bulgarians to kill.' My breath catches in my throat. 'I'll find you another dragon, someone who can heal you with their Koinamens, the wyverns— Daria! I know you love her. You must be bonded, you must.'

'Our bond is not strong enough for that, not yet,' Chumana says. 'It is the price I pay for having left her all those years ago.'

'Then me!' I say. I thrust up the sleeve of my jumper to the deep wound in my arm. 'Take my blood, as much as you need. Go on, do it.'

'We have needed each other, you and I,' Chumana says quietly as she stares into my face. 'To teach each other the importance of a second chance. I have seen you live out your own on this island, just like you said you would. I have watched you from afar, fighting for the rebels, even as you struggled to fulfil the part you thought you were supposed to play. You don't know who you are without the labels other people give you. Identities that are rooted in the very system you are fighting to bring down. Daughter, student, criminal. Translator, rebel, Swallow.'

'Chumana, please.'

'Will you let me say my piece?' she snaps. She runs her tongue across her bloody lips. 'Like a dragon, you itch to shed your old skin. You are human, so you cannot, but you *can* try metaphorical skins on for size, to see which fits you best.'

My breath comes faster as Chumana's begins to labour and I force myself to stay silent, to cling to every word that comes from her mouth.

'Who are you if not a Draconic translator?' Her whole body heaves in a nonchalant shrug. 'It is nothing more than a career, after all. The essence of who you are, who you have always been, remains the same. As for the rest of you . . . you have a whole lifetime to find out.'

'And you?' I ask her, my voice thick with tears. 'You've shed your skin a hundred times over since the Massacre, trying to forgive yourself. Have you found out who you are?'

'I have been dragonling and dragon, lover and murderer, criminal and commendable. But in the face of death, none of these really matter. No one is the sum of their mistakes or their achievements.' She sighs. 'I am Chumana.'

'Snake Maiden,' I whisper.

She breathes, her lips stretching into a smile as her eyes close. 'Just Chumana. Like you are just Vivien.'

'You've never called me by my name before today.'

'I never thought it suited you,' she growls. 'Until Daria, in her studies of the British Latin maxim tradition, told me it means *alive*. And that is how I wish you to stay.'

I lay my head on her snout and force myself not to cry.

'When Krasimir and Goranov are dead and this war is over,' she says, 'you must stop trying to *be* someone. You will not find yourself until you do. There is no one singular title to define you, *just Vivien*. And you may feel broken to begin with, but as Britannia rebuilds itself, so will you.'

I nod. 'Atlas has been trying on different selves, too. Seminarian. Boyfriend. Traitor. Earlier, I think he was going to tell me he loves me.'

'And is the feeling mutual?'

'Yes,' I croak. 'But what if, once I've rebuilt myself, I don't feel the same? Translation took up such a huge part of me, too big a part. And now I think it's gone. What if it's the same with my love for Atlas? Or what if, after this war, he finds out he's someone different, too?'

I blink the tears away and see the golden orbs staring at me intently.

'Of course you will be different. This war will shape you, human girl. But this is not the first time you have remade yourself. And it will not be the last.'

I sniff, my eyes on the pitiful, bloody knife on the ground.

'If you choose to dig that bullet out of me when I'm gone, be sure to use a better blade. We both know we cannot count on your teeth.'

I smile at the old joke and for a moment I'm back with one of my old selves, the frightened, confused, angry little girl who was about to release a criminal dragon and begin a war. Then I look down at the familiar, spiked face and realise I can't feel her breath on my skin any more.

'Chumana?'

The golden orbs close.

The cries of battle carry from the other side of the cliff and I know I cannot stay. I feel a tender ache in my throat. A series of sharp pains in my chest threaten to crack me open.

'But I love you,' I whisper, biting back sobs. 'I love you, so you can't leave.'

I stare at the tremendous creature who deigned to make a deal with me, who flew across the sea to find me, who sat with me in a watery ditch and told me I was worthy of a second chance. She glows pink-orange in the sunset. Fiery, even in death. I plant a kiss on Chumana's warm snout as a flight of swallows dip and dance above us.

I stand up, my most recent memories of her flooding my mind. Flying with her in the sunrise. Watching her burn Wyvernmire's camp to free me. Lying next to her in the sugar house, my unlikely roommate, her presence a path of light through the darkness of my nightmares.

'You once had the honour of being like her,' I murmur to the birds. 'Watch over her. She's not used to sleeping alone.'

Twenty-Two

A HIGH CHIRRUP.

A chatter.

A dracovol zips around my head, fluttering its wings and breathing out a puff of grey smoke.

It lands on my shoulder and I jump as I see someone walking towards me. Her hair is gold in the sunlight and her eyes linger on the dead dragon behind me.

'Ruth?' I say.

'This way,' she tells me, beckoning towards the sea.

I follow her. 'How did you know I was here?'

'Atlas.'

'Atlas?'

We reach a series of rocks just out of reach of the waves and Ruth crouches down. 'In here.'

I frown, peering closer, and she disappears between the rocks. The dracovol follows her. I drop to my knees and look down. What I thought was a small pool is actually a hole. I sit on the low rock, dangle my legs over the edge of the sandy tunnel and jump down. It's a short drop and when I stand up I'm in a dark but wide space.

'Ruth?' I whisper.

There's the sound of a match striking and then a small flame fizzes to life. Ruth lights a lamp and lifts it up to my face. Atlas is standing beside her and behind them, the walls are covered in faded tweed.

'Viv!' Atlas says, grasping me by the shoulders. 'I saw you fall. I thought . . . I thought . . .' His eyes land on my bleeding arm. 'Are you all right?'

'I'm fine,' I say, but my voice breaks. 'What are you both doing here? Where are we?'

'Abandoned wyvern tunnels,' Ruth says.

'They go all the way to Sanday,' Atlas tells me.

'Across the whole island, actually,' Ruth says.

I stare at her. 'These tunnels are how you get around?'

'Yes. The dracovols scout out the tunnels. They can navigate in the dark like bats.'

'With echolocation,' I whisper.

'That's how you found the dracovol looking for me,' Atlas says slowly. 'All the way on the other side of Canna.'

Ruth nods.

'Do the wyverns know?'

'Of course not,' Ruth says. 'Once they abandon a tunnel, they never return.'

'I wouldn't count on that any more,' I say, thinking of Abelio. 'Your Sanday caves. They weren't built by old islanders, were they?'

Ruth smiles and shakes her head.

'Where does this tunnel lead?' Atlas asks.

'Back to the battle,' Ruth says. 'If that's where you want to go?'

'No,' he says, shaking his head. 'No, we don't.'

I frown. '*Yes*, we do,' I tell Ruth.

Atlas grabs my arm so hard I feel it bruise. 'What are you doing?' I snap.

'We've got to go,' he says, casting another look down the tunnel. 'To the other side of the island. Now. I know you don't want to, Viv, but you've got to trust me. You've got to go with me, because you have no idea what's coming and I don't have time to—'

'Atlas,' I say. 'Chumana is dead.'

A small noise comes from his throat. His eyes sharpen in shock. 'How?'

'Ralph shot her.'

Atlas stares at the tweed behind me. 'Then it might already be too late,' he whispers.

'No!' I say. 'Krasimir is weakened. Chumana saw to that. And Goranov is as good as dead. He and Ralph . . .'

At the thought of Ralph, my mouth turns dry.

He fired the Speerspitze that killed Chumana, injecting a poison that even my blood wouldn't have been able to counteract.

I'll make sure there's no second chance for him.

But Atlas is still shaking his head. He looks at me as if he's drunk, as if he doesn't know who I am. And then suddenly he focuses.

'I'm sorry,' he says. 'I'm so, so sorry.'

What is he talking about?

'I've told you more lies than I can count. But it was all to save you, Viv, and you have to let me try. You have to come with me. Please.'

I blink. 'To save me?'

Atlas's jaw trembles. 'The rebels *do* have a Plan B, in case the wyverns couldn't be convinced to use their Koinamens.'

I feel a small rush of relief. 'What is it?'

He stares at me. 'Goranov has agreed to call off his war on Britannia. He agreed months ago, before you even left London. There's this dragon in Bulgaria, head of a council of regals. He drinks human blood to stay alive and his . . . his current human has died. He needs a new one, but there are no people left in Bulgaria.'

'I know about the council,' I say, remembering what Daria told us on Sanday. 'But how do you?'

'Hollingsworth,' he says. 'Goranov asked her for ten humans per year to be sent to Bulgaria as blood perfumers for the head of the council. In exchange for an immediate Bulgarian retreat. And the first human Goranov wants,' Atlas says hoarsely, 'is the brasstongue.'

My head spins. 'Me?'

Atlas nods as Ruth stares at him in horror.

'That's why I accepted Hollingsworth's secret mission. She told me about Plan B, told me how crucial it was that the wyverns help the rebels. That's why I lied to you, Viv. Why I was still lying to you in Canna House. I had to get you to convince them, because I can't let the alternative happen.'

He's crying now and the image of Hollingsworth on the hillside flashes through my mind.

'You mean that, because the wyverns refused to use their Koinamens – because I wouldn't ask it of them – I'm going to be *sacrificed* instead?' I place a hand on the wall to steady myself. 'Why didn't you tell me?'

Atlas's gaze meets mine. 'Would it have changed anything? Would you have tried to *force* them to use their echolocation? I know you wouldn't, Viv.'

'We could have come up with a different plan,' I say angrily. 'You, me, Marquis—'

'What plan?' Atlas explodes. 'How do a bunch of kids stop a Bolgorith from taking you? How do we convince the entire rebel movement that their leader has made an unspeakable deal from a secluded Scottish island? And what about Ursa? Would you have tried to escape, leaving her to be eaten by Bolgoriths?' He snorts. 'You would have rather offered yourself to Goranov willingly.'

He's right.

'Who knows about this plan?'

'Hollingsworth, Cormac, Dr Seymour and me.'

I pale. 'Dr Seymour?'

'That's why she sent you Clawtail's journal and the coded directions,' Atlas says. 'She knew what Hollingsworth would do if we failed and that she wouldn't be able to stop the plan once it was set in motion.'

'So Hollingsworth's intention,' I say shakily, 'is just to give me up?'

'Along with nine other people,' Ruth spits. 'Every year.

Another corrupt offering of human flesh in exchange for peace.'

I shake my head. None of this makes sense. Hollingsworth is a rebel who cares about human and dragon equality, about the individual people who make up the oppressed Third Class. Surely she wouldn't do this?

Take her! Take her now!

My eyes land on Atlas. 'Back on the beach, everything you said about hesitating over the priesthood, about . . .'

'It was all true,' Atlas says fiercely. 'I *was* lost for a while, after Bletchley. But none of it mattered any more once Hollingsworth told me of her plan. She knew I would do everything in my power to keep you safe, including exploiting the wyverns.' He reddens with shame. 'And I knew it too. That's the only reason she told me. And it's why I went looking for Chumana when we got out of the wyvern tunnels. I was going to tell her everything, ask her to fly you away, but then we found her imprisoned. Now, please, Viv, come with me.'

He holds out his hand.

'Where to?' I say. 'And what about Britannia?'

'I don't care about Britannia any more!' Atlas roars. 'If Goranov takes you to Bulgaria, Bolgoriths will feast on your blood for the rest of your life.'

'But Britannia would be safe,' I say quietly. 'Ursa would be safe.'

He sinks to his knees.

'You would burn the world for your sister, wouldn't you?'

I nod.

'I would burn it for you, Viv,' he sobs.

I drop down next to him, tears pricking my eyes. 'But we have to do the right thing, Atlas. We can't simply save ourselves.' I think of who I was back at Bletchley Park, how I almost refused to join the rebels out of fear for my family. 'I tried that before, remember?'

I press my lips to his cheek and we kneel in the silence, crying.

'You 'ent going to give yourself up?' Ruth says to me in disbelief.

I shake my head. 'Not while we still have a chance at winning.'

'You think we do? Have a chance?'

'Thanks to Chumana, yes. Krasimir and Goranov are both injured. Surely the rebels have enough dragons to finish them off.'

I pull Atlas to his feet.

'This way, then,' Ruth says.

She turns and heads down the dark tunnel. I move to follow her, but Atlas grabs my hand. His cheeks are red from crying and his mouth is a taut, quivering line.

What is it?' I say.

'If we fail, I won't let you give yourself to Goranov. You know that, don't you?'

'I won't have to, Atlas,' I lie.

He kisses me gently, tentatively and then, when I don't pull away, his mouth turns hard and deliberate. I kiss him back, my lips scorching, my mind clouding with surprise and desire.

The edges of the wound in my arm burn. Will feeding my blood to a dragon hurt more than this?

'For God's sake,' Ruth shouts. 'Can't you save the snogging for when you're sure you're actually going to survive?'

We come apart, our faces tearstained, the wyvern-spun tweed at our backs. I take Atlas's hand and we follow Ruth's voice towards the battle.

*

The sky is black with dusk and dragonsmoke when we emerge from a cave in the cliff face. We're standing on the beach where Wyvernmire's camp was, every tent around us burned to ash with only their metal pegs remaining, glinting in the torchlight that pierces the gloom. The rebels have dragged out the torches used in Chumana's prison tent to help them guide the Speerspitzes. I see a black hole in the sand – the detonator must have exploded. On the hills above, a fire-breathing plane lies on its side. The battle is still raging and the sand is littered with bodies. The bodies of Guardians and rebels. The bodies of dragons.

Ruth sinks down to the ground to crouch over a small figure wrapped in furs, then looks up at me with tears rolling down her face.

The bodies of children.

I let out a small, horrified cry.

Marquis, Serena and Freddie are still fighting, their faces caked in blood and soot. Beside them are Hollingsworth, Sophie, Gideon and Cormac, and a whole group of rebels and

Guardians. And yet the air is still full of Bulgarian dragons.

'Viv!' Marquis shouts as we approach the Speerspitzes.

He jumps down and embraces me, his clothes slick with sweat. He smells of gunpowder and his eyes are red-rimmed with exhaustion. He glances at Atlas, then Ruth.

'Where have you been?' Serena says as she loads another poisonous sphere into the barrel of a Speerspitze.

Freddie stands behind her and reaches around to adjust the positioning of the gun's muzzle. Rebels run past as a shadow drops across the beach. Krasimir flies over us, his neck still dripping with blood. His talons reach for a human in his path, lifting them into the air before flinging them back down against the rock.

'Incoming!' Freddie shouts.

Krasimir turns and glides back towards us, his huge body glistening, his talons trailing innards. I see Aodahn, Cindra and Aberdine move across the sky. They strike from above, so much smaller than Krasimir but slicing wounds into his skin like hungry vultures. More wyverns attack from the ground and when Krasimir swoops down on them they disappear into the sand, tunnelling out of sight before I can blink. Freddie swings the gun in Krasimir's direction but the Bolgorith veers sideways as Serena fires.

Another Bolgorith sends flames careening towards the wyverns and when Aberdine shoots upwards to avoid them, Krasimir catches her by the neck. She convulses for several seconds before he clamps his jaw closed, then lets her drop unceremoniously to the ground. Cindra lets out a heartbroken yowl and flies at Krasimir again just as several other rebel dragons join her. I recognise Yndrir, another Bletchley dragon, among them. As they attack, the rest of the Bulgarian dragons swarm around Krasimir. I count about over fifty, all battle-worn but still going strong.

'Retreat!' someone bellows.

Cormac is ordering a huge crowd of gun-toting rebels to shelter as the body of a British dragon slams on to the sand. Above, its murderer breathes a ring of fire around the remains of the tents. Rebels scream, fleeing across the beach.

My eyes meet Atlas's wild stare. 'No human will survive this.'

He turns to Ruth and says something. She runs into the crowd and begins leading people towards the cave we just came from.

'Where's Chumana?' Sophie shouts at me.

A glint of orange fizzes in the corner of my eye and I pull her into the sand. The Speerspitzes to our left erupt into flames and Serena screams, the left arm of her jacket on fire.

'Serena!' Marquis bellows.

Freddie throws his body on top of hers, smothering the flames with his hands, then pulls her up and drags her away from the raging fire.

I crawl across the sand to reach them. 'Is she okay?'

Serena is sobbing, holding her arm as violent tremors take over her body.

'We have to go back to the caves,' I say, looking around until I spot Hollingsworth, firing with Cormac.

Freddie nods and lifts Serena off the sand as Atlas runs for Hollingsworth. I see her argue with him beneath the flickering shadow of flames. Then her eyes land on me. I feel something inside me shrivel. Does she have a way of contacting Goranov from here? Atlas shouts something at her. She gives a small nod, abandoning the Speerspitze, and he hurries back towards me.

'What did you say to her?'

'I told her Chumana knows about her plan,' Atlas says. 'And that if she tries anything, she'll soon be dead.'

'Chumana is—'

'She doesn't know,' Atlas says. 'Let's keep it that way for now.'

'This way!' Ruth shouts, leading us back in the direction of the tunnel.

I seize Atlas's hand and run, then stumble on a body in the sand. I leap backwards as I stare into a cold, dead face.

Ralph.

My eyes land on his empty gaze and I feel nothing. His skin is smooth and pale, marked only by a spot of blood left from a shaving cut. His chest is oddly sunken. He must have been crushed when he and Goranov fell from the sky.

But where is his master?

'We're losing,' I gasp as Freddie and Marquis carry Serena past me and through the cave entrance. Ruth is running to and fro along the cliff face, gesturing to rebels and children to follow her.

'Viv!' Atlas says.

He pulls me into the cave. We flatten ourselves against the cold wall as more people rush inside. Awful roars sound on the beach and inside the cave, fearful eyes glint in the darkness.

I stare out at the battle, every patch of sky and hilltop lit by fire. Ursa is hidden away somewhere with Dr Seymour and her baby. If the Bulgarian dragons take over tonight, will they have to live underground forever?

There are hundreds of people inside the cave, a mix of Guardians, uniformed rebel soldiers, Canna children and civilians who must have flown in from the mainland. I see a huddle of kids armed with flint knives and spot Jasper among them. He nods at me as he watches Freddie bandage Serena's arm. I pick my way through the crowd towards them. Serena has stopped shaking but her face is twisted in a grimace of pain. Freddie has wrapped her burn in a wet handkerchief and is helping her hoist her arm into a sling.

'That'll keep it from getting infected,' he mutters as she blinks in surprise.

'We were promised planes,' I hear someone shout. 'Fire-breathing ones. So where in God's name are they?'

I turn around.

'We flew in here on a suicide mission,' the man is yelling, his voice echoing through the humid cave. 'We're all going to burn.'

I close my eyes and wipe the sweat from my brow. Outside, steam is rising off the sand.

'Our fleet of fire-breathing planes was sabotaged when the Bolgoriths attacked Eigg a few days ago,' says a clipped voice. Hollingsworth strides into the middle of the cave. 'Every plane we built on Eigg over the last month, save for two, was torched.'

'Shit,' Marquis mutters.

A soft moaning comes from the corner of the cave. It's

Edward, stretched out on the ground with George's jacket over his shoulders, a pool of blood seeping out beneath him. I go to him, then take a step back in shock. Vomit rises in my throat. His leg is gone.

'Pen?' he says, looking up at me, his face as pale as sand.

'Edward,' I whisper.

I drop down beside him and take his hands.

'Bolgorith,' he says shakily, looking down at his missing limb. 'Beecham had to tourniquet it. I'm lucky it didn't devour me whole.'

I look at George, who stares at me with glassy eyes.

'What are you even doing here?' I turn my head towards Hollingsworth. 'Have you made a habit of sending untrained soldiers into battle?'

Her eyes narrow. 'The rebellion accepts any willing volunteer. And we were desperate.'

'You should have stayed in London, Ed,' I say miserably. 'Both of you.'

'We had to fight for our country,' George says. 'Looks like we're about to die for it.'

'It was those bloody pamphlets of yours that made me join.' Edward squeezes my hand. 'Your name isn't Pen, is it?'

The pamphlets. My tiny act of rebellion actually moved people to action. I blink back tears.

'Hyacinth always thought there was more to you than you were letting on.'

A deafening roar comes from outside and horror settles in my stomach. This is it. The battle has barely begun, but we've already lost.

Why did we think we could win against Bulgarian Bolgoriths?

'Where's the Swallow?' someone mutters. 'I thought she was supposed to be leading us.'

Hollingsworth gestures towards me. 'The Swallow is—'

'Shut up,' Atlas snaps at her. 'Just shut up.'

The cave goes quiet and I see Marquis reel in shock. But Hollingsworth hasn't so much as flinched. She takes a step forward and gestures to me again.

'Here is your Swallow,' she says, her voice steady. 'For months, she has worked tirelessly to win this war. She has rebelled both in the shadows and in the light, operating undercover in London and on Canna with the Hebridean Wyverns. But heroism is not always met with the victory it deserves. You have heard of the Swallow's bravery on the radio, seen it brought to life in the lines of her likeness that fill the rebel newspapers. And now you will witness it with your own eyes. For she has chosen to sacrifice herself for her beloved Britannia.'

Atlas's hand clasps mine as my mouth turns dry. The sketches of me in Hollingsworth's office, Serena's radio reports . . . they were all for this. To turn me into a personality.

A martyr.

'What's she talking about, Viv?' Marquis says.

'The Bolgoriths have agreed to retreat, if they can take the Swallow with them,' Hollingsworth says.

'No!' Marquis cries. He looks from her to me and then at Atlas, his eyes burning with rage. 'Did you know?'

'She will be honoured by the Regal Vasil, living a life of

luxury and security in exchange for her blood, which has the power to keep him alive.'

Horrified gasps fill the crowd. Ruth steps out in front of me.

'You shan't have her,' she spits. 'You and Wyvernmire, you shan't have any of our kids. We 'ent yours to take.'

'I am no Wyvernmire,' Hollingsworth says coldly. 'I have campaigned to reverse the Canna project for years. *I am the one who sent you those books through the smuggling caves, Ruth, along with the materials for my father's grave. Canna's children owe nothing to Britannia, I'll give you that.'

Ruth scowls.

Hollingsworth's eyes land on me and I wonder how it has come to this. Back in London, when we were studying the wyverns together, we really thought we were going to win. Her Plan B, despicable as it may be, makes sense. But I know she doesn't want it any more than I do.

'I'm so sorry to have to ask this of you, Vivien,' she says softly. 'To leave your family and live among Bolgoriths is no easy fate.'

'No easy fate?' Marquis snarls. 'You call having your blood sucked by a twenty-foot reptile *no easy fate?*'

'The Swallow will not be harmed,' Hollingsworth says sharply. 'I made sure of it. She will remain fed and healthy, dignified and courageous. She is of great value to the Regal Vasil, and not merely for her blood. She is what the Bolgoriths call a brasstongue. A speaker of many tongues. For the Bulgarians, who have been shunned by the rest of the world, she is an invaluable political pawn.'

I feel my eyes narrow. Is this still all I am? Hollingsworth's Swallow, a bird to be caught in a snare? Goranov's brasstongue, a translator in a gilded cage? Am I destined to live by other people's definitions of me for the rest of my life?

'And the same goes for any of the men or women who volunteer to go to Bulgaria with her, this year and every year after.'

Someone swears at Hollingsworth, a barrage of insults that land on deaf ears.

'This is the price Britannia must pay to keep her loved ones safe! Ten humans per year, in exchange for financial compensation for their families.'

'Only the Third Class need that,' someone mutters. 'So I guess they're the ones who'll be doing the paying.'

'No one will be forced to go. And no children,' Hollingsworth glances at Ruth, 'will be permitted to volunteer.'

'You'll have Viv when hell freezes over,' Atlas snarls. He looks to Cormac, the man who trained him to survive on Canna. 'Are you going to let her get away with this?'

'I don't like it one bit, boy,' Cormac replies. 'But I've never seen an invasion like this. The Chancellor is acting for the greater good.'

'You go, then!' Serena shouts.

'Dr Hollingsworth can go,' Sophie snarls.

'Oh, I intend to,' Hollingsworth replies. 'You didn't think I was going to send Vivien alone? I will be one of this year's sacrifices, too.'

The cave falls silent again.

'I'll volunteer,' George Beecham says, stepping forward.

'I'm nineteen. Not a child.'

I shake my head, my eyes filling with tears. Surely this isn't the only way?

A figure appears in the cave entrance.

It's Wyvernmire, her face covered in soot and her eyes wide with panic. Immediately, the girls from Sanday surround her, their charred furs engulfing her like a black cloud.

'How did you escape the Bolgoriths?' I demand.

The Prime Minister looks at me, then at the rebels, and sways. 'There was no guard.'

'You're of no value to them,' Marquis says darkly. 'I'm surprised you're still alive.'

'Not for long she won't be,' says Ruth. She steps towards Wyvernmire, her face so close that their noses almost touch. 'Her name was Clemmie. She was thirteen years old and she's dead because of you.'

I remember the dead child on the beach and catch Ruth's eye. There's a flash of a challenge, as if she's daring me to interfere. But I have no intention of it. Footsteps sound as Jasper and Freddie join her, followed by what is left of their own groups.

'Look at her!' Ruth shouts. 'This doe-eyed, trembling old lady is the woman who sent us here. She's the reason we've all watched kids die. Why we had to make poison pouches. She let the Bulgarians in and fed Clemmie to them!' Her voice cracks as more people gather round. 'And now, this Hollingsworth woman wants to do the same thing. I say we kill 'em both.'

Atlas is no longer by my side. My gaze flits around the

cave. He is standing just outside the cave entrance, the shape of him illuminated by the orange flames. He's pointing to the sky, whispering to Cormac who is nodding as they follow the trajectory of a Bolgorith. I touch my necklace as I see him say something to two rebels. He points at their guns, then at the dragons outside, and the rebels are nodding, obeying his order to bring him their weapons. When he lifts his hand again I see the curve of each finger in the moonlight, hands that have held a gun, held a prayer, held me.

And something unfurls inside me. Everything he has done on this island was to save me, to save his country. Atlas never went to university, never won any awards or cracked any codes. He's *more* than what people wanted to make of him, more than a priest or a rebel; just like I'm more than a brasstongue or a symbolic bird. Chumana was right about that. I love him, but not for what he has achieved. It's *who* he is – a dragon-hearted boy whose lies were an act of devotion – that makes me want him.

So perhaps there's still hope for me.

'*We*, Canna's children, are walking proof of Wyvernmire's corruption,' Ruth shouts, drawing my attention again. '*We* are the secret clause in her Peace Agreement. And we will be her downfall.' Her eyes flash. 'This 'ent her island. It's ours. And she'll watch us take it back, you'll see.' She casts a look outside. 'We don't know how many dragons we have left, so it's up to us to bring Krasimir down. He can't fly high – we have that British Bolgorith to thank for that.'

I smile, knowing that Chumana would like this description of her.

'I want Speerspitzes set up in a circle,' Ruth says, climbing up on to a rock.

Every rebel, every Guardian is watching her. She looks to Cormac.

'When Krasimir flies over, you fire together. Understood?'

'You heard the lass,' Cormac growls as he turns to the rebels. 'What's the ammunition count?'

'Your poison pouches are your final weapon,' she says to her girls. 'If you're about to die, you can at least put a Bolgorith out of action for the rest of the battle!'

Marquis is nodding, his eyes alight. I meet his gaze and know, with a sudden certainty, that he would have followed Ruth in her plan to kill both the Prime Minister and the leader of the Human-Dragon Coalition.

Better that than lose me.

'Something to consider,' I say, taking an awkward step forward, 'is that the Bolgoriths have poor eyesight. They hunt in packs because they can communicate, er –' I glance at Hollingsworth – 'telepathically.'

Everyone stops to look at me and my voice rings clumsily throughout the cave. I promised the Koinamens would remain a secret, but I can't keep this crucial information from the rebels. Not if it could save their lives. 'Some of you already know this and some of you don't, but I'm afraid there's no time for questions. What one of them can see, albeit poorly, the others can see. A Bolgorith could be preying on you here on this beach, watching your every movement while simultaneously seeing you from his brother's vantage point. It makes them almost impossible to escape. Except for the fact that their weakness lies in their telepathy, too.'

Atlas meets my gaze and smiles. He gestures to a group of Guardians holding rifles. 'You can't kill a dragon with those guns, but you *can* aim for the eyes. If they lose the ability to see in two places at once, they lose their advantage. Right?'

One of them, a man almost as young as Atlas, nods.

'We've really got to go back out there?' George asks.

His face is ashen and full of terror.

'No one's going to make you,' Marquis says. 'The whole point of rebellion is freedom. But if you want to protect that freedom for Britannia, not just for its Third Class but for all its humans and dragons, we have to kill that Bolgorith. Krasimir *must* fall.'

'Speerspitzes and any guns or arrows that will take out their eyes,' says Ruth. 'Leave your knives behind.'

The man who complained about the planes is nodding as the cave rings with the clatter of weapons. Atlas points at two of Freddie's kids, his eyes darkening. 'You keep one of the Speerspitzes on Goranov, understand?' He glances at me. 'You don't let him near her. You shoot on sight.'

They nod. The rebels surge towards the entrance and Ruth lifts her crossbow.

'For Canna!' she bellows as children spring out on to the sand.

I feel Hollingsworth watching me. I turn to her slowly, then point to Ruth, to Jasper and Freddie and Marquis and all the other kids.

'I was never your Swallow,' I say. 'They are.'

But if this doesn't work, I know what I'll do. I'll slip away from the battle and find Goranov. It's not a death sentence. I'll just be some Bolgorith's pet. I force myself to imagine a burning Britannia, Marquis and Sophie cowering like prey, Ursa lying still and cold.

These are far worse fates.

'We have thirty Speerspitzes,' Cormac tells Ruth outside. 'Twenty on the shoreline and another ten on the hillside.'

'And we have ten,' Freddie says, walking across the beach.

'Serena?' I say as she follows him. 'You can't shoot with that arm.'

'Don't patronise me, Featherswallow,' she says, tightening her sling. 'I can still load.'

I step out on to the sand and Atlas grabs me by the sleeve. 'Stay close to me.'

Cindra and a group of wyverns swoop above us towards Compass Hill. I stare at the sky. I count a few dozen Bulgarian dragons between here and the sea, all airborne. And half their number of ours.

'Wait for the dragons!' Atlas calls out to the rebels. 'Wait until it's safe to cross the beach.'

The rebel dragons rise up to meet the wyverns and together they fly towards the Bolgoriths, forming a defence line in the sky. I see the glint of jewels in the twilight. Krasimir joins his Bulgarian battalion, although his neck is half severed.

'Now!' Atlas shouts.

We run across the sand, his hand still in mine, until we reach the lapping waves where the Speerspitzes are positioned. Atlas swings one away from the sea and points it upwards towards Krasimir, but he's disappeared. I drop to the ground, fumbling in the sand for one of the shells I've seen piled high. It's cold and menacing in my hand, full of the same poison that killed Chumana. I want to throw it into the sea, but I load it into the Speerspitze as Marquis does the same beside me. Atlas and Sophie move the barrels of their Speerspitzes across the sky, searching for Krasimir, but in his absence Sophie fires hers and only narrowly misses a Bolgorith flying towards us.

'Shit,' she squeaks.

The Bolgorith picks up speed, bringing its talons up to stretch them outwards.

'Marquis!' Sophie screams.

Marquis swears as he reloads and Sophie fires again. The shell hits the Bolgorith in the chest. It plummets and hits the sand, then lies there breathing slowly.

'It won't die until the poison—'

My voice is drowned by a furious shriek as a Ddraig Goch swoops low over the Bolgorith and snaps its neck.

'Where's Hollingsworth?' Atlas mutters.

I glance back at the empty cave entrance, then shake my head.

'Have you stopped for a picnic, Featherswallow?' Serena screams. She loads another shell into Freddie's Speerspitze and whips around to glare at me.

'Sorry,' I say.

I reach for one of the cold spheres as Guardians fire their rifles into the sky on either side of me, aiming for the Bolgoriths' eyes. I fling it into the waiting Speerspitze. A wyvern streaks past, leaving a trail of smoke and blood. The Bulgarian battalion reconverges, flank to flank, a wall of scales moving across the sky. Wyverns and dragons attempt to attack, but the Bolgoriths simply rip them from the air. I reel at the sight of them advancing towards us. The rebels have been reduced to about ten dragons, the rest injured, dead or fleeing.

'There's no way we'll be able to fight this many Bolgoriths with nothing but the Speerspitzes!' I scream, but nobody hears me.

The Bolgoriths are making an awful grunting sound, like a chant.

'Where the hell is Krasimir?' Marquis shouts.

'He's inside,' Serena says calmly.

I swing around to look at her as she points at the sand beneath the battalion. It's pooling with blood, a steady stream raining down from above.

'They're shielding him.'

'Like a Trojan horse,' Atlas murmurs.

A Bolgorith drops from the formation, straight into the sea.

'What the . . . ?'

The space it leaves is filled as the Bulgarians move close together, but before they do I see a flash of colour. Another Bolgorith drops. It spirals out of control as it lands, crushing two Speerspitzes, a dead weight.

Cormac lets out a furious bellow. The Bolgoriths pull closer together, filling the gaps.

'Atlas!' I grasp him by the jacket and pull him towards me, but he swings the Speerspitze around again, looking for a gap in the shield.

'Fire!' Ruth shrieks.

Six girls are manning two Speerspitzes. Jasper and Roy canter through the smoke, their horses dragging nets full of bullets through the sand. A few feet away, Jasper's friend Henry lies dead beneath a mauled Western Drake.

I see Goranov dragging himself across the sand, his back to us, a thick river of blood trailing behind him. I don't think he could fly me to Bulgaria even if I asked him to. The Bolgoriths breathe fire across the sky, a continuous blaze that lights up the night. I see a Guardian carrying one of Ruth's girls back towards the caves, blood trailing behind them. Cormac is shouting orders at several rebel men as they attempt to dislodge one of the Speerspitzes from beneath the body of a Bolgorith.

'Atlas,' I beg.

He looks at me and I shake my head, my eyes filling with tears.

'It's too late,' I shout. 'We need to run.'

Atlas looks up at the fire, then back at me, then nods. 'Marquis,' he shouts, wrapping his arms around me. 'Fall back.'

My cousin's eyes are stricken with despair. Another Bolgorith drops from the sky.

Then two more.

Then another.

The shield is falling apart.

I stare up, searching for their rebel attackers, but most of our dragons are lying on the beach.

Krasimir drops lower, exposed as his protection momentarily disperses, then descends with him. I let go of Atlas.

Among the black and red scales are slivers of blue.

Hebridean Wyverns.

Ten Bolgoriths crash into the sea. I hear a tormented scream. At the far end of the beach, Goranov is writhing in the sand. He contorts as if burned by invisible flames. And at the same time, Krasimir lets out an excruciating roar.

'What's happening to them?' Sophie shouts.

Goranov shudders twice, then lies still. The sky fills with wyverns. I scan it for Daria, feeling a surge of panic as I remember what Sophie told me about her sibling bond. But she's nowhere to be seen.

'They're echolocating,' I whisper as half the Bulgarian battalion collapses into the sea. 'The wyverns are emitting a kill call.'

Above us, the surviving wyverns soar between the fiery clouds. They dart and glide in a breath-taking dance, their bodies moving together like a pair of synchronised wings, rising and falling in harmony as two separate groups come together to drive the remaining Bolgoriths towards the waves. They drop dead, one by one, into the water.

'Incoming!' someone screams.

Krasimir is plummeting, spinning out of control. He skitters, jerking like a fish caught on a line.

'Rebels, disperse!' Marquis roars from his Speerspitze.

Krasimir lands on the sand making a bone-chilling yapping sound.

What does a kill call sound like? What must it be like for Krasimir to hear death approach in his own mind, to have his own brain turn against him and implode? He lurches towards the Speerspitzes, screaming like a skua.

We stumble back into the sea as his black body towers over us. Roy drags one of Ruth's girls out of the way as Krasimir's neck, almost drained of blood, swings out of control. My boots fill with water as the waves lap around my knees. Sophie reaches for my hand and Atlas shouts something I can't hear. Krasimir keels over with a sickening thud.

'What's he doing?' Marquis shouts.

Atlas is running across the beach towards Krasimir, surrounded by clouds of disturbed sand. I blink it out of my eyes, my vision blurring, then stumble out of the water after him. His shirt, rolled up to his biceps, is soaked with seawater and splattered with dragon blood. I stare in horror as Krasimir twitches, then sways to his feet again.

He isn't dead.

The wyvern Koinamens didn't kill him.

I cast a desperate look at the sky for Cindra or Aodahn, but the wyverns are far across the sea, chasing the other Bolgoriths. Only a few remain above, divebombing Krasimir ferociously.

There aren't enough of them to emit a final kill call, and the remaining rebels have evacuated the beach.

My stomach lurches.

I run after Atlas as Marquis and Sophie scream at me, my waterlogged clothes slowing my movements. Krasimir limps towards him. Atlas drops to the ground, searching, his eyes still on the Bulgarian regal. Krasimir's blood pours on to the sand, turning it black. I reach Atlas and grab the back of his shirt.

'Viv?' he says, his eyes wild. 'Get back!'

There's a shell in his hand.

I grab the end of the Speerspitze and swing it round, my arms straining against the weight. Krasimir stares down the barrel with a snarl. I look him in the eyes as Atlas loads the shell.

'Who,' Krasimir breathes, 'are you?'

I feel Atlas climb up behind me and his hands come down over mine.

'She's the Swallow,' he spits.

I shake my head as we guide the barrel together.

'I'm just Viv,' I say.

I fire.

Twenty-Three

THE BULLET HITS KRASIMIR IN THE face, blowing off his jaw. He drops dead with a quake that knocks us both off the Speerspitze. My ears ring. I sit up, spitting out sand, and the beach is momentarily swathed in silence.

A monstrous yapping fills the air.

I blink, my eyes straining in the smoke. My gaze meets Atlas's as he shakes his head in disbelief.

No.

More Bolgoriths emerge from across the hills.

'How?' Atlas croaks.

I let out a desperate sob as I try to think. 'A back-up battalion, made up of different family groups,' I say slowly. 'Krasimir must have known what the wyvern echolocation can do. Wyvernmire must have found out and told him. He planned his battalions so that the Bolgoriths in the second are unbonded to those in the first.'

I shiver.

'The wyverns took out the first battalion, family group by family group, while the second waited, unaffected.'

Which means that we're dead.

The wyverns are gone, the rebels defeated and Atlas and I are lying beneath a fresh horde of uninjured Bolgoriths. Time slows as Atlas crawls in my direction, the blue sea at his back and a red bank of blood-soaked sand between us. His arms wrap around me and he pulls me to my feet.

'I love you,' he says, his hot breath in my ear.

I blink, marvelling at the irrational confidence that made me believe I might ever get to say it more than once. 'I love you.'

My vision blurs as I scan the beach. Marquis is firing the last remaining Speerspitze, taking aim at the new Bulgarians in the sky. He dives into the sand as a rush of fire engulfs it. Jasper and Sophie are dragging Ruth between them towards the caves, her long hair streaked with blood. Marquis, Serena and Freddie run after them. Everywhere smells of burning; burning gunpowder and burning flesh, and as a Bolgorith snarls Atlas screams at me to move. I stumble in the hot sand, my head spinning.

Britannia is going to be overrun by Bulgarian dragons. I'm never going to see my sister again.

'I'll go with you!' I scream into the sky. 'I'll go with you to Bulgaria!'

Atlas lifts me bodily from the ground, enveloping me in the smell of sweat and dragonsmoke as he drags me across the sand. 'Move!'

I try to breathe but the air is full of fumes, filling my

lungs as I imagine Ursa growing up in the darkness with Dr Seymour, forgetting about me, about our parents.

'Wait!' I choke. 'Listen.'

'Viv, hurry!' Marquis has turned around and is running towards us, tears rolling down his nose.

But I tear away from Atlas and turn my face to the clouds. I can hear something.

The steady beating of wings.

'More Bolgoriths,' Marquis breathes.

'Have you gone insane, Featherswallow?' Atlas snarls, grabbing my arm as Marquis wrenches me towards the caves by the other.

'Three beats, not two,' I mutter.

My heart quickens.

'It's not Bolgoriths.'

Shadows drop across the sand and the hazy light of the dragonfire is momentarily extinguished as hundreds of dragons surge from behind the cliffs. And then they're everywhere, pouring in from Sanday, from behind Compass Hill, from across the sea.

'That's . . . that's a Double-winged Sapphira, a Spanish dragon!' Marquis shouts. 'And an Austrian Solar-tail.'

I shake my head. That's impossible. We don't have those species in Britannia.

Two British Sand Dragons reach the beach and wrench a Bolgorith from the air, twisting its neck before it hits the ground. They're followed by a dragon with a long yellow mane.

A Pyrenees Python?

I see a flash of pink and my stomach plummets, because I know what I'm seeing is impossible. The dragon soars through the torchlight and I realise that I'm not looking at Chumana, but Daria.

'Foreign aid,' she purrs as she lands beside me. 'Bolgoriths really *are* the most hated dragons in Europe.'

I watch as a Western Drake fights beside a Vermeil Viper, and their tails lock together to protect an Italian Tortoiseshell from a lethal Bulgarian blow. They're from different cultures, speak different languages . . . but solidarity like this doesn't need translating.

We reach the cave as Europe's dragons join forces with what is left of Britannia's troops. The moon is high, its white light bursting through the dragonsmoke. The Bolgoriths are outnumbered, fleeing in droves, and I see Daria and Aodahn bring one down together, their scales glittering in the pearly night. Atlas turns to me, his face creased with exhaustion. I take his hands in mine.

'I'm not going to Bulgaria,' I breathe.

He laughs quietly. 'No, Featherswallow, you're not. You're going home.'

My shock turns to sobs as I try to hold myself together. Atlas wipes a smear of blood from my cheek and kisses me. Wyverns and dragons soar along the silvery coastline as the Bolgoriths retreat. The sea shimmers in the moonlight. I think of Clawtail's last description of the island, an ode to his home before he was killed.

Such a heavenly rock is Canna.

I scan the cave, lit by the fires flickering outside. My eyes linger on each bleeding rebel and I'm unable to stop myself from counting, from searching for missing faces. I can't see Hollingsworth anywhere. Wyvernmire is sitting against a wall, her head in her hands. The noise outside is deafening as I sink down beside her, dizzy with exhaustion. I glance at Atlas and Marquis, watching the last of the battle from the mouth of the cave, then at the Prime Minister.

'How did you know what the wyvern echolocation could do?' I ask her.

She looks up. 'My nephew worked it out. We knew you were looking for wyverns, and when Atlas refused to give him the loquisonus machine in Canna House, he put two and two together.'

'He knew before I did, then,' I mutter. 'But why did he tell you?'

'He thought that if I gave the information to Krasimir, he might keep me alive. He was right about the Bolgoriths turning against me. I should have listened.'

I glare at her. 'Ralph tried to save you, then. You always underestimated him. If you hadn't, perhaps he wouldn't have become who he was. Perhaps he wouldn't have killed Chumana.'

Wyvernmire stands up, brushing the dust from her trousers. 'Perhaps. And perhaps I underestimated you, too. Rita Hollingsworth certainly did.'

I shake my head. 'She knew exactly who I was.' I get to my feet. 'But I'm going to rebuild myself, Prime Minister. I don't want to be a brasstongue. I think I'll give the languages up for now. Without them, I can be someone new.'

Wyvernmire gives me a look of surprise. Then she jolts forward, her eyes widening in shock.

'Prime Minister?'

Wyvernmire staggers sideways, a small flint knife sticking out of her lower back. I pale as Ruth steps out from behind her.

'Help!' I shout as Wyvernmire collapses.

I drop down beside her, reaching for the knife. She shakes her head at me, her eyes huge, her hair unkempt. I watch her pupils dilate.

'Help me lift her, quickly,' I hear Marquis say to Atlas.

Wyvernmire lets out a small gasp, then shudders.

'Shit,' Marquis whispers.

Ruth eyes meet mine in a long, hard stare.

'Told you I'd make her pay.'

She steps back into the shadows.

*

Rebels crowd the blood-soaked beach, warming cold hands by the dragon-lit fires in the dawn. A chilled mist gathers around them, purging the air of the smoke. The smell of fried pigeon makes my mouth water. I keep walking, Atlas by my side. I can't bring myself to sit still, to rest. Not until I've found what I'm looking for.

A sign that the Bulgarian Bolgoriths are really gone.

We walk hand in hand, past Jasper and Philippa, past Freddie draping a blanket over Serena's shoulders and Ruth's girls who are sipping something hot from bowls that Sophie and George are handing out. Edward is being hoisted into a small rowing boat by two medics, and as more reach the shore I see Marquis leap up from the sand and stumble towards them, his arms outstretched. Karim steps out of one of them, looking ten years older, and they fall into each other's embrace.

'Reports coming from the Inner Hebrides, home to the Human-Dragon Coalition Headquarters, tell us that the war is over.' A voice crackles through Serena's radio. 'Indeed, as we look out of our window now, we can see the foreign allies landing in London. It took them long enough, didn't it, Drake?'

'Look, there are the Bulgarian oafs, rising above the city, fleeing as the mothership calls them home. Britannia has won the war, Sandy! I repeat, the war is officially over.'

'Is it, do you think?' I say quietly to Atlas. 'Is it really over?'

Dragons are dragging dead Bolgoriths towards a great fire between two cliffs, an honour they don't deserve. As their scales crack and bend I see the grim finality of it, of this war we very nearly lost. So what now? Above us a group of Western Drakes keep watch, as sceptical as I am. Atlas squeezes my hand and we keep walking.

There is a line of bodies, surrounded by flowers and seashells that more of the Sanday girls are quietly arranging. Among them I see Cormac Mackenzie and Roy. Atlas releases a heavy breath. The sea rises up to kiss the body of a Sand Dragon who could merely be sleeping.

'His sister is over there,' I hear Gideon saying. 'Burn them together.'

We watch as a dragon drags Addax towards Soresten,

several Guardians holding her tail. My heart wrenches.

'Viv!' Gideon shouts when he sees me. 'Where's Chumana?'

The mention of her name is like a punch in the stomach.

'She died,' Atlas says softly.

Sorrow shadows Gideon's face but before he can reply, we hear voices. People are marching down the cliff towards us, a mix of rebels and Guardians carrying gas masks, led by Hollingsworth. In the aftermath of battle, with her untamed hair and a limp she didn't have before, the leader of the Human-Dragon Coalition looks almost frail. I see Cindra beside her, black smoke rising from her mouth. They come to a stop in front of us and Hollingsworth's eyes search mine.

'You convinced the wyverns to use their Koinamens,' I say stonily.

'Convinced?' Cindra snarls. 'Have you learned nothing of the Hebridean Wyverns, Vivien Featherswallow?'

Hollingsworth nods. 'Cindra made the decision herself. We owe her our lives.'

'And how are you going to save hers?' Atlas asks. 'Now that the world is about to find out that the wyverns killed the Bolgoriths?'

'What are you talking about, King?' Hollingsworth says. 'It was the foreign aid that killed the Bolgoriths, and just in time. The Regal Goranov was defeated by the great Chumana, who died for her country, and the Regal Krasimir was killed by *two* of our Swallows – Vivien Featherswallow and Atlas King, using those marvellous guns the late Prime Minister had made in Germany. I saw it with my own eyes.'

So that's her story. That's how she's going to protect the wyverns. By covering up how they used their Koinamens with a newspaper-worthy story: not one but two Swallows triumphing over the Bolgoriths, witnessed by every rebel present. The wyverns won't be in danger, will be able to come out of their concealment without being seen as a threat to the world. I gaze at Hollingsworth's wrinkled face and determined smile. She has done it again. Twisted the truth to ensure that she wins.

'You should pray that the rest of Britannia never finds out what you tried to do, *Chancellor*,' Atlas says scathingly. 'You would be more hated than Wyvernmire.'

In some ways, I admire her obstinate refusal of Wyvernmire's government, of a Bulgarian regime, of a war between humans and dragons. But I'll never trust her again. Like Wyvernmire, the founder of the Academy for Draconic Linguistics is not who I thought she was.

Perhaps, I think to myself, *this war has changed us all.*

Cindra steps aside, gesturing with her snout.

'Your tunnel-detecting machine,' she tells me in Cannair with a glint in her eye.

I pick the loquisonus up off the sand and it's cold and hard in my arms.

'Thank you, Cindra. Your tunnels. Are they—'

'Still inhabitable, according to Abelio,' she replies. 'But we have no use for them now.'

She stares across the beach at the wyverns, who are curled up in a blue pile on the beach, sleeping. There are so few of them now. Their kill call would have only been able to reach one Bulgarian at a time, unless they were part of a bonded group. Such repeated concentration must have cost the wyverns all their energy and by the time they got to Krasimir, there simply wasn't enough left.

As Cindra slinks away to join them, I look at Hollingsworth. 'Did they find your father's journal, too?'

Hollingsworth nods. 'Cindra returned it to me, along with her own writings. And I found more of my father's sketches in Canna House. I was born there, you know.'

I remember the watercolours of the wyverns.

'It's all going straight to the Academy to be preserved. The first known study of the language called Cannair. I believe you added some of your own, too, Vivien?'

'They're more like trans-estimations,' I say. 'I've never known a language to have so many layers of meaning. I don't know if an accurate translation will ever be possible.'

Hollingsworth nods. 'I was going to offer you a job, in the event that—'

'In the event that you didn't have to turn Viv into a blood sacrifice?' Atlas says coldly.

I lay a hand on his arm as their eyes lock.

'But,' Hollingsworth continues, 'I'm afraid we won't be going back to our old lives just yet.'

I stand up straighter.

She lowers her voice. 'We have made a mockery of the Bulgarian Council of Regals. The Bolgoriths that died here today were from Krasimir's regality, but there are numerous others.'

'What are you saying, Dr Hollingsworth?' I ask as fear rises in my stomach.

'The war isn't over,' she replies. 'How could it be?'

'But Krasimir's army is defeated.'

Hollingsworth's mouth trembles. 'The Council of Regals didn't take Krasimir's invasion of Britannia seriously, Daria tells me. They knew that he was not of sound mind and so refused to send their own regalities to war. But now that he is dead, they will be forced to retaliate. And rumour has it that Krasimir was one of the most . . . accommodating of the regals.'

'Then we need to tell everyone to stop celebrating!' Atlas bursts. 'We need to warn—'

Hollingsworth holds up a wrinkled hand. 'Parliament is already calling an emergency session. We need not alarm the people yet. Let them rest a little first. And do not despair, both of you.' She watches an Austrian Solar-tail soar through the sky. 'This time, we have allies.'

I sigh and sit down against the cliff, setting the loquisonus in the sand. Atlas sinks down next to me and we watch Hollingsworth congratulate another group of rebels. They eye her warily. I'm not the only one who has lost my faith in her. The oyster-catchers begin their song and out on the sea a ship is sailing towards us.

'That's what we're going home on,' Atlas says, pointing to it. 'Seeing as the Bolgoriths took out our planes.'

I cradle my bloody arm, wincing at the thought of stitches. 'Do you think there's anything left of London?'

'If new Bolgoriths are coming, they won't arrive for several days,' Atlas says grimly. 'That will give us time to assess, to set up some new defences.' He throws an arm around me. 'The first thing we'll do is find Ursa. We'll send a dracovol, to tell Dr Seymour where we are.'

I give him a tiny smile, the anticipation of seeing my sister again rising above my renewed terror.

'Viv?'

'Atlas?'

'I – I once told you the priesthood was how I was called to love. But I was wrong.'

He's looking at me sheepishly, letting sand trail through his fingers.

'God wouldn't ask you to make a vow you don't want to make, Atlas. The priesthood is—'

'Is *not* the vow I'm talking about.'

'It's not?'

'No.'

Atlas reaches to touch the swallow around my neck and I feel heat creep across my skin.

'I joined the rebellion because my conscience urged me to, and I told myself it was fine to be breaking the law and shooting Guardians as long as I became a priest after,' he says. 'Surely, that was what God had led me to Father David for. But then you came along, Featherswallow. Every time I tried to clear my mind, to pray, you were there. Your smile, the smell of your hair, your infuriatingly stubborn personality. I begged God to let *you* be his will for me, to change my vocation. But when I woke up on Eigg after Bletchley Park, you were already gone.

'And then a letter came from Hollingsworth, detailing the orders for a secret mission and the Plan B that would ensue if I failed.' He grimaces. 'It was cruel of her. She knew I wouldn't tell you the truth about needing the wyvern Koinamens to win the war, because you'd refuse to ask it of them and then Plan B would be enacted. And she knew I wouldn't tell Chumana about Plan B, because she would have killed Hollingsworth and the rebel movement would have fallen apart.' He closes his eyes. 'There was no way I was going to tell *you* about it, either, in case you turned round and bloody volunteered.'

When he opens his eyes, there's a depth to them I've never seen.

'I realised, as soon as I saw your name in her letter, and then again at the egg-choosing ceremony, that God had heard my prayer. That my calling was to something – someone – else.'

My heart flutters like a dracovol's wings. 'You told me mine was languages,' I say before he can continue. 'But you were wrong about that, too.'

'You're still a translator, Viv. Just because Cannair was—'

I shake my head. 'It's okay,' I tell him. 'I don't think I want to be any more. Some things are only meant to form a small part of us and yet we let them become our entire identity.'

Atlas frowns.

'Don't you think?' I say.

'I think there are big vocations and small vocations,' he says. 'The type we're meant to dedicate our lives to – like the priesthood for Father David, or fatherhood for Aodahn.' He hesitates. 'And the type that is only one piece of a larger puzzle, a job or a state of mind that is the means to a higher end. Maybe you thought translation was the former, when really, it's the latter.'

I nod.

'If we're about to head into another war, then I don't want to wait, Featherswallow.'

I meet his gaze. 'Wait for what?'

'I don't have a ring . . .'

I stop breathing.

'Atlas—' I begin.

'You don't have to answer me yet,' he says quickly. 'But I know what I want. And it's not this, Viv.' He gestures to the destruction around us. 'It's not the priesthood, either. My vocation is you. It's been you ever since Bletchley Park.'

I want to say yes, want to fall into his arms and whisper it a hundred times into his ear. But I shake my head, my throat dry as I try to find the words.

'I'm not ready to get married, Atlas,' I say softly.

His face falls.

'For years, I convinced myself that my languages were the most important part of me. And then I thought I was the face of the rebellion, thought I was going to win the war through translation. I was vain and naïve and selfish.'

Atlas stares at the sand. I take his hand and kiss it.

'I don't know myself,' I say. 'I need to figure out who Viv Featherswallow is, and that will take time. I need to learn to like myself, Atlas. For who I am, not what I can do.'

I lean in as he looks up and our faces are so close I can see the tiny grains of sand in his eyelashes.

'All right.' He smiles his crooked smile. 'But don't give

up your languages completely. I've always wanted to talk to a Pyrenees Python, so I'm going to need you to teach me Drageoir.'

Later, we step on to the ship. Its sails billow in the wind as the skippers, two Scottish rebels, help people embark.

'Welcome aboard *Provident*,' the woman says, pushing a tin at us. 'Shortbread?'

'God bless the Scots,' Marquis mutters as he takes two slices.

I watch as Serena says goodbye to Cindra on the shore. Aodahn disappeared after the battle and I feel a pang of grief as I think of him mourning his egg up in the hills alone. What will this next war mean for the wyverns?

We find the others by the stern. Rebels file past us and down below decks, where beds and hot coffee are waiting. I see a big group of Canna kids, their pockets full of shortbread and other treats. Not one of them glances back at Canna and I realise it's because for the first time ever, the prospect of returning to London, where many of them were Third Class, is not more terrifying than calling a dragon-infested island home.

But that's only because they have no idea that the Bolgoriths will be back.

Ruth and her girls have disappeared, too. I stare over at Sanday, still and silent in the drifting smoke, and I know they're waiting underground until they're alone once more. Marquis, Karim, Gideon and Sophie are watching as the rebel dragons depart the beach in flight towards London. Serena and Freddie join them, talking quietly, and Jasper is lifting

Philippa up to touch the red sails. When they turn towards us, Atlas and I whisper the news given to us by Hollingsworth.

'So London is just another battlefield?' Serena says, blinking back tears. 'I thought we were going home.'

Marquis stares out to sea, a pulse flicking in his jaw. I watch the anger and disappointment building in his eyes and don't dare speak to him. A communal despair has drained any energy from the air. Freddie pats Serena's back awkwardly as she begins to cry and Sophie swears before flouncing away below deck.

'And here I was thinking I'd never have to see a Bolgorith again,' Gideon mutters.

I concentrate on the thought of Ursa. I imagine her running towards me, probably a head taller than she used to be. I imagine spinning her around and inhaling the warm scent of home. When we get back to London, Hollingsworth will have my parents released from Highfall. This war may have changed my life forever, but I'm about to get the most important part of it back.

I glance at Atlas. 'Your mother. Doesn't she think you're dead?'

He nods. 'I'll go to Bristol when we're back, take her somewhere safe.'

This time will be different, I tell myself as we sail into open sea. *This time, we are different. And we won't be fighting alone.*

I reach down to the loquisonus machine at my feet. Its metal is now warm from the sun and I stare at its dials, at the speaker used to hear the whisper of the wyvern Koinamens and Chumana's greeting as she arrived on Canna to save me.

I want to clutch it to my chest and keep it with me, but I know that won't bring her or the dead wyverns back. I stand it on the edge of the boat. This isn't the machine I learned to understand echolocation with, but it's the one I had with me when I realised that languages – ultrasonic or otherwise – are not the sum total of who I am.

Marquis looks at me. 'Viv, what are you doing?'

I push the loquisonus machine into the sea. We all watch in silence as it gets tossed by the swirl, a glint of gold on blue. Then it sinks, and with it, a version of Viv I'm leaving behind.

Both of them lost to the Hebridean waves.

A breeze hits my face. I see movement out of the corner of my eye but before I can turn, wings spread out in front of me, a canopy of black leather. An outstretched talon extends towards my face and next to it, slightly higher, a bloody stump.

'Bolgorith!' someone screams.

Around me, people hit the deck with their hands above their heads.

I move slowly, as if I'm still trudging through sand.

The wyvern Koinamens was supposed to have killed him.
Why isn't he dead?

The talon scrapes my shoulder, but misses. I drop to the floor, feel Atlas's arm around my waist. For a moment, there's nothing but the sound of gulls and waves. I lift an arm and blink out at the sky.

'Viv!'

As the talon descends again, someone lands on top of me. I'm crushed against the deck and then suddenly the weight lifts. I roll to my feet, then stagger.

No.

Please, no.

Blood splatters the deck as Goranov's remaining talon sinks into the shoulder of his prey, lifting him higher. The Bolgorith flounders before regaining his balance. His roar drowns out the screaming as he carries his struggling victim out to sea and I sink to my knees, sobbing.

He couldn't have the Swallow, so he has taken someone else instead.

Goranov has taken Marquis.

Epilogue

MY HAND GRIPS THE RIBBON OF Marquis's class pass so tightly that the velvet edges cut into my skin. It dropped from his pocket as Goranov snatched him, landing softly on the deck like a whispered goodbye. Perhaps he kept it all this time as a reminder of the life we left behind. A reminder of what he was fighting for. I step off the boat and on to the London Docklands, my body still feeling the rocking of the waves. It has been three days of silence, three days of replaying the scene in my mind as Atlas tried to coax me to eat, to sleep. Goranov won't make it to Bulgaria, Hollingsworth says. Daria is already out looking for him, along with a dozen rebel dragons.

But if the Regal Vasil is coming to Britannia to collect his new blood perfumer, I might never see my cousin again.

The port is chaos, newspaper sellers shouting about a general election and people calling the names of missing family members. Telegraph boys on bicycles and children carrying gas masks swerve between colossal dragons. They're everywhere, dragons of various species, perched on every rooftop and on every street corner. Trucks are parked up on the road, full of foreign soldiers exchanging cigarettes with the rebels getting off the boats. I hear English and Dutch, French and German, Italian and Spanish. So many countries have come to our aid.

Atlas squeezes my hand as we walk past them, towards the hotel where Ursa is waiting. I should be excited, but all I feel is dread. How am I going to tell her that Marquis is gone?

I concentrate on putting one foot in front of the other, my bloodstained boots striking the flagstone street as I fight to stay upright.

Will Ursa even recognise me? I'm thinner than when she last saw me, with short hair and innumerable cuts and bruises. And my love for her is different, shaped by our separation. It's a fragile, wounded, possessive love. The same goes for Marquis. The Viv I am in this moment, standing in a war-torn London with nothing left of her cousin but a velvet ribbon, would stare down the fiercest Bolgorith before she loses him.

Some things never change.

We pass by a half-demolished theatre hall, only the separate stone entrances for humans and dragons still standing. The dragon entrance is marked in Wyrmerian. I think of the love of dragon tongues that I shared with Clawtail. My languages will always be a tiny part of every version of myself I'll ever be. And my mind is already racing in an attempt to decide how I might use them to get Marquis back, despite promising myself that I'd give it all up.

Because if anyone can save him, it's me.

While we await the election of a new Prime Minister, most of the British population, and our foreign allies, will defer to Hollingsworth. She can access every resource we could need to find Marquis: Scotland Yard's special investigators, the Army and Royal Navy, the Academy, and all our dragon power.

And if I have to play the role of Hollingsworth's Swallow one last time to sway her hand, then so be it.

I know nothing about who I truly am, except for who I love. But while I try on and shed countless different skins, I'll remember what Chumana told me.

This is not the first time Vivien Featherswallow has remade herself.

And it won't be the last.

Atlas pushes open the door to the Feodora Royal Hotel and ushers me into the busy lobby. I see her immediately: a little girl in a yellow coat with a braid hanging down her back.

A radio crackles to life on a nearby table. 'This is London. Bulgarian Bolgoriths have been sighted on the coastline. All soldiers to report for duty. All civilians to take shelter immediately.'

Outside, the attack siren sounds.

'Little bear?' I breathe.

Ursa turns around.

EULOGY FOR A DRAGON

Age her scales shall not subdue
Nor time fade the pink from her wing.
In the flight of the swallows and
in our victory roar
we will remember her.

Author's Note

Some of the storylines in this book are inspired by real historical events, which are important to acknowledge.

The islands of the Inner Hebrides have changed hands many times throughout history, often with devastating consequences for the islanders, who were frequently forced to leave their homes.

The Highland Clearances began after the Battle of Culloden in 1746 and affected both the Scottish Highlands and Islands. Clan-based, Scottish Gaelic-speaking communities had lived on the Small Isles, including Canna, for centuries. But in the eighteenth and nineteenth centuries, many tenants were forcibly evicted by landowners seeking to resolve financial debts. Thousands emigrated to Canada, particularly to places like Nova Scotia, where Scottish Gaelic survived longer than in Scotland itself.

In the fictional world of this book, Canna is cleared to create a prison for 'criminal' children. As in real life, such upheavals led to the erosion of the customs and oral traditions related to the Gaelic language and its draconic descendant, Cannair – a cultural decline that still echoes in our own world today.

In the twentieth century, Canna was purchased by John Campbell Lorne, a scholar of Gaelic on whom I modelled Patrick Clawtail, and his wife Margaret Fay Shaw. I first heard of John Campbell Lorne on a research trip to Scotland. My friend Eve and I went on a week-long sailing trip along the West coast of Scotland, from Oban to Mallaig, with a night spent sleeping on Loch Ness, where I scanned the water for a dragon-shaped monster. From Mallaig we took the ferry to Canna and spent the day exploring the island, and our return trip involved a long train journey and a stop in a Waterstones, where I spotted a section dedicated to the Small Isles. The book *The Man Who Gave Away His Island* by Ray Perman caught my eye, and Patrick Clawtail was born.

John and Margaret devoted decades to collecting Hebridean folklore, song, poetry and oral traditions, recording it all in Gaelic. These traditions included the waulking of the cloth, a practice undertaken by women and girls, which involved telling stories through song while shrinking the tweed.

After the 1872 Education (Scotland) Act introduced mandatory state schooling, Gaelic was excluded from the curriculum and lessons were taught in English. The Campbells were critical of this and of attempts to 'civilise' Gaelic by reshaping its songs and grammar to fit English or Classical norms.

They purchased the island in 1930 as a deliberate attempt to preserve the Gaelic language and traditions and donated it to the Scottish National Trust in 1981. Canna House, which was unfortunately closed for renovation when I visited, contains archives of their work and reflects the Campbells' understanding that a loss of language equals a loss of culture. These archives, as well as the lives they lived on Canna, are a reminder that linguistic preservation requires both documentation *and* practice.

If you would like to learn more about Scotland's cultural heritage, *Tobar an Dualchais/Kist o Riches* and *National Trust for Scotland* are excellent online resources.

Scotland is far from the only country to have experienced linguistic suppression. My research took me across centuries and continents, revealing how language has been used as a tool of control and erasure.

In nineteenth- and twentieth-century America, residential schools were explicitly designed to strip Indigenous children of their native languages and cultures, forcing them to speak English and sever ties with their communities. In eighteenth-century Sardinia, the ruling Savoy government replaced Sardinian with Italian in all areas of public life, from administration to education.

My research also led me to Donald Trump's 2016 presidential campaign, during which white supremacists publicly told Spanish-speaking Latin Americans to 'speak English'. Among Native American communities today, many young people favour English because their tribal languages are marginalised or outright rejected in schools.

In 2000, Arizona voters chose to end bilingual education, replacing it with an untested 'English immersion' model promoted under the slogan 'English for the Children'.

And in 1847, the infamous Welsh Blue Books – officially titled *Reports of the Commissioners of Inquiry into the State of Education in Wales* – condemned the Welsh language as backward, claiming it hindered moral and economic development.

Through this research, I learned just how widespread and damaging language assimilation can be. As sociologist Van C. Tran defines it, language assimilation is a 'one-way process whereby members of ethnic groups acquire English and abandon their mother tongue, with the endpoint being English monolingualism'.

My final note is on Viv's understanding of the fictional theory pertaining to the translation of dragon tongues. This theory, with its linguistic 'subordination' and 'domination' is based on Lawrence Venuti's 'domestication' and 'foreignisation'. My Grandma, a social historian who studied our family's

Scottish heritage, took great interest in my education and sent me Venuti's books when I was writing my undergraduate dissertation on the invisibility of the literary translator. Venuti's work has influenced both my understanding of and passion for translation and I dare to hope he wouldn't mind this small act of fictional theft.

I owe deep thanks to the communities whose histories have inspired this book. If you've enjoyed the linguistic themes present in both *A War of Wyverns* and *A Language of Dragons*, I'd encourage you to listen a little more closely to the languages you encounter as you go about your lives, especially the ones at risk of being lost forever.

Acknowledgements

Second books are notoriously difficult, and this one was no exception. Thank you to my husband for his steady encouragement as I birthed both the first draft of this book *and* our first child, within weeks of each other. I can't decide which was harder.

To my parents and siblings for being as excited about this second book as they were the first, but especially for providing hours of precious childcare without which this novel would not exist. A special mention to all the mums – my mother, my mother-in-law and my step-mother – and to my brother Harry, whose patience with the baby knows no bounds. Harry, without you I don't think I would have found the courage to finish this book. Thank you for letting me run my every idea by you, for being both my first and final editor.

To my writing group – Eve, Kate, Zulekhá, Anika, Lis and Fox. Kate and Zulekhá, our writing calls and WhatsApp check-ins kept me going. Eve, our trip to Canna is a memory I will carry in my soul for a lifetime. Thank you for inviting me.

To Em, Hattie and Emma, my soulmates, for helping create the launch party of my dreams for *A Language of Dragons*, to the team at Mr B's Emporium of Reading Delights for helping send Viv out into the world and to everyone who bought a copy of the first book in this series.

To my friends in France for your support and for surprising me by showing up in the crowd on the evening of the French launch. To Anthony, for reading my book even though you don't read and to Chloé, for travelling to celebrate it with me mere days before your wedding. To Justine, Clem, Grace, Alice and Clarisse, for being my cheerleaders, for being my sisters. To Meg, my companion in motherhood, for your weekly 'how's the book coming along?'

To my agent, Lydia Silver. There's no one I'd rather brave the publishing world with. To Head of Rights, Kristina Egan – your love for Chumana makes me love her even more. To my North American agent, Becca Langton and to the rest of the team at Darley Anderson Children's.

To my UK editor, Tom Bonnick, for telling me 'I think this book might be better than the first' when I was genuinely afraid you were going to ask me to start over. I cannot describe the relief I felt. To my US editor, Erica Sussman, whose comment in a phone call sparked the development of an entirely new plotline. Thanks to both of you for allowing me to make some very last minute changes to this story!

To the whole team at HarperCollins Children's Books UK, including Jasmeet Fyfe, Aisling Beddy, Leah Wood, Dan Downham, Caroline Fisher, Rosie Catcheside and Sandy Officer. Special thanks to Laura Hutchinson, for her patience coaxing this introvert author through many online videos in order to answer reader questions about Britannia and Dragonese, and to my publicist Charlotte Winstone, who plied me with coffee and dragon-themed cocktails while guiding me through my first book tour. I still owe you a beer on a sunny terrace somewhere in France. And thank you to you both, and to Iona Richards, for treating me like one of your gang during that crazy week.

To my US team, Sara Schonfeld, Heather Tamarkin, Mary Magrisso, Meghan Pettit, Allison Brown, Lisa Calcasola, Abby Dommert and Audrey Diestelkamp.

To Ivan Belikov and Nekro for the striking UK and US cover illustrations, to Matthew Kelly and Jenna Stempel-Lobell for the cover designs and to my copy editors and proofreaders, Anna Bowles, Dan Janeck and Sara Marchington.

To all of my translators, your work is an art of its own and deserves more recognition than it currently receives.

To Catriona MacRae, a native speaker of Scottish Gaelic, for checking the Gaelic words and phrases used in this book, and for helping me adjust several Gaelic-inspired Cannair words. It was important to me to represent the language accurately and respectfully.

To all the readers patiently waiting for this sequel. Your messages, reviews and gifts have brought me so much joy.

And finally, to my little boy. I write slower than ever with you around, but I couldn't have wished for a more beautiful distraction. To borrow words from this book, my Vocation is you.